The Horsemen's Gambit

TOR BOOKS BY DAVID B. COE

THE LONTOBYN CHRONICLE

Book 1: *Children of Amarid*
Book 2: *The Outlanders*
Book 3: *Eagle-Sage*

WINDS OF THE FORELANDS

Book 1: *Rules of Ascension*
Book 2: *Seeds of Betrayal*
Book 3: *Bonds of Vengeance*
Book 4: *Shapers of Darkness*
Book 5: *Weavers of War*

BLOOD OF THE SOUTHLANDS

Book 1: *The Sorcerers' Plague*
Book 2: *The Horsemen's Gambit*

The Horsemen's Gambit

✦┼✦

Book Two of Blood of the Southlands

David B. Coe

A Tom Doherty Associates Book
New York

THE HORSEMEN'S GAMBIT
BOOK TWO OF BLOOD OF THE SOUTHLANDS

Copyright © 2008 by David B. Coe

Edited by James Frenkel

Maps by Ellisa Mitchell

A Tor Book
Published by Tom Doherty Associates, LLC
175 Fifth Avenue
New York, NY 10010

www.tor-forge.com

Tor® is a registered trademark of Tom Doherty Associates, LLC.

Library of Congress Cataloging-in-Publication Data

Coe, David B.
    The horsemen's gambit / David B. Coe.
        p.   cm.—(Blood of the Southlands ; bk. 2)
    "A Tom Doherty Associates book."
    ISBN-13: 978-0-7653-1639-4
    ISBN-10: 0-7653-1639-0
  1. Plague—Fiction.   I. Title.

    PS3553.O343H67   2009
    813'.54—dc22

                                          2008038198

First Edition: January 2009

Printed in the United States of America

0 9 8 7 6 5 4 3 2 1

May 2009

For Elyse, Amy, and Alan.
This is but small thanks for all you've given me over the years.

Acknowledgments

As always many thanks to all who have helped me with this book and those that have come before, including Tom Doherty, Liz Gorinsky, Alan Rubsam, Leslie Matlin, Carol Russo and her staff, Romas Kukalis, Terry McGarry, Harold and Margie Roth, my wonderful agent, Lucienne Diver, my fine editor and good friend, Jim Frenkel, and of course, Nancy, Alex, and Erin.

—D.B.C.

Border
Seawind Range
M'SAAREN
A'VAHL
Berylline Forest
Western Sea
The Shipsbane
Bay of Jispal
Fallow D
Sindaal's Spur
Strait of Senkora
D'KRAD
J'BALA
Lost Bay
Weeping Wood
Senkora Island
Looking Glass Lake
Lake Qira
A'Vahl River
Wraith Range
Gulf of T'Saan
TALM'ORA
Djindsamme Mountains
Upper H'Bel River
B'QAHR
Claia River
R'TROTH
Lower H'Bel River
Tejony River
H'BEL
East Fork
Forest of Raqasse
Lake Sabaak
I'PRAEL
NORTH
Tejony Peninsula
NID'QIR
Nahraida Inlet
Nahraidan Peninsula
Gulf of T'Saan
Cape of
Morna's Ocean

The Southlands

Border Range

The Companion Lakes

Bear Lake

Porcupine Lake

Owl Lake

Skunk Lake

Lowna   Tivston

Turtle Lake

C'Bijor's Neck
Runnelwick   Kirayde

STELPANA

K'Sahd River

Thraeds River

THE HORN

Sentaya

Greysford

D'Raqor   S'Vralna   N'Kiel's Span   Bred's Landing

Silverwater Wash

FAL'BORNA

Qalsyn

Central   Plain

Major's Wash

Thamia

Ravens Wash

Ofirean City

J'BALANAR

Ofirean Sea

Siraam

2007 Elisa Mitchell

The Companion Lakes Region

The Horsemen's Gambit

Chapter 1

First blood, the rules said. Beyond that, they didn't specify. A nick of the skin, the severing of a limb, a fatal strike to the breast; any of these would do. First blood. That was all a warrior needed to win.

Every person understood how Qalsyn's Harvest Tournament worked. From the youngest child, dreaming of the day when she might step into the ring and bow to His Lordship, to the oldest man, his memory of that first bow to the lord governor a fading memory, they all knew. A battle could turn with a single thrust, be it the desperate last lunge of a weary guard or the methodical advance of a skilled swordsman. The ring, it was said, was as unforgiving as steel, as merciless as the Growing sun. One mistake, one momentary lapse of concentration. First blood.

Even as she circled her opponent, watching for his next assault, Tirnya was conscious of the spectators shouting and stamping all around the arena. She had watched enough matches as a child to understand the rituals of those in the boxes: the wagers, the exchange of coin at the end of each match, the constant shifting of fortune among men and women hoping to profit from each new wound. But while the spectators made sport of the contests, there could be no doubt: the tournament was a matter deadly serious to all who watched.

And yet, the earnestness of those in the boxes was nothing compared with the gravity of those in the ring. Each contest began the same way. The two combatants entered through the doors at opposite sides of the ring, walked to the center, and turned to face His Lordship, who sat in the main box. Each warrior bowed to the lord governor, the flat of his or her blade pressed to the forehead in salute. Then they bowed to each other. And then they began to fight.

Tirnya had fought dozens of battles in the ring, and had watched more than she could count. Some began and ended with a single devastating assault or in a blindingly quick frenzy of metal and flesh and the obligatory spilling of blood. Other matches began slowly, as this one had, the warriors turning slow circles, eyeing each other, looking for any advantage. Attacks in such contests came in quick bursts; swords dancing suddenly, fitfully, bright blurs in the sunlight, chiming like sanctuary bells each time they clashed, whistling dully as they carved through air.

Standard Qalsyn army blades and Aelean bastard swords; Tordjanni broad blades and the famed shillads of Naqbae; silver dirks and bodkins; curved Qosantian daggers and narrow-bladed knives concealed in a sleeve or a boot: Tirnya had faced all sorts of steel in the ring. She herself might use three or four different swords and as many short blades in the course of a single tournament. But every warrior knew that the weapon itself meant nothing; it was the hand wielding the blade that mattered. There was a saying that was heard quite often this time of year, both in the arena itself and in the chambers beneath, where the combatants awaited their turn. "You can arm a fool with the finest Aelean steel, and at the end of the day he'll still end up bloodied."

Like all sayings of its sort, this one carried the weight of truth. Tirnya remembered a battle tournament from her tenth or eleventh year, when she still sat in the boxes with her mother and brothers, watching with the women and children and the men who had grown too old to fight. A warrior had appeared in the ring whom none could remember seeing before. His coat of mail, the only armor the combatants were allowed, was dull and fit poorly. The clothes he wore beneath the forged ringlets were tattered and travel-stained. And, most memorably, his sword was rusted and notched, a weapon barely adequate for a road brigand, much less someone who hoped to be the last man standing in Qalsyn's famed Harvest Tournament and take home the crystal blade and twenty gold sovereigns.

No one who saw him step into the ring for the first time thought the stranger would last more than a round or two.

"Even the Tordjanni army would turn away a man who looked like that," said one older gentleman who was sitting behind Tirnya and her family.

His companion agreed. "One round with a Qalsyn guard will send him back into the wilds, where he belongs."

But this unknown warrior surprised them all, defeating his first opponent with elegant ease. His swordwork was restrained and efficient, his winning strike a controlled blow to the neck that drew blood, but caused the vanquished man no serious injury.

"The first man was no one," the older man assured himself and his companion. "I'd never seen him before, either."

His companion might have nodded his agreement. Tirnya wasn't certain. She knew only that he said nothing.

When next the stranger entered the ring, it was to face a soldier from the Qalsyn army. Coaf Vantol wasn't the finest swordsman in His Lordship's force, but he was a good fighter, a big, strong, genial man, and a favorite among the city people. Surely the stranger would fall to Coaf. But no. With astonishing speed this man no one knew, this so-called warrior, who looked more like a troubadour desperate for coin than a fighter, had Coaf on his heels. In mere moments, the city's man was bleeding from a cut on his cheek. First blood; second victory. No one cheered, until at last His Lordship himself stood and began to clap his hands for the stranger. Slowly, the applause spread through the arena, growing louder and louder.

After that the man became the favored warrior in the tournament. And he didn't disappoint. Nine more times he stepped into the ring, and nine more times he raised his rusted blade in victory, bowing graciously, first to the central box and then to the rest. Even the old man began to cheer for him, cataloging in a loud voice the man's fine attributes as a fighter: his agile footwork, his skilled use of the long-handled dagger in his off hand, the fluid grace of his sword arm. One might have thought that the old man had instructed the stranger in swordplay, so extravagant was his praise.

Eventually the stranger did lose, to Tirnya's father, as it happened. Her father was a marshal in His Lordship's army, and one of the finest swordsmen in all of Stelpana. He was also well liked in many parts of the city; usually a victory for Jenoe Onjaef would have elicited a mighty roar. But on this day, the defeat of the stranger left the arena strangely quiet. The men and women in the boxes cheered for her father as he raised his blade, but even Tirnya could sense their disappointment. This once, they had been pulling not for Jenoe, but for the other man. Tirnya couldn't deny that even she had felt the briefest pang of regret at the stranger's loss.

Her father won the tournament that year, the last of his seven championships. He could have fought for several years more; there were some who said he could still fight in the ring to this day and compete for the crystal dagger. But his duties in His Lordship's army had begun to lie heavy on his shoulders and he had grown bored with the ring. Besides, a few years later Tirnya was ready to take her place in the tournament, and only one member of any family could enter the ring in a given year. Still, though that was Jenoe's last year as champion, forever after that tournament was remembered for Stri Balkett's appearance in Qalsyn. Stri had since become a captain in her father's battalion and one of the city's most renowned soldiers.

But for Tirnya, it was the warning inherent in Stri's success that remained freshest in her mind. Never again would she look at any warrior and underestimate his or her prowess in battle on the basis of a worn blade or tarnished armor. Nor would she assume that a man or woman couldn't fight simply because he or she didn't look the part of a warrior.

Others in the Qalsyn tournament had been slower to take this lesson to heart, and she had benefited from their carelessness. The first year she entered the Harvest Tournament, the year she came of age, the other combatants looked at her and saw the daughter of a great warrior, beautiful, graceful, but too weak and too lovely to be a swordswoman of any consequence. Like Stri, she proved them wrong, making it through seven rounds before finally being beaten. She still bore the scar from that tournament. In fact, she bore scars from every tournament she had entered, for though she had established herself as one of the best fighters in all the land, she had yet to win the crystal blade.

The last two years she had made it to the final match, only to be beaten on both occasions by Enly Tolm, son of Maisaak, the lord governor. Tirnya fully expected that they would meet again this year, though with a different result.

First, though, she had to defeat this giant of a man stalking her in the center of the ring. She had never learned his name; like most of the other fighters she knew him only as the Aelean. But she had seen him fight several times, and she knew that this was not a victory she could take for granted.

The Aelean was a full head taller than she, with huge shoulders and long, muscular arms. For a man of his size, he was fairly nimble: he moved his feet well and reacted quickly to his opponents' attacks. Usually, against so powerful an opponent, she would have circled continually toward his off hand and the smaller blade. But the Aelean had won more than a few of his matches with the dirk he carried in his left hand, which lashed out like a serpent at any foe too concerned with his great sword.

His greatest asset as a warrior, though, was his strength. One stroke of his bastard sword, it was said, could hew through an oak tree two hands wide. Tirnya wasn't certain that she believed this, but there could be no denying the power of the man's sword stroke. If she tried to parry more than one or two of his attacks, her arm would end up numb, or broken.

Best, then, to keep moving. Not toward his dirk, but to her left, his right. She took care to keep outside of his sword hand, so that any blow he landed with the bastard sword would be backhanded. He eyed her warily as they turned their slow circle in the dirt. He might have been twice her size, but he knew as well as she that Tirnya had her own advantages in the ring.

She was strong for one so little, though not nearly as powerful as the

Aelean. But she was quicker and more skilled with her shillad, the long, thin blade used by the horsemen of Naqbae. It wasn't the weapon she used when leading her soldiers; it wasn't even the sword she usually carried into the ring. But she always brought it with her to the tournament, knowing that it would be the perfect weapon against an opponent like the Aelean. The blade was light and perfectly balanced, and its length allowed her to keep her distance, to dance at the edges of her opponent's reach. She was tall and long-armed. With the shillad she became elusive as well.

In her off hand she carried a second sword—short-bladed, but longer than the dagger she usually used. Anything to keep her distance. Some of the more powerful combatants in the tournament could fight the Aelean on his terms; she didn't dare. "A clever warrior guards against his opponent's strengths," her father had once told her, "and watches for his weaknesses. More often than not, the clever ones live to fight another day."

The Aelean struck at her and she parried with the short blade. It wasn't a particularly hard blow, but still it made her arm sting from her wrist to her shoulder. She swiped back at him with the shillad, but he jumped away and she missed. Once more they began to circle. The crowd had been loud a moment before, but with the man's attack they had grown quiet and restive. Even His Lordship seemed intent on their battle. He leaned forward in his chair, his chin resting in his hand, his eyes narrowed.

Perhaps sensing that she had allowed herself to be distracted for the briefest instant, the man suddenly lunged at her, leveling another backhanded blow at her head. She parried this one as well, but nearly left herself open to the dirk, which flicked out at her side, like silver lightning. The crowd gasped. Tirnya spun away, unmarked. Two blows she had parried, and already her arm was beginning to ache.

The Aelean began to stalk her once more, and again Tirnya circled, trying to stay outside his sword arm. She waved her blade at him, trying to reach the side of his neck, but he knocked it away disdainfully with the bastard sword.

"Fight him!" someone shouted from behind her. Others murmured their agreement. She was losing them.

Early in one of her first tournaments, several years before, she had won a contest against a larger opponent by drawing blood at the knee. Whistles and shouts of "coward" chased her from the ring that day, and she never did such a thing again. Nor did she have any intention of doing so today. She wondered, though, if those shouting at her now remembered that day as clearly as she did.

"I hope you learned something," her father had said to her that evening, after the tournament was over.

She had been dejected and humiliated, stung far more by the reaction from the boxes than by her loss in the next round. "I won't go for someone's leg again, if that's what you mean."

"It's not."

She looked at him.

"People often liken the ring to a real battlefield," he said. "What you experienced today should make it clear to you that they actually have very little in common."

Tirnya frowned. "I don't understand."

"When you're fighting in a war, your object is to win. It's that simple. You win for your sovereign, you win for your people, you win for the soldiers under your command. Nothing else matters. But here, in the ring, there are times when the cost of victory is higher than that of defeat. You lost the respect of a good many people today. You'll have to earn that back, even if it means losing contests that trickery might let you win."

It was another lesson she'd never forgotten. If she couldn't defeat the Aelean fairly, warrior to warrior, she would take pride in the manner of her losing. She smiled to herself. *But I have no intention of losing.*

He aimed another blow at her head and for the third time she parried. This time, however, she didn't dance away, nor did she circle to the outside of his sword hand. Instead she remained in front of him. The man's eyes widened and he raised his bastard sword again to deliver a chopping strike that might well have sundered her short blade. Before he could hammer at her, however, she delivered a sideways blow of her own with the shillad. The Aelean blocked it with his dirk, but by then Tirnya had struck at him with her short blade, coming in under his raised sword to cut him just below the ear.

The Aelean winced, closing his eyes, knowing that she had baited him, and that he had fallen for the ruse. But it all happened so quickly that the people in the boxes didn't seem to understand until the Aelean lowered his blades and turned to face the center box. Seeing the blood on his neck, the spectators began to cry out Tirnya's name again and again, the timidity of her earlier attacks now forgotten.

Over the years many in the city had grown to love her. She was, after all, the daughter of Jenoe, the Eagle of the Ring, as he had once been known, for his long reach and the swiftness with which he pounced when seeing a weakness in his foe. In recent years, as she had become more skilled with her blades and more successful in the tournaments, they had given her a name as well: the Falcon. Not as formidable as her father, but faster, more agile.

She heard that name now, amid the cries of her given name. They would be pulling for her to win the final match.

She turned to the lord governor, bowed with the Aelean, and then left the ring, though not before glancing up at her father, who smiled at her as he applauded with the others.

Once in the chambers beneath the boxes, Tirnya didn't wander far from the doorway. She assumed that Enly would make short work of his next opponent. Instead, she checked her shillad for notches, and exchanged her short sword for a dagger. Enly was not nearly as big as the Aelean, nor was his reach as long, but he was as quick as she, perhaps quicker. The short sword would slow her down.

Satisfied that she had the right weapons for the final match, she sat on the floor a short distance from the entrance to the ring, closed her eyes, and cleared her mind of thoughts of her match with the Aelean. Instead, she reflected on her past encounters with His Lordship's son, scouring her memory for any pattern in his attacks, any tendencies on his part that she might use against him this time.

In truth, though, Enly was too good to be predictable. He never fought the same way twice. He was as creative as he was skilled, as clever as he was swift of hand. The first time they fought he overwhelmed her with the speed and intensity of his attacks, defeating her in mere moments. Their second battle, in last year's final match, he fought more cautiously, confounding her with feints and counterassaults. It was a longer fight, but it ended the same way.

Not this year.

Tirnya heard the roar of the crowd and then sustained applause, and she knew that Enly's match had ended. She stood and made her way back toward the door. She glanced down to make certain that her coat of mail hung correctly, though of course it did. She examined her blades yet again, though both were polished and honed. She looked at her boots, her belt, and her gloves to see that they were properly fastened, though she had no doubt that they were. Habits, all; they calmed her, steadied her breathing, slowed her pulse.

"Onjaef!" called the old guard by the doorway.

She stepped forward, stopping just beside the man, waiting for the door to open. Padar, the guard, said nothing to her, as was proper. He had once served under her father, and for the past six years he had stood by these doors and ushered her into the ring. But he was bound by the rules of the tournament to treat all combatants the same way.

She stood for several moments, listening to the cheers of the crowd, waiting. At last, the door opened, flooding the chamber with brilliant sunlight, so that Tirnya had to shield her eyes. A tall Qosantian soldier stepped past her, scowling bitterly, blood running from a cut along his jawline. Enly had won, as if there had ever been any doubt. The warrior paused and glanced back at her.

"Ya'd do us all a favor if ya beat 'im, ya know. Jest this once."

"I'll try," she said mildly.

He stared at her another moment before shaking his head and walking away. "Ya'll lose," he muttered. "Jest as ya did last year. No one can beat 'im."

Tirnya smiled faintly. The Qosantian wasn't alone. Those looking to wager on this last match would have a hard time; there couldn't have been more than a few dozen people in the entire arena who gave her much chance of bloodying the lord governor's son. A far smaller number than that would have been willing to risk their hard-earned gold and silver on her.

Because Enly had just finished his match, the rules of the tournament allowed him to take as much time as he needed to rest and prepare for this final contest. Tirnya knew, however, that he'd want to fight her immediately. A delay of any length would have been an admission of weakness. It would have given her cause to think that he was concerned about their encounter. Even had he needed some time, he never would have taken it. And chances were he didn't need the rest.

"They want t' know if ya're ready," the guard said, his voice level.

"I am."

He nodded, held his arm up high, and gave a short, single wave to the guard across the ring. A moment later, the second guard waved back.

"Time to go, then," Padar said.

She started past him, and as she did he winked at her once and offered a barely perceptible nod.

"Thanks, Padar," she whispered, and entered the ring.

Enly hadn't yet stepped out of the other doorway. That was his way, and though she generally thought him arrogant and full of himself, she could hardly begrudge him this small extravagance. He was, after all, the champion for two years running. Still, Tirnya slowed her gait. She had no intention of standing in the middle of the ring looking like a fool as he sauntered toward her with the crowd cheering.

As it was, the cheers that greeted her entrance were loud and sustained. While few thought she could defeat Maisaak's heir, a good many of the people watching the match would have given up gold if they thought it would help her win. Enly was better thought of than was his father, but he was still a Tolm.

Perhaps hearing how she was greeted and fearing that his own entrance would be met with less enthusiasm if he waited too long, Enly entered the ring from his doorway. Immediately, the sound coming from the spectators changed. Taken together, the cheers didn't grow quieter or louder, but some who had been cheering for her fell silent, and others who had offered little response to her appearance cried out seeing the lord's son.

Tirnya chanced a quick glance at the lord governor, and saw that he was scowling, his gaze wandering the crowd, as if he might remember the face of each person who cheered more enthusiastically for her than for his son. She looked toward her father, who was merely staring back at her, his expression deadly serious. "Stop worrying about the rest of us," he seemed to be telling her. "You should only be thinking about Enly."

Right.

They met in the center of the ring, turned to face the center box, and bowed to Maisaak.

"They'd cheer more for me if you were uglier," Enly said under his breath. "You know that, don't you?"

"They'd cheer more for you if you weren't such an ass," she answered in a whisper.

"Well, that's obvious."

She couldn't help but giggle.

"But I was speaking of you," he went on, still not looking at her. "You look beautiful today, your cheeks still flushed from your last battle, your hair tied back the way I like it. Just lovely."

"Shut up," she said.

He raised an eyebrow, but said nothing more. Maisaak nodded to them, a smug smile on his handsome face. Clearly he assumed that his son would win again.

She and Enly turned to face one another, bowed, and raised their swords.

In their previous meetings, Tirnya had fought carefully, even tentatively, knowing how dangerous Enly could be with either hand. This time, she immediately launched into a ferocious assault, her blade flashing like sorcerers' fire. Enly tried to counter with his dagger as he parried her blows, but she struck at him with both blades, making it impossible for him to do anything more than defend himself. He gave ground slowly, grudgingly, but give ground he did.

The boxes seemed to be quaking, so loudly were the people there shouting at what they saw, but Tirnya concentrated solely on Enly. He tried to pivot to throw her off balance and then attack her from the side, but she had seen him do this before, and she spun as well, still pressing him.

Beads of sweat stood out on his forehead and ran down his temples. He wasn't breathing hard yet, but his face was reddening. Tirnya was sweating, too. The muscles in her arms were starting to burn. But she had him on the defensive, and she refused to relent.

He tried to strike at her again, using the momentum of his retreat to carry him into a spin and an assault of his own. Again, she was ready, parrying with the shillad and lunging at him with her dagger. He jumped away, and she was on him once more, her steel a glittering beast, like something called forth by the gods.

Enly tried his spin maneuver a second time, stumbled, and sprawled on the ground. Tirnya leaped forward, putting one foot on his sword and the other on his dagger, and laying the edge of her blade against his neck.

She could have won then. First blood.

A few people shouted for her to end the match, to take the crystal dagger as her own. But she didn't want to win like this. She took a step back, and then another.

"Get up," she said.

She heard someone groan in the boxes, but then people began to call her name again. "Tirnya!" they called. "Falcon!"

Enly climbed to his feet slowly, and picked up his weapons. He stared at her for a moment, his grey eyes ghostly pale in the sunlight. Then he bowed to her.

Tirnya started forward, intending to renew her assault, but Enly wasn't willing to let her gain that advantage again. He attacked as well, and for long moments they stood face-to-face, their blades lashing out, clashing loudly. And then Enly began to advance on her, forcing her back.

She tried to parry and strike, to find once more the energy she'd had when they began. But she was tired, her arms and legs heavy. Enly must have sensed her weariness, but his expression didn't change, nor did the speed of his attacks. He had been known to talk to some of his opponents. It was said that he often taunted them, hoping to provoke them into mistakes. But he had never done anything of the sort to her, nor did he now. He merely kept after her. And when she tried to spin to the side and strike over his off hand, he was ready.

Tirnya saw both attacks, the chopping blow with his sword and the thrust with his dagger. But the pivot had left her off balance; not much, but enough. She managed to parry the sword strike, but she could do nothing about the dagger as it darted out at her cheek. An instant later, she felt the sting on her flesh and the hot trickle of blood running down her face like tears.

Enly stepped back and looked at her, his brow creased, as if he had surprised himself with the assault.

"I'm sorry," he mouthed. Then he raised the dagger over his head and turned a slow circle so that all could see, stopping when he was facing her once more.

At first there was silence. No one seemed to believe that he had won. The fierce smile on the lord governor's face began to fade as he looked around the arena. After a few moments, those sitting in the boxes seemed to realize that they ought to be cheering, and they began to call out Enly's name. But His Lordship still didn't look pleased. And Tirnya heard her name being shouted as well.

She turned to face the center box.

"We have to bow," she said under her breath.

Enly turned smartly toward his father and made himself smile. They bowed in unison and then they walked their separate ways back toward the doors.

As she walked, not bothering to wipe the blood from her face, Tirnya looked up at her father. He was staring back at her, looking both proud and concerned. She smiled, and he did as well. But she felt her eyes starting to well. She'd come so close to beating him. And then she'd let him win. She shook her head. That wasn't quite how it had happened, but it felt that way.

Padar was waiting for her at the door.

"Ya had him," he said grimly.

She'd hear a lot of this in the next few days. "Yes."

"Ya did th' right thing."

"There are those who will disagree."

The old guard shrugged. "Wha' d' they know? Ya don' bloody a man when he's down, even if i' 'tis fer th' crystal blade."

Tirnya nodded, fearing that she might weep. The crystal blade! She'd come so close! "Thank you, Padar." She started to walk away.

"Captain, wait," the guard said.

She halted. He crossed to where she stood and looked at her cheek.

"I' doesn' look too bad," he said after a moment. "Probably feels worse than i' 'tis. It'll heal before ya know it."

Tirnya smiled bravely, though a tear slipped from her eye. "Right," she agreed. "Just another scar." Just another tournament; just another year.

But this time, she had come so close.

Chapter 2

✦-I-✦

Before leaving the chambers beneath the boxes, Tirnya stopped by to
see the healer who treated the wounds of all the combatants. Left to
decide on her own, she would have ignored the cut on her cheek, but she
knew that her father would be waiting for her outside the arena, and he
would make a fuss if she left the wound untended.

The healer examined her in silence, using a warm, damp cloth to wipe
away the dried blood. He then dabbed a different cloth in spirits and gently
patted the cut. Tirnya winced, sucking in air through her teeth.

"It cleans the wound," the healer said, holding her chin with a firm
hand. He dipped the cloth in the spirits again and dabbed at the cut a bit
more.

"I know what it does," she muttered, still wincing. "That doesn't make it
burn any less."

The healer put down the cloth and eyed the cut, clicking his tongue as
he did. He was a heavy man, only a few years older than she, with brown
curls and short, fat fingers that were more deft and gentle than she would
have thought possible.

"We can leave it to heal as it is, or we can stitch it up," he said after several moments. "Either way you'll wind up with a scar. It may be less notice-
able if we use the sutures."

She pointed at the scars on her chin and temple. "What do I care about
one more scar?"

"Will you at least let me put a poultice on it?" he asked, though from the
tone of his voice it seemed clear that he knew she'd refuse this as well.

"And have me walking around the city looking like Enly sliced off half
my face? No, thank you."

The healer shook his head. "Very well, then. You can go. Try to keep it
clean. If it starts to hurt more, or the skin around it turns red and fevered,
get yourself to a healer. Any healer. You understand me?"

Tirnya nodded sullenly and stood, grabbing her swords and striding
toward the door. Taking hold of the door handle, she paused and looked

back at the man, who was clearing up his medicines, herbs, and bandages. Naturally, she was the last. No doubt he'd had a long day.

"Thank you," she said.

He looked up a smiled wanly. "You're welcome, Captain. You know," he said a moment later, stopping her as she began to open the door. "I understand that you're disappointed. Anyone would be. But there's no shame in losing the final match to the lord heir."

Surely the healer was trying to help, but his words stung more than did his spirits. She merely nodded and left the chamber.

Her father was waiting for her just outside the arena, chatting amiably with passersby and flanked by several of his men. There had been an attempt on Jenoe's life several years before—a single attacker who came at the marshal with a dirk while Jenoe was drinking in a small tavern near the river. Tirnya's father had killed the man himself and there had been no further attempts. But since then, Jenoe's captains had each assigned a man to guard the marshal in shifts, so that he always had four armed guards at his side.

There was nothing to indicate that the attacker had been anything more than a drunken soldier who sought to exact revenge for some imagined slight, but some believed that he had been sent by the lord governor, or one of his subordinates. The Onjaef and Tolm families had mistrusted each other for more than a century, and Maisaak had long been envious of Jenoe's stature among Qalsyn's soldiers and subjects.

While Tirnya was not so naive as to deny that the lord governor might well be jealous of her father, she didn't believe that Maisaak would resort to murder to rid himself of a rival. Jenoe's popularity might have bruised His Lordship's pride, but her father could hardly be considered a threat to Maisaak's power.

The Onjaef family had come to Qalsyn a century and a half before, during the darkest days of the Blood Wars between the Eandi of the eastern Southlands and the Qirsi, the white-haired sorcerers who controlled the western lands. House Onjaef held the great city of Deraqor, the family seat, where Tirnya's ancestors ruled as lord governors. They also controlled the Horn, a narrow strip of fertile land between the Threades and K'Sahd rivers. At the time, the Horn might well have been the most valuable land still under Eandi control. But as the Fal'Borna, a clan of fierce horsemen, who were as skilled with their blades as they were with their magic, pushed eastward, the leaders of the Eandi found themselves forced to cede territory. The Blood Wars of the northern plain were among the bloodiest fought during the long, violent history of the conflicts, and in the end the Onjaefs, led by Mehp, Tirnya's grandfather four times removed, had no choice but to abandon their ancestral home. They fled eastward, into what remained of Stelpana, settling eventually in Qalsyn. And they didn't come alone.

To this day, descendants of the other families that came from Deraqor still saw the Onjaefs as their leaders, and they still hoped that someday the families of Deraqor would reclaim the city for the sovereignties. In the eyes of the sovereign and most of those who lived elsewhere in Stelpana, the On-jaef clan was disgraced, a family in exile, the vanquished stewards of a lost city. Only here in Qalsyn, where Maisaak was seen by some as a strong but capricious ruler, and Jenoe was revered by so many for his prowess with a blade and his easy manner, would anyone even stop to wonder if a rivalry existed between the two men.

When Tirnya emerged from the stone doorway, her father ended his conversations and walked toward her, a sympathetic smile on his lips. He was still youthful, despite the fact that he no longer considered himself young enough to fight in battle tournaments. His brown hair and beard were unmarked by grey, and he remained trim and muscular, an imposing figure on the battlefield as well as in the city streets. Reaching her, he put his arms around her and kissed her forehead.

"You fought well," he whispered.

She closed her eyes, fearing that she might start crying again. He wouldn't have tolerated that—a warrior shed tears for lost comrades and fallen lead-ers, not for matches lost in the arena. He had made that clear to her years ago.

"Not well enough," she managed to say.

He pulled back and made her look him in the eye. "Yes," he said. "Well enough. Everyone in the boxes knew that you had the tournament won, that you could have bloodied him as he lay on the ground. The rest is . . ." He waved his hand vaguely. "The rest means nothing."

Only a father could say such a thing.

"It means nothing that Enly won?" she asked. "It means nothing that I'm going to have another scar on my face?"

"You're right," he said. "That will mean something. If nothing else, it'll mean that your mother will have a new reason to berate me for ever teach-ing you to hold a sword."

Tirnya smiled, but only briefly. "What are they saying about me?"

"Who?"

She shrugged. "Everyone. Your men. The people in the boxes. Enly."

"You think I've spoken to Enly?"

"Of course not," she said. "But the rest of them. Come now, Father. You know what I'm asking."

"They're saying that you should have won. Some of them mean it kindly; others don't."

"The ones who don't—"

He shook his head. "You shouldn't trouble yourself about them."

"What are they saying, Father?"

Jenoe ran a hand through his hair, and wound up rubbing the back of his neck. "They're saying that you made . . . that you made a womanly choice."

"Womanly!" she repeated, her voice rising. "Womanly?"

"I think they mean—"

"I know what they mean!" Tirnya said. "I was weak. I took pity on him when I just should have won."

"They're wrong," Jenoe told her.

"Are they?"

"Yes. What you did was honorable, not weak. Had you struck at Enly as he lay on his back, they'd be calling you a snake and worse." He laughed mirthlessly and gave a small shake of his head. "I know it didn't seem this way at the time, but Enly's fall was the worst thing that could have happened for you, and the best that he could have hoped for. Had I not seen it all with my own eyes, I might have thought that he stumbled intentionally."

"He wouldn't do that."

"I know. But still, it gave him a respite from your attack. It changed everything about the match."

"I can only imagine what they're saying about him," Tirnya said, her voice low.

"I don't think he could care less what anyone other than his father is saying."

She frowned. "I imagine his father had quite a lot to say."

Jenoe grinned. "Yes, well be thankful your father is such a kind, reasonable man. Because a more exacting teacher might want to know what you were thinking in your third match, when you fought with your sword in your off hand, and the dagger in your right."

"It worked, didn't it? Craevis had probably never seen anyone do such a thing before."

"You might well have lost, taking such a risk."

Tirnya shook her head. "Not to him. You saw how easily I won. Admit it, Father: It was a fine idea, and it worked perfectly."

Her father laughed and shook his head. "He did look confused, didn't he?"

"By the time he understood what I had done, and why all my attacks seemed so different, he was already bleeding."

"Speaking of bleeding," Jenoe said, his brow creasing as he examined her wound.

Tirnya pulled away. "I'm fine."

"I'm sure you are. It looks like a clean cut. The healer saw you?"

"Yes, Father."

"Fine, then. I won't mention it again. You're going to the Swift Water?"

She'd forgotten. Each year, after the tournament ended, the lord governor hosted a supper at the largest tavern in the city, the Swift Water Inn. Nearly all the combatants went—it wasn't often that anyone offered free food and ale for as long as one could eat and drink—and usually Maisaak himself put in an appearance. As one of the lord governor's captains, Tirnya was expected to attend; as one who had fought in the final match, her absence would have been conspicuous. She wanted only to go home and sleep, but that would have to wait.

"Yes," she said, the word coming out as a sigh. "I'm going." After a brief hesitation, she asked, "Are you?"

Tirnya knew the answer already. Jenoe hadn't gone to the supper since his last year as champion, although as a marshal in the army and a former winner of the tournament he had every right to attend. Others of lower rank—men who had never set foot in the ring—showed up every year and drank themselves into a stupor. But Maisaak hated him, and Jenoe knew it. The lord governor tolerated him as marshal because he and every other person in Qalsyn understood that no one in the city, perhaps in all the land, was more suited to command than Jenoe. But this was another matter.

"No," he said, his smile fleeting and forced. "I should be getting home to your mother. She'll want to hear all about your matches."

Tirnya looked away. "Then she should come herself."

"She doesn't like to watch you fight," he said. "You know that. It frightens her."

"It doesn't frighten you."

"I don't love you as much." He grinned, to soften the gibe. Not that it was necessary; they both knew it wasn't true. "I've been through enough tournaments," he said a moment later. "I understand the risks and the strategies. To your mother it just looks . . . dangerous. But she would have been proud of you today. She will be, when I tell her about it."

"All right," Tirnya said, not wanting to talk about this. "I'll see you later."

Before she could walk away, Jenoe caught her hand and raised it to his lips. "I'm proud of you," he told her. "You should be proud, too."

She smiled. "Thank you, Father." She kissed his cheek, and walked away.

By the time she reached the Swift Water, the sun had almost set, and long black shadows stretched across the city streets, darkening the stone façades of homes and shops. The door to the tavern was open, and raucous laughter from within spilled out into the lane, along with the scent of roasting meat and musty ale. Tirnya wouldn't be the only woman there—a few had entered the tournament this year, though she was the only one to have gotten beyond the sixth set of matches. But in all ways that mattered, she would be awash in a sea of loud, arrogant men. Her mother would have laughed had she known how much Tirnya dreaded this. "You see?" Zira would have said. "If you had listened to me, and concerned yourself less with swordplay and more with the finer crafts, you'd be home now, resting comfortably with a cup of wine." Too late for that, by more years than she cared to count.

Steeling herself with a long breath, Tirnya stepped inside.

As soon as she entered the tavern, the other warriors began to stare at her, turning one by one as they realized who had come. Gradually conversations stopped, the din fading toward the back of the tavern like a receding tide. Maisaak stood near the bar, a slight smile on his face, as if he were enjoying her obvious discomfort. Enly stood near him, with the Aelean and several other warriors. His expression was far more difficult to gauge than his father's. Concern, embarrassment, even a touch of resentment: Tirnya saw all of these in his pale grey eyes, in the lines around his mouth. Enly resembled his father superficially. Both men had light eyes and black hair. Both were blandly handsome, though Enly had broken his nose as a boy and its crookedness made his face more interesting than his father's. But Maisaak always seemed to be scowling, and on those rare occasions when his expression softened there remained a touch of contempt and condescension, so that even his kindest smile seemed mocking. Enly was more open, kinder, softer, and thus, in his father's view, weaker. Today's victory couldn't have been easy for either of them.

After a silence that lasted for what seemed an eternity, Enly began to clap, stepping forward and raising his hands so that others could see him. Others began to applaud as well, until the sound grew so loud that it compelled even the lord governor to join in. After a few moments, Maisaak stepped forward, raising his hands to silence the throng. For once, Tirnya was deeply grateful to him.

"Yes, yes," the lord governor said, nodding as the applause died down. "She deserves no less." He faced her, the smile on his face appearing genuine. "Welcome, Captain Onjaef. We were starting to fear that you might not come at all, and thus deny us the opportunity to congratulate you on your fine performance today."

Tirnya bowed to him. "Thank you, Your Lordship, and forgive me for being late. Unlike my opponent in the final match, I had to spend some time with the healer afterwards."

That drew a laugh from all, and an approving nod from Maisaak.

"Well, you're here now. And I hope you'll enjoy yourself."

"I will, Your Lordship. I intend to avail myself of as much of your free ale as time will allow."

More laughter followed, and slowly the other discussions resumed, leaving Tirnya in the uncomfortable position of having to make conversation with the lord governor.

"You handled that very well, Captain," he said quietly. "Someone with less courage and grace would have stayed away entirely."

It was a rare courtesy from the man, and she didn't bother to hide her surprise. "Thank you, Your Lordship. You're most kind."

"Not really. I'm just not the monster your father has made me out to be."

And there it was: the hidden knife slipped between exposed ribs. No matter the circumstance, Maisaak and Jenoe were both incapable of putting aside their animosity, even for an evening.

"Yes, Your Lordship."

Fortunately, Enly chose that moment to join them.

"She said she wanted an ale, Father. And you know she's too polite to get one so long as you're talking to her. Leave the woman alone."

A brittle smile touched His Lordship's lips. "Yes. I think I understand. I'll leave the two of you."

He walked away, joining a knot of soldiers near the back of the inn, and leaving Enly and Tirnya alone, or at least as alone as two people could be in a tavern so crowded.

"Thank you for that greeting," Tirnya said after a brief, strained silence. "It's not often that people applaud when I step into a tavern."

"Really?" Enly said. "I would have thought it happens all the time."

She raised an eyebrow.

He sipped his ale, shrugged. "It was nothing." He looked away, taking another pull of ale.

She frowned slightly. It wasn't like him to be so diffident. Stepping past him to the bar, she ordered an ale, then turned to face him again. He was already watching her.

"Why are you looking at me like that?" she asked.

He looked away again and drank more. "I'm not looking at you in any particular way."

She smiled. "You beat me, Enly. It's as simple as that. You should be used to it by now. You should be gloating, as you do every other year."

"Oh, I am used to beating you," he said, with a hint of his usual swagger. "But I'm not used to winning this way."

"And what way is that?"

He started to drink again, but stopped himself. After a moment he met her gaze, though it seemed to take some effort on his part. "By accident. By sheer, dumb luck."

"It was a good strike," she said, unsure of why she was being so generous. "You cut me cleanly."

"That's not what I mean and you know it. I was losing. If I hadn't fallen down when I did, you would have bloodied me, probably with your next attack."

"Did you fall on purpose?" she asked.

He frowned. "I'm not that clever, Tirnya."

She laughed. "No, I don't suppose you are."

Enly's expression didn't change. If anything, he looked more and more troubled by the moment. "Everybody here knows that you should have won," he said. "My men know it. Yours know it. Certainly my father knows it."

"Good," she said. "Maybe next year a few people in the boxes will wager their gold on me."

He regarded her sourly.

"What is it you want me to say, Enly? That I'm sorry I almost beat you? That I didn't mean to fight so well?"

"That's not . . ." He stopped, shaking his head.

"Then what?"

He stood still for several moments, the muscles in his jaw bunched.

When he faced her again anger and wounded pride burned in his eyes. "Why didn't you bloody me when you had the chance?"

"You mean when you were down."

"Yes, when I was down! The match was yours! You should have ended it then and there!"

All around them, conversations ceased and people began to stare. Tirnya felt her face growing hot. She grabbed Enly by the arm and dragged him out into the street. The sky overhead had turned to a soft indigo, and the first bright stars shone down on the city. She could hear people singing in another tavern and two men staggered past, both of them drunk, both of them laughing at something. This was a night of celebration in Qalsyn, and not only for those who had fought in the tournament. The Harvest had begun, and this year's crops promised to be bountiful. Tirnya, Enly, and Maisaak might well have been the only unhappy people in the entire city.

"You were saying?" she asked wearily, making herself meet his glare.

"Why didn't you end our match when you had the chance?" He sounded calmer now, but there could be no masking the intensity of that look.

"An Onjaef doesn't strike at a defenseless opponent. My father wouldn't have done it, and neither would I."

"So it's all about pride. Stupid Onjaef pride."

She threw her arms wide. "Of course it is! And so are these questions of yours! You know very well that I couldn't win that way. You know what people would be saying about me. You won, Enly! The crystal dagger is yours again. The only reason we're even having this conversation is that I wounded your pride when I let you get up. Well, that's too damn bad!"

He blinked, then looked away. "This is . . ." He shook his head, looking very young. "It's our fathers, isn't it? This is all about them."

"Not entirely. I'd want to beat you even if your father was a cloth peddler."

"You know what I mean."

"I'm not having this discussion again, Enly."

"We have to—"

"Don't!" she said, shaking her head.

"We have to marry. You know it just as I do. It's the only way to end their feud and all the rest of this foolishness."

"You just don't want to have to fight me again next year." She smiled. He didn't. After a moment she shook her head. "That was supposed to be a joke."

"I'm serious, Tirnya."

"We've talked about this."

A small smile touched his lips. "We've done more than talk about it."

"Yes, and we saw how that turned out, didn't we?"

He gave her a coy look. "Was it really all that bad?"

"It didn't work, Enly. And I have no interest in being any man's wife. Not even yours. You'd expect me to give up my command, to have children, to be the dutiful wife of the lord heir."

"It wouldn't be that terrible, would it?"

She gestured at the mail coat she still wore and at the weapons hanging from her belt. "Look at me, Enly. Do I look like the marrying kind?"

They were about the same height, and now their eyes met. It was only for an instant—she quickly made herself look away—but she saw enough to know that he meant what he was saying. He might well have loved her.

"I'd marry you in a heartbeat," he said, his voice dropping to a whisper.

She made herself look at him again. He deserved that much from her. "No," she said. "I'm sorry, Enly, but the answer is still no."

He held her gaze for a moment longer before shaking his head. He smiled again, but it looked pained. "Onjaef pride," he said.

"Call it what you will."

"You'll change your mind someday."

Tirnya shrugged, far less certain of this than he seemed to be. "Maybe."

"By then it might be too late."

She straightened. "I suppose that's the risk I'm taking."

They stood in silence for several moments. Enly continued to eye her, but Tirnya refused to meet his gaze again. Finally, he took a long breath. "All right, then." He held out a hand to her, somehow managing a smile. "Shall we go back in?"

Tirnya had to laugh. However disappointed he might have been, he recovered quickly, or at least hid his pain well. By midnight he'd be in bed with some barmaid or one of the other swordswomen.

"All right," she said. She took his hand, and together they reentered the tavern. Once inside, he released her hand and joined some of his men, leaving Tirnya to reclaim her ale from the bar. She didn't much feel like drinking it. In fact, she would have preferred to leave, but after the way the others had welcomed her, and after her exchange with Enly, which so many had overheard, she didn't feel that she could. Not yet, at least.

"Captain!"

Tirnya turned and searched the tavern, wondering if this was someone calling for her.

"Captain Onjaef!"

She saw a man near the back of the Swift Water wave a hand over his head. After a moment she recognized Oliban Hert, one of her lead riders. His shirt was stained red on the sleeve, from a wound she had dealt him today in the seventh match. Still, he was smiling. She waved in return, picked up her ale, and walked back to where he was standing. When she reached him, she realized that several of her riders were there. They raised their glasses in salute and she drained hers, the proper response under the circumstances. The men cheered, and immediately one of them rose and hurried to the bar to get her another.

"Ya made us proud today, Captain," Oliban said with a grin. "I only wish ya'd been as gentle with me as ya were with th' lord heir." Immediately his face fell. "Wh-what I meant was—"

She patted his shoulder. "It's all right, Oliban. I know what you meant." But her throat had tightened. People in Qalsyn would be speaking of what she had done for a long time. It might well become a lasting part of Harvest Tournament lore, like Stri's first competition, or the year when Enly's older brother, Berris, won the final match, only to fall to the ground dead a few moments after, the victim, the healers said, of a defective heart. She'd be remembered, too: the woman who had her chance to defeat the lord heir, only to squander it.

The rider returned with Tirnya's ale and handed it to her. She drank a bit, taking the opportunity to compose herself.

"Ya did what ya had to, Captain," Oliban said, eyeing her. "All of us knows it."

The other men nodded their agreement.

"Ya showed ya was th' best, an' ya showed ya have honor." Oliban raised his cup. "T' th' captain!" he said.

"Hear, hear!"

Tirnya grinned and sipped her ale as the others drank. "Thank you," she said. They cleared room for her at their table, and she sat.

All of them, including Oliban, started to ask her questions about her matches. How had she beaten the Aelean? What weapons had she used? Who was quicker, Enly or the Tordjanni swordsman she fought in her eighth match? She answered as many of their questions as she could before finally raising a hand to forestall the next one.

"Actually," she said, smiling to soften the words, "I really don't want to talk about the matches anymore. It's been a . . . a long day."

Oliban glanced around the table at the others. "Our apologies, Captain. Maybe we should leave ya alone."

Tirnya shook her head. "No. I don't want that." She looked at them each in turn. "You can't tell me that the tournament is the only thing you know how to talk about."

They laughed, but it sounded forced, a response intended to please their commander. And she understood. It wasn't all they knew to talk about, but it was certainly all they wanted to talk about. Every other conversation in the Swift Water was about the day's events; why shouldn't theirs be as well? They could speak of more mundane matters every other day of the year. But today . . .

Tirnya smiled again, this time at her own foolishness.

"Enly's quicker," she said. "Although the Tordjanni isn't bad. His off hand is only average—Oliban here is quicker on the left. But his sword . . ." She shook her head, and the men all leaned in, waiting, eager. "His sword is *fast*. Lightning quick." Tirnya grinned. "Not as fast as mine, of course, and no match for Enly's. But very quick."

They wound up talking for hours. Once Tirnya forced herself past her self-pity, she understood that talking about her matches and those of her men was just what she needed. Before she knew it, most of the other combatants had left the Swift Water, though Enly and his father were still there, talking to separate groups of soldiers, trying to ignore each other.

"It's late," Tirnya said, standing and stretching. Despite all the sword-work she did every day, during the tournament she always seemed to exercise muscles she had forgotten since the previous year. She'd be sore come morning. "We have training at first bells."

The others stood as well. "Yes, Captain," Oliban said.

"We also have patrol two nights hence," she said. "I want the assignments set by tomorrow evening."

Oliban nodded. "They will be."

"Good night, Oliban."

He grinned and nodded. "G'night, Captain."

She watched her men leave before draining her cup—her fifth ale of the night—and starting toward the door herself.

"Captain Onjaef."

She turned. Maisaak was watching her, and, she now realized, Stri Balkett was standing with him.

"A word please."

She crossed to where he stood and nodded to Stri. "Yes, Your Lord-ship."

Enly looked up from his conversation and immediately joined them. Maisaak raised an eyebrow, but he didn't order his son away.

"Captain Balkett was just telling me that there's been trouble on the roads south of the city. Brigands from the sound of it. Groups of them, dis-ciplined and clever. They've been striking at peddlers making their way to-ward the Ofirean and the lower sovereignties. Have your men heard anything?"

"Not that I know of, Your Lordship," Tirnya said. "But I'll ask them about it first thing in the morning."

Maisaak nodded. "Yes, do. And I want patrols doubled until further notice." His eyes flicked toward Enly. "All patrols. Even those in the north. I don't want anything interfering with Harvest trade. There's also talk of the pestilence to the west. Much of it seems to be in white-hair lands; the Fal'Borna mostly. But all it takes is a single peddler to bring it across the Silverwater into our lands."

"Yes, Your Lordship."

"Tournament's over now. It's time we got back to more serious matters." He seemed to direct this at his son, but he hardly looked at Enly at all. "I'm off to bed. I'd suggest the rest of you do the same."

"Good night, Your Lordship," Stri said.

Maisaak left the tavern with Enly in tow, but Tirnya hardly noticed. *Pestilence in white-hair lands . . .*

"You fought well today."

Tirnya looked up. Stri still stood beside her, his eyes shining in the lamplight.

"Thank you."

"Your father was pleased, as much by what you didn't do as by what you did, if you follow."

"I do," she said. "Thank you."

Stri was usually quiet. So much so, that many of the men in her com-mand thought him proud and superior. She knew better. He simply was not given to idle chatter. But since becoming one of Jenoe's captains, he had become a fixture in the Onjaef home, where he was as garrulous as Tirnya's younger brothers. He was a large man, with a broad, plain face and dark eyes. His light brown hair was long and straight, and though he was muscu-lar, he looked soft, his shoulders rounded, his head slightly bowed, as if he were afraid of bumping it on the top of every doorway. Early on, he had doted on Tirnya, as if taken with her. But as time went on, and he came to accept that she didn't return his affection, the two of them settled into a comfortable friendship. He was now more like a big brother than a friend, and she trusted him as she did few other people.

"You probably don't want to talk about the matches anymore, do you?"

She smiled and shook her head. "Not really, no."

"Fair enough." He gestured at the door with a large hand. "I'll walk you home."

Tirnya nodded, but didn't move. "What do you know about this pestilence His Lordship mentioned?"

"Not a lot," he said. "A peddler mentioned it to me two or three days ago. Three, it was. And then I heard talk of it again today from one of the other combatants. A swordsman from western Stelpana."

"Do you know where it's struck?"

"Well east of the Horn, it sounds like. Not near Deraqor, not yet at least, if that's what you're wondering."

It was. The Qirsi had renamed Deraqor D'Raqor, as was their way. Tirnya had never seen the city, though to this day it was said to be one of the most beautiful and impressive of all the cities on the northern rivers. But like her father, and his father before him, Tirnya still thought of Deraqor as her family's home. Though she knew no one who lived there, and cared not a whit if every Qirsi on the plain died tomorrow, she was oddly relieved to know that the pestilence had not struck there. She was tied to the place, as were all Onjaefs. One day, she had sworn long ago, the Onjaefs would take back Deraqor for the Eandi. Yes, there was peace between the races, and no one wished to return to the terrible days of the Blood Wars. But by the same token, Deraqor was theirs; it belonged to the Eandi and it was meant to be ruled by her family.

"Did they know people who were sickened by it?" Tirnya finally asked.

"Who?"

"The peddler you mentioned, and the swordsman."

He shook his head. "Not that I know of. It seems from what they told me that it's mostly white-hairs who've been getting sick."

She tried to muster some sympathy for them. They were people after all, and she knew, mostly from tales told to her by her father and by other soldiers, how horrible the pestilence could be. No one should have had to endure such suffering. But her heart seemed suddenly to have turned to stone. What did it say about her that she couldn't bring herself to feel anything?

"I guess that's too bad for them," she said, feeling that she had to say something.

"You hate them very much, don't you?"

She looked at him, hearing something in his voice. "Don't you?"

"Not really."

"But the wars . . ." Tirnya trailed off, not quite certain what she had intended to say.

"I never fought in the wars."

She frowned, then shook her head. "No, of course not." She started to say more, but stopped herself. She felt herself growing angry with him, and for the life of her she didn't know why. Unlike so many men under her father's command, Stri had no ties to Deraqor. He had come to Qalsyn from the south, near the Ofirean; his family had never lived in the western lands now held by the Fal'Borna. Deraqor probably meant nothing to him. It was just one of many cities taken by the white-hairs.

But for Tirnya, who had been brought up on tales of her family's former glory, and for others whose ancestors fought and died in the battles for the Horn, Deraqor was both a wound that never healed, and a name that carried within it the promise of redemption.

Stri should have known that. Or was she being unreasonable?

"Come along, Captain," he said, starting toward the door. "It's late and this has been a long day for all of us."

She followed him out of the tavern, lost in thought. Stri didn't say much as they walked. He might have commented on how clear a night it was, and how fine the crop fields outside the city looked, but that was all. He seemed to understand that Tirnya was barely listening. When they reached the home she still shared with her family, however, he turned to face her.

"Did I say something wrong?" he asked. "You've been very quiet."

She made herself smile. "No, I'm just . . . I'm tired."

"You're certain?" He was frowning, the light of the two moons shining on his face.

"Yes." She touched his arm lightly. "Thank you, Stri. I'll see you in the morning."

"All right." He started to walk away. "You fought well today. Your father was very proud."

She nodded and forced another smile. But the cut on her cheek burned like a brand.

Chapter 3

The cold winds of the Harvest had come early to the plain, carrying with them steel grey skies and bands of hard rain that could soak through the thickest woolen wraps in mere moments. Even during the warmest, most pleasant days of the Growing, when soft breezes stirred the grasses and wildflowers bloomed on the hillsides in more shades of red, purple, orange, and yellow than one could imagine, these were inhospitable lands. Few trees grew among the boulders and grasses, and when the days turned hot, travelers found little shelter from the Growing sun. The Growing storms, when they struck, were harsh, violent affairs: hail, wind, lightning that seemed to make the air crackle, and thunder that could cause the mightiest warriors to cringe.

But only when those warm days gave way to the Harvest, with its drenching rains and merciless gales, did the weather on the plain begin to bare its teeth. And yet even the Harvest was mild when compared with the cruelty of the Snows. Judging from this year's rains, it seemed that the cold turns ahead would be truly monstrous.

For Lariqenne Glyse, these lands were doubly dangerous. Apart from the climate and the terrain, she had to contend with the hostility of nearly every man and woman she encountered. Such was the fate of an Eandi merchant looking to make her gold in Fal'Borna lands. The Qirsi warriors of the plain were among the most fearsome of all the white-hairs of the Southlands, and they were second to none in their hatred of the Eandi. Yes, Lariqenne—Lark, as she was known—was a merchant, and of all the people of the sovereignties, traders were most accepted by the sorcerer race. But still, her arrival in a Fal'Borna sept never failed to cause a stir. It didn't help matters that she was a woman. The Fal'Borna of the plain were strictly patriarchal—women were expected to serve their men in all ways imaginable. This made haggling with Qirsi men over the price of her wares interesting, to say the least.

Yet Lark had survived, even prospered. There were times when she had to endure cold glares and insults. Men who found her too unyielding in striking a bargain often walked away bitter, their pride wounded. Over the years, some had called her a whore. A few had threatened to kill her and one, a young warrior in a village near the Fallow Downs, had tried to make good on his threats. Only the timely intervention of an older Fal'Borna who knew her from her previous visits had kept him from succeeding. She still bore a scar on her breast from the first thrust of his blade.

Over the years, she had learned the ways of the Fal'Borna. She always sought out the a'laq—the sept leader—sometime on the day of her arrival in any settlement. She suffered the tales of men who thought it amusing to recount their romantic conquests in vivid detail, and on those occasions when she found herself haggling with Qirsi men, she always did so in even, respectful tones. On the other hand, she no longer lowered her eyes when dealing with Fal'Borna men. Early on, she had done so as a matter of course, thinking it safest to appear respectful, lest the men think that she was challenging them. She had learned, however, that the warriors often took this as a sign of weakness, as license to treat her as they would a Fal'Borna woman. By meeting their gazes straight on, by letting them see the dark brown of her eyes, she reminded them of who and what she was. *You may not like me,* she told them with her directness, *but you will not take advantage of me.*

Perhaps as a result, she had earned something of a reputation among the septs of the Central Plain, not only for the quality of her wares, but also for her courage. Her friends among the other Eandi peddlers might have called her Lark, but to the Fal'Borna she was K'Lahm, so named for the small, wild dog of the highlands known for its fearlessness.

On those few occasions when she returned to her native Stelpana to visit with family and old friends, her conversations turned invariably to the difficulties of trading with the Qirsi.

"Why would you want to do business with the white-hairs," her father often asked her, "when you can just as easily trade here, with your own kind?"

She always responded the same way. "There's more gold to be made on the plain than in any Eandi city."

This was true in a sense. Certainly there were riches to be made in the large cities of Stelpana, but there were also far more merchants there, competing for their share of the gold. Out here, on the plain, she was one of only a small number of Eandi merchants bringing Eandi goods—Qosantian blankets, Tordjanni wines, smoked fish from the shores of the Ofirean—to the Qirsi clanfolk. She would have to work harder, travel farther, endure hardships unknown to the merchants of the sovereignties, but she would grow rich more quickly here than she could anywhere else.

Her father could only shrug when she argued thus, because he knew she was right. But this wasn't the real reason she returned to the plain again and again. The truth was, she liked the challenge, the danger. She enjoyed returning to her home village with tales that left her father and brothers wide-eyed, wondering that their little Lariqenne should see and say and do such things. The scar she still bore high on her breast had been enough to win her brothers' unwavering admiration. Trading in the cities of Stelpana would have bored her to death, so instead she risked her life trading with the Fal'Borna.

Her goods were always of decent quality; not to the level of Torgan Plye, or even Brint HedFarren, Young Red, as he was known in their circle, but good enough that she was now known as a merchant who could be trusted, no small thing among the clans.

Today, though, she was carrying in her cart items of such quality that she didn't quite know how to trade them. When she first saw Young Red's baskets at the bend in the river, where she often gathered with her fellow merchants to share food and wine and good conversation, she had been overwhelmed. Never had she seen baskets of any sort, Mettai, Aelean, or B'Qahr, that could match these in both color and tightness of weave. Usually Lark wasn't one to carry items that would fetch too high a price. She preferred to turn over her stock with some frequency, as opposed to someone like Torgan, the one-eyed Eandi trader, who was willing to hold on to goods for several turns, even as long as a year, until he got the price he wanted. But these baskets had called to her, and she had purchased sixteen of them from Young Red, at a price of one and a half sovereigns apiece.

It had been an extravagance, one she had regretted ever since. Such baskets made the rest of her wares appear coarse by comparison, and if she were to make any profit at all, she'd have to charge at least two sovereigns for them, making them easily the dearest items in her cart. And so, she'd kept them packed away in the first two settlements she visited. Better to save them for the proper setting, she told herself. But really she was afraid, though she couldn't say why. Maybe she feared that she'd been duped by young HedFarren, though she knew the man better than to think that he'd take advantage of his friends in such a way. But what if she had made an error in buying them? What if she had squandered her twenty-four sovereigns on baskets that looked pretty, but were worth only a fraction as much? Or what if they were just as fine as Brint and the others had said, and she sold them for too little? What if she got her two sovereigns for each, only to learn later the Stam Corfej had sold his dozen for twice that amount?

She kept them hidden away, pretending she didn't have them, only taking the time to look at them again when she was alone on the plain. In truth, she would have liked to keep them all. Regardless of what they were really worth, she thought them beautiful.

At last, though, she resolved to sell them, or at least to try. She was close enough to the Thraedes that she could venture all the way to its banks and stop in some of the larger established settlements there. Selling such finery in the septs might have proven difficult, but the men and women of the Qirsi cities were every bit as willing to spend their gold as those who lived in the largest cities of the Eandi sovereignties.

On this morning, the third of the waxing, she had come within sight of S'Vralna, one of the more hospitable cities in Fal'Borna lands. It seemed as good a place as any to try to sell the baskets.

Like so many of the fortified settlements in the central plain, S'Vralna had once been an Eandi stronghold. Silvralna, the Eandi had called it, until it was taken from them during the last of the Blood Wars. As with most other cities lost by the Eandi—Ubrundai, Deraqor, Raetel—Silvralna had been renamed by its Fal'Borna conquerors. Not drastically, but rather just enough to be familiar and yet clearly Qirsi. It almost seemed that the white-hairs sought to taunt the former denizens of the settlements. "It was yours once," these new names said, "but now it belongs to us."

S'Vralna, or Silvralna, as Lark preferred to think of it, sat at the elbow of a small bend in the Thraedes, its stark white walls ghostlike against the dark clouds that hung overhead. Gates along the north, south, and east walls, six in all, were guarded by armed Fal'Borna warriors, though no army had threatened the city in more than a century. Towers rose above each gate and also above each of the four corners of the city walls. Two archers stood in every parapet. Lark couldn't help feeling that all these guards and weapons were merely for show, and yet she also couldn't deny that she was impressed by the Fal'Borna's continued vigilance, even in the face of more than a hundred years of peace. It bespoke a strength and discipline that her own people would have been hard-pressed to match. And the thought came to her with the power of a revelation: *This is why we lost.*

As she approached the east gate, Lark noticed that the guards were stopping peddlers' carts and searching them and for a moment she thought about passing the city by and continuing on to the south, toward Deraqor. But the guards appeared to be making quick work of their searches, and she had already come a long way in the past few days. She needed food and wanted to find a bit of wine as well, something other than the pale Qosantian honey wine she was selling. Best just to remain here.

Before long, she had reached the front of the column. One of the guards approached her, his eyes so pale they appeared white, just like his hair, which was tied back from his face.

"What are you selling today, dark-eye?" the man asked, sounding bored.

"My usual wares," Lark told him, refusing to flinch away from that wraithlike gaze. "Blankets, cloth, a few blades, some smoked fish, wine—"

"Any baskets?" the guard demanded.

Lark blinked. "Yes. Several."

Instantly, the man's entire bearing changed. "Where did you get them?" he asked, his tone crisp. Had his hand strayed to the hilt of his sword?

"From another merchant," she said. "What's this about?"

"The merchant's name?"

"I won't tell you that until I know why you're asking."

His blade was out and leveled at her neck before she could draw breath. "The a'laq takes this matter most seriously, dark-eye," he said, low and menacing. "Don't toy with me. Now I'll ask you one last time, who sold you your baskets?"

She swallowed, reluctant to give Brint's name to this Qirsi, but knowing that if she defied the man again, angering her friend would be the least of her worries. "His name is Brint HedFarren."

The soldier appeared to relax somewhat at the mention of Brint's name. "And where was this?" he asked.

"East of here, on the plain."

"How long have you had them?"

"Half a turn perhaps."

"And have you stopped in other Fal'Borna septs in that time?"

"Yes, a few."

"And you've noticed nothing unusual."

Lark shook her head. "No, nothing."

He nodded and lowered his blade. "Very well." He stepped away from her cart and motioned her through the gate. "You can pass."

She frowned. "Can't you tell me what this is about?"

"Apparently some are trading baskets that carry the pestilence with them. Obviously, we don't want any of them in our city."

The pestilence? In baskets? "No," Lark said, still not quite understanding. "Of course you don't."

"Get moving there!" came a voice from behind her; one of the other merchants no doubt.

Lark flicked the reins and clicked her tongue at Ashes, her dappled grey gelding. The old horse started forward through the archway. But still Lark shook her head, her brow furrowed. How could the pestilence come from baskets, except through some dark magic? Were the Fal'Borna at war with one of the other clans? Were they fighting their own kind?

She steered Ashes through the broad stone lanes to the large market-place in the center of the city. This late in the morning, the market teemed with peddlers and buyers alike. Her mind fixed on what she had heard from the Qirsi guard, Lark noticed immediately that few of the other peddlers had any baskets for sale. She should have been pleased. Stam or Brint or any of the others would have been. Her baskets were sure to fetch a good price and sell quickly. But as before, Lark wondered if she should just leave them in her cart for today. Perhaps people here would be afraid to buy them. They might even be offended if she displayed them with her other wares.

She found a small space between two Eandi traders. She guessed that they were from Tordjanne, or maybe the southern shores of Qosantia: both were fair-skinned, with well-groomed beards and yellow hair that they wore short. They displayed goods from every other sovereignty except Tord-janne, but this wasn't all that unusual. Tordjannis were born merchants; they made few articles themselves.

The men nodded to her as she took her place between them, spread a blanket on the ground, and began to put out her goods.

"Good day so far?" she asked the one on her left as she worked.

The man shrugged and grimaced, then gave a slight shake of his head. Looking at him again, she saw that his hair and beard weren't so much fair as white, and his face was more deeply lined than she'd first noticed.

"Not so good," he said. "It's harvest time. Everyone's selling; no one's buying."

Qosantian. Definitely. She'd know that accent anywhere.

"You're from Ferenham," she said. "Or maybe Harborton."

The man grinned at that, revealing crooked yellow teeth. "Ferenham. And you're from north shores of the Ofirean. Stelpana, if I had to guess."

She smiled. "I'm Lark."

"Lark, is it? The woman who sings so well. I've heard of you." He tapped his chest. "The name's Antal Krost."

"Nice to meet you." She glanced over at the merchant on her other side, but he seemed intent on ignoring them. She cast a questioning look at Antal, who merely shrugged again, an amused grin on his face.

"What are you selling, Lark?" Antal asked, pulling out a skin and taking a small drink. He offered it to her. "Wine?"

She shook her head. "Too early for me, thanks." She gestured vaguely at her old display blanket, which was already half covered with bolts of multicolored cloth and heavier woolen blankets. "Nothing that unusual," she told him. She hesitated, but only for an instant. "I have some baskets in my cart, but I'm wondering now if I should just leave them there."

Antal raised an eyebrow. "Baskets, you say?"

Lark nodded.

He stood and walked to her cart. "Let's have a look."

She joined him at the back of her wagon, and pushed aside the cloth that covered her goods. Seeing the baskets, Antal whistled through his teeth.

"You'd be mad to leave those in the cart. They'll bring a good price, even this time of year." He glanced at her. "If you hadn't noticed, there's a bit of a shortage of good baskets in S'Vralna."

"So I heard. What's this about the pestilence?"

"I'm not certain I understand it," Antal said. "Seems there's been pestilence east of here, near the wash. Somehow the Fal'Borna have convinced themselves that the baskets are spreading it. They think it's some Mettai curse, and they think that our kind are using the baskets to attack the septs."

"It's no' jest any pestilence."

Lark and Antal turned to look at the other merchant, who continued to sit just as he had, staring straight ahead, as if still ignoring them.

"What do you know about it?" Antal demanded.

"Jest what I's heard. It's no' a pestilence like any other. It's a white-hair plague." He looked at them, dark eyes peering out from beneath a shock of yellow hair. He wasn't a young man, but neither was he as old as Antal. "It don' touch our kind," he went on. "Jest them. That's why they's so scared. It only kills them." He stared at them another moment. Then he faced forward, his expression unreadable. Had Lark not seen him speak, she might have thought that the words had come from someone else.

She turned back to Antal. "Those baskets are Mettai," she said in a low voice. "And I was near the wash when I got them."

Antal smiled and shook his head. "Don't let him scare you," he said, dropping his voice as well. "Mettai curses? White-hair plagues? If you ask me it's all nonsense." He nodded toward her cart. "What did you pay for them?"

"One and a half sovereigns for each."

"You'll get three for them here. Two and a half at least. And they may well be the only things you sell." He shrugged. "It's up to you of course, but if it was me, I'd have them out already."

Lark knew Antal was right. Ignoring her lingering doubts, she retrieved the baskets from her cart and placed them on the blanket, pushing aside goods of lesser quality in order to make room for them. She started by putting out eight of them, but at Antal's urging, ended up with all sixteen on display.

"That's it," the older merchant said as she laid out the last of them. "Let them be seen. No one ever bought any goods of mine that they didn't see first." He winked at her and smiled.

Even with her baskets out for all to see, it proved to be as slow a morning as Lark could remember having in any of the larger Fal'Borna cities. It seemed that the cold winds had people frightened of the coming Snows. Or maybe word of the pestilence had scared folk so much that they were refusing to buy any goods from Eandi peddlers. A few people wandered past and some lingered over her display, but none of them so much as touched any of her wares, and many of those who did pause to look at her goods stared warily at those colorful Mettai baskets.

"Maybe I should put them away," she muttered, as the midday bells echoed through the marketplace. "I think they're scaring people."

But Antal merely shook his head. "Give it time. They'll come around."

Not long after, a young Fal'Borna woman stopped in front of Lark and surveyed her offerings. Like so many of the women in the plains clan, she was short and muscular, with bronzed skin that would have been quite unusual for a daughter of any other Qirsi nation. She planted her feet and crossed her arms over her chest before nodding toward the baskets.

"Where did you get those?" she demanded.

"The eastern plain," Lark said. "I bought them from another merchant."

"You know what's been done to our people with baskets like those?"

"I do now. I heard about it today for the first time."

"Yet you continue to display these. No doubt you hope to make a tidy profit by selling them."

"That's what we do," Antal said, drawing the woman's glare. "We're merchants."

The Fal'Borna woman twisted her mouth sourly.

"They're as fine as any baskets I've ever sold," Lark said. "You're welcome to pick one up and look at it. I'm sure you'll agree that they're beautifully made."

"I'm not certain I want to touch them at all," the woman said.

Two other Fal'Borna had stopped near Lark's blanket and were listening to their conversation.

Lark nodded, taking care to hold the woman's gaze. She wanted to keep the other two interested as well, but she knew that the woman was the key. If she could be convinced to buy, the others would follow her example. And once people in the marketplace saw that some had bought the baskets, their fears might be allayed somewhat. "I understand why you might be afraid of them," she said. "If I'd heard all that you probably have, I'd be scared, too. But the guards at your gate let me through. They asked me questions about the baskets, but they came to the conclusion that your people have nothing to fear from them. Even if you don't trust me, you must trust them, right?"

Lark sensed Antal nodding his approval.

The woman hesitated, then squatted down and reached for one of the baskets. Her hand paused over the handle, but then she took hold of it and stood. It was a deep basket, with a simple arching handle and grass osiers. It was brightly colored—reds, blues, yellows—and the coloring was as even and vivid as any Lark had ever seen. Had she the means to keep some of the baskets for herself, this would have been one of them.

"How much for this one?" the woman asked.

All of them were watching her—the other Fal'Borna, Antal, even the ill-tempered merchant on her right. Still, Lark held the woman's gaze.

"Three sovereigns," she said.

The Fal'Borna frowned and shook her head. "Too much." But she didn't put the basket down. "One and a half."

Lark smiled. "No." She turned to the Fal'Borna who were standing nearby. "Can I interest you in a basket? Perhaps two?"

The first woman glanced at them, taking a small step toward Lark, as if to put herself between the merchant and the other Qirsi. "Wait, now. We're not done here. How much for this?"

"The price is three sovereigns," Lark said evenly.

The woman pressed her lips thin, looking angry. "I'll pay two and a half. Not a silver more."

Two and a half was a good price, and though she agreed with Antal that the baskets might well fetch three somewhere, they wouldn't bring that much here, not with all that had been said about Mettai baskets on this day. She made a show of mulling over the offer, but she'd made up her mind almost immediately.

"Very well," she said after a suitable pause. "Two and a half."

The Fal'Borna pulled a small coin pouch from within her wrap and counted out the money. After handing the coins to Lark, she turned and walked away, saying nothing more. Typical Fal'Borna manners.

Lark pocketed the coins and turned to the other Qirsi, who had already begun to sort through the remaining baskets. Within the next few moments she sold six more of them, all for two and a half. She also sold a blanket and two bolts of cloth. Antal sold several items as well, and for a short while it seemed like a normal day in any market. Then, just as quickly, their flurry of sales ended, and the merchants were alone again, the crowd of customers gone.

"There'll be more," Antal said, looking around, a slight frown creasing his forehead. "It's early yet."

Lark just nodded, hoping he was right.

"I was surprised you let the baskets go for so little," the man added a moment later.

She nodded, then sighed. "I know. There are others who might have held out for three."

Antal shrugged, but she could guess at what he was thinking.

"I just thought that with all these tales of the pestilence flying around, I was lucky to be selling them at all."

The man's eyebrows went up. "Well, you might be right about that. Hadn't looked at it that way."

Before either of them could say more, a second cluster of buyers came by, and many of them were drawn immediately to the baskets. This time Lark held out for three sovereigns, and though two of the Fal'Borna walked away, refusing to pay that much, three others paid the price, and two of them bought a pair each.

"Seems you were right," Lark said after they'd gone. "From now on, I'll take nothing less than three."

Antal grinned and nodded.

The rest of the day passed in much the same way. Occasional waves of buyers interrupted long periods when the merchants had little or nothing to do. It made for a long, slow day, but by the time sunset neared Lark had sold several blankets, some cloth, a bit of wine, and much of her smoked fish. Best of all, she had sold all but five of her baskets—eleven in all. And aside from the first few, she'd managed to sell each of them for three sovereigns.

"Looks like you had a good day after all," Antal commented, as he packed up his wares. "Better than I did, that's for certain."

Lark smiled. "I did pretty well," she admitted.

"Well, I'm glad for you. You moving on, or will you be here tomorrow?"

"I'm moving on," she said. "I'll sleep outside the gates tonight and head toward D'Raqor in the morning."

"More's the pity."

Lark paused over her goods, glancing at the old man. Her travels had been lonelier than usual since that night at the bend when she supped with her fellow merchants. Until today, that is.

"How 'bout if I buy you a meal before I go?"

Antal looked up at her and grinned. "I have some food with me as well. I can supply a bit of cheese, some dried breads maybe."

She shook her head. "No, I mean I'd really like to buy supper for you—in a tavern here in the city. An ale as well."

The man frowned, though he appeared interested. "You certain?"

"I had a good day, and thanks to your prodding, I got a few extra sovereigns for those baskets. Supper and an ale seems the least I can do."

Antal nodded once, smiling once more. "All right, then. You convinced me. Supper it is. Where?"

She shook her head. "I don't know the city all that well. You'll have to choose."

He laughed. "I can do that. In fact, I know just the place."

It was called simply the River House and it was tucked away on a narrow lane near the quays, at the southern end of the city. They drove their carts to a small alleyway near the river, and left them there, Antal assuring her that their wares and their horses would be safe.

"I've done this before," the man said. "Never had any problem."

The River House didn't look like much from outside, but within it was brightly lit with candles and oil lamps and the bar and tables were clean and well tended. It smelled of fresh bread and roasted fish.

"Best river bass in the city," Antal said, with a nod and a knowing look. "Trust me."

Lark had to smile. One might have thought from the way he was acting that he would be the one paying for their meals. Too late it occurred to her that Antal might have taken her invitation as something more than just a friendly gesture. She would have to tread carefully; she had no interest in a romance with the man, but neither did she wish to hurt his feelings.

As they sat at a table near the back, Antal signaled the barkeep for a pair of ales.

"So you're off to D'Raqor, eh?" Antal said, after a brief, awkward silence.

"Yes. And then south to the Ofirean."

"You been there before? D'Raqor, I mean."

Lark nodded and smiled. "Many times. I've been selling in Fal'Borna lands for the better part of twenty years."

"Then I needn't tell you that the white-hairs aren't any friendlier there than they are here. In fact they might be worse."

"Yes, I—" She stopped, frowning. She could hear the gate bells ringing again. "Now what's that about?" she said, looking toward a small window by their table.

Antal shrugged. "Probably the twilight bells."

"No," Lark said, shaking her head. "They rang the twilight while we were driving our carts over here."

Antal frowned in turn. "You're certain?"

Lark nodded. After a moment she stood and walked to the door, thinking that she could hear . . . Yes. When she reached the doorway, she was certain of it. People were shouting, and the voices were coming from several directions.

"What do you suppose it is?" Antal asked, joining her at the door.

Lark shivered, feeling the hairs on her arms stand on edge. Something about this troubled her. "I don't know," she muttered.

"It's probably—"

She cast him a look, silencing him. "Listen!" she said. "Can you make out what they're saying?"

He closed his eyes, as if in concentration. Lark did the same. At first, she still could not make out what was being said. But gradually, as those who cried out moved closer to the river, certain words began to stand out among those that remained unintelligible.

". . . Gates . . . Market . . . Fever . . . Healer . . . Eandi . . . Pestilence . . ."

Lark's eyes flew open. Antal was already watching her, looking pale and frightened.

"It can't be!" she whispered. Abruptly she was trembling, her stomach tight and sour.

"Those baskets—"

"No! It's not possible!" But she knew it was, had known all day, from the time the guard first alerted her to the possibility. Had she visited other septs with those baskets? he had asked her. And she had told him the truth: that she had. But she'd neglected to tell him all. "I never took them out of my cart in the other septs."

"What?" Antal demanded.

Lark hadn't even known that she was speaking the words out loud. "Nothing," she muttered, shaking her head. "I need to find the people who bought those baskets."

"It's too late for that," the old merchant said. "You need to get out of this city, before the Fal'Borna find you."

"But all those people—"

"They're dead already," he said, his words striking at her like a fist. "If this really is the pestilence, there's nothing you can do for them now, even if it did come from your baskets."

"We're not sick."

"No," Antal said. "We're not. What was it Kary called it? A white-hair plague? Seems he was right."

She turned to look at the man, raking both hands through her dark hair. "So, you're saying that I should run away?"

"It's all you can do." He said. "You can't help them, but you can save yourself. We'll find—"

Suddenly there were voices nearby. Antal grabbed Lark's arm and pulled her into a narrow byway not far from the tavern entrance. They pressed themselves against the building wall as a pair of uniformed Qirsi walked by.

"There's pestilence in th' city!" one of the men shouted, his voice echoing through the lanes. "Th' gates ha' been closed, an' so has th' market! Stay in yer homes! If'n ye has a fever, light two candles an' leave 'em by yer door! A healer will be along! Stay away from Eandi merchants! If'n ye bought somethin' from one, burn it now! There's pestilence in th' city. Th' gates ha' been closed . . ."

"How do I leave now?" Lark asked when the men were gone. "You heard them: The gates have been closed."

Antal rubbed a hand over his mouth, his eyes trained on the wall behind her. "They'll have to open them again, eventually. You have no choice but to wait them out."

"Wait them out? Where? I have no place to stay! They'll be looking for our carts! For all we know they've taken them already."

"I doubt that," Antal said. "But I take your point. Let's get back to them and see if we can't find a better place to hide. We can't be the only Eandi left in the city."

They hurried back to the river and, to their profound relief, found the horses and carts just where they'd left them. Unfortunately, while they were still on the small byway where they'd left them, they heard another pair of guards approaching.

Once again, it seemed the gods were smiling on the merchants: the guards turned off the broader avenue before reaching their alleyway. But it was clear to Lark that she couldn't evade the Fal'Borna forever. She didn't know the city well enough, and though Antal did, so long as they remained together, they would be easier to spot.

"Maybe I should just go to them," she said. "Give myself up."

Antal shook his head vehemently. "No. They'll kill you. You've been trading with the Fal'Borna long enough to know their ways. You'd be better off . . ." He trailed off, gazing toward the water.

"What is it?" she asked, twisting around, trying to see what he was looking at.

"I was going to say that you'd be better off throwing yourself in the river. But maybe that's not such a bad idea after all."

"The river?"

"It's deep here. Too deep to cross. But if we can stay by the river and get to the north end of the city, we might have a chance. It's still deep, but not as."

"How do you know?"

"I used to work the trading boats between here and the Ofirean. I have some knowledge of these waters." He climbed onto his cart and took up the reins. "Follow me," he said. "And try to keep your animal quiet."

Lark nodded and whispered a soothing word to Ashes before climbing into her seat and starting after the man. By this time it was growing dark, and the lanes by the quays were narrow and poorly lit. Again, though, Antal's knowledge of the city served them well. He navigated the alleys and byways confidently, and Lark surrendered all to faith and simply followed. They had no more near encounters with guards, but they could hear shouted warnings in the distance. Occasionally they also heard low conversations coming from the quays or the ships moored there, but whoever was speaking didn't seem to notice the merchants.

After some time Lark asked, "How much farther?," taking such care to keep her voice low that she wasn't even certain Antal had heard her until he swiveled in his seat to look back at her.

Before he could say anything, however, a streak of fire blazed overhead. An instant later, a second beam carved through the darkness at a different angle, and then a third. At the same time, more voices rose from the city. These were nothing like the shouted litany of the Fal'Borna soldiers. People were screaming in terror, crying out in pain.

"What is it?" Lark asked, her voice rising as well.

Antal just shook his head. Shafts of flame continued to arc above them, and a baleful orange glow began to illuminate the low clouds. Fire. The city was burning.

The smell of burning wood reached her and a moment later something else. Flesh. She gagged. She heard a strange moaning sound and then the rending of wood. It seemed that the city was being ripped apart.

"Magic!" she called to Antal. "It's all magic. The fire, the buildings—"

Before she could say more, Ashes reared, kicking out his front legs and neighing in terror. Antal's horse did the same.

"Easy, Ashes!" Lark called to her beast. "Easy!" But the animal continued to rear and kick. They were in yet another narrow lane, and Lark feared that the animal would hurt himself. Antal struggled to control his horse as well.

"Off your carts, dark-eyes!"

Lark twisted around, still struggling with the reins as Ashes continued to buck.

There were six of them, all men, all Fal'Borna from the look of them. Four of them held long blades; the other two were unarmed, although Lark wasn't sure that really mattered with sorcerers.

"I said, get off your carts!"

They weren't soldiers. Most likely they had come from the quays. But Lark felt certain that they had heard the warnings.

Ashes reared again, drawing her gaze once more. "I can't get off until I calm my horse," she said over her shoulder. "If you can calm him, great. Otherwise you'll just have to wait."

Almost immediately the two horses began to calm down.

Lark took a long breath.

"Now," the Qirsi said. "For the last time, get off your carts."

Slowly, Lark and Antal climbed down from their seats and turned to face the men.

"Eandi merchants," the Fal'Borna said grimly. "I don't know what you've done to my city, but we're going to find out."

Chapter 4

✛

The men led Lark and Antal away from the river, up a hill, to the marketplace. Bolts of flame still streaked across the night sky, and smoke drifted among the buildings, stinging Lark's eyes and nose. She could still hear the shattering of wood and glass. Winds whipped through the city streets, seeming to come from every direction at once. Ashes, though calmer than before, remained on edge, his ears laid flat as he shook his head impatiently again and again. In part this was due to the fact that a Fal'Borna had led him through the lanes to this point. He was a fairly docile beast, but he didn't like to be handled by anyone other than Lark. Even so, he was behaving oddly. Whatever magic had been unleashed by the pestilence was still at work. She still heard voices; forlorn cries, moans of despair and pain. Had she not known better, she might have thought that the city was under siege.

Surveying the marketplace, Lark saw that other Eandi merchants had been brought here as well. Antal had been right to think that they weren't alone among the Fal'Borna. It seemed, though, that the others of their race were in similar straits.

"There! That one!" Looking toward the voices, Lark saw a guard pointing at her, leading several others in her direction. His clothes were stained with soot and blood, and he had a gash on his forehead, but as he drew near, she recognized the man who had questioned her earlier this day at the gate.

The man and his comrades stopped a short distance from her, seemingly unwilling to come nearer. It almost struck her as funny that they should be so afraid of her. They were the ones with magic.

"Your baskets did this," the man said, glaring at her. "You know it's true."

"I don't know anything for certain," she said, an admission in the words. "When I saw you this morning, I didn't think any of this would happen. That's the truth."

One of the other guards nodded toward her cart. "Is that one yours?" he asked. His uniform bore markings on the chest; it seemed he was an officer, a captain probably.

"Yes," Lark said.

"Are there more baskets inside?"

She nodded.

Lark knew immediately what he would do. She nearly opened her mouth to beg him to spare Ashes, but she needn't have bothered. These were Fal'Borna. As merciless as they would be with her and her wares, they would take good care of her horse. They removed the beast's harness and led him a short distance away. A moment later, her cart exploded in flame. Even expecting it, Lark started.

"My gold!" she said, remembering the leather pouch that held her coins. She'd had it with her in the tavern, but had placed it on the seat beside her when she and Antal returned to their carts. She started toward the cart, but Antal caught her around the waist.

"No! It's too late."

"That's everything I have!" She struggled to break free of his grip, but the old man held her fast.

"Please!" she sobbed. "I'll have nothing!" She looked at the Fal'Borna, desperate now. "Can't you stop it? Just long enough for . . ."

The captain shook his head, a hard expression on his face. "Fire magic doesn't work that way." He opened both hands, turning slowly and glancing up at the sky, a simple motion that seemed to encompass all that was going on around them: the fires and smoke, the screams of terror. "Don't you think we'd stop these other fires if we could?"

"But my gold," she said weakly.

She saw his jaw muscles bunch.

"You won't need it."

Lark felt her knees buckle. *You won't need it.* Had it not been for Antal, she would have fallen to the ground.

The Fal'Borna turned to the other merchant. "What's in your cart?"

"No baskets, if that's what you mean?" When the soldier didn't respond, Antal shrugged. "Much the same as her. Blankets, cloth, a few blades, some boxes and other woodwork. But no baskets. I swear it."

The captain looked toward the gate guard, a question in his pale eyes.

"She was the only one with baskets," the gate guard said. "At least that I saw."

For several moments, the captain merely stood there, eyeing Antal, as if trying to decide what to do with him.

Lark took a breath, fighting a wave of nausea. *You won't need it.* She felt herself going numb. But she couldn't allow what she had done to doom

Antal as well. The merchant was still holding her, and now she pulled herself from his grasp and straightened. "I only met this man today," she said. "Whatever it is you think I've done, whatever vengeance you plan to exact, that's between the Fal'Borna and me. He had nothing to do with it."

"He's with you now," the captain said, his voice flat. "He did nothing to stop you. He might well have been helping you."

"He did nothing for me. We met today. We chatted, but that was all."

"They were on the river road," said one of the men from the quays. "I'd wager they were trying to get out of the city by crossing at the north end."

The captain nodded once. "See to his horse."

"You're making a mistake!" Lark shouted, tears on her face. "He's just a merchant."

The captain ignored her; the other guards quickly unharnessed Antal's nag from his cart.

Lark heard the jangling of coins and, glancing over at Antal, saw that the merchant held his money pouch in his hand. Antal tried to smile, but it looked pained. "At least I have my gold," he said, tears shining in his eyes.

The Qirsi led Antal's horse over to where they had tied Ashes. In mere moments, the merchant's cart was engulfed in bright, angry flames.

"I'm so sorry, Antal," Lark whispered.

The man said nothing.

For several moments all of them just stood there, watching the carts burn. The wood snapped and popped so that glowing embers flew in all directions. Black smoke billowed into the night, buffeted by the winds so that it shifted first one way and then another until finally it mingled with the dark, pungent cloud that now hung over S'Vralna.

Finally the captain looked away from the flames and regarded the two merchants.

"Bring them," he said, turning on his heel and walking out of the marketplace.

Two guards approached Lark and, taking her by each arm, steered her after the captain. Antal walked behind her, also held by two Fal'Borna soldiers.

"Where are you taking us?" Lark called to the captain.

He cast a quick look over his shoulder before facing forward again. "To the a'laq," he said, his words nearly lost amid the wind and the screams and the desperate whinnying of horses coming from a nearby farrier shop.

The a'laq. Would he be the one to execute them? Or would he merely pass judgment and leave the killing to another?

Once out of the marketplace, Lark saw even more evidence of the damage being done by the white-hair plague. Houses were in ruins. A building seemed to tear itself apart in front of them. One moment it was standing dark and silent against the glowing sky; the next it crumbled to the ground as if crushed by some great, unseen fist. Lark heard voices calling out for help within the rubble, but the captain and his men didn't stop to help.

"Aren't you going to do something?" Lark demanded. She tried to halt, but the men holding her arms forced her to keep moving, until they were practically dragging her along the lane. "They need help!" she shouted at the captain's back.

Finally, the man stopped, turning to stare at her. What she saw on his face silenced her, made her ashamed for having spoken at all. Rage, grief, hatred; tears shone on his cheeks. She half expected him to walk to where she stood and strike her. "If we help them, we'll be sickened as well," he said, the calmness of his voice chilling her. "There's nothing we can do."

They walked on and soon stopped in front of a large, fortified house. A stone wall surrounded the structure, and guardhouses sat at each corner as well as at the front entrance. It seemed a strange home for a Fal'Borna leader until Lark remembered that S'Vralna had been built and ruled by the Eandi long before the Qirsi took it for themselves. In all probability this structure had once housed an Eandi governor or a marshal in the Stelpana army.

"Wait here," the captain said to the guards. He disappeared through the gate, leaving Lark, Antal, and the other soldiers standing in the street.

"I'm sorry, Antal," Lark said again, knowing that she had apologized already, knowing as well that any apology she offered would be inadequate.

"Why baskets?" the man muttered in response. "What kind of evil is it that would put such an illness in baskets and send them out into the world?"

She turned to face him, forcing herself to meet his gaze. "I don't know."

"Baskets," he said again, shaking his head. His eyes had a strange, otherworldly look to them, and Lark found herself fearing for the soundness of his mind.

The captain returned a few moments later, pausing at the front gate and beckoning to his men to bring the merchants forward.

"The a'laq will speak with you," the captain said. "You will remain standing while in his presence, and you will answer every question you're asked. Do you understand?"

"Yes," Lark said.

"Good. Follow me."

She remained where she was. "What's the a'laq's name?" she asked.

"You will address him as A'Laq. Now come along."

"What's his name?" she asked again.

The captain pressed his lips thin and glared at her. "P'Crath," he finally said. "Son of P'Rajh."

He turned and started walking again. This time, Lark followed.

After passing through the gate, they followed a narrow stone path to the door of the building. Two more guards stood there, and one of them pulled the door open as they approached. They entered a broad hallway that led them into a large room with a high ceiling. A small man sat in an ornate chair at the center of the room, watching them approach. He had long white hair that hung to his shoulders. In the dim light of candles and oil lamps, his skin looked surprisingly dark and leathery and his large eyes seemed to glow like golden coins. He gripped the arms of his chair, eyeing Lark as she walked toward him. The captain held out a hand, stopping her.

"This is the merchant, A'Laq. The man was with her, but he himself had no baskets."

The a'laq nodded once, never taking his eyes off of Lark. "What's your name?" he asked.

"I'm called Lark, A'Laq. My full name is Lariqenne Glyse."

"Where did you get these baskets you sold?"

"I bought them from another Eandi merchant, east of here, near the Silverwater."

"What merchant? Give me a name."

Lark straightened and took a breath. "No."

The a'laq didn't appear surprised by her refusal, but the captain shot her an angry look.

"Answer him!" he commanded.

"Or what?" she said. "You'll kill me? You've made it clear that you intend to do that anyway. I won't doom my friends as well." She faced the a'laq again. "I've known the . . . the person who sold me the baskets for some years now. He didn't know what he was doing any more than I did. He certainly bears no ill will toward the Fal'Borna. Someone has done a terrible thing to your people, A'Laq. I understand your rage, your need for vengeance. But I'm not your enemy. Whoever made this pestilence used me, and they used this other merchant, as well. Killing me or him won't accomplish anything."

The a'laq stared at her for what seemed a long time. Then he nodded again, and turned to the captain. "Cut off the man's hand."

Lark gaped at him. "*What!*"

"A'Laq?" the captain said, clearly discomfited.

"I don't care which one," P'Crath said, his voice even. "Just do it."

"Wait!" Lark said. "You can't—"

"*Be silent!*" the a'laq said, his voice echoing through the chamber.

Suddenly, she couldn't speak. She couldn't even breathe. It seemed that someone had wrapped a powerful hand around her throat.

"You feel that?" P'Crath demanded. "That's what we call mind-bending magic. I could command you to claw out your own eyes or to gut yourself with that blade you carry. I can command you to tell me what I want to know, but right now, I'd rather see you suffer. I'd rather see your friend here maimed. You say you understand my need for vengeance? You understand nothing! My daughter . . ." His voice broke on the word and he paused, then swallowed. "My girl was in the marketplace today. She bought nothing, but it seems she encountered one of your baskets. Perhaps you showed it to her. Perhaps it was someone else; someone she knew, someone she trusted. It doesn't matter. She's sick now. She can't eat or drink." He opened his hands and stared at his palms. "Fire pours from her fingers, and she can do nothing to stop it. She's new to her power—it can't be more than two or three turns that she has been wielding any magic at all. Now it will kill her. And you say you understand my need for vengeance?" He looked at the captain again. "Cut off the man's hand."

The captain hesitated, but only briefly. He pulled his sword free and strode toward Antal. The merchant shrank away from him, but he was held fast by the guards standing on either side. There was nothing he could do to save himself.

"No!" Lark said, released for the moment from the a'laq's magic. She was crying again. "You bastard!" she said, flinging the word at P'Crath. "The merchant's name is Brint HedFarren. He's from Tordjanne. He said that he bought the baskets in a village near the Silverwater. He didn't tell us more than that. I swear it."

It was a betrayal, she knew. The Fal'Borna would be after Young Red now, but what could she do? Antal had nothing to do with any of this, and it seemed likely that he'd be dead before the night was out. She couldn't allow him to be tortured, as well.

"Us?" the a'laq asked.

"What?"

"You said, 'He didn't tell *us* more than that.' He sold baskets to others?"

She nodded, struck dumb by the realization of what this meant.

"Their names. Quickly."

The anger she had felt moments before was gone, replaced by guilt and panic. What had she done? What had all of them done? "Yes, of course. There was Stam Corfej, and me, and . . . and Barthal Milensen. There were two others, but I don't know their names. I'd never seen them before and I haven't seen them since. They were headed east, into Eandi lands. I don't think you have anything to fear from them. But Barthal and Stam were going south, toward the Ofirean."

"What other cities have you visited? Where else have you sold these baskets of yours?"

"This is the first place."

The a'laq frowned.

"It's true, A'Laq. I've had them for some time now, but I didn't sell them anywhere else. I didn't even display them before today. I don't remember all the septs I visited between the bend and here, but there were several, and I never showed anyone the baskets."

P'Crath narrowed his eyes. "So you did this to get at me? At my city?"

"No!" Lark said, taken aback by the question. "I told you before, I had no idea that the baskets would hurt anyone!"

"Then why would you wait to sell them?"

"I didn't know how . . ." She shook her head, certain that he wouldn't understand or believe her explanation, wondering if it really mattered anymore. "I wasn't sure how much to ask for them, and I was afraid that they'd make the rest of what I sold look common by comparison."

"So you just carried these baskets with you, ignoring the gold you'd spent to get them, thinking nothing of the gold you'd make when you sold them. Is that what you want me to believe?"

"I can't make you believe me, A'Laq. But that's the truth. You can use your mind-bending magic on me and I'll tell you the same thing."

He stared at her a moment longer, perhaps considering whether or not he should do just that. But then he turned to Antal. "How did you end up with this woman, dark-eye?"

In a flat voice, the merchant briefly related how he and Lark had met that day.

"What did she tell you about the baskets?"

"Basically the same thing she told you. She'd been carrying them for a while, but had yet to sell them. She said that she was reluctant to display them here. Seems she had an encounter with one of your gate guards that scared her off of them. I encouraged her to put them out. I thought she'd get a good price for them, and she did."

Lark closed her eyes and shook her head. What little doubt might have remained as to Antal's fate was gone now.

"What about that?" the a'laq asked, turning back to Lark. "How did you convince the guard to let you through?"

"I told him that I'd had the baskets when I visited other septs, and that nothing had happened to make me believe they posed a threat to your people."

"You lied to him, didn't you?"

A denial sprang to her lips and she nearly gave it voice. But she could see from the look on P'Crath's face that he understood as well as she what she had done.

"Yes," Lark said. "I lied to him."

Antal whirled on her. "*What?*"

"I tried to tell you before," she said. "I did take the baskets to other septs—that's what I told the guard," she added, glancing at the a'laq. "But I didn't take them out while I was in any of those places. I didn't display them. The guard assumed, because of what I said, that the baskets were safe, but they weren't."

"And you knew that," P'Crath said.

"No," she said. "I didn't know that they were dangerous. But I didn't know that they were safe, either."

"Surely that's not her fault," Antal said, looking first at Lark and then at P'Crath.

"Not entirely, no," said the a'laq. "The guard will be punished for his carelessness. But there is a price to be paid for her crime, as well."

"And mine?" Antal asked. He looked pale, but he didn't shy from the a'laq's gaze.

"Yes," P'Crath said. "And yours." He glanced at the captain. "What have you done with their wares?"

"Their carts have been burned, A'Laq. Their wares are gone. That seemed the prudent course to take."

P'Crath nodded. "Very well." He regarded Antal, looking thoughtful. Then he nodded again. "Yes, very well. You can go, dark-eye. The loss of your wares and cart seems punishment enough. Return the man's horse to him," he said to the captain. "When the gates are opened again, he's free to leave the city. For now . . . take him back to the marketplace."

"Yes, A'Laq." The captain sheathed his sword again. "What of the woman?"

"Leave that to me."

The soldier's eyes flicked toward Lark, but then he bowed. "Yes, A'Laq." He turned to leave the chamber. "Bring him," he said to the guards.

Antal's guards started to lead him away.

"Wait!" the merchant called, twisting his neck to look back at Lark and the a'laq. "What are you going to do to her?"

The a'laq didn't answer.

"Just go, Antal," Lark said. "Get away while you can."

"She didn't mean any harm! You know she didn't." He fought to break free, but the guards held him firmly and dragged him out of the building. "You bastards! She's done nothing wrong! You have no right to do this to her!"

Even after the guards had taken him out of the building, Lark could still hear him shouting. For several moments the a'laq said nothing, and Lark realized that she could also hear the wretched cries of the sick and grieving, the terrified, unearthly screams of horses, the harsh rending of wood. The pestilence had not relinquished its grip on the city; if anything, matters had worsened in the time Lark had been in P'Crath's home.

"My people are dying," the a'laq finally said, his eyes fixed on a small glazed window that overlooked his gardens. The sky above his home still glowed with that same malevolent orange. "For all I know my daughter is dead already." He faced Lark again. "You understand: Someone must pay for what's been done to us this night."

"Are you asking me to forgive you for killing me?"

His expression hardened. "No. I don't give a damn if you forgive me or not. When the time comes I'll answer to Bian, and to him alone."

"There's no need to be angry with me, A'Laq," she said, surprising herself with her calm. "I'm just trying to understand what it is you were trying to say."

He looked away again. "This pestilence has moved across the plain faster even than my people feared it would. It was set upon us by the Mettai and spread with aid from Eandi merchants like you and your friend." He glanced at her before averting his gaze again. "My people are warriors. In all our history, we've never hesitated to defend ourselves. We've never surrendered to any foe. But with this . . ." He opened his hands, then let them drop to his side again.

His eyes met hers again, and this time he didn't look away, though it seemed to take some effort. "Perhaps I am seeking forgiveness. You tell me that you had nothing to do with the poisoning of these baskets, that you mean us no harm. And I believe you. But you're Eandi, and no matter your intentions, you brought this illness into our city."

A door behind the a'laq opened and a small, white-haired woman with wide, pale eyes appeared. Lark couldn't be certain, but there seemed to be tears on her face.

P'Crath turned at the sound, stared at the woman for several moments, and nodded once. She withdrew and closed the door.

"I have no more time for this," the a'laq said. "Draw your blade."

Once more, Lark found that she hadn't the power to disobey. It seemed as if her hands were no longer hers, that they were guided by some other will, stronger than her own. She felt tears flowing down her face again, and she couldn't even wipe them away.

"Please," she said, her voice quavering.

"I'm sorry." The a'laq didn't sound contrite, but he wore a troubled expression. "This will be quick. I promise you that much."

Lark stared at him, her entire body trembling. All except her hands, which were perfectly still. "I don't deserve this."

"My daughter doesn't deserve her fate, either. Turn the blade and place the tip over your heart."

She did as she was told, though she fought the man's magic with every bit of strength she possessed. Never in her life had she felt so powerless.

"I hope your daughter lives," she said. "I hope that one day, you'll have to explain to her what you're about to do."

The a'laq opened his mouth, then closed it again. "She's Fal'Borna," he finally said. "I won't have to explain." He exhaled and looked away. "Take your life."

She battled as she never had before. She tried to release the blade, to let it fall to the ground. She tried to move its tip so that her heart wouldn't be pierced. She tried to flee the chamber. But her hands were not her own, her feet, it seemed, were held by invisible shackles, her aim was perfectly, lethally true.

"No!" she screamed, her voice echoing off the ceiling and walls.

And still, her hands, steady, strong, sure, guided the blade into her chest, as if they had been waiting to do so all her life.

It hurt less than she thought it would. Mostly she felt cold. Her legs gave out and she dropped to the floor.

"Damn you," she managed to mutter, as darkness took her.

But already the a'laq was getting to his feet and leaving the chamber. He gave no indication that he had heard.

The guards were at the door before he reached it, concern etched on their faces.

"We heard a scream, A'Laq," one of them said. "Are you all right?"

P'Crath nodded. He had no time for this. He wanted only to find Z'Feni, his wife, and see his daughter. Z'Feni had looked so frightened a few moments before, when she came to the chamber seeking him. Was their beloved child dead already? Or was there still time to save her?

"I'm fine. The Eandi woman is dead. Have her removed from the chamber."

"Yes, A'Laq," the man said.

P'Crath was already past him, striding toward the inner courtyard. He quickly navigated the corridors of the old Eandi palace, until he came to the arched entranceway to the court. Cold air crept into the hallways through the open door, but P'Crath didn't care. Z'Feni stood just outside, tears on her face reflecting the glow of a bright fire that burned on the far side of the court. The small pool at the center of the space reflected the flames and the dark orange sky, the waters rippled by the wind. Between the fire and the pool lay B'Asya, covered by several blankets, her face damp with sweat, her eyes closed.

"She's finally asleep," Z'Feni said, her eyes fixed on their child. "We have to do this now."

"The healers gave her a tonic?" P'Crath said, looking at her.

"It was the only way. As it was, she nearly killed the man who gave it to her. And now he fears that he'll become ill as well."

"Did he get that near to her?"

Z'Feni grimaced and nodded.

"Where is he now?" P'Crath asked.

"I sent him away and told him not to return for ten days."

The a'laq nodded. "Good." He looked out at B'Asya again. "Let's get started then."

"What if it doesn't work?" his wife asked, taking his hand. "What if you can't heal her? Maybe she needs to be awake."

"I don't know," the a'laq said. He was leader of the sept. He was a Weaver; he could wield all forms of Qirsi magic. But in the face of this pestilence, P'Crath felt utterly helpless. It was an unsettling sensation for him, one that he felt compelled to hide from his wife, though as a Weaver herself, she probably felt much the same way. "I choose to believe that it will work."

She nodded, giving his hand a squeeze. "Yes, all right."

P'Crath released her hand and closed his eyes. He took a long, steadying breath, and then reached to his daughter with his mind and magic. Sensing her, feeling immediately how weak she had grown, he stepped into her dreams.

He had done such a thing many times before. Weavers often communicated with each other in this way, reaching forth with their minds over many leagues to enter the dreams of those who led other septs. In this way, the a'laqs of all the Fal'Borna could work together against a common enemy or alert one another to approaching danger. This was how he had first learned of this pestilence that was sweeping across the plain.

But never before had P'Crath experienced anything like this. His daughter's thoughts were disjointed and alien, as if the fever that gripped her body had also addled her mind. He saw and heard things he didn't understand. B'Asya stood before him surrounded by a blazing, swirling cloud, as if she were in the midst of a storm of flame. She writhed, her mouth open as if she were howling in pain, though P'Crath heard not a sound from her. Her eyes were open, panicked, unseeing. He called to her, but she didn't respond.

He took a step toward her, but before he could draw nearer, without warning, it struck at him. He doubled over, the abrupt pain in his gut enough to bring tears to his eyes and make him gag. He dropped to his knees and retched until his throat ached. He knew this was not some image conjured by his daughter's fever; this was real. He tried to break away from her, to sever the connection he had forged between his mind and hers, but he couldn't. It seemed that she clung to him, though whether she did so blindly or out of fear or out of some delusion-induced malice, he couldn't say. He knew only that however weak she had seemed a moment before, her grip on him was impossibly strong.

He forced his eyes open, but still could see only the vision in B'Asya's mind. Z'Feni was calling his name, sounding terrified. That much he knew.

"Get away from here!" he shouted.

He felt her hand on his back and he shrugged her off.

"Get away from me! Now! While you still can!"

Gods! His stomach hurt! But more, he felt it creeping through his body, like molten rock in his veins. And he knew. Bian help him, he knew.

B'Asya had only just come into her power. She might well have wielded all the magics of a Weaver someday, if only the pestilence hadn't taken her. But P'Crath remained at the height of his powers. Fire, shaping, healing, mists and winds, language of beasts. He had them all, and he sensed that all of them were being unleashed. He tried to resist, to hold back his magic, at least until Z'Feni could heed his warnings and get away. But he felt as if he were standing in the middle of a river, attempting to block the current. He hadn't the strength or the will; he didn't even know how to make the attempt.

"Get away!" he called out again.

Even as the words crossed his lips, he felt the magic slip out. Shaping. He heard the stone wall of the house collapse, heard Z'Feni, his wife, his love, cry out in terror.

Too late, he understood. Just as this pestilence struck at Qirsi magic, as well as at the body and the mind, it was passed along by magic. That was why this was happening to him. He hadn't gone near B'Asya—B'Asya, who was lost to him!—but he had touched her mind with his own, her magic with his. And in forging that bond, he had opened himself to her affliction.

P'Crath felt the power building inside him again, terrible and immense, overwhelming and irresistible. He tried to steer the power into one of the less destructive magics; away from shaping or fire or even wind, which, if uncontrolled, would do nearly as much damage as the other two. Before he'd even made a conscious choice, he felt the air around him growing cold and damp. Yes, a mist. What harm could come from a mist?

"P'Crath, stop it!" Z'Feni cried out. "You're killing the fire! You're going to kill her!"

It was getting colder and colder. Z'Feni was right. Still linked to his daughter, he could feel her shivering, and worse, he could feel her reaching for her fire magic again, even as she slept. The urgency she felt as she tried to access her magic was almost a match for the force of power within him. How could he hope to stop her when he couldn't even stop himself? All this from his mist. What harm, indeed. He forced his eyes open, trying again to break free of B'Asya's mind.

"Can't you stop?" Z'Feni asked him.

"No!" he managed to say. "I can't! Don't you see? It's got me as well. You have to get away from me; away from us!"

His wife gaped at him. She seemed so far away already, though he knew that she was right there with him, close enough to breathe the air he breathed, to feel his magic, to be killed by this disease that would surely kill him.

"You . . . You mean you have it now?"

"Yes. I have it. You will soon enough."

"What about B'Asya? Can you save her?"

He felt the pulse of magic building and knew from his daughter, from the bond they shared now, just where it would go. "Get down!" he shouted, dropping to the ground. "Z'Feni, get down!"

She did, just in time. Fire burst from B'Asya's hands, lashing out at the walls surrounding the courtyard like bright, angry serpents, burning through his mist, which continued to build. He turned his power to something else: language of beasts. It would make matters worse for those beyond his home, but what choice did he have? The power was still inside him, clamoring to get out. Eventually he'd weaken and die, but he was a Weaver; his power went so deep. Always he'd seen this as a boon, a gift from Qirsar, the god of Qirsi magic. Now it was his curse, and that of the people he loved most.

Eventually, B'Asya's burst of magic ran its course, leaving the poor girl even more exhausted and ever closer to death. P'Crath was able to break free of their connection, but that was no consolation to him now. He'd failed; she'd passed her illness to him.

"Both of you," Z'Feni muttered. "I'm going to lose both of you."

He wanted to reassure her, to tell her that they'd find a way through. But she was right: She was going to lose both of them. And she deserved more from him than false hope and empty words of comfort.

"You must leave here!" he said instead. He had found the strength to stop the flow of magic from his body, but already he could feel it building once more. It wouldn't be long until he lost control of it again. "It's the magic, Z'Feni. That's what will kill me. That's what will kill all of us. As soon as I touched her mind I was sick, too. It's the magic."

She shook her head, her pale golden eyes wide, her skin as pale as starlight. "Then there's nothing we can do. We can't save her."

"No," he said. "We can't. But you can save the rest of them, the ones who aren't sick yet."

Z'Feni shook her head again, tears streaming down her face.

"You have to listen to me," he said. The power was building quickly now. He couldn't hold it back much longer. "We haven't much time. The power . . ." He swallowed. No time to explain that now. "You can't help us. We're lost already. But the others. Get them away from here. Not together. And you have to keep your distance from them, too. You're not sick yet, but . . . but you probably will be soon." Gods, it was hard to keep his mind on what he was saying. All he wanted to do was unleash his magic, let it pour from him. "Send them away. Tell them that if they're still alive in ten days, they can return and start rebuilding the city. It's the only way. Otherwise we'll simply kill one another. Do you understand?"

She nodded. "I think so."

"Good. Then go."

She looked at B'Asya, and P'Crath knew that she wanted only to go to the girl, to hold her, to stroke her hair and kiss her brow.

"Go, Z'Feni. Please."

She must have heard the strain in his voice, because she turned her gaze on him, the tender expression of a moment before giving way to a look of terror. "What is it?" she asked.

"My magic. I can't hold it much longer. Go! Save yourself! Save our people!"

Still on her hands and knees, she backed away from him, never taking her eyes off his face.

"I love you," she said. "I have since the day we first met, when we were just children. Do you remember?"

He nodded, and suddenly there were tears on his face, too. For just an instant, his hold on his magic slipped and a wind whipped through the courtyard. Gritting his teeth he clamped down on his power again, but he knew he couldn't hold out for more than a few seconds.

"I love you, too," he said, his voice hoarse. "Always. Now go!"

She stood, took a step toward the door, then stopped and looked one last time at B'Asya. The wind began to rise again. She stifled a sob and ran from him.

With her gone, P'Crath surrendered to the power surging through him. A gale swept through the courtyard, keening in the stone, roughening the water in the pool so that it lapped over the sides. Fire flew from his hands, just as it had from the hands of his child. One of the stone walls shattered like glass at the touch of his mind. His was powerful magic, and now, for the first time, it was completely unbridled. There was no telling what he might do before he died.

At the same time, the a'laq reached for B'Asya again. They would spend these last hours of their lives together. Perhaps she would draw comfort from knowing that her father was there with her, suffering as she did. She would grieve for him as he did for her, particularly if it occurred to her that he had gotten sick trying to help her. But at least she wouldn't be alone. And neither would he. The thought eased his mind, just a bit. It wasn't much, P'Crath knew, but it was all that either of them had left.

Chapter 5

✦‡✦

At times it seemed to Grinsa jal Arriet that the dark clouds hanging over the plain had no end, that this chill wind bending the grasses and scything through his damp clothing would never cease. The rain had stopped for the moment—a small grace that did little to raise his spirits or those of his companions. Their days were grey monotony, their nights tense and restless.

The two Eandi merchants, Torgan Plye and Jasha Ziffel, kept to themselves, speaking in quiet tones or riding silently, side by side. What little Grinsa had seen of them prior to their departure from E'Menua's sept, had convinced him that they didn't like or trust one another. But they were prisoners now, their executions certain should this mission fail. And because their captors were Qirsi, because they were alone and friendless in Fal'Borna land, they could look only to each other for fellowship.

Grinsa and the other Qirsi, a young Fal'Borna Weaver named Q'Daer, couldn't even take that much comfort. They trusted neither the Eandi nor each other. They had clashed several times before leaving the sept—Grinsa had gone so far as to strike the man the day before they began their journey—and though they had come to an accommodation that allowed them to speak civilly to one another, each remained wary of the other.

They had been riding for six days, but they had not yet encountered any Eandi merchants, much less the baskets that supposedly had spawned the outbreak of pestilence on the plain. Nor had they seen any sign of the Mettai witch who was said to have spread this evil curse across the land. The Harvest winds were blowing. The rains were upon them. Grinsa suspected that by now those Eandi merchants who usually spent the warmer turns among the Fal'Borna would be headed back to the Eandi sovereignties. With each day that passed, his hopes of finding either the Mettai woman or the traders who had her baskets faded.

The previous night, Q'Daer had given voice to similar doubts, even suggesting that they were wasting their time and should return to E'Menua's sept.

"These winds are cold for a Hunter's Moon," he had said, his square, youthful face illuminated by their small fire. "The Snows will be coming early this year, and I have no desire to be out here when they arrive. It's time we turned back."

Both merchants had looked toward Grinsa, gauging his response, fear in their dark eyes. Certain death awaited them back at the sept. Torgan, the older man, with his hulking frame and one eye, had sold cursed baskets in a Fal'Borna settlement on the Silverwater Wash, and hundreds had died. He claimed he hadn't known that the baskets posed any danger to the Qirsi, but under Fal'Borna law he was responsible for their deaths. Jasha had done nothing, but the law of the plain was merciless and unyielding. Because he traveled with Torgan, he too was held responsible.

Grinsa had argued for both men's lives and that, in large part, was why they were out here now, searching for the Mettai woman. But that wasn't the reason Grinsa replied as he did. He had far more at stake than merely his sense of justice and his desire to save the lives of two innocent Eandi. He and Cresenne wished only to leave the Fal'Borna, to find another Qirsi clan among whom they might make a new life for themselves and their daughter. E'Menua, the a'laq, had made it clear that only if Grinsa found the Mettai witch and killed her would he and his family be allowed to leave. Otherwise they would live out the rest of their days as Fal'Borna, which meant, among other things, that Grinsa would have to marry a Weaver, for though he considered Cresenne his wife, their joining was not recognized under Fal'Borna law, which required that Weavers be joined to other Weavers.

So, when Q'Daer suggested that they go back to the sept, Grinsa made it clear that he wasn't about to end their search for the Mettai so soon.

"We told the a'laq that we'd find the baskets and the woman who made them," he said, keeping his voice low. "Once we've done that, we can turn back."

"We don't even know where to look," the young Weaver said. "She could be anywhere!"

Grinsa glanced at the man. "All the more reason to find her. Your people are in danger, Q'Daer. That should mean more to you than a cold wind and some snow."

The Weaver cast a dark look his way. "You've never been on the plain when the Snows come, have you, Forelander?"

"No," Grinsa admitted. "I haven't."

"Then you have no right to mock me."

"I'm not mocking you, Q'Daer. I'm merely telling you that we've yet to do what the a'laq asked of us. And until we do, I'm not turning back."

That effectively ended their discussion. Grinsa wasn't certain that Q'Daer accepted him as the leader of their small company. But in the short time he had spent among the Fal'Borna, he had come to understand that E'Menua did not tolerate failure. No doubt the young Weaver knew this better than any of them. Grinsa didn't know for certain that the a'laq really wanted them to succeed in this endeavor—the man seemed to care little whether the merchants lived or died—but he was intent on keeping Grinsa in his sept. Grinsa thought it possible, even likely, that Q'Daer had been instructed to do what he could to keep Grinsa from earning his freedom. Clearly though, regardless of what Q'Daer's purpose might have been, he had yet to achieve it. That had to be why he stopped arguing for an end to their search.

Grinsa shared Q'Daer's eagerness to return to the sept. He was cold and tired; he slept poorly every night and awoke each morning thinking only of Cresenne and Bryntelle, his stomach hollow and sour, his chest aching with longing for them. Occasionally, during the night, when sleep wouldn't come, he considered using his magic to reach back to the sept and enter Cresenne's dreams, just to be with her, to hear how Bryntelle was faring, to make certain that E'Menua was honoring his promise to keep them both safe. But this was a poor substitute for actually being able to hold his daughter and kiss the woman he loved, and it robbed Cresenne of her sleep. Most nights he resisted the urge to speak with her.

He also shared Q'Daer's frustration. Every day that went by made it more likely that others would fall prey to the Mettai curse that was sweeping across the plain. And if it truly was a pestilence, all of them were at risk, including every person in E'Menua's sept.

When they broke camp this morning, Grinsa reminded the merchants of this, not bothering to mask his impatience.

"You've probably been trading on this plain for twenty years," he said to Torgan.

The Eandi, who was saddling his mount, didn't so much as glance at him. "More."

"Fine. More than twenty. Then you must have some idea of where other merchants go this time of year."

"They go where the gold is, as always."

"And where is that?"

"It depends."

The Eandi could save themselves only by helping Grinsa and Q'Daer find the Mettai woman. Failing that, their best hope lay in stalling, in keeping to the plain long enough for them to be rescued or to escape. Like Grinsa, the two merchants were prisoners of the Fal'Borna. But despite this shared circumstance, Grinsa's interests and those of the Eandi often diverged, as they did now.

His patience running thin, Grinsa used language of beasts to make Torgan's horse rear and kick out. The Eandi jumped back, then whirled toward Grinsa, his face reddening.

"You made her do that!"

"Yes," Grinsa said mildly. "I take it I have your attention now."

For a moment, Grinsa actually thought the man would take a swing at him. Then Torgan seemed to remember the other magics Grinsa could wield against him. He frowned, his gaze wandering, but he nodded.

"Where are we most likely to find merchants this time of year?" Grinsa asked again. "Clearly they're not on the Central Plain."

"Probably the rivers," Torgan said reluctantly. "Either the wash—"

"The Silverwater, you mean?"

"Right. Either there, or the area around the Horn."

Grinsa frowned. "The Horn?"

"It's a strip of land between the Thraedes and the K'Sahd," Jasha told him. "Very fertile. Lots of cities. Many merchants pass the Snows there."

"So that would be west of here?" Grinsa asked.

Jasha nodded. "And north."

"Do the Mettai trade there, too?"

The younger merchant shrugged. "Some might. The Mettai don't usually stray far from their villages. That's why those baskets were in such demand. They're hard to find, particularly ones of such high quality."

"So, the woman's not as likely to be at the Horn," Grinsa said.

Jasha appeared to consider this. "No, probably not. She'd probably stay closer to the Silverwater. It would be unlike a Mettai to journey so far into Fal'Borna land."

Discouraged, Grinsa shook his head. "Then I suppose we should just keep to the course we've been following."

"I take it we're ready now?" Q'Daer said, in a tone that indicated he'd known all along where their conversation would lead. He was already astride his dappled grey, a rilda skin pulled tight around his broad shoulders.

Grinsa didn't bother answering. He merely mounted his bay and started riding, following the same northeastern tack they'd been on for days. In a few moments, Q'Daer had caught up to him. He could hear the merchants' horses a short distance behind.

"This is folly, you know," the Fal'Borna said. "You won't find the Mettai woman, and you probably won't find any of her baskets. This is a vast land; looking for a single person, or even a handful . . ." He shook his head. "You haven't a chance."

"We," Grinsa said, staring straight ahead.

"What?"

"You keep saying 'you,' as if you're not a part of this. We're in this together." He looked at the man. "I don't know what E'Menua told you to do. And if your purpose is to keep me from succeeding so that I have to remain in your sept, I don't know how I'll manage to defeat you. But I will. I've faced down more formidable men than you. So you might want to consider whether you're on the wrong side of this."

Q'Daer stared at him, tight-lipped and pale.

"You want to save your people," Grinsa went on. "I know you do. I also know that you want to be rid of me. And I'm sure you want to return to the sept as soon as possible. I want all of those things as well. If we work together, we can see that all of them happen. But one way or another, we're not turning back until we've found the woman and saved these two men from execution."

Q'Daer eyed Grinsa for another moment before facing forward once more. He looked as if he might speak, but said nothing. Grinsa thought, not for the first time, that he looked terribly young and unnerved, and utterly out of his depth.

"I know that E'Menua is your a'laq," Grinsa said after a brief silence. "But I also know—"

"Enough!" Q'Daer said. "You're right. E'Menua is my a'laq. There is no 'but.' There's nothing else you can say beyond that. He is my a'laq. To us, that's everything." He shook his head, looking away again. "I wouldn't expect a Forelander to understand."

"What did he tell you to do?" Grinsa demanded.

He didn't expect that the man would meet his gaze, but Q'Daer surprised him, looking him right in the eye. "Nothing. He sent me with you to help you find the woman and the baskets, and to keep watch on the Eandi."

"And to keep watch on me?"

The man grinned, though the look in his pale eyes remained hard. "There's no need to watch you. Your woman and your child are back in the sept. You're not going anywhere."

Grinsa couldn't really argue the point. "No, I don't suppose I am. But the fact remains we both want and need the same things, at least for the most part."

"I'm Fal'Borna, Forelander," Q'Daer said, his voice tight. "You're not. The a'laq offered you the chance to be one of us, to join our sept, commit yourself to our ways. You refused. What I want and what you want can't possibly be the same."

He knew the man was wrong, but he also knew that nothing good would come of discussing the matter further right now. He held his tongue, and they rode side by side in uneasy silence.

The wind hissed in the grasses and an occasional drop of rain darkened Grinsa's riding cloak. He could see squalls to the west, faint blurs of rain hanging from that unrelentingly grey sky, and he wondered how long it would be before he and his companions were soaked again.

They stopped at midday to eat some dried meat, drink a bit of water, and rest their mounts. As always, the Eandi took their food from Q'Daer, but otherwise kept to themselves. Though they said little to one another, it almost seemed that each took comfort in knowing that the other was nearby. Grinsa and the young Weaver ate without speaking a word. The Fal'Borna refused even to look at him. Soon they were mounted and riding once more.

A light drizzle began to fall on them, coating their clothes and saddlebags with a silvery sheen, and chilling them further. Grinsa threw a hood over his head and huddled within his cloak, staring at the ground in front of him and merely trying to stay warm. He thought of Cresenne and Bryntelle and of the many friends he had left in the Forelands; he thought of his sister, Keziah, who served in a noble court in the kingdom of Eibithar. Not for the first time, he wondered if he and Cresenne had been wrong to leave their home for this strange, hard land. He felt a sudden longing for the simplicity of his old life in Bohdan's Revel, the traveling festival in which he had once done gleanings, using magic to determine the fates of the young boys and girls of each village the Revel visited. That was where he had met Cresenne.

"Look at that!" he heard Q'Daer say.

Grinsa's eyes snapped up. The Fal'Borna was a short distance ahead of him, pointing toward the northern horizon. Looking in the direction Q'Daer indicated, squinting in the soft rain, he could barely make out some odd, dark shapes.

"What is it?" he asked.

The young Weaver shook his head, his eyes still fixed on the distant forms. "I don't know." He glanced back at Grinsa and the Eandi. "Come on." He kicked his mount into a gallop.

Grinsa did the same, looking back to make certain that the merchants were following.

Even as they advanced on the dark shapes, Grinsa couldn't make them out distinctly. Ahead of him, Q'Daer drew a thin blade from his belt.

"What is it?" Grinsa called.

"I still don't know."

Grinsa nodded, though the man wasn't even looking at him. A moment later, he, too, drew his dagger.

"What's going on?" Torgan called to him from behind.

"We're not certain," Grinsa told him. "You see those shapes up there?"

"Barely," came the reply. Grinsa wondered how much the man could see out of his one good eye.

"I can see them," Jasha said. "What are they?"

Before the gleaner could answer, Q'Daer reined his horse to a halt.

"Damn," he whispered. His blade hand dropped to his side.

"What, Q'Daer? What is it you see?"

"You can't make it out?" the younger man said, his voice thick. He pointed to a large clump near the front of the shapes. A blackened pole jutted from it, as if it were some great, dark beast that had been felled by a huge spear. "That's a z'kal, or what's left of one."

A z'kal. It took him a moment. The word had been new to him when they reached Fal'Borna land, and he hadn't heard it used in days. Z'kals were the temporary shelters the Fal'Borna constructed from rilda skins and wooden poles. He wouldn't have recognized this blackened mass as one, but as soon as Q'Daer pointed it out to him, he knew that the young Weaver was right. He saw as well that this wasn't the only one that had been destroyed. Far from it. Knowing what to look for, he realized that the flat in front of them was filled with the remains of shelters, as well as what once had been a horse paddock.

"I don't understand," Torgan said, his brow furrowed as he stared at the scene, clearly still trying to make out what Q'Daer had seen. "What's happened here?"

Q'Daer didn't answer.

"It looks like a sept has been destroyed," Grinsa said, quietly.

"Destroyed how?"

"We don't know yet."

Q'Daer clicked his tongue and his mount started forward again, slowly this time. The rest of them followed.

As they drew nearer to the ruins of the sept, Grinsa began to see more than just shelters and the shattered wood of the paddock. There were human remains everywhere. Many of the bodies had been charred, probably by the same fires that destroyed the z'kals, and these remained largely intact. But of others, all that was left were bones and scraps of clothing. Perhaps they had died some other way; perhaps their remains had been more appealing to the crows and vultures and kites that would have descended upon such a feast. Several wild dogs still stood amid the ruins, eyeing the riders warily, their ears laid back. A few, particularly close, bared their teeth and growled.

The Fal'Borna halted and dismounted, heedless of the animals.

"Q'Daer," Grinsa said, drawing the man's gaze. "Don't touch anything. It might not be safe."

The man's eyes widened slightly and he quickly glanced down at his feet, as if expecting to find that he was standing in a cluster of Mettai baskets. He looked at Grinsa again and nodded.

Grinsa dismounted and indicated to the Eandi that they should do so as well.

"What are we doing here?" Torgan asked as he stretched his back and surveyed the carnage around them.

"We're going to search the settlement," Grinsa said.

The merchant wrinkled his nose, as if disgusted. "For what?"

"For anything that might tell us what happened to these people."

"Isn't it clear?" the man said, opening his hands to indicate the ruins. "That same pestilence has been here. And this time you can't blame me for it."

"Torgan," Jasha said softly.

"What?" the older man shot back at him. "You know they'll try to. They'll say that we destroyed this sept, too, and they'll use it as an excuse to kill us right here, without waiting to go back to E'Menua."

"Nobody's looking for an excuse to kill you, Torgan," Grinsa said, though in that moment he wondered if the man was worth saving. "Even if the baskets caused this, we know you weren't responsible. But we have to know who was. You know what these baskets look like?" he asked, shifting his gaze to Jasha.

The young merchant nodded. "I'd recognize them."

"Good. See what you can find. I'll be watching you both," he warned.

"And as you already know, I can control your animals, even from a distance. So don't try to run."

Jasha nodded again. Torgan merely scowled at both his fellow merchant and Grinsa.

Grinsa left them there and followed the young Fal'Borna. Normally, he preferred to keep his distance, but he feared that Q'Daer might become so enraged by the destruction of this sept that he would seek vengeance against the merchants, simply because they were the only Eandi there.

Q'Daer gave Grinsa a puzzled look as he approached, but he said nothing.

Together, they walked past one destroyed z'kal after another, eyeing the bones and corpses, stepping over shattered bowls, broken spears, and all other manner of debris. It looked far more like the scene of a fierce battle than it did the detritus of an outbreak of pestilence.

Fractured bones lay scattered among many of the skeletons—Grinsa couldn't be certain whether they had been shattered before or after death. Dead horses lay in what had been the paddock; several living beasts grazed near them. But Grinsa saw no evidence that any people had survived.

"Even after the a'laq told us about S'Plaed's sept, I didn't believe it," Q'Daer said, his words barely carrying over the wind. "I knew he wasn't lying, but I didn't imagine it could be like this."

"Is there any chance that this wasn't the pestilence, or whatever the Mettai woman is spreading?"

Q'Daer cast a sharp look his way, narrowing his eyes. "What else could it be?"

He shrugged. "I don't know. A battle?"

"No." The man shook his head. "No, I've seen battles. They don't look like this. Nothing has ever looked like this."

Grinsa had to agree. "I'd like to find proof."

"What do you mean? What proof?"

"A basket, I suppose. Just to see one; just to be certain."

He expected that the Fal'Borna would argue, but Q'Daer merely nodded. "All right."

They continued forward, carefully stepping through the ruins, scanning the remains of the z'kals. Occasionally, Grinsa glanced back to check on the Eandi, but neither of the merchants had made any attempt to get away. Jasha seemed intent on all that he saw around him. Even from a distance, he looked pale and very young, a pained expression on his face. Torgan was harder to read. At one point he looked up and saw that Grinsa was watching him. For several moments he stared back at the gleaner with his one good eye. Then he looked away.

"How long ago do you think they died?" Q'Daer asked.

"I don't know. Nothing's smoking. There aren't many crows or vultures left here. I'd say it's been several days, at least."

"I was thinking the same thing." He nodded toward the Eandi. "They could have done this."

"I don't think so, Q'Daer. It's been at least half a turn since they could have been this far from E'Menua's sept."

"We just agreed that this happened several days ago."

"Several days, yes. But I don't think it's been half a turn."

"You don't know that. Neither of us does. You may not want to believe that these two were responsible, but it is possible."

Before Grinsa could argue the point further, he heard Jasha call out. Both he and the Fal'Borna turned to see the young merchant gesturing frantically for them to join him. They hurried toward him, slowing as they drew near.

"What is it?" Grinsa asked.

"Part of a basket." Jasha pointed at the ground a few fourspans from where he stood.

Grinsa spotted it immediately. He felt his blood run cold, and yet he also was fascinated, unable to look away as if he had just spotted a venomous snake. It sat in a pile of blackened rubble beside yet another ruined shelter. Most of it was burned to ash, and much of the rest of it was charred. But a small bit, perhaps as large as the palm of Grinsa's hand, remained unmarked. And even Grinsa, who knew nothing of basketry, could see that when whole, this basket had been beautiful. Its osiers were straight and tightly woven, and they had been dyed brilliant shades of green, gold, and blue.

"Is that her work?" Q'Daer asked. He turned to Torgan. "Does that look like one of the baskets you sold?"

"I was never here!" the merchant said. He stood a short distance off, staring sullenly at the three of them. Grinsa wasn't even certain he could see the basket from where he was.

"I haven't time for your games, dark-eye," the Fal'Borna said. "I'm asking you if this is one of the Mettai woman's baskets."

"I know just what you're doing, and I'm not going to let you!"

"What are you talking about, Torgan?" Grinsa asked.

"He wants me to answer so that he can claim I admitted it all! And I won't do it! I've never been here, and you won't get me to say otherwise!"

Grinsa raised his hands, trying to placate the man. "He's not saying you were here, Torgan."

"Yes, he was! He asked if I sold that basket!"

Q'Daer shook his head and turned to face Jasha. "You saw the baskets, too, didn't you?"

The young merchant hesitated, his eyes flicking in Torgan's direction, as if he feared how the man would respond to his answer. "Yes," he finally said. "Briefly. I only had one; I bought it from Torgan, and I sold it that same day. But I saw others."

"And this one?" Q'Daer asked.

Again he glanced Torgan's way. "It's hard to say from such a small piece, but it looks to be the right quality." He squatted down and pointed at the basket. "See how tight the weave is? How vivid the colors are? That's good work. The Mettai baskets looked like that."

Neither of the Qirsi stepped any closer to the basket, but both nodded.

It began to rain lightly. Grinsa, glancing westward, saw that the sky had darkened.

"If there's one here," Jasha went on, "chances are there are more. If I see one that's still whole I may be able to give you a better answer."

"All right," Grinsa said, checking the skies again. "Look around a bit more. But I want to be moving again soon."

"It's not like I don't care," Torgan said.

All of them looked at the man.

He shifted his weight to the other foot, clearly uncomfortable under their gazes. "I mean, I didn't want any of this to happen. I'm sorry that . . . I'm sorry they're dead. All these people, I mean."

For several moments, none of them offered any response, until finally Grinsa decided that someone had to say something.

"We all are, Torgan."

"Right. Of course. It's just . . . I really had nothing to do with this. We were never here, were we, Jasha?"

Grinsa just shook his head and started to walk away. He sensed that Q'Daer was just behind him.

"What?" Torgan demanded, his voice rising. "I said I was sorry! But there's nothing we can do to help them anymore! And I'm fighting for my life!"

"Stop it, Torgan," Jasha said.

"They want us dead! You think they're trying to help us, but they're not! The Fal'Borna see this and they have to blame someone. They want to blame me; they want to blame both of us. You watch. You'll help them find those baskets and then they'll turn around and cut your throat!"

"Damn it, Torgan!" Jasha shouted.

The two Qirsi halted and turned to stare back at the men. Jasha stood just in front of the older merchant. Torgan was the bigger man by far; nearly a full head taller. But Jasha had his fists clenched, and despite their size difference Grinsa wondered if they'd come to blows.

A moment later, though, Jasha seemed to realize that Grinsa and Q'Daer were watching. He opened his hands slowly and shook his head. Then he turned away from the man.

"Just shut up, all right?" he said over his shoulder.

Torgan glowered at the man's back and opened his mouth, as if to say more. Then he appeared to think better of it.

Convinced that the two Eandi were content simply to avoid each other for a time, Grinsa turned and started walking again.

"Do you still think he's worth saving?" Q'Daer asked.

Grinsa gave a small, rueful laugh. "I don't think this is the time to ask me."

The Fal'Borna stopped and held out a hand, forcing Grinsa to halt as well. "You're wrong, Forelander. This is the perfect time to ask." He gestured in Torgan's direction. "What you just heard; that's his truest self. And I'm asking you, is that man worth saving? Is he worth leaving your family for? Is he worth this rain and wind?"

The rain started falling harder, darkening Grinsa's cloak and breeches. It almost seemed that the gods themselves were asking the question.

"He doesn't deserve to die," Grinsa said.

"Doesn't he?"

"No. He may be an ass, but he's not a murderer."

Jasha called out again and beckoned to them.

Neither of the Qirsi even looked his way.

"It seems the young merchant knows just where to find these baskets," said the Fal'Borna.

"They weren't here, Q'Daer. You heard what Torgan said."

"Yes, I heard." The young Weaver regarded Grinsa briefly, the rain soaking his long hair and running down his face. "I've heard talk about you, Forelander. I know that you had Eandi friends back in your old home. That may be why you trust these men as you do. But I assure you, the dark-eyes of the Southlands are demons. They're not to be trusted. The sooner you accept that, the better off you'll be."

He started toward Jasha before Grinsa could answer. Grinsa wasn't sure what he would have said if the Weaver had waited.

*D*amn them all! Torgan thought, his rage threatening to spill over into violence. In that moment he wasn't sure who he hated more: Jasha or the Qirsi.

He'd had enough of the white-hairs and their suspicions, their certainty that he was a monster. Yes, he had sold the Mettai woman's baskets, but he hadn't known what they would do. He'd tried to explain this countless times—first to E'Menua and later to these two—and still they didn't believe him. They thought him a monster and worse. Sure, he hated the Qirsi. Who among his people didn't? But that didn't mean that he would do . . . this. He looked around him, at the burned shelters, at the bones of the dead, and he shuddered.

And Jasha! Who was that whelp to tell him when he could speak and when he couldn't? There had been a time—could it have been only a turn before?—when Torgan had been the wealthiest, most famous merchant in all the land, and Jasha had been little more than a common peddler, trading wares of questionable value and eking out meager profits. He made as much gold in a day as Jasha made in half a turn. And now Jasha was telling him to shut up? Torgan should have throttled the little bastard when he had the chance.

This search of theirs was futile. Not that they couldn't find the Mettai woman—it seemed unlikely that they would, but he supposed that it was possible. No, the futility of it lay in the fact that all hinged on the Fal'Borna keeping their word. Even now, the Qirsi were using them, getting Jasha to search through the ruins for baskets as if he were a hound. They'd let the merchants lead them to the Mettai woman, just as they had agreed. And then they'd execute them anyway. That was the Qirsi way. Torgan had thought that maybe this white-hair from the Forelands was different, but now he knew better. They were all the same, no matter their clan, or their homeland.

The worst part of it was that poor Jasha was making it easy for them, being as trusting as a pup.

Well, Torgan had no intention of following along. He'd save Jasha if he could, but he wasn't going to risk his life for the young fool. But how to get away?

It came to him suddenly, and he felt his knees give way, so that it was all he could do to stay on his feet. He'd never done such a thing before. True, he had brought this white-hair plague to C'Bijor's Neck and S'Plaed's sept, but he hadn't done it on purpose. He'd been selling baskets, trying to make some gold, doing what all merchants do. He hadn't known that hundreds would die until it was too late to save even one of them.

But this was different. This was murder.

No, a voice said in his mind. *This is war. They're holding you against your will. They intend to execute you for crimes you didn't commit. You're defending yourself.*

He couldn't bring himself to move. Jasha had wandered off a ways, and was scanning the ground for more baskets. The white-hairs had walked away and were speaking in low tones, probably about him, about how much longer they would keep him alive.

The rain began to fall harder, but Torgan stood there, staring down at it: his hope, his weapon, his freedom. If only he had the courage to reach down and take hold of it.

Jasha called out. He waved the Qirsi over to where he stood. Another basket, no doubt. Probably there were several of them here.

The white-hairs started in Jasha's direction, ignoring Torgan for the moment. This was his chance. And yet he didn't move.

It's murder.

It's the only way.

It might not even work. Who was to say how long such a thing could last? But he watched the Qirsi walk to Jasha. The young merchant bent down to look at this newest discovery. He said something that Torgan couldn't hear and he pointed. The Qirsi looked, they nodded. But they had halted two or three strides shy of Jasha, and they continued to keep their distance. They didn't squat down. They certainly didn't get close enough to touch it. They still feared the Mettai woman's magic.

And so at last, while his three companions spoke among themselves and looked at this new basket, Torgan bent down quickly and picked up the first scrap of basket they had seen. He straightened, slipping the burned osiers into his pocket. It couldn't have taken him more than a moment, a heartbeat or two, and it was done. The others didn't notice a thing.

He walked over to them, keeping his trembling hands in his pockets. Jasha looked up at him as he approached and nodded at the basket they'd found. This one was nearly whole. It had been dyed in earth tones and it had a long, curved handle. It was as fine a basket as Torgan had ever seen; it had to have been made by that Mettai witch he'd seen in the Neck.

"What do you think?" Jasha asked.

"It's her work," Torgan said. "I'm sure of it."

The Forelander looked Torgan in the eye. "Thank you." He turned to the Fal'Borna. "At least we know we're heading in the right direction."

Q'Daer didn't seem pleased, but he nodded and started back toward the horses. "Then let's get going. If I'm going to be out here in the rain, I'd rather be getting somewhere."

The rest of them followed the man, Torgan bringing up the rear. He was still shaking, even as his fingers caressed the osiers hidden within in his coat. He felt sick to his stomach, as if the woman's plague was making him ill. He had to fight an urge to throw the basket back onto the ground.

I don't have to do it, he told himself, trying to ease his nerves. *Not yet; not ever, if that's what I decide. But at least now I know that I can.*

This thought calmed him. By the time he reached his mount, he felt composed enough to pull his hands from his pockets and reach for the pommel of his saddle. As he climbed onto his horse, he realized that for the first time since being captured by the Fal'Borna, he had some hope of getting away.

Chapter 6

They were losing ground with each day that passed, held back by cold and wind, by the madwoman who rode in the old peddler's cart, rocking back and forth, mumbling nonsense to herself, and by Besh's own physical limitations, which humiliated and appalled him. The trader who had bought Lici's cursed baskets, who was no doubt selling them to the Fal'Borna already, was by now days ahead of them.

Perhaps he knew what he carried; perhaps he understood the peril that lurked in those innocent-looking wares. But even if that was the case, he could only know this from experience, from having sold the baskets to unsuspecting Qirsi and then having watched them die.

It seemed more likely that he had sold some baskets in a marketplace in some sept on the northern plain, and then had moved on, determined to sell more. There was no telling how much damage the merchant had done without intending to, without even being aware that he was hurting anyone. At this point, if Besh could have stopped the man at the cost of his own life, he would have done so gladly, so much did he suffer for every moment delayed, every hour wasted.

Sirj, the husband of Besh's daughter, Elica, did his best to keep them moving. He woke early each morning to restart their fire and prepare food for breakfast. While Besh and Lici ate, he readied the horse and cart, so that they could leave quickly after eating. And in the evenings, he gathered wood, started a cookfire, and set up their simple shelter of tarpaulin and wood.

Still, despite the man's efforts, they barely covered a league each day. Besh had thought that having Lici's cart would allow them to travel faster, but with Lici's cart came Lici herself. It sometimes seemed that she actually wanted to slow them down, so that her baskets might do as much harm as possible. She would make them stop in the middle of their travels so that she might relieve herself behind a rock or in a small copse, and then she would wander off aimlessly, picking blades of grass and saying that she needed to weave new baskets. Besh and Sirj usually tried to coax her back into the cart, and on some days she complied. At other times she didn't. On one such occasion Besh tried to force her bodily back toward the wagon, and she turned on him viciously. They had taken away her knife, for their protection and hers, but she was preternaturally strong and her fingernails were long enough to rend flesh. Besh still had marks on his face and neck from his fight with her.

There were other days, however, when she wailed inconsolably at the mere thought of the plague she had loosed upon the land and seemed to be in as great a rush as Besh and Sirj to find the merchant to whom she had sold her baskets. And at still other times she spoke to herself, rambling on seemingly about nothing. In short, she was part demon, part doddering old witch, part madwoman. From one day to the next—sometimes from hour to hour—the two men couldn't be certain which Lici they would encounter.

For several days now, Besh had tried to get Lici to tell him something—anything—about the merchant to whom she had sold the baskets. He also needed to know how to stop the plague she had created, but that was a far more complicated matter, and it seemed to Besh that finding and stopping the merchant ought to be their first priority. He often asked Lici about the man: his name, what he looked like, what other wares he carried in his cart. Anything that might have helped them if they happened upon a sept or other merchants. But Lici would tell them nothing. Whenever he pressed her for more, she began to scream about how the man had lied to her.

"He said he was going to the Y'Qatt! That's what he told me! But he lied! He lied! He lied! He lied!" She would then lose herself in sobs and incoherent babble, punctuated now and again by her cries of "He lied!" It was much the same litany they had heard the first day they found her near the ruins of Sentaya, her home village, which had been ravaged by the pestilence more than sixty years before. At this point, Besh was torn between his desperate need to know more about the man and his reluctance to raise the matter at all. More than once it occurred to him that she might engage in such hysterics for just that reason. Perhaps, while regretting that some Fal'Borna would die as a result of her curse, she still held out some hope that the merchant would take the baskets to the Y'Qatt and thus fulfill the dark ambitions that had led her to conjure her plague in the first place.

From reading the journal of Sylpa, the Mettai woman who had taken Lici in when she was newly orphaned, Besh knew that the Y'Qatt, Qirsi who eschewed all use of magic, had refused to help Lici save her family and friends. She had gone to them in the hope that Qirsi magic might do what

Mettai magic had been unable to do: cure the people she loved who were dying of the pestilence. But the Y'Qatt feared the disease as much as she did, and they sent her away, even threatening to kill her if she refused to leave their village. Since that day sixty-four years ago, Lici had hated the Y'Qatt. Knowing her as he did, Besh wouldn't have been surprised to learn that she had been planning this twisted vengeance ever since.

"I have to stop."

Besh was walking alongside the cart. Most of the time, he rode in it, resting his aging legs. But he'd been cold today, and he felt restless. Sirj walked a short distance ahead, leading Lici's white nag.

"I have to stop," Lici said again.

"Why?" Besh asked wearily. It wasn't yet midday, and already they had stopped twice since breakfast.

She smiled at him shyly, her expression that of a little girl, though with her wizened face and long white hair, the effect was ghoulish. "You know," she said, sounding coy.

The old man sighed. "She wants to stop again," he called to Sirj.

Sirj halted and ran a hand over his face, looking as frustrated as Besh felt. But he simply shrugged and said, "All right."

Lici scrambled down off the cart and started off toward a cluster of grey boulders.

"Just do what you have to do and come straight back," Besh called after her.

She glared at him over her shoulder, but said nothing.

It had been so long since last they saw the sun or the moons that Besh found it difficult to keep track of the days. One seemed just like the last, and since Besh couldn't see the moons to mark their progress through their cycles, he was reduced to guessing what day it might be. But if he was right, this was the fourteenth day of the waxing. Tonight, both moons would be full, and tomorrow would begin the waning. They were halfway through the Hunter's Moon, and they'd found nothing.

Besh could hear Lici speaking, her voice rising and falling as if she were arguing some point or chastising herself. Sirj walked back to where he was standing and shook his head.

"She's going to run off again," he said.

"I know. But I can't very well tell her that she's not allowed to relieve herself, can I?"

"I know it doesn't seem right," Sirj said, not even looking at him.

"But that's what you think I should do."

"It's what *we* should do," Sirj said. "But yes, that's what I think."

"You're probably right. Next time then."

Sirj nodded.

"In the meantime," Besh said, "how do we get her back in the cart?"

Lici stepped out from among the boulders, her eyes bright and alert, like those of a wildcat.

"Come along, Lici," Besh called to the woman. "We have a long way to go today."

She grinned and began to back away, as if daring them to come after her.

"Lici!" Besh said, warning her with a tone he usually reserved for his grandchildren.

She laughed, turned, and started to run. For an old woman, at times she could be surprisingly nimble.

"Damn!" Sirj said, starting after her.

Besh followed, though he was probably slower than both of them. As they ran, he saw that Lici was scratching at her hand; picking at it actually. *She's trying to draw blood!*

"She's drawing on her magic!" he shouted to Sirj.

He heard the woman mumble something, a spell no doubt. An instant later, just as Sirj was pulling his own blade free, probably to conjure a spell of his own, she stopped and spun around thrusting out her hands. Bright golden flames leaped from her fingers, catching Sirj full in the chest and knocking him backward and to the ground.

Somehow Besh had his knife in his hand; he didn't remember pulling it free. He dragged it across the back of his hand and bent to pick up a handful of dirt. Mixing the dirt and the blood from his hand in his palm, he chanted the first spell that came to mind. "Blood to earth," he said. "Life to power, power to thought, earth to stone!"

With these last words he flung the dark crimson mud from his hand. Instantly the mud turned to a fist-sized rock that flew at Lici with unnatural speed. It struck her in the back of the head and she fell heavily to the ground.

She was old enough that such a blow might well have killed her, but at that moment Besh didn't care. He rushed to Sirj's side with hardly a glance at the woman.

The younger man had managed to extinguish the flames that had engulfed his overshirt and he lay on his back, panting, his eyes closed. His clothes were blackened and still smoking. He had burns on his face and hands, and probably elsewhere on his body.

"Are you all right?" Besh asked, looking him over, searching for any other wounds.

Sirj nodded, although he kept his eyes closed. "I have burns," he said, sounding weak. "My chest, my neck."

"Yes. Your hands and face as well."

He nodded again.

"All right. I'll . . . I'll heal you."

Sirj sat up slowly, grimacing with the effort. Then he removed his shirt, inhaling sharply through his teeth several times, so that Besh found himself wincing along with him.

Besh had never been good with healing magic, but right now he didn't have much choice. Lici certainly wasn't going to help him, and Sirj was in no shape to heal himself.

"Use the magic slowly," Sirj said, as if reading his thoughts. "That's the secret to healing. Just let it seep from your hand."

Besh nodded, recalling how skillfully Sirj had healed him after his first encounter with Lici just outside Sentaya. "I'll try," he said.

He cut himself again, took hold of another clod of dirt, and mixed the blood and earth in his hand.

"Blood to earth," he murmured. "Life to power, power to thought, power to life."

He felt the mud in his hand change, felt it come alive, as if he were holding a handful of bees. Not that it stung, but it . . . it hummed. It vibrated. Besh had to fight the urge to release it all at once. Instead, he placed his fist over Sirj's chest and let the magic run from his hand like wet sand. It was an ugly burn, blackened and angry-looking. It seemed that Sirj's skin had just melted in places.

The younger man winced again as the magic started to penetrate the wound, and Besh jerked his hand away.

"What? What did I do?"

"Nothing," Sirj whispered. "It's supposed to hurt, at least at first. You're doing fine."

Besh swallowed and took a breath before putting his fist over the burn again.

Sirj winced again. Besh tried to ignore him, concentrating instead on keeping the flow of magic even and slow.

"Where's Lici?" the younger man asked after some time.

"Over there in the grass."

Sirj craned his neck. "I don't see her."

"No, I don't imagine. She's on the ground. I'm hoping she's just uncon-
scious."

"As opposed to . . ."

"As opposed to dead," Besh said.

"What did you do to her?"

"I hit her in the head with a rock. It was the best I could think of in the
moment."

Sirj raised an eyebrow and nodded. "I wish I'd thought of it. That's good
enough," he said, looking down at his chest. "My neck now, and my face."

Besh shifted the position of his hand, still keeping a tight hold on the
magic.

"We can't keep on this way, Besh. She's a demon, and eventually she's
going to kill one or both of us. We thought taking her knife would work,
but clearly we were wrong. We can cut her fingernails to stumps, but then
she'll just use her teeth, or a scrap of wood, or something else that you and I
can't even imagine because our minds don't work as hers does. The point is
if she wants to use magic against us again—and of course she does—there's
really nothing we can do to stop her."

Besh could hardly disagree with anything the man said. "So, what
would you suggest?"

Sirj shook his head. "I really don't know." But he wouldn't meet Besh's
gaze.

"There's nothing you could say that I haven't already thought of. Nothing."

Sirj did look at him then.

"Before we found her, you spoke of killing her. You said that if that was
what it took to stop her from spreading her curse, you'd do it."

"I remember," Besh said.

"Do you still feel that way?"

Besh frowned, even as he continued to heal the man's burns. For several
moments, he didn't answer.

"That's better," Sirj said eventually, gently probing the wounds with his
fingers. "Thank you."

Besh sat back and wiped sweat from his brow with the back of his hand.
The magic had dissipated, although he still felt a faint tingling on his palm.
He rubbed it with his other hand.

"If I thought she still posed a danger to the land," he finally said, choosing his words with care, "I wouldn't hesitate to do everything necessary to
stop her. And that includes killing her. But she doesn't pose a danger to the

land anymore. In fact, at this point, she may be the only one who can find this merchant she talks about, which makes her the land's best hope. She only poses a danger to you and me, and that's not reason enough to take her life."

"I know that," Sirj said, sounding weary. "I needed to hear you say it, but I know it's true."

"But it doesn't solve our immediate problem."

Sirj reached for his shirt. "It doesn't solve either of them."

"Either of them? What's the other?"

"We need food. We've enough to last another day or two, but after that we're going to need to find a settlement where we can buy more." He shrugged and gingerly put his shirt back on. "Now that we're feeding three, we're going through our stores faster."

Besh exhaled, looking toward Lici, who still hadn't stirred. Perhaps he'd killed her without intending to. Despite what he'd just said to Sirj, he couldn't deny that he felt a surge of hope at the thought.

"I want to go home," Besh said, his eyes suddenly stinging. He could almost smell Elica's cooking. He could hear the laughter of his grandchildren—Cam and Annze, and of course Mihas, the oldest, with whom he passed so many of his days in the garden or wandering through the small marketplace.

"Then let's," Sirj said. "Let's leave her here and just go home. She can have her cart and her horse. Her baskets are gone and I don't think she has it in her to make more and spread her plague again."

Besh said nothing. He didn't have to. Once, not very long ago, he had thought Sirj a fool and had lamented Elica's decision to be joined to the man. Perhaps he had wished for a richer husband for her, someone who could have given her more than Besh himself had been able to give his beloved Ema. Or perhaps, as Ema had once told him, he wouldn't have been satisfied with any man Elica found. No matter the reason, he had always dismissed Sirj as someone unworthy of his respect or even his consideration.

He knew better now. Sirj was strong and kind. His quiet manner masked a keen intelligence and simple wisdom. And in their present circumstance, it wouldn't take him long to come to the same conclusion that Besh had reached. Now that they knew about the baskets Lici had made, cursed, and sold to her mysterious merchant, they could not stray from the path they were on. Even if Sirj was right, and Lici was no longer capable of making new baskets and casting her dark spell on them, she had done enough harm to keep them on the plain, and away from their home.

For several moments neither of them spoke. At last, Sirj climbed stiffly to his feet and heaved a sigh. "Well, it was a nice thought, anyway."

He smiled, and Besh grinned in return. Lici gave a low moan and rolled onto her back.

"It seems I didn't kill her." He glanced at Sirj. "Sorry."

The younger man shook his head and laughed.

They both walked to where the woman lay and squatting beside her they helped her sit up.

"What happened to me?" she asked, her voice weak.

"You used magic to set Sirj on fire," Besh said. "So I hit you in the head with a rock."

She stared at him for a moment and then looked at Sirj's blackened shirt. "I did that?"

"Yes. And the next time you do anything of the sort—in fact, the next time you use magic at all—I'll kill you."

Her eyes snapped back to his face, narrowed and glinting dangerously. "You really think you can?" she asked.

It often amazed Besh how quickly Lici could go from seeming addled and confused, to speaking with the grim assurance of a hired blade. Besh could never be certain what she feigned and what was real. He wouldn't have been surprised to learn that she couldn't remember what she had done only moments before, or that she herself was awed and slightly embarrassed by some of her more outrageous actions. But this voice that he heard now—hard, fearless, and so malevolent that it chilled him just to hear her speak—this struck him as her truest self. Not long ago she might have cowed him with the look she gave him, but not on this day. He was leagues away from the only home he'd ever known, from the only people left on Elined's earth whom he cared about. She'd taken enough from him.

"Yes," he said, refusing to flinch from her gaze. "I can do it with magic, or with a knife, or with my bare hands, if you prefer. But I will do it."

"I don't believe you." But there was doubt in her voice, and in her dark eyes.

"Actually, I think you do. I think you understand just how serious I am. And if I'm wrong, if you really are foolish enough to try conjuring again, you'll realize, in the moment before you die, what a terrible mistake you've made."

Her eyes held his for a moment longer, her expression now more sullen than menacing. Then she looked away and rubbed the back of her head.

"It hurts here," she said.

Besh hesitated, trying to keep up with her ever-shifting moods.

"Would you like me to heal you?" he asked her.

Lici nodded, more child than demon, at least for the moment.

Besh glanced at Sirj and shrugged. Then he cut himself again, mixed his blood with a bit of dirt, and placed his hand over the lump that had formed on the back of Lici's head. Now that he understood how to wield it, he found that he liked healing magic. Within just a short while, the lump had vanished. Lici touched the back of her head again and smiled.

"Is that better?" Besh asked.

"Yes."

That was all. She didn't thank him; perhaps she remembered that he had dealt her the injury to begin with. The two men stood and helped Lici to her feet. They led her back to the cart and soon were on their way again, angling southwestward into the heart of Fal'Borna land.

The rest of their day passed without incident. Lici asked them to stop once, again to relieve herself. Besh and Sirj were reluctant to do so, but they relented. Amazingly, Lici saw to her needs and immediately returned to the cart; the entire stop delayed them for only a few moments.

Besh wondered if he had actually scared the woman when he spoke of killing her. It had been a ploy born of desperation; he'd had little hope that it would actually change anything. But with Lici suddenly so compliant, he had to reconsider. He said nothing to Sirj, fearing that the old witch would overhear. Still, as they resumed their travels Sirj glanced at Besh, his eyebrows raised in surprise and the hint of a smile playing at the corners of his mouth.

They ate a small supper before making ready for sleep. As usual, Besh slept first, while Sirj kept watch on Lici. In the middle of the night Sirj woke him, and Besh watched the woman until daybreak. Lici appeared to sleep through the night, though she cried out in her slumber two or three times.

With their breakfast that next morning, they finished most of their remaining food. There were small copses scattered across the plain along streambeds and in shallow dales where they might find roots and harvest berries. Sirj had brought a snare with him, so they could hunt for small game. Before long, though, they would need to find a sept and buy some food; the sooner the better.

Lici seemed unusually quiet this morning. She hardly looked at either man, but from what Besh could tell she wasn't actually avoiding eye contact with them. She simply appeared withdrawn. She ate what they handed to her; he and Sirj had no trouble getting her into the cart. Once again, Besh wondered if his threats of the day before had reached her, and he decided to use this new docility of hers to his advantage.

As they started out from their camp, Lici riding in the cart and Besh walking just beside it, he asked her how she was feeling.

"I'm fine," she said quietly. "A little sore."

"Where are you sore?"

"All over."

He nodded. She had taken a hard fall the day before. It made sense, really.

"My head especially."

Besh glanced at her and saw just a hint of her old malice in those dark eyes. But as suddenly as it appeared it vanished again, leaving her looking old and weary.

"Lici, I'm wondering if you remember anything more about the merchant who bought your baskets."

"The merchant?"

He frowned, unsure, as usual, as to how much of her forgetfulness was genuine and how much she put on simply to frustrate him. "Yes. You met him in Sentaya and he bought the rest of your baskets from you. He was supposed to sell them to the Y'Qatt, but instead he took them into Fal'Borna land."

"He lied to me."

"Yes, Lici, he lied. What else do you remember about him?"

"I remember everything."

Besh shot her a look, but Lici kept her eyes trained on the road before. He glanced at Sirj, who walked ahead of them, leading the cart horse. The younger man was watching them over his shoulder and he nodded encouragement to Besh.

"What did he look like, Lici?"

"Tall, a bit fat, even for an Eandi. He had red hair."

"What else?" Besh asked, eager now that she was talking.

"He told me which one of the sovereignties he came from." She shook her head. "I don't remember now."

"Try."

She frowned, her brow furrowing. After a time she shook her head a second time. "I can't"

"Was it Aelea? Stelpana? Tordjanne? Qo—?"

"Tordjanne!" she said, her eyes wide. She actually smiled, looking happier than Besh had ever seen her. "It was Tordjanne!"

"Good, Lici," he said. "Is there anything more you can remember? Anything at all?"

"His name," she whispered. "He told me his name."

This was almost too much for Besh to believe. "What was it?" he asked, his voice dropping too, as if he feared scaring the recollection away.

"H—" she said. And then again, "H—" Her eyes darted from side to side, giving her a wild, insane look. "Hed . . . Hed . . . HedF . . . arren! Hed-Farren! That's it! Brint HedFarren!"

"You're certain?" Besh asked.

She nodded and cackled. "Brint HedFarren! Brint HedFarren!"

"Well done, Lici! Well done!" Besh cast a quick smile at Sirj, who was beaming as well. "We'll find him now for certain. I know we will."

She didn't answer, but she was smiling still, repeating the name to herself again and again. "Brint HedFarren. Brint HedFarren."

"Can you tell me something else?" he asked her. "Do you know how to defeat your curse? Do you know how to stop it?"

No response.

"Lici? Can you tell me how to stop it?" He tried to look her in the eye, but she avoided his gaze, all the while repeating the merchant's name. "Very well," he finally said. "Maybe later."

He hurried forward and fell in step beside Sirj.

"How did you manage to do that?" the younger man asked.

"I'm not sure. She's been behaving differently since yesterday. I thought I might as well try."

"Well, it was brilliant."

Besh dismissed the compliment with a wave of his hand. "It means nothing if we can't stop her curse from spreading, but at least now we have a better chance of finding the merchant and her baskets. We need a settlement of some sort. I'll stay with Lici. You go in, buy us some food, and ask around a bit. With any luck at all, Brint HedFarren has come this way."

Besh's spirits were higher than they had been at any time since he'd left his home in Kirayde. Even if they didn't find a sept, this had already been their most successful day of the journey. And yet, it seemed that their good fortune was just beginning. Before midday, they came within sight of a small settlement that fronted what must have been a tributary to the Thraedes.

They steered the cart into a small wooded hollow, where it would be hidden from view. However cooperative Lici had become in the last day, they weren't ready to take her into a village of any sort, and if they left the cart out in the open while Sirj walked into the sept, it would arouse suspicions.

They were Eandi—Mettai, no less—in Fal'Borna land. Even these precautions seemed inadequate.

"Have a care," Besh said, as Sirj unhitched the horse from the cart. "The Fal'Borna don't like our kind."

"Nobody likes our kind," Sirj said with a grin. "Why should the Fal'Borna be any different."

Besh remained serious. "They are, and you know it. If they know of Lici and her curse, they'll be especially hostile."

Sirj nodded. "I'll be careful. Don't worry." He patted Besh's shoulder and started toward the sept, leaving Lici and Besh in the small copse.

Lici didn't seem to pay much attention to what they were doing. She sat on her cart, gazing into the trees, her expression unreadable. Besh eyed her briefly, then followed Sirj up the small rise leading out of the hollow, so that he might mark the man's progress toward the sept. Sirj was walking quickly, appearing a bit too eager. Besh had to resist an urge to shout to him to slow down.

He'll be fine, came Ema's voice in his head. *He's smart and he's strong, and he'll be just fine.* Still Besh watched him until at last Sirj neared the edge of the settlement. He saw several riders set out from the village in Sirj's direction, swiftly covering the distance between them. He and Sirj should have anticipated that. The Fal'Borna wouldn't just allow a man to walk into their sept. They'd want him to state his business first.

"Damn," Besh muttered.

There was nothing he could do to help Sirj now. He had to trust that the younger man could convince the Qirsi that he was merely a traveler in need of food. He recalled pledging to his daughter that he would keep Sirj safe. Now, remembering, he scoffed at how arrogant he had been to make such a promise.

"Don't anger them," he said, as if Sirj could hear him. "Don't push too hard. Better we should go hungry."

He was still watching, trying to determine from Sirj's stance and the actions of the riders what was being said, when he heard a footstep behind him, far closer than should have been possible. He whirled around and found himself face-to-face with Lici. She had one hand balled into a fist and blood oozed from a fresh wound on the back of her other hand. He should have pulled his own blade free, but he simply froze, like a rabbit caught in the hungry glare of a wolf.

Earlier in the day she had appeared withdrawn, even meek, and both

Besh and Sirj had been all too willing to believe that they had tamed her. Clearly she'd been deceiving them yet again.

All pretense had vanished now, and with it any semblance of submissiveness. Her eyes glittered like emeralds in the grey light, bright and angry, and she wore a cruel grin like a gash across her face.

"So," she said, in a voice as cold as death, "you think you can kill me."

Chapter 7

✦—✦

𝕳 alfway between the copse of trees and the Fal'Borna sept, Sirj wished that he'd remained behind and left it to Besh to enter the settlement. He could handle a trade, of course. He'd been trapping and selling skins for nearly sixteen years. He could deal with the Fal'Borna as well. They might hate the Mettai, but gold was gold and trade in the Southlands crossed all boundaries.

But Besh wanted him to learn what he could of the merchant, of this Brint HedFarren, who had bought Lici's baskets. Sirj didn't do well with people, at least not with people he didn't know. That was Besh's strength, and Elica's as well. Even Mihas, his eldest, was better than he at making conversation and winning people's trust.

He very nearly turned around and went back to the hollow where Besh and Lici waited for him. But Besh was old to be wandering so far from Mettai lands, and his appearance in the settlement would have raised more questions than Sirj's. And the last thing they needed was to draw attention to themselves and to Lici. Reluctantly, he continued toward the settlement.

He'd had few dealings with the Fal'Borna, none of them in Qirsi lands. They were said to be a hard people—arrogant, cold, fearsome in battle. Those Fal'Borna he'd encountered in the marketplaces of Kirayde and other Mettai villages around the Companion Lakes had struck him this way. They showed little humor; they rarely even smiled. It always seemed to Sirj that they charged too much for their goods and refused to entertain even the most reasonable counteroffers. He scoured his memory, but he couldn't remember a single pleasant exchange with a Fal'Borna peddler.

"That bodes well," he muttered under his breath.

Fortunately, Besh had taken a good deal of gold from Lici's hut before leaving Kirayde, and Lici had been carrying a great deal more when they found her near Sentaya. He'd pay a lot for the food he bought this day, but they could afford it.

As he approached the sept he realized that it was smaller than he'd expected it to be. There were perhaps a hundred shelters clustered near a meandering stream. Beyond them he could see a large paddock holding several dozen horses and a series of rectangular plots of land that were now bare, where the Fal'Borna probably had grown their crops.

He hadn't yet reached the shelters when four figures ran to the paddock, leaped onto horses, and started riding in his direction. All of them carried spears. With his heart abruptly pounding in his chest, Sirj raised a hand in greeting. The riders, all of them men, halted a short distance from him.

"Stop there, dark-eye," one of the men called.

Sirj stopped and lowered his hand. Lici's horse let out a low whinny, and he stroked her nose, all the while keeping his eyes on the Fal'Borna.

"Who are you?" the man demanded. "What do you want here?"

"My name is Sirj," he said. "I come from Kirayde. It's a village on Ravens Wash, near the Companion Lakes. I was hoping to buy some food."

Too late, it occurred to him that he had been planning to buy a good deal of food, far more than a lone traveler would need. Probably he would be better off buying some here, and then finding another sept in which they could buy more. It wasn't an appealing proposition, but he thought it wiser to risk a second encounter with the Fal'Borna than to raise the suspicions of these folk. That is, if he survived this first encounter.

"Kirayde," the man said. "I don't know that place."

He tried to smile; failed. "It's very small."

"Are you Mettai, Sirj?"

For just an instant, Sirj thought about denying it. It quickly occurred to him, though, that the men had only to look at the back of his hand and see the scars there to know the truth.

"Yes, I am," he said.

"What do you have in the carry sack?"

Did these men know about Lici and her baskets? Is that why they were asking these questions and keeping their distance?"

"A second overshirt, a change of clothes, some rope, a waterskin, what little food I have left, and . . . and a pouch of gold."

"That's all?"

"That's all."

"Then you won't mind opening the sack and showing us."

They were as much as calling him a liar, but Sirj didn't say anything. He merely opened the sack and began to pull out every item it held. When he was done, he held it upside down and shook it.

"Satisfied?" he asked.

"I believe that your sack contains nothing more than what you told us it did," the Fal'Borna said. "But I still can't allow you to enter F'Ghara's sept."

"Why not?"

"Our people have had dealings with the Mettai in recent turns. We know how dangerous your kind can be. Any of the things you just pulled out of your carry sack could be cursed."

"Cursed?" he said, trying to sound surprised. But inwardly he despaired. They did know about Lici. He'd buy no food here, or anywhere on the plain for that matter.

"That's right. Your blood magic clings to all it touches. And it sickens my people. There are those in my sept who would kill you where you stand, just for being Mettai. Fortunately for you, the a'laq isn't one of them."

"I'm grateful to your a'laq for his mercy. But I need food. I don't have to enter your sept. I don't even have to get near you. If you can bring me food to buy I can leave gold here. You can take it when I've gone."

"And if your gold is cursed?"

"It's not!" Sirj said.

The Fal'Borna shook his head. "I'm afraid I can't take you at your word. Not about this."

"You have magic that can tell you if I'm lying, don't you?"

The man narrowed his eyes and regarded him for several moments. Finally he nodded. "The magic you speak of is called mind-bending. It doesn't tell us when you're lying, but it can compel you to tell the truth. And I don't wield it; our a'laq does."

Compel you to tell the truth. About anything? Sirj didn't dare ask the question aloud for fear that it would give away too much. But he wished he had left the Fal'Borna while he still had the chance. He and Besh could look for roots and use the snare. If need be, they could go hungry for a night or two. Now, though . . .

"You would consent to this magic?" the man asked.

Having raised the possibility himself, how could he refuse?

"If it's the only way I can enter your village and buy food, yes, I'll consent to it."

The Fal'Borna seemed to consider this briefly. He glanced at the man beside him and said something in a whisper that Sirj couldn't hear. His companion nodded and responded, also in a whisper.

"Remain here, Sirj of the Mettai. We'll return shortly with an answer for you. If you come any closer to our sept, you'll be killed. Do you understand?"

"Yes," Sirj said.

The four riders wheeled their mounts around and rode back toward the shelters.

Watching them ride away, Sirj wondered whether he should flee or await their return.

And where would you hide? he asked himself. *Now that they know to look for you, you'll be easy to spot.*

The horse shook her head and stamped a foot impatiently.

"Yes, I know," Sirj said. "Besh would have been smarter. So would Lici for that matter."

If the Fal'Borna only asked him about the things he carried and if they were cursed, he'd be fine. But if they started asking him other questions—Do you know who's responsible for the pestilence that's killing our people? Can you lead us to her?—he'd be in trouble. He couldn't be certain what the Fal'Borna would do to him and Besh. But they'd kill Lici for sure, and chances were they'd be just as ruthless with her companions.

He shook his head, his stomach knotting itself like wet rope. *Besh should have come instead of me.*

Soon—far too soon—he saw the riders returning, with a fifth man at the head of their party. This man's horse might have been slightly larger than those of the warriors, but otherwise Sirj saw little in his appearance or attire to mark him as the a'laq.

Again the Fal'Borna riders stopped a short distance from where Sirj stood. The a'laq dismounted and stepped a bit nearer, but he seemed as leery as the others of coming too close. He appeared older than the warriors. His face was lined, his white hair somewhat thinner than that of the other men. But he stood taller than the rest, and was broader in the chest and shoulders. Even from this distance Sirj saw no tokens of his authority in his clothing, save for a small white stone that he wore at his throat on a thin cord.

"My name is F'Ghara," he said. "This is my sept. I understand that you wish to buy food from us."

Sirj nodded, wondering if custom demanded that he do more. Should he bow, or drop to one knee? "Yes, A'Laq. I've come a long way and have far to go. I need a good deal of food and will pay well for it."

"My warriors have told you why you can't enter the sept?"

"Yes. And I've told them that I mean your people no harm. You can use your magic to confirm that if you like."

"I intend to."

Sirj took a breath and nodded. "All right, then. What do I . . . how does this work?"

"Where are you headed?" the a'laq asked.

He considered how to answer without giving away too much. To say simply that they were headed west would hardly satisfy the man. Sirj knew this.

It took him a moment to realize that he was already responding, that his mouth and his mind were no longer connected to one another.

"West," he said, unable to stop himself.

The a'laq frowned. "Where in the west?"

"I don't know."

The frowned deepened. "You don't know?"

"No."

"What is your business here?"

Sirj felt panic building inside him, like floodwater against an earthen dam. But somehow, through force of will, or, more likely, sheer dumb luck, his answer revealed nothing at all.

"I need food," his mouth said.

The a'laq opened his mouth, closed it, and shook his head. "Have you come here to spread the pestilence that's striking at my people?"

"No."

"Do you have any items with you that could harm us?"

"I carry a knife. All Mettai do."

"That's not . . ." The man shook his head again. "Are any of the items you carry cursed or poisoned or enchanted in any way?"

"No."

"So, you've just come here to buy food?"

"Yes."

"All right then," the a'laq muttered.

Other than finding that he had no control over what he said, Sirj hadn't been aware of the a'laq's hold on his mind. But when F'Ghara released him, he recognized the sudden absence of magic.

"You have a light touch, A'Laq," he said.

Abruptly the magic was on him again, more forceful this time, more intrusive.

"What are you doing here?" F'Ghara demanded, his expression deadly serious. "Why have you come to the plain?"

"We're looking for a merchant," Sirj said, again unable to stop himself.

"A merchant? Why?"

"Because he's selling cursed baskets. We have to stop him."

The a'laq blinked. "Who's 'we'?"

Sirj cringed, wondering how his mouth would answer. "Besh and me."

"Besh?"

"My wife's father."

"And where is he?"

"In the hollow, east of here."

"Why didn't he come with you?"

And that's when Sirj knew he was a dead man. The other questions he'd somehow been able to answer honestly, without revealing too much. But not this one.

"He's with Lici."

"Who is Lici?"

"A madwoman, also Mettai."

F'Ghara's eyes widened and he took a step back, as if staggered by a blow. "A Mettai witch! Is she the one?" he asked. "Did she curse the baskets you're after?"

"Yes."

"And you're protecting her."

It wasn't a question. Sirj said nothing.

The a'laq appeared to realize his error. "Are you protecting her?"

"No. Well, yes. We captured her. We went after her to stop her from doing more harm. Now we're hoping she can help us find the merchant and undo her curse."

The a'laq rubbed a hand over his face. After a moment he glanced back at his warriors. "Leave us," he said.

"But, A'Laq—"

"I said, leave us. He can't hurt me, and I want to speak with him in private."

The warrior hesitated another moment, then inclined his head and steered his horse away. The other warriors followed him.

Once the others were away, the a'laq released Sirj from his magic once more.

"You know what you've told me," F'Ghara said. "And you know that I can control you again if I need to."

Sirj nodded, too frightened to speak.

"I want to understand. You and this . . . this Besh, you went after the woman because you knew what she was doing?"

"We didn't at first. Besh figured it out. She left our village one night, without anyone knowing why. Besh spent almost two turns trying to figure out where she had gone. It only came to him when word reached us of what was happening to the Y'Qatt near the Companion Lakes."

"It started with the Y'Qatt?"

"Yes. She—Lici, that is—she had cause to hate them, and this was her vengeance."

"And now her curse has spread to us."

"Has it already?" Sirj asked. "We know there's a merchant who's carrying her baskets, but we didn't know that it had already struck at your people. I'm . . . I'm very sorry."

"My warriors will expect me to kill all three of you. That's our way."

An image of Elica and the children flashed in Sirj's mind, and suddenly he was blinking back tears. "We're trying to do the right thing," he said, his voice wavering. "We guard her night and day to keep her from doing more harm. We've left our family behind so that we could stop more Qirsi from dying. Doesn't that count for anything?"

"No. Not to the Fal'Borna."

"Then you're a cruel people," Sirj said, his grief giving way to anger.

"What you see as cruelty, we see as strength," the a'laq said, pride in his voice. "The Fal'Borna rule the Central Plain because we have never shown mercy to our enemies. We didn't during the Blood Wars and we don't now."

"But we're not your enemies. Lici might be, but not me, and certainly not Besh. If it wasn't for him, she might still be spreading her plague across the land."

The a'laq looked as if he might argue the point further, but he stopped himself and looked away, his lips pressed thin. He appeared older in profile, his forehead steep, the hint of loose skin beneath his chin.

"We are a small sept," he said after some time. "I've no sons, though both of my daughters will be Weavers. I hope to marry one or both of them to Weavers before I die, so that my people will be assured of having an a'laq after I'm gone." He faced Sirj again. "I can't do anything to disgrace my sept or weaken it in the eyes of other a'laqs."

Sirj shook his head. "You mean to tell me that I'm going to die so that your daughters can marry well?" He closed his eyes not certain whether to laugh or cry. "Fathers really are idiots, aren't they?"

F'Ghara's expression hardened. "Judge me if you will, but it changes nothing. You will lead my warriors and me to your companions."

"And if I refuse?"

"You'll die where you stand and we'll find them anyway."

There was nothing Sirj could say. He'd known from the start that the task Besh had given him was beyond his abilities. And now his failure had doomed them all.

So, you think you can kill me."

"What are you doing, Lici?" Besh asked, holding her gaze. He eased his hand toward the hilt of his blade.

Lici noticed the movement and shook her head. "Don't."

Besh didn't stop. "Where's the fairness in that, Lici?" He found the smooth wood of the knife handle and wrapped his fingers around it. "Why should you be the only one of us with access to magic?"

"I said don't!" Her eyes widened, and she began to mumble to herself—a spell, no doubt—though she also took a step back.

Besh dropped to one knee and grabbed a handful of dirt. Before he could cut the back of his hand, though, Lici threw the blood-soaked dirt at him, yelling, "Earth to dagger!"

The mud coalesced into a single blade and Besh barely had time to wrench himself out of the way, sprawling onto his back and dropping both his knife and the dirt he'd picked up. The dagger flew just past his head and buried itself in the ground.

Besh crawled to his knife and grabbed another handful of earth. He sensed that Lici was getting more dirt as well.

"Blood to earth, life to power, power to thought, earth to sleep!" He threw his dirt at her, watching as it transformed itself to something akin to sand.

"Earth to fire!" he heard her shout.

Flames erupted from her slender hands, forming a wall that guarded her from his spell. When his magic struck the fire she had conjured, it flared like sunlight, forcing him to shield his eyes and shy away from the sudden heat.

An instant later, the blaze had vanished, leaving them both blinking in the somber gloom of the morning. At the same time, both of them reached for more of the dark brown soil. Besh cut himself and Lici clawed at the back of her hand with the stubs of her finger nails, which were already stained with blood. Besh backed away slowly, drawing a grin from the witch.

"Frightened, Besh?" she asked, giving him that odd, coy grin he found so disturbing.

"I don't want to hurt you, Lici. I certainly don't want to kill you."

"Funny. I want very much to hurt you, *before* I kill you."

"All I've done is try to help you find that merchant you've been looking for."

She laughed mirthlessly. "Is that all?" She held up her bloodied hand. "Look at me. Where's my knife? What have you done with it?"

"You tried to hurt us. You nearly killed Sirj. We had to take your blade."

"Damn you both! And damn the white-hairs, too! I don't care about that merchant! I don't care if my baskets kill every Qirsi on the plain!"

"You don't mean that," Besh said, because he knew he should. But he couldn't help thinking that she did mean it, that again, as when she had spoken to him with such malice the day before, when she set Sirj on fire, he was seeing the true Lici. Whatever she had once been—a frightened orphan alone in the world, her family taken from her by the pestilence; a strange old woman taunted by Kirayde's children and shunned by its adults; a conjurer driven nearly to madness by guilt for all the darkness she had unleashed upon the world—this woman before him, this creature of anger and vengeance, was all that remained.

She muttered to herself again, and Besh began his own incantation, preparing to defend himself against any conjuring she might try next.

This time, though, she didn't throw anything at him. One moment she held a fistful of blood and dirt; the next she held a spear. She jabbed it at him, aiming for his heart. He stumbled back, just beyond her reach. She advanced on him, looking more like a warrior from one of the sovereign armies than an old Mettai witch. This time, rather than trying to stab him, she slashed at his leg with the spearhead, catching him just below the knee.

Besh grunted at the pain and collapsed to the ground, dropping both his blade and the dirt he held in the other hand. Lici grinned darkly and thrust the spear into his other thigh. Again Besh cried out, clutching at his leg, feeling warm blood run over his fingers.

"You made me your captive," Lici said. "Now I've made you mine."

And just for good measure, she stabbed him again, this time high on the chest, just below his shoulder. It wasn't a killing blow. It was simply meant to hurt, and to show Besh that he was at her mercy. It did both.

He gritted his teeth, reaching now for that wound, his hand stained crimson.

"I remember everything, you know," Lici said, standing over him, menacing him with the bloodied spear. "I remember how you stared at me when you were just a boy. You thought me beautiful then. I know you did. Later, after you married that woman—what was her name?"

He didn't answer her. After a moment she swung the spear so that the butt end struck him across the temple. For a second he could see nothing but white light, and he nearly toppled onto his side.

"What was her name?" she asked again.

"Ema," he said thickly.

"Yes, of course. Ema. I remember her, too. Pretty thing. But after you married her, you stopped looking at me. You pretended I wasn't there, just like the others. How does that happen? How does a man go from lust to indifference so quickly?"

Again, Besh didn't say anything, but this time she didn't seem to care.

"I'd wager you even warned your daughter away from me," she went on, "and your grandchildren as well."

Besh's legs and shoulder screamed at him, and his head hurt as well, though dully, unlike the searing pain of the stab wounds. He'd lost a good deal of blood, and the world around him was beginning to spin. He couldn't help thinking that a younger man would have borne the injuries better.

"What were you thinking you'd do with me?" Lici asked him. "After we found the baskets, I mean. Were you going to kill me? That's what the others told you to do, isn't it? They sent you to kill me."

"No, they didn't," Besh said, closing his eyes to keep from growing any dizzier. He understood immediately that this wouldn't work, that with his eyes closed he felt even more light-headed. He opened them again, blinking to clear his vision. Doing so, he braced himself against the ground with his hand. Dirt. Earth. Power. "They merely sent me to stop you from killing anyone else," he said. "They were concerned about you. We all were."

One hand on the earth and the other gripping his bloodied shoulder. How to switch without Lici noticing?

"That's a lie," she said. "They want me dead. If they didn't before, they will now, to punish me for what I've done."

He let the bloodstained hand drop to his lap, and then began to slide it toward the ground.

"Stop," Lici said. She shifted the spear point so that it hovered like a hornet just before Besh's eyes. "If you move that hand anymore, I'll kill you."

"That's what you plan to do anyway, isn't it?"

"Perhaps not," she said, coy again. "You still think I'm beautiful, don't you?"

Besh shuddered. He couldn't help himself. "Of course," he said.

She laughed, harsh and high-pitched. "Liar. But that was good. You almost sounded like you meant it."

"What do you want from me, Lici? Do you want to go back to Kirayde? Do you want me to plead for your life before the eldest and the rest of the council? I can . . ."

He trailed off. She was laughing again, though her eyes held nothing but rage.

"Why would I go back there? To be taunted again by the children of fools? To be looked down upon by people whom I hold in contempt?" She shook her head. "No, I don't want you to plead for my life. But before this day is through, I'll hear you plead for your own."

"Then what?" Besh asked, his voice sounding weak and thin to his own ears. How long could a man his age endure torture? "You don't want to go back? You don't care about finding the merchant anymore? What's left?"

"I could make more baskets," she said softly. "I could start again. There are more Y'Qatt, you know."

Besh shook his head. "You don't want that. You sold all your baskets. I know you did, because you told me so. And I think you did it because you were tired. You don't want to go back to that."

It was a guess on his part, and nothing more. But he could see by the way her brow creased and her eyes strayed off to the side, that he was right. Once more he began to ease his hand toward the earth.

The spearhead flashed past his eye so quickly that he had no time to react. Only when the blood began to flow down his face did he understand that she had cut him high on his cheek.

"I told you not to move that hand. Next time you lose an eye." She regarded him briefly, then examined the weapon she held, nodding her approval. "It's a good spear, don't you think? I've come to realize that I'm very good at conjuring. Better even than I am at making baskets." She grinned. "You're right," she went on a moment later. "I don't want to go back to baskets and the Y'Qatt."

"How did you create this pestilence, Lici?"

"It doesn't matter. It can't be undone, if that's what you're thinking. There's no spell you could make that would defeat it."

Besh didn't want to believe her. So much of what Lici said could be dismissed as nonsense or false pride or pure vitriol. But he sensed that she was telling him the truth about this, and he despaired. It struck him as odd that the harm she had done to so many nameless white-hairs should disturb him more than his own impending death.

"But it occurs to me," the woman said, "that I could create a similar plague for the Mettai."

He felt himself growing cold. "Why would you do such a thing?"

"Why wouldn't I?" she asked. "It would have to be a bit different from this one: a plague of the blood rather than the mind. But in other ways it would be much the same."

"If you're doing this to torment me, there are other ways. Cut me again. Hit me, burn me. But don't harm our people."

"The trick would be to keep myself from being afflicted as I spread it to others. But I'm certain there's a way. With magic, there's always a way."

"Sylpa would be angry with you," he said. "She wouldn't want you to speak of it, much less do it."

Her eyes flashed dangerously, her attention fully on him once more. "What do you know about Sylpa?"

"I know how much she cared about you. But I also know that she loved our village and our people. She devoted her life to leading us. How do you think she'd feel about this magic you're talking about?"

It was a gamble, he knew. Sylpa had been like a mother to Lici, taking her in when she was just a girl, only a turn or two removed from the death of Lici's entire family. But Lici guarded her memories of the woman; the one other time Besh had even mentioned Sylpa's name to her, Lici hadn't reacted well. He hadn't dared reveal to her that he carried Sylpa's daybook with them. He had discovered it in Lici's hut after she left Kirayde, and he had read through a good portion of it, trying to learn what he could of Lici's past.

"Sylpa's been dead a long time," Lici said. "There's much that she doesn't know, that she couldn't possibly understand."

"Like what?"

But she shook her head. "That won't work." She squatted and picked up a handful of dirt, all the while keeping the spear point level with his eyes. Then she scratched at the back of her hand again. Once more blood began to flow from the marks there. "What would it take?" she asked, seemingly speaking to herself. "How would I make this curse?"

"What are you doing?"

"I've told you. I'm making a new spell. I have you here; I can see what works and what doesn't."

Besh reached for the ground with his bloody hand.

"Stop it!" Lici said, smacking the side of his face with the flat of the spearhead.

Besh glared up at her, but he kept his hand moving.

"Stop!"

He ignored her. She could hurt him all she wanted, but he wasn't going to allow her to use him to make a Mettai plague.

He placed his hand on the ground and wrapped his fist around a clod of dirt. "Blood to earth, life to power," he started to chant.

"*No!*" she screamed.

And raising the spear shaft over her head, she stabbed down on his hand, the point piercing flesh and bone and flesh again, before digging into the ground.

Besh howled, the agony in his hand nearly robbing him of consciousness. His stomach heaved and he vomited down the front of his shirt. But even through the haze of anguish that enveloped him, he was aware of the blood running from his hand into the ground. He didn't have to make a fist—he couldn't have had he tried—but the magic was there. He wouldn't have much control over it, not in this state. But the time for that had passed. Any hopes he had for Lici and what she could do for them were gone. He cared now only for his family and his village, and yes, here at the end, for his own survival.

"Power to thought," he gasped, finishing the spell he had begun. "Magic to magic!"

He couldn't throw the magic at her. He didn't have to. It shot up the shaft of the spear like a bolt of crimson fire, crashing into Lici's chest and knocking her backward as if she were but a child's doll. She sprawled to the ground, her eyes still open wide, but she didn't move again and smoke rose from a blackened spot over her heart.

Besh took hold of the spear shaft and tried to pull it free of his hand, but all he managed to do was grind the base of the metal tip against the shattered bones in his hand. His vision swam and he fell back into darkness.

"Besh?"

The voice reached him first—Sirj's voice—but immediately he became aware of the blazing agony in his hand.

"Heal me," he muttered. "Take that damn thing out of my hand and heal me."

He heard Sirj say something, realized that the younger man wasn't alone, but he couldn't even bring himself to open his eyes.

He must have passed out a second time. The next thing he knew, he was sitting up, and someone was giving him water to drink. He forced his eyes open and found himself looking into Sirj's concerned face. Several Qirsi stood behind him. Fal'Borna. The pain in his hand had dulled to a throbbing ache; his shoulder and legs felt better, too. No doubt he looked a mess.

"Thank you," he said.

"I only did part of it," Sirj said, glancing toward the white-hairs. "And I wouldn't thank them, yet. I think they're going to kill us."

Besh looked past Sirj at the nearest of the Fal'Borna, an older man with long white hair and a white stone hanging at his throat. The Qirsi stared back at him until at last Besh faced Sirj again.

"It seems you haven't done much better than I have today."

Sirj shrugged. "I haven't done very well, but I managed not to get stabbed, so I think I'm still ahead."

Besh had to grin. "Help me up," he said.

"I don't think you're ready."

"I don't care. Before these men kill me, I want to look them in the eye."

Sirj nodded and helped him to his feet. His legs trembled and the pain in his thigh returned, but after a moment he found the strength to stand without Sirj's support.

The old Fal'Borna gestured at Lici's body. "This is the witch who cursed my people?"

"Yes," Besh said.

"And you killed her."

"I had no choice. She was going to kill me. She was going to curse the Mettai as she did the Y'Qatt."

Sirj gaped at him, but Besh kept his attention fixed on the Fal'Borna.

"Your friend said that a merchant is still wandering the plain selling her baskets."

"We believe he is, yes. We know his name and what he looks like, but we have no idea where he is right now."

"Is it still your intention to search for him?" the Fal'Borna asked.

"A'Laq—" one of the warriors said in a low voice.

The Fal'Borna raised a hand, silencing him. "Is it?" he asked again.

Besh nodded. "Yes. I swore an oath to the leader of my village that I would find Lici and stop her. I found her and she's dead. But I won't have fulfilled my oath until I've ended this plague she loosed upon you."

The a'laq nodded. "Then you'll need food."

Sirj gave him a puzzled look. "I thought that Fal'Borna law gave you little choice but to kill us."

"That was before," the a'laq said. "Now, your friend has killed an enemy of the Fal'Borna. By custom that makes him an ally, and you as well." He smiled, the change in his expression transforming his appearance. All the severity vanished, leaving a face as friendly and open as any Besh had ever seen. "Come, friends. We'll feed you and give you more food for your travels."

"We can pay you," Sirj said.

The a'laq grinned. "Oh, you will." He turned and started toward the Fal'Borna's mounts, which stood clustered together a short distance off.

"What about her?" Besh asked.

The a'laq paused and glanced at Lici once more. "We leave her to the crows."

Not long ago Besh would have objected. He thought he'd come to understand Lici; not to sympathize with her, but at least to recognize the dark path that led her to the terrible things she had done. He could tell that Sirj expected him to argue with the Fal'Borna, to plead for a more dignified end for the woman. But his hand ached, and his legs and shoulder still pained him, and he couldn't stop thinking about what might have happened to Elica and his grandchildren and the people he had known all his life if she had made good on her final threat.

Silently, he followed the a'laq. And as he passed her body, he tapped two fingers against his lips four times: the Mettai warding against evil.

Chapter 8

For the first several days after the Harvest Tournament it seemed to Tirnya that nobody in the city spoke of anything except her failure to draw blood from Enly while the lord heir was down, and her subsequent defeat in that final match. Most thought they were doing her a kindness by telling her how honorably she had fought. Others made it clear that they thought she was too soft to be an effective warrior, or an effective captain in His Lordship's army, for that matter. As her father had counseled that first day, she tried to listen only to those who saw the virtue in what she had done, but ignoring her doubters proved nearly impossible.

Soon enough, however, her days and nights were occupied with more pressing matters. The brigands who had been harassing peddlers on the roads south of the city were expanding their assaults, striking at travelers from the north as well. At any time, the lord governor had little patience for such lawlessness in his lands. But with the Harvest trading well under way, he seemed to view these attacks as a personal affront, as if the brigands were plundering gold from His Lordship's treasury. He ordered his captains to rid the lands around the city of all the outlaws and he made it clear that he didn't care if any of his soldiers ate or slept again until his orders had been carried out. He even went so far as to offer a bounty of ten sovereigns for each brigand killed or caught.

Needless to say, Tirnya's soldiers spent nearly as much time planning how to spend the gold they expected to earn as they did actually hunting for the road thieves. To their credit, Oliban and the other lead riders in her company kept the foot soldiers on task much of the time. As a result, Tirnya's riders claimed a good portion of His Lordship's gold as their own. As had always been her way, Tirnya ordered that any gold earned by soldiers in her company be shared equally by all, regardless of which man struck the wounding or killing blow. She had learned this policy from her father, who had once told her that the worst thing a commander could do was to pit one of his men against another.

"They live and die as a company," he had told her, when she was first learning the rudiments of command. "They ought to share equally in every-thing. The glory of one is the glory of all; the same is true of failure."

Maisaak's rewards struck her as being no different, and her men appeared to agree. That said, she took no share of the gold for herself. She earned enough as their leader.

Enly's company and that of Stri Balkett also claimed a fair amount of Maisaak's gold, but by the end of the waxing, small bands of brigands still remained at large. His Lordship's patience, as all of them knew, was far from boundless, and most days Tirnya and her men were on duty from midday to dawn. In the few hours afforded them in the mornings, they slept and ate, and saw to whatever other duties their lives demanded. Her men were ragged with fatigue, and Tirnya was not much better off.

Her father complained bitterly about how hard the lord governor was pushing them, but when Tirnya pressed him he admitted that, if he were ruler of the city, he would do much the same. The brigands' attacks had taken a heavy toll. Dozens of peddlers had lost their gold and their wares over the past turn and a half. Many had been wounded, and, to date, eleven people were known to have been murdered. The thieves had also taken a heavy toll on trade throughout the city, and would continue to do so until they were wiped out. Already there was talk in the marketplace of merchants avoiding Qalsyn, of traders in other towns and villages saying that the city was no longer safe. Crafters in the city and farmers from the surrounding countryside had goods to sell; they needed gold so that they could buy their provisions for the coming Snows. Tirnya was desperate for rest, and though she had no affection for Maisaak, she understood why he was demanding so much of her and her company.

Yet, even with all of Qalsyn gripped by talk of the brigands and the skirmishes being fought beyond the city walls, Tirnya also managed to listen to other tales being bandied about among the peddlers' carts and stalls of the city marketplace. These stories had nothing to do with thieves, or for that matter with this city. Rather, they pertained to the outbreak of pestilence in the Central Plain.

Since hearing of the pestilence at the Swift Water Inn just after the tournament, she had thought about it in odd moments, and had sought out any who might bear tidings from that part of the land. Word from so far off was hard to come by, but occasionally she found merchants, many of them Qirsi, who had journeyed from the West. She generally avoided white-hairs—her family had fought against the Fal'Borna for centuries and though she had never so much as had an argument with one, she hated them for what they had done to Deraqor. But she would have spoken with the a'laq of her beloved city if only he could tell her something about what was happening on the plain.

From what little she did learn, it seemed that the pestilence had struck most fiercely at the Y'Qatt settlements near the Companion Lakes, but that it had spread westward as the Harvest went on. She had not heard of it striking any villages to the east of the Silverwater.

On this morning, she had circled twice through the marketplace looking for merchants to question and was debating whether to walk around a third time or return home to snatch a few hours of sleep before beginning her next patrol. She had nearly made up her mind to make her way to bed when she saw another merchant steering his cart into the market. He was an older man, Eandi, with brown hair that was thinning and turning silver. His cart looked to be nearly as old as he, and his horse could hardly be called young. His clothes fit him well, but they were plain and threadbare. In short, there was little about him that would have caught her attention on any other day. But she noticed immediately that he carried animal skins prominently displayed on his cart. Rilda skins.

She watched as he selected a spot to stop his cart—a narrow space between two other Eandi merchants, both Qosantians by the look of them. The newcomer looked to be one of the Wolf People as well. He had the fair complexion of the lowlanders, and his horse, a small roan, also put her in mind of the mounts she had seen from Qosantia. As he began to set out his wares, Tirnya approached him.

One of the other merchants must have said something to him, because he turned quickly and smiled.

"What can I do for you, Captain?" he asked, his accent subtle, but definitely Qosantian. "A sword perhaps?" He began to search through those items that he had yet to remove from his cart. "I've shillads, Aelean steel, bodkins from Tordjanne." He glanced back at her, a conspiratorial grin on his angular face. "I even have a few daggers forged by the T'Saan. Very rare in these parts."

She shook her head, wondering if there were really Eandi soldiers who would deign to carry a white-hair blade into battle.

"No," she said. "I'm not looking for a new blade."

"Of course. Jewelry then. A woman as lovely as you—surely there's more to your life than training and battles."

"No, I'm not interested in jewelry either." Tirnya raised a hand to keep him from offering more goods. "I need information."

His face fell, and he went back to sorting his goods, setting some out on his blankets, leaving other items in the cart.

"I have precious little of that," he said, his voice flat.

Tirnya grinned at how quickly he'd gone from charming to sullen. "You've been in Fal'Borna land."

"What makes you say so?"

"The rilda skins. Only the Fal'Borna can tan so well."

The man straightened, smiling again, perhaps sensing that he might make a sale after all. "They are fine ones, aren't they? Four sovereigns apiece, and that will also buy all that I know about the Fal'Borna, and anything else you might ask."

"Four is high, for the skin and the information." She scanned his blankets quickly, her gaze coming to rest on a curved knife with a polished stone handle. She pointed at it. "But I'll give you two for that. And some answers."

He shook his head and frowned as if the tale he was about to tell her was too sad to bear. "Would that I could sell it for so little, Captain," he said. "But that's as fine a blade as you'll find in Qosantia, and what's more, it may well be the last of its kind. The man who made it, a smith named Clarton, died this past Growing. Tragic tale, actually. His poor wife and children—"

"I haven't time for tales, tragic or otherwise," Tirnya said. "And I won't pay more than two. Now, I can ask you questions with your blade on my belt and my gold in your pocket, or I can simply ask. One way or another, I intend to have answers. It's your choice."

"He had children, you know," the merchant said, looking wounded. "Now they're orphans."

She raised an eyebrow. "His widow died, too?"

"What?"

"The children are only orphans if both parents have died."

He opened his mouth, then faltered, his brow creasing.

"You might want to work on your story a bit more," she said. She heard one of the other merchants snickering.

He stared at her another moment, his mouth twisting sourly. Then he picked up the blade, handed it to her, and held out his other palm for her coins. "What do you want to know?"

She didn't give him the money right away. "Where were you before you came to Stelpana?"

"The plain, just as you said."

"And you were trading with the Fal'Borna?"

The man nodded. "I was after skins: rilda, wildcat, wolf. Didn't find much by way of cats or wolves, but they had plenty of rilda. I also found some wooden bowls and a good deal of the grain the white-hairs grow. It fetches a fair price as you head farther east. I had some blankets, beaver and stoat pelts, baskets, even a bit of Tordjanni wine. I did well, considering."

She narrowed her eyes. "Considering what?"

The merchant shrugged. "Considering that I was trading with the Fal'Borna. They're a difficult people."

That much Tirnya knew. "Was there any talk of the pestilence in the septs you visited?"

"There's always talk of the pestilence, Captain, particularly when it's been found in other places, like the Y'Qatt villages." He frowned. "But now that you mention it, I did hear, a few days after stopping in one sept, that it had been destroyed by disease of some sort. They weren't calling it the pestilence. It was some white-hair plague that they talked about."

"Who talked about it?"

He shrugged. "Other merchants. They say it strikes at their magic. It makes them sick—the white-hairs, that is—and then it attacks their magic, so that they destroy themselves and their homes." The man shook his head. "Bad business, if you ask me. I'm no friend of their kind, mind you, but I'm a merchant before anything else, and I'm telling you that if we can't trade with the Qirsi, there's going to be a good deal less gold in the sovereignties."

"You can't expect it to kill all the Qirsi," Tirnya said, thinking that the man must have been listening to some wild tales.

"No, I don't. But I know for a fact that the Fal'Borna are starting to turn merchants away. They think that the plague is being spread by Eandi traders."

Tirnya shivered in spite of herself, as if a frigid finger had traced the length of her spine. "Why would they think that?"

"Because none of us even gets sick, and all of them die."

"None of us . . . ?"

"By all rights, I should be dead, Captain," the merchant said. "I was there just before the outbreak started. I heard things about it—" He broke off, swallowing and looking away briefly. "I should be dead," he finally said again.

Tirnya wasn't certain what to say. In the end, she merely nodded once, placed the coins in the man's hand, and walked away.

She didn't have long before her next patrol was to begin, but still she returned to her home and lay down for a time, hoping to sleep just a bit. She barely even closed her eyes. It didn't help that Zira, her mother, made no effort to lower her voice when speaking to Tirnya's brothers. But Tirnya doubted that she would have slept in any case. She spent the entire time turning over in her head again and again all that the merchant had told her. As when she first heard of this outbreak of the pestilence, she couldn't say why it occupied her mind so. There seemed to be little danger of the disease coming to Qalsyn; the Companion Lakes, where it seemed to have begun, were far from here, and the disease was spreading westward, away from Stelpana. She wasn't afraid, either for herself or for her people.

But she couldn't stop wondering about the fate of Deraqor, or rather, D'Raqor, as the Fal'Borna now called it. When Stri first told her of the pestilence that night in the Swift Water, Tirnya was relieved to hear that the disease had not reached her ancestral home. But now her feelings were more ambivalent. What might it mean if Deraqor were struck by the plague the merchant had described? It seemed, from what the man had told her, that this strain of the pestilence unleashed the white-hairs' magic, which might well damage the city. That would be unfortunate. But he had said far more than that. *None of us even gets sick, and all of them die.*

Surely he couldn't have meant that the pestilence killed every white-hair in those cities it struck. Could he? She had never heard of the Fal'Borna turning away merchants. As hard and unwelcoming as the horsemen of the plain were said to be, they rarely turned down a chance to trade. They must have been terrified of this plague to go to such extraordinary lengths to keep it away. And Tirnya knew that the Fal'Borna feared nothing.

"They fear this," she whispered to herself.

She heard bells tolling from the city gates. Midday: time to resume her patrols. She rose from her bed and left the house, not bothering to say anything to her mother.

She and Zira rarely spoke. As a girl Tirnya had taken up swords and daggers rather than dolls and pretty clothes, and that decision had forever marked her as Jenoe's daughter rather than Zira's. During her fourth four, as she grew from a coltish, long-limbed girl to the woman she was now, her mother had tried to lure her away from Jenoe's influence.

"Swordplay is fine for children," Zira told her on Tirnya's twelfth birthday. "But a young woman must turn her mind to other pursuits. You're beautiful, Tirnya; you must know that. You've a lovely face, fine hair, a good figure." She offered these observations not as compliments, but rather as statements of fact, as if she were the lord governor's treasurer, cataloging

His Lordship's holdings. "I feared that all that time you wasted wrestling with your brothers and playing with arms would spoil your looks, but you've been fortunate. Now it's time for you to put away your blades and put on your dresses."

"There are women in His Lordship's army," Tirnya had argued.

"Common women. Daughters of farmers and smiths and farriers. Not the daughter of a man like your father."

"Papa doesn't mind. He likes it that I'm good with a sword."

Her mother's expression hardened at that. She was a beauty as well; Tirnya looked just like her. She had pale blue eyes, a wide, sensuous mouth, and honey brown hair that fell to the shoulder in waves. But when Zira grew angry, her beauty became as dangerous and forbidding as that of a highlands lion.

"He indulges you," she said, as if it were the worst crime a father could commit.

"He loves me. He wants me to be happy. Why is it you don't?"

Tirnya left the house before her mother could respond, and for a long time afterward, they didn't discuss dresses or swords again. There were times when she heard her parents speaking about her, and those discussions usually ended in fights. But her father never said anything to her; he certainly never tried to change her. Eventually, Tirnya's relationship with her mother improved; they were cordial with each other, though not warm. Occasionally Zira would speak to her of how important it was that she marry well, and how difficult it would be for her to find a husband so long as she insisted on training with common soldiers. Tirnya pretended to listen, but she rarely responded, even to argue the point, and she continued to hone her skills with a sword. Her best revenge was that she took to calling her mother "Zira" to her face, rather than "Mother." Her mother hated it, which was why she did it. Her father begged her to stop, but she refused. It was a habit that had become so ingrained that she couldn't have stopped even if she had wanted to. And the truth was she didn't.

She made her way to the palace armory where every day she met the soldiers in her company. Oliban and the other lead riders had already gathered the men in formations of eight, and the stableboy had saddled her sorrel, Thirus.

"G'day, Captain," Oliban said, raising a hand in greeting and smiling. "All present and ready to ride."

"Good."

She walked among the men, checking their weapons and armor, making certain that their mounts were properly harnessed, though she had little doubt that they would be. Her lead riders would have seen to it before she arrived.

She'd been fortunate with the men assigned to her, or perhaps her father and his commanders had chosen them with extra care. Despite what she'd told her mother all those years ago—that there were other women in the lord governor's army—few women became captains. Oliban, Qagan Fawler, Dyn Grathidar, and her other lead riders could easily have chosen to make command difficult for her. She would have disciplined them, but if they had worked together to disrupt her company, they could have made it seem as if she was incompetent. She knew of riders under other captains who would have done just that if they had been assigned to her. Many soldiers chafed at the idea of serving under a woman, particularly one as young as she. To this day, some in the army claimed that she'd been promoted quickly, not because of her fighting skill or abilities as a leader, but solely on the basis of being Jenoe Onjaef's daughter. And truth be told, Oliban and the others had seemed skeptical when she first took command of the company. But from the start they obeyed her orders and gave her every opportunity to succeed rather than looking for ways to make her fail.

They may have done this out of respect for her father, rather than in response to anything she did as their captain. Tirnya didn't care. At this point, more than a year since she had been promoted to captain, her men liked and respected her, and their company had earned a reputation as one of the finest in Maisaak's army.

Finishing her inspection, she nodded to her leads. "Excellent." She swung herself onto Thirus and faced the men again. A light, misting rain had begun to fall, but the air was warmer than it had been for several days. Certainly not ideal weather for a patrol, but not the worst either. "We have the south road today," she told them. "Enly reported trouble there yesterday, as did Stri the day before, but neither of them managed to capture anyone." She allowed herself a sly grin. "I won't presume to comment."

The men laughed.

"But I expect that we'll find brigands there today, and I have every confidence that the next time we drink ales at the Swift Water, they'll be bought with His Lordship's bounty."

All of them cheered.

Wheeling her mount around, Tirnya led them out of the palace courtyard, through the city lanes, to the south gate. Once outside the city walls, they rearranged themselves into tighter, diamond-shaped formations and spread out to cover the lane leading from the gate as well as the sparse woodlands on either side of the road. Tirnya, as was her custom, remained on the lane, beside Oliban at the head of the first diamond.

They rode in silence, watchful, alert to any sound. Road brigands generally roamed in bands of ten to twenty men; they wouldn't engage a force as large as Tirnya's if they didn't have to. Instead, they'd try to keep out of sight and hope that the soldiers would pass by without noticing them. Like all His Lordship's soldiers, Tirnya's men had been trained not to let that happen. They knew these woodlands well, and they knew what to search for: disturbed patches in the leaf litter, clusters of shrubs and trees that appeared unusually dense, freshly broken twigs and plant stalks. Such signs were as likely to be made by woodland beasts—deer, fox, boar—as by outlaws. More often than not, soldiers investigating such signs would find no one. But still they investigated every lead.

This day was no different. In the first few hours of their patrol, they followed several trails into the forest, only to find that they led nowhere. One rider and his group stumbled upon a herd of elk, and another saw what they believed was a fox den. But they encountered no brigands.

"These last holdouts are th' clever ones," Oliban said in a low voice, as they continued to ride. "They've gone this long without being caught. If they've stayed this close t' th' city, they won't be on th' main road."

Tirnya nodded. "I'm listening."

Oliban pointed toward a narrow, overgrown path coming up on their right. There was a lattice of such trails in the woodland, nearly all of them leading off the main road. They were little more than footpaths, worn into roads by repeated use by those on foot, and the occasional rider. Some led to favored hunting grounds, others to spots where rare herbs or roots were known to grow. Some were even used by petty thieves who preyed on travelers singly or in small bands. They would make fine hiding places for the outlaws.

"All right," Tirnya said. "We'll have a look."

She halted, raising her hand over her head, signaling her company to stop and gather around her.

"We're going to check some of these smaller paths," she said, once all her men were close enough to hear. "Oliban has suggested that the brigands have retreated farther into the woodland to evade our patrols."

"We've already passed several paths," said Dyn, his red hair dampened by the rain and clinging to his brow. "We would have noticed if they had been traveled."

Another of her lead riders, a man known simply as Crow, for his raven black hair, his black eyes, and his willingness to eat anything, shook his head. "They wouldn't be so obvious. They'd avoid the main road, and find the paths in the woods."

Dyn nodded. "Right. Of course."

"We'll split up," Tirnya said. "Two groups on this path, two on the next. The rest of you remain here and listen for sounds of engagement. If we have trouble, you'll be our reinforcements."

Dyn and Oliban exchanged a look. Tirnya knew what they were thinking.

"Uh, Captain," Oliban began, looking unsure of himself. "Ya ought t' stay here. For all we know, we'll be ridin' into an ambush."

"All the more reason for me to be leading you," Tirnya said, though she knew what they'd say to this as well.

"That's no' th' way His Lordship would see it," Dyn said, taking up the argument, "or . . . or th' marshal."

The marshal: her father. Dyn and Oliban were both right. This was precisely the reason why captains had lead riders, soldiers they could trust with command in situations that called for smaller companies. Still, it went against all of her instincts. She had great faith in Oliban and the others. But given the choice between putting herself in danger and risking the lives of the men who served her, she would always choose the former. And, she had to admit, she enjoyed the excitement of this kind of work. She *wanted* to go down these paths; every one of them.

"All right," she said. "Oliban, Crow, you take this one. Dyn and Qagan, you and your men take the next. The rest of us will wait here. If you don't see any evidence of activity on the path in, say, a thousand fourspans or so, come back. There are plenty more for us to search."

"Yes, Captain," Oliban said, speaking for them all, as he so often did.

"Have a care. You're right: You could be riding into an ambush." She nodded toward the horn Oliban carried on his belt. "At the first sign of trouble, you blow that, understand?" She looked at her other lead riders. "That goes for all of you."

"Of course, Captain."

The four groups quickly arrayed themselves into columns and started down the two paths. Soon they had disappeared from view, though for a few moments longer Tirnya could still hear the jangling of harnesses and the occasional snort of a horse. Before long she no longer heard even that much.

"The rest of you can get off your horses for a bit," she said. "But stay near your mounts, in case we need to ride in quickly. And keep the noise to a minimum. If we can't hear them, we can't help them."

Some of the men dismounted; others didn't. Tirnya remained on Thirus, listening intently for any sound of combat. She was sure that she would hear a skirmish if one began, but the longer she waited, the less certain she felt. Angry with herself for allowing Dyn and Oliban to talk her out of going with one of them, she was just about to lead a group of men down the first of the paths when Dyn and Qagan emerged from the wood, leading all of their men.

"Nothing?" Tirnya asked, masking her relief.

Qagan shook his head.

A few moments later, Oliban and Crow returned as well.

Tirnya was not yet ready to give up on the idea, and she sent her other four lead riders down the next pair of paths. Again they found no sign of the brigands. Reaching a third pair of trails, Tirnya decided to try it one last time. Once more, she sent Crow and Oliban in one direction, Dyn and Qagan in the other.

As before, she found the wait interminable, but by this time she had grown less convinced that they were apt to find anything. She was still listening for any sound of struggle, but her mind had begun to wander back to her conversation with the merchant and all he told her about the pestilence. So when the first shouts and clashes of steel reached her, it took her a moment to locate the sound. An instant later she heard a horn blow, and then a second, both of them from the eastern side of the road. Oliban and Crow.

Recovering quickly, she shouted "This way!" to her men, kicked at Thirus's flanks, and plunged into the woodland, the remaining half of her company just behind her.

She heard the horns again, and more sounds of fighting. They weren't far; five hundred fourspans at most. And she was about to ride into the thick of it. Even knowing this, though, she didn't slow down. She'd been frustrated and impatient all day long, waiting for her men to return from their forays into the woods, wondering if she'd been wrong not to go with them. Now they'd found the brigands, and she refused to let Crow and Oliban face them without her. At that moment she couldn't have said if she was driven by fear for her men or by battle lust or simply by pride. Nor was she certain that she wanted to know.

Emerging into a small clearing, she saw her men battling perhaps a dozen of the outlaws. Several men already lay on the ground, most of them brigands, though at least one man down was wearing the blue and green uniform of Qalsyn. She had no time to notice more, for at that moment an arrow caught her full force just above her right breast, knocking her off her mount and onto her back. The impact of her fall stunned her momentarily, though she had sense enough to cover her head with her arms, lest she be kicked by one of the horses trailing her.

In the next moment several of her men were beside her, concern on their faces making them look so young. When had they gotten so young?

She heard fighting all around her, tried to get up so that she could join in. But she could barely make herself move at all. Steel on steel, war cries and neighing of horses. All around her. Yet the sounds seemed to be receding, and the light with it.

"Captain?" one of the men said, sounding so scared, so young. Not one of her lead riders, but another one. What was his name? She knew all of their names. At least she had. "Captain?"

"I'm all right. Don't be scared." That's what she tried to say. "What's your name?"

She wasn't certain, though, that she managed to say anything. And then all was darkness.

She was on foot, carrying her shillad and dagger, as if ready for a match in the Harvest Tournament. But rather than being in the ring, surrounded by a cheering audience, she was in the city.

No, that wasn't right either. She was in *a* city, but it wasn't Qalsyn.

The two thoughts reached her together, like some twin-headed creature from the Underrealm. *I'm dreaming*, and *This is Deraqor.* She heard a thin cry above her, looked up, and saw a falcon circling overhead, black against a bright blue sky.

"I am dreaming, aren't I?" she asked the bird.

It cried out again, a hawk's plaintive note. And yet she heard words within the sound. "Yes, a dream." And then it said, "Deraqor," anticipating her next question.

She nodded, and began to walk. There should have been an army with her. Where were Oliban and Dyn, Crow and Qagan? This was folly, trying to take back her family's city by herself. The white-hairs would defend it to the death. They would attack her with blades and arrows and, most dreaded of all, their evil magic.

But no attack came. The streets were empty.

Again, that wasn't right. Or rather, it was, until she formed the thought. Now, though . . .

There were bodies. Hundreds of bodies. They lined the street, arrayed neatly in rows, as if they had gathered to watch a parade. Every corpse was Qirsi, every one of them dressed in a white robe, so that they looked like sleeping wraiths. Tirnya felt that she should have been terrified, but there was nothing gruesome about the bodies, nothing to give any indication of what had killed them. Yes, sleeping wraiths. That's what they were.

And the city! Looking away from the bodies, Tirnya lost herself in reverie at the beauty of that city. Buildings constructed of red and pink stone—river stone, they called it; her father had told her that much. Lofty spires from the sanctuary soaring upward, seeming to pierce that blue like blades; the low jumble of houses, some stone, some wood, sprawled at the feet of the God's shrine, like supplicants bowing before a prelate; the gentle curve of the city walls, punctuated at regular intervals by arched gates. She had never seen a city so lovely.

"It is yours," the falcon said. "If you want it." The bird wheeled above her, angling its wings, twisting its tail slightly, its flight as effortless as thought. "But there is a cost."

She didn't care. This was Deraqor! Her city! Her family's ancestral home! The Onjaefs belonged here. How pleased her father would be when he learned that she had taken it back. But she knew she had to ask, that the falcon expected it of her. And this was a dream, with a logic of its own.

"What cost? Tell me, and I'll pay it."

The bird wheeled a second time, tucked in its wings to dive, pulling up just above her and hovering there. "Look!" it said, the cry both sharp and mournful.

Tirnya lowered her gaze once more.

Bodies; even more than there had been. But not dressed in white anymore, not neatly arrayed, not only Qirsi. Bodies everywhere. Hacked, broken, brutalized. Severed limbs, spilled innards, and so much blood. More blood than Tirnya had known existed, coursing through the streets like the Silverwater in flood, running over her feet, soaking through the leather of her boots. She took a great breath, opened her mouth to scream.

And woke, her eyes fluttering open.

"Gods be praised!" a voice said. Her father. That was her father who spoke.

"Captain?"

She peered up into the thin, tanned face of an older man. She was in her own bedroom. Her chest hurt, as did her head.

It came back to her in a rush. The arrow. Falling back off Thirus. Thirus!

"My horse," she said, her voice sounding thick.

She heard her father chuckle. "That's my daughter."

She tried to make herself sit up, but her body didn't respond.

"Hold on there, Captain," the older man said. "You've taken a nasty fall and you had an arrow in you. You're not going anywhere for a while."

"My men?

"You lost two," her father said, stepping to the side of her bed and looking down at her. "Four more were wounded, but they'll be fine. Thirus is unhurt and in the stable, and the brigands you encountered are all either dead or captured. Twenty-one in all. Your men have a good deal of gold coming to them."

Two men dead! She turned her face away, feeling tears on her cheeks. That simple motion made her stomach heave, and she almost was ill. Two men. She wondered which ones.

"She's past the worst of it now, Marshal," the older man said. "Keep that poultice on her wound for the rest of the night; the betony will keep the bleeding to a minimum and ease the swelling, and the lavender will keep it from becoming fevered. And keep giving her that brew. Sanicle and sweetwort. It'll keep the pain in check and help her sleep. That's what she needs most now. Rest."

"Thank you, healer."

Tirnya knew that voice, too.

"Mother?" she said, looking past Jenoe.

Her mother stood near the door, her face pale in the lamplight.

"I'm glad you're better," she said, smiling, though she appeared to be blinking back tears. After a moment Zira looked away. "Come, healer. I'll show you out."

The older man nodded. He glanced down at Tirnya again. "I'll come back to see you tomorrow, Captain."

"Thank you."

He left the chamber, followed by Tirnya's mother.

Her window was slightly ajar, and she could see that night had fallen.

"How long was I . . . ?" Her thoughts were so scattered. What had she just been dreaming?

"It's nearly time for the gate close," her father said. "They brought you back here several hours ago."

"Mother was here."

He frowned, but there was a smile on his lips. "Yes, of course. What did you expect?"

"Do you know . . . what were the names of the men who died?" She didn't want to answer his question.

"I don't know. I'm sorry."

"I've never . . . I've had men wounded before, but I've never lost any."

Her father brushed a strand of hair off her forehead, looking sad and relieved and much older than she'd ever seen him. "Think about that tomorrow. Tonight you need rest." He straightened.

"Do you think I was wrong to search the paths?" she asked quickly, afraid he would leave her.

Again he frowned, and shook his head. "No. It was a fine idea."

"Oliban thought of it."

"Then he's to be commended."

"But if we hadn't searched there . . ."

Her father shook his head. "A commander can't think that way. You lost two good men, but you did what was expected of you, and more. Every soldier knows that his next battle could be his last. I don't know the names of the men who died, and even if I did, I probably couldn't tell you much about them. But they knew the risks of what they were doing."

She nodded, knowing he was right, knowing as well that it would still take some time before her guilt and grief went away.

"As long as we're on the subject, though," her father went on, "I can't say that I like the idea of you leading a charge like that. You're fortunate to be alive."

"You'd have me ride at the back of the column instead of the front?"

"A company needs its captain. When a commander, any commander, falls in battle, it places all the men in a company at risk."

"I see," Tirnya said. "And I take it you always ride at the back when your men charge into battle."

"He never has that I know of." Zira walked to her bedside. "I can't tell you how to lead soldiers into a battle," she said. "But I can say that your father has never ridden at the back of a column in his entire life."

Tirnya had to smile. "I didn't think so."

"No more talk of soldiers or battles," Zira said. "She needs sleep."

Her father kissed Tirnya's forehead, and then her mother did the same. Tirnya couldn't remember the last time she had done such a thing. Zira sat beside her and held the cup of the healer's brew to Tirnya's lips. Tirnya drank as much of it as she could before turning her face away. It was too heavy and too sweet.

"No more," she said.

Her mother nodded and stood. She took Jenoe's hand and they started toward the door.

Tirnya closed her eyes, feeling sleepy. But as soon as she closed them, she saw the city again, the shadow of a falcon flashing across the face of a red building.

"I dreamed of Deraqor," she said, opening her eyes once more.

Her parents stopped and faced her again.

"What?" her father said.

"I had a dream. I was in Deraqor and I'd . . . I'd won the city back for our family." She could see the bodies again, and the blood. She swallowed, forcing herself past the memory of that part of her dream.

"What made you think of Deraqor?"

"There's been pestilence there," she said. "Not in the city itself, but on the plain. The Fal'Borna. It's . . . They've suffered."

"That much I had heard." He shook his head. "That's a long way from here. I don't think we have anything to worry about."

"No, that's not . . ." She wasn't certain what she was trying to say. "I'd like to see it someday. Deraqor, I mean."

Jenoe nodded. "So would I. Good night, Tirnya."

"Good night."

Zira extinguished the oil lamps and they left her in the darkness.

Again Tirnya closed her eyes, and immediately she felt herself drifting toward sleep, slipping back into the dream. She heard the falcon calling to her from a distance. She could see the walls of her city. And though she feared seeing the blood and the bodies again, still she started up that street once more.

Chapter 9

The rain had stopped and for the first time in days, a few pale blue gaps had appeared in the blanket of grey that covered the sky. The wind still blew hard out of the north, and if anything the air had turned colder, but still Grinsa was thankful for any break in the somber weather they'd endured since leaving E'Menua's sept.

Yet even warm breezes and clear skies would have done little to lift his spirits or those of his companions. It had been several days now, and Grinsa still was haunted by what he had seen in the devastated sept they found. Several times, he had awakened from nightmares in which he was dying of the pestilence, destroying the z'kal he shared with Cresenne and Bryntelle. Even awake, he had only to close his eyes and he could summon images from the sept: ruined structures, charred bodies, shattered bones stripped bare by scavengers and the elements.

Q'Daer had said nothing to him about what they saw that day, but the young Weaver had been unusually subdued since. He made no effort to engage Grinsa in conversation. He had also stopped taunting the Eandi merchants, though, judging from the cold stares he cast their way, he seemed to hate them more than ever.

For their part, Jasha and Torgan had behaved differently, too. Jasha had become far more talkative, taking every opportunity to tell Grinsa and Q'Daer, if the Fal'Borna would listen, all that he could remember about the one Mettai basket he had briefly owned and then sold. Whatever reservations he had harbored about helping the Qirsi with their search for the cursed baskets and the Mettai witch who had created them seemed to have vanished. Torgan, on the other hand, had grown more reserved. Before they came across the sept he had said little to the Qirsi, but had spoken freely with Jasha. Now he kept to himself, saying little to any of them, and almost appearing to flinch when one of them spoke his name. Torgan's protestations of innocence that day, as they stood amid the devastation, had been self-serving and offensive. But Grinsa couldn't help but wonder if he and the others had driven the man into this sullen silence by responding too vehemently.

If anything vaguely positive had come from that awful day, it was that none of them spoke anymore of returning to E'Menua's sept; not even Q'Daer. They rode each day for hours, stopping only to eat and drink, or to rest. But though they covered much ground, they didn't see any other septs, ruined or whole. The Night of Two Moons came and went, marking the beginning of the waning, and still they were no closer to finding the witch or her baskets. Grinsa's frustration grew with each day that passed and he could tell that Q'Daer's did, too.

Today, again, they had been riding since early morning, and with twilight approaching they had nothing to show for their efforts. Or so it seemed, until Grinsa and the young Weaver topped a small rise and saw in the distance a curving stream, and, by its banks, a cluster of eight or ten peddlers' carts.

Immediately, Q'Daer raised his hand, signaling to Jasha and Torgan, who were behind them, that they should halt. Grinsa and Q'Daer retreated back down the incline, hoping that the merchants hadn't seen them.

"What is it?" Jasha asked.

Grinsa waited until he and Q'Daer had ridden back to them before answering. "Merchants," he said in a low voice. "Several of them."

Torgan, suddenly alert, looked past Grinsa toward the top of the hill.

"Eandi?" Jasha asked.

"I think so." Grinsa glanced at the Fal'Borna, who nodded.

"We should speak to them," the younger merchant said.

"It's not quite that easy," Grinsa said. "Q'Daer and I can't just ride into their camp. If any of them are carrying the woman's baskets, we could be infected with her pestilence. And even if they don't have any, I can't imagine they'll tell us anything." He hesitated, knowing how Q'Daer would respond to what he was about to say. "We need for you to speak with them."

"We'll do it!"

"Are you mad?"

Torgan and Q'Daer said the words simultaneously, then eyed each other.

Grinsa turned to Q'Daer. "What choice do we have? We can't go ourselves, and we can't simply pass those merchants by without finding out if they've encountered the woman or her wares."

"They'll try to escape," Q'Daer said, shaking his head. "They'll get help from their friends, and they'll try to escape."

Grinsa knew that the man had a point. "Then we'll send only one of them." He looked first at Torgan and then at the younger man. "We'll send Jasha."

"No!" Torgan said.

A harsh grin spread across the Fal'Borna's features. "You see how eager he is? He knows that this may be his best chance to get away from us."

Torgan's face shaded to crimson and he looked away, shoving his hands into his pockets.

Grinsa couldn't help thinking that Q'Daer was entirely right about this. Torgan's reaction had been too immediate, too fervent. He looked at Jasha.

"You'll go," he said. "Find out what you can and then return here. If you try to run . . ." Grinsa trailed off. He'd never been good with threats of this sort.

"If I run," Jasha said, "I'll be leaving Torgan at your mercy. I'm not about to do that."

"And what's he going to tell them?" Torgan demanded. "How's he going to explain when they ask what he's doing out here alone, without so much as a cart?"

Silence. Grinsa and Q'Daer exchanged a look, but neither of them answered.

"I tell them the truth," Jasha said. "At least, as much of the truth as I can. The Fal'Borna are looking for the woman and for anyone who's selling her baskets. They took my cart and told me to find her. If I don't, I lose everything."

Torgan shook his head. "They won't believe that."

"You have a better idea?" Jasha asked.

They glared at each other for several moments, until Torgan turned away again, dismissing the younger man with a wave of his hand.

"Fine. Do what you will. I don't give a damn."

"They'll ask me to make camp with them for the night," Jasha said, looking at the Qirsi again. "It's the way of merchants out here on the plain. They'll offer me food and a place by their fire."

Grinsa shrugged. "Tell them that you can't stay, that you have to keep moving."

"I'm not sure they'll believe me."

"Then convince them. We'll expect you to be back here by nightfall."

"And have a care what you say to them," Q'Daer said. "The Forelander and I keep watch every night. If you tell them where we're camped, and they come looking for a fight, they'll die. All of them. And their deaths will be on your head."

Jasha eyed him, and finally nodded. After a moment he looked at Grinsa again. "This isn't going to work. You know that."

He did know it. But he knew as well that Q'Daer's warning and his own restrictions on what Jasha could and couldn't do were necessary. They couldn't just allow the young merchant to run away; they needed him, perhaps more than they needed Torgan, if for no other reason than because he was trustworthy. The irony wasn't lost on Grinsa. They were sending the one merchant they could trust not to betray them, and they were dooming him to failure by refusing to have faith in him.

"What would you have us do?" he asked.

Jasha looked surprised, as if he'd expected only more threats. "I'm not sure. I suppose it might help if you let me stay with them and win their trust. That's the only way I'm going to learn anything of value."

"Do you think we're fools?" Q'Daer demanded. "Do you think we'll just let you go free?"

"We should let him do it," Grinsa said, his eyes still on Jasha.

"You are mad!" the Fal'Borna said. "You can't really think he'll keep his word."

"Yes, I do. Because he knows that if he doesn't, I won't be able to keep you from killing Torgan."

Q'Daer shook his head. "You've seen the way they are. He'd trade his life for Torgan's in a heartbeat."

Grinsa faced the Fal'Borna. "No. You or I might, but Jasha won't."

"So I can go?" Jasha said.

It was getting dark. Before long it would be too late for Jasha's arrival at the merchants' camp to be believable.

"No," Q'Daer said. "No, you can't."

"Go ahead," Grinsa said. "We'll look for you come first light."

"No!" the Fal'Borna said.

Jasha flicked his horse's reins, but the animal didn't move. Language of beasts.

"Let him go," Grinsa said.

The young Weaver shook his head again. "I won't. I've let you have your way again and again on this journey. You want to feel like you're leading us, and I've been fine with that. But I won't let you do this."

Grinsa reached for his magic and using language of beasts, touched the mind of Jasha's mount. He didn't scare the animal; he merely told it to walk. Immediately he felt Q'Daer try to stop the creature, but he blocked the young Weaver's magic. Q'Daer was powerful, but his magic lacked precision, and Grinsa had little trouble mastering it.

"Damn you!" Q'Daer said.

Grinsa felt the Fal'Borna gathering his magic for a more substantial challenge. He could only guess what the man had in mind, and the last thing he wanted was a battle of magic. Yes, he could prevail in such a contest, but it would accomplish nothing, and quite likely it would alert the merchants to their presence.

"Don't do it, Q'Daer," he said. "I'll best you again, just as I did with language of beasts."

"You don't know that!"

"Yes, I do. The fact is, you haven't let me have my way, and I haven't been leading us because of some abdication on your part. I'm leading and getting my way because, quite simply, you're not as powerful as I am. It's time you made peace with that."

Even in the gloaming Grinsa could see Q'Daer's face darkening.

"Fine then," the Fal'Borna said. "Let him go. And when he doesn't return, we can kill Torgan and be done with this folly. You can explain it all to the a'laq once we're back in the sept."

With that he stalked off, his shoulder brushing past Torgan's so hard that he almost knocked the merchant to the ground.

Jasha had halted a short distance off, and had watched their exchange.

"I will come back," he said now. "You have my word on it."

"With first light," Grinsa said.

Jasha nodded to him and rode off toward the merchants.

And Grinsa whispered to the gathering night, "Just learn something from them. Anything."

Perhaps he should have been looking for some way to exploit the tensions he had just witnessed. The white-hairs were his enemy, his and Torgan's, assuming of course, that Torgan was his ally. They were prisoners of the Fal'Borna, and he should have been looking for any means of escape he could find. Torgan himself would have told him to run, even if it meant leaving Torgan to be executed by the Fal'Borna.

Jasha smiled to himself and shook his head. Well, at the very least, he thought, that's what Torgan would have done if their positions had been reversed.

But Jasha had seen too much to take that path. He'd been in S'Plaed's sept near the Companion Lakes when the Mettai witch's pestilence struck there. He knew what this plague did. He'd seen shaping power shatter homes and peddlers' carts and bodies. He'd stared, helpless to do more, as fire magic laid waste to houses, killing entire families. He'd looked on in horror as a healer's magic tore his own body apart from the inside. And in case he had forgotten—as if he ever could—he had also seen the ruins of the sept they'd come across just a few days ago.

He had no love for the white-hairs. He might not have hated them as some did, but they held no special place in his heart. Still, no people, no matter what they might have done, no matter what color their eyes, deserved to suffer as the Qirsi had under this curse.

So he would speak with these merchants, and he'd learn what he could from them, and then he would return to Torgan and the two Qirsi. Torgan would call him a fool and worse. He'd rail at Jasha for being weak. Let him. Where was the weakness in trying to save lives?

Alone, on this unfamiliar horse given to him by the Fal'Borna, with no cart rattling behind him, Jasha could have ridden right into the camp before the merchants noticed him. Having no wish to startle them, he called out long before reaching their circle.

A man stood and peered into the darkness. Others turned toward the sound of Jasha's voice.

"Who's that?" the man called.

"A friend," Jasha said. "A fellow merchant." He dismounted a short distance from their fire and led his mount on foot the rest of the way.

The man stood and turned to face him, as did the other merchants. They watched him warily, no doubt wondering what one of their kind would be doing way out here on the plain without any cart or wares.

"Hello, friend," the man said, and though Jasha sensed no irony in the stranger's use of the word, he sensed no warmth either. "What can we do for you?"

"I'm hoping you can help me," the young merchant said. "My name is Jasha Ziffel. I've been trading on the plain and in the lands around the Companion Lakes for several years now." He looked at each merchant as he spoke. There were nine of them in all, all of them Eandi, all but two of them men. A few he recognized, and he sensed that they knew him as well, though he couldn't recall any of their names. "A few of you have seen me before, and you'll know that I'm no thief and I'm no cheat. I'm just a man in need of information."

"Where's your cart, Jasha?" the man asked. He was a bit older than the others, a tall man with a thick shock of white hair. His broad shoulders were stooped, but he was still trim, and Jasha thought that he must have cut an imposing figure in his youth.

"The Fal'Borna took it from me."

"The Fal'Borna?" the man said, clearly surprised.

"Why?" one of the women asked him.

Jasha wanted to ask if he could sit with them around their fire. The air had grown colder with nightfall, and he could smell roasted fowl, which reminded him of how hungry he was. He could tell, however, that the merchants weren't yet ready to welcome him into their circle. He had some work to do before they would trust him that much.

"Because they think that I can lead them to a Mettai woman who's been selling cursed baskets in their lands."

"Cursed baskets?"

The tone of the question carried more than mere surprise at such an idea. Jasha knew it immediately, and it seemed that others noticed as well, for several of the merchants turned to glance back at the man who had spoken. He was a big man, not quite as tall as the white-haired merchant, but far heavier, with a large gut and an open, youthful face. He couldn't have been much older than Jasha. He wore a wide-brimmed leather hat, which hid most of his hair. But what little Jasha could see appeared in the firelight to be red. Jasha was certain that he had seen this man before in marketplaces along the Silverwater, or perhaps in one of the Eandi sovereignties, but he couldn't recall his name.

"Yes," Jasha said. "Do you know something about them?"

"No," the man said. "Not a thing."

"What's your name, friend?"

"Don't answer that," the white-haired merchant said, glancing back at the other man. "Not yet at least." He faced Jasha again. "I want more answers from you first. I've had enough dealings with the Fal'Borna to know that if they consider you an enemy, they won't just take your cart and goods and leave it at that. There's more to this tale, and I want to hear it."

Jasha nodded. "Yes, there's more. The Fal'Borna captured me as well as another merchant named Torgan Plye."

"Torgan?" the red-haired man said.

Several of the others exchanged looks; clearly all of them knew who Torgan was.

"Torgan had traded for some baskets and was near a Fal'Borna sept that suffered an outbreak of the pestilence. The Fal'Borna found us together, took our wares, and threatened to kill us if we didn't find the Mettai woman they believe is responsible for cursing the baskets. We've been searching the plain for her ever since, but thus far we've found neither the woman nor her goods. The only thing we have found is the ruins of another sept, and we did find scraps of Mettai baskets there."

The white-haired man eyed him for several moments before finally shaking his head again.

"I believe you're telling us the truth as far as it goes. But much of this still doesn't make sense to me. I think there are things you're keeping from us."

Jasha briefly considered denying it. In the next moment he rejected the idea, knowing that there was nothing to be gained by doing so. The man didn't believe him, and for good reason. Best to be as honest as he could be and see if that at least convinced the merchants to speak with him further.

"There are," he admitted. "I'll answer your questions as best I can, but there are certain things I can't tell you without endangering my life, as well as Torgan's."

"The Fal'Borna still have him?" the white-haired man asked.

"Yes."

The man considered this briefly. Then he stepped forward and offered Jasha his hand. "Very well. My name is Tegg Lonsher. I'd wager that I've been trading in the clan lands since before you were born."

Jasha shook his hand and smiled. "It's a pleasure to meet you, Tegg."

Tegg began to introduce the other merchants, but Jasha had trouble remembering all the different names. Except for one: The red-haired man was called Brint HedFarren. Jasha recognized the name immediately. He was said to be one of the most successful merchants in all the Southlands. Though far younger than Torgan, he was already considered nearly Torgan's equal in terms of both the quality of his wares and his skill as a bargainer. Jasha found it easy to believe that, like Torgan, Brint might have seen the Mettai woman's baskets and been drawn to them by their vivid colors and fine workmanship.

When the introductions were done, the merchants returned to the fire, making room for Jasha in their circle and offering him food and wine. Tegg remained by his side though, and the old man peppered him with questions. Where had he been when the Fal'Borna caught up with him? To whose sept had he been taken? Why would the a'laq have been willing to let him leave on his own, without Fal'Borna guards? Had he considered returning to one of the sovereignties and getting help from the armies there? Who was this Mettai woman he was after, and how certain was he that she had actually cursed her baskets? Was this pestilence of hers the same one that had ravaged Y'Qatt villages near the Companion Lakes?

Jasha told him what he could, gauging Tegg's reactions and those of the people around him as he spoke. Several of the merchants were listening intently to their conversation; others were speaking among themselves, ignoring them.

Brint gave the appearance of doing neither. He stared at the fire, chewing on a piece of dried meat and occasionally taking a pull of wine from the skin that was making its way around the circle. But Jasha knew that he was listening to every word they said. The man's indifference to their conversation seemed too studied to be convincing.

Eventually, Tegg relented, satisfied that Jasha posed no threat to him or his friends. Free finally to pose his own questions, Jasha began by asking the most obvious.

"Are any of you selling any Mettai baskets right now?"

None of them were.

But when he next asked if any of them had seen Mettai baskets of high quality in the last turn or two, several of the merchants said that they had. One woman in particular—her given name was Ghella; he couldn't recall her family name, though he knew that he had seen her before in his travels—recalled seeing more than a dozen of them in the cart of another peddler.

"It was Lark, Tegg. You remember. That woman who sings so well."

Tegg nodded, though he was frowning. "Of course I do. She had baskets? You're certain?"

Ghella nodded. She was heavy, with long, auburn hair and a friendly, round face. "Yes, I'm sure of it. We were north and east of here when I saw her, and she had several of them. She said that she hadn't put them out yet, that she was still trying to decide what to ask for them. I tried to buy a few, but she wanted two sovereigns for each, and I couldn't buy enough of them to make it worth my while." She shook her head. "Shame, really. They were lovely."

"Do you know where she was headed?" Jasha asked.

"The Horn, I think. But I can't be certain."

The Horn. Jasha shuddered. That was the center of the Fal'Borna clan lands. There was no telling how many people would die if those baskets reached D'Raqor, or one of the other cities there.

Another man claimed to have seen the baskets as well, but he proved far less helpful than Ghella. He couldn't recall the name of the peddler who had been carrying them, and his description of the baskets he'd seen was vague enough to leave Jasha wondering if they had been made by the same woman. Not long after, the man returned to his cart to sleep.

Tegg watched him go before turning to Jasha again.

"Don't put too much faith in what Kalib tells you. He doesn't like it when he's not the center of a conversation. I'd be surprised if he even knew what a basket was."

Jasha grinned. "Thank you." He nodded toward Brint. "What about him?" he asked, dropping his voice to a soft whisper.

"Young Red?" Tegg answered. "He's a good man. If he tells you something, you can bet it's the truth."

"All right. Again, my thanks." Jasha stood, and walked over to where Brint was sitting, his eyes still fixed on the low flames of their campfire. "Mind if I join you?" he asked.

Brint looked up at him for just an instant and shrugged. Jasha sat beside him and rubbed his hands together before holding them out to the fire.

"If I didn't know better, I'd say it feels like snow."

"We've another turn before the Snows come," Brint said. "But they'll be hard this year, that's for certain."

Jasha nodded. "Before, when I first got here, I had the sense that maybe you know something about these baskets, or maybe about the woman who made them."

Brint shook his head, but he didn't meet Jasha's gaze. "I don't know anything more than the rest of these folk. I'm just a merchant trying to make some gold on the plain before the Snows send me back south."

"You're being modest, Brint. I know Torgan, remember? I know that the two of you are more than just merchants. You have an eye for quality, and a knack for finding the treasures in a crowded marketplace that the rest of us would miss. That's how he came by the baskets—he spotted them, and immediately he knew their worth." Jasha looked at the man. "I think that's what happened with you, too. You saw them, and you knew instantly how valuable they were. I had one of them, briefly, before I sold it again. It was finer than any basket I'd ever seen."

"I wouldn't know," Brint said. "I haven't seen any of her baskets."

"Really?" Jasha asked. "I could have sworn that you had."

At that Brint finally turned to look at him. "What's that supposed to mean?"

"Just that you reacted pretty strongly when I first mentioned them."

The man turned back to the fire. "I don't know what you're talking about."

"I wasn't the only one who noticed." Jasha indicated the other merchants with a small bob of his head. "They were looking at you. They heard it in your voice."

"I'm telling you, there was nothing to hear."

Jasha shrugged. "All right. If you tell me it's so, I believe you. It's a shame, though."

A silence hung between them for some time, until Jasha began to wonder if he had handled this poorly, or if perhaps he had been wrong about Brint in the first place. Maybe he didn't know anything about the woman. Still they sat, and neither of them spoke. At last, unsure of what else to do, Jasha stood, intending to speak with some of the others. Perhaps there was more that Ghella could tell him.

"Well, good night, Brint."

"What's a shame?" the merchant asked him before Jasha could walk away.

"What?"

"You said before, 'It's a shame.' What did you mean by that?"

Jasha sat again. "I just meant that a lot of people have died already. A lot more are going to. I was hoping you might be able to tell me something that would keep that from happening. It seems I was wrong." He paused, eyeing the man. "You did say that I was wrong, didn't you?"

"It's just white-hairs, isn't it? The ones who are dying?"

"So far, yes. But it's a bad death. I've seen it, and I wouldn't wish it on anyone. Not even the Fal'Borna."

"And what happens to you if you don't find . . . what you're looking for?"

"Probably they'll execute me, and Torgan, too."

Jasha didn't even have to look at him. He could feel the man fighting himself. Brint did know about the woman; it was just a matter of getting him to admit it. And Jasha knew with equal clarity that there was precious little he could do in that regard. This was up to Brint.

"I'm sorry to have disturbed you," he said, standing once more. "I'm going to speak with some of the others. They might be able to help me. Thank you, Brint."

"For what? I didn't do anything."

"Well, thank you anyway."

Jasha left him there, stepping around the circle, and went to sit beside two other merchants. He didn't remember the name of either and he didn't expect that they would be able to tell him anything of value. But he chatted with them for a long while, until most of the others had gone to sleep. At one point Tegg approached Jasha, and told him that he was welcome to bed down for the night beside their fire. Jasha thanked him and said that he would.

Through all of this, Brint remained awake, doing much the same thing he had done all night. He stared at the fire and he drank wine, and said nothing to anyone.

Finally, the last of the merchants went off to sleep, leaving just Jasha and Brint. Still the red-haired man didn't speak, and though Jasha knew better than to press the matter, his frustration mounted. He was tired, and he feared that whatever Brint knew might be of little consequence, in which case he would have wasted the entire night.

The fire popped loudly, and a swarm of glowing sparks rose into the night. Jasha picked up a long stick and stirred the embers, trying to coax a bit more light and warmth from them. When he looked up again, Brint was staring at him.

"Tell me about this pestilence," he said.

"What is it you want to know?"

The big man hesitated, appearing unsure of himself. "Why does it strike at their kind but not at us?"

"I don't know," Jasha said.

"Before, you said that the sept you found had been ruined."

Jasha nodded. "Yes. By magic. It seems that when the Qirsi are stricken they lose control of their power. Their fire magic, their healing, their shaping—all of it runs wild, destroying everything and everyone around them."

Brint nodded and began once more to stare into the dying flames.

After what seemed an eternity he said, in a voice that barely carried over the settling of the coals, "She told me this would happen."

It took Jasha a moment. "Who did?"

The red-haired merchant just looked at him.

"You mean the Mettai woman?" he whispered, his eyes widening.

Brint chewed his lip, looking, for all his bulk, like a boy caught in a lie. Finally, he nodded.

"Where did you see her, Brint? You have to tell me."

"I thought she was mad. You have to believe that. One moment she was selling me baskets, and the next she was shouting this nonsense at me about how they would destroy everything. It made no sense."

"You have to tell me everything, Brint. All of it. Every detail matters."

"'Death and ruin.' That's what she said to me. That's what she said the baskets would bring."

It was as if they were carrying on different conversations.

"Brint!" Jasha said sharply, forcing the man to look at him again. "Tell me everything. Where were you?"

"I found her among the ruins of some old village. The place looked to have been deserted for decades. It was right near N'Kiel's Span on the Silverwater."

"What did she say to you?"

Brint shrugged. "We talked for a long while. She seemed fine at first. Sane, that is. She asked me about where I was from and we bargained over the price of the baskets. It was only when I told her that . . ." He stopped, chewed his lip again.

"When you told her what?"

"I . . . I think I said at first that I had been looking for Mettai and Y'Qatt goods. Later, after she'd sold me the baskets, I told her that I was headed to the plain to trade with the Fal'Borna. That's when she started talking like a madwoman."

"What did she say exactly?"

"I told you already," Brint said, sounding sullen. "'Death and ruin.' Nonsense like that."

"That was all?" Jasha asked, certain that it wasn't, that she'd told the man a great deal more than that. "She sounded mad, you said. I'm sure that all of it sounded like the ramblings of a crazy woman."

Brint pressed his lips then, but he nodded. "She said thousands would die, that entire villages would be destroyed. She said that I couldn't take them to the Qirsi, because she hated them. I think . . . I think she wanted me to take them to the Y'Qatt."

Jasha frowned. "The Y'Qatt?"

"Yes. That's when she got so angry; when she realized that I wouldn't be taking the baskets to the Y'Qatt."

It made no sense. Jasha could understand why an Eandi, even a Mettai, might hate the Fal'Borna enough to loose this plague upon them. But the Y'Qatt were ascetics, Qirsi who refused to use their magic for any reason at all. They were peaceful, and they kept to themselves.

"You're sure of this?" Jasha asked.

"Yes. I know it makes no sense. None of what she said did. That's why I didn't think much of it."

Jasha considered this for a few moments longer, but he could think of no reason why the Mettai would hate the Y'Qatt so much. Eventually he decided that this was something the Fal'Borna would have to figure out for themselves. He'd found out what he could.

"Do you still have the baskets?" he asked.

Brint shook his head. "She tried to buy them back from me when she found out where I was taking them." Suddenly the big man couldn't stop talking. "She offered me all the gold she had, plus what I'd just paid her."

"And you refused."

Brint looked at him. "You saw those baskets. You know how fine they were. And at that point I just wanted to get away from her as quickly as I could."

"Where are the baskets now, Brint?"

"I sold them to other merchants."

Jasha had been afraid of this. He passed a hand through his hair. "Where did you sell them?"

"Around a fire, much like this one. I met up with some other merchants and decided I didn't want anything to do with that crazy woman or her wares. So I sold them all."

"To who?"

Brint named several merchants. A few of them—Stam Corfej, Lariqenne Glyse, Grijed Semlor—Jasha knew. He tried to commit to memory those names he didn't recognize.

"And how many baskets were there in all?" Jasha asked.

"Forty-seven."

Jasha felt his mouth drop open. Perhaps it shouldn't have surprised him. The Mettai woman was selling her wares throughout the land; no doubt she had dozens of them. But somehow hearing this number—forty-seven!—and knowing that they were being spread across the plain, like seeds blown from a harvest flower, struck him dumb. He and his riding companions had seen the remains of two or three in the ruined sept they'd found days before. How many more villages could be ravaged that way? Would one basket do it, or did it take two or three or even four? Even if it took more—six or eight—that meant half a dozen villages might suffer the same fate as the one they had seen. And that assumed the baskets Brint had bought from the woman were the only ones still out there.

"It didn't seem like that many at the time," Brint whispered after some time.

"No. I'm sure it didn't."

Jasha had to resist an urge to climb back on his horse and return immediately to Torgan, Grinsa, and Q'Daer. Forty-seven baskets! He wanted to find them now, this night.

We can't do anything tonight, he told himself. *I need to rest so that we can be moving again with first light.*

"You probably don't know where the merchants who bought them were headed, do you?"

"No," Brint said. "There were several of them. They were all headed in different directions. Some were going west, others south, toward the Ofirean."

Jasha winced and closed his eyes. The Ofirean. If those baskets reached Thamia or Siraam or one of the other major settlements on the inland sea . . . He shuddered.

"I didn't mean for this to happen," Brint told him.

"I'm sure you didn't." Jasha stood, too weary to say more. "I'll see you in the morning."

Brint nodded.

Jasha lay down beside the fire, stretching out on the hard ground and wrapping the blanket he'd brought with him around his shoulders. But for a long time sleep wouldn't come. Whenever he closed his eyes, he began to see once more the devastation of S'Plaed's sept and the ruined settlement they'd seen south of here. So he kept them open, staring at the baleful orange glow of the embers. After a while, he heard Brint walk off to his cart. One of the other merchants mumbled something in her sleep, and an owl called from far off.

Death and ruin, the woman had warned. Yet clearly that was what she had been hoping for when she first conjured this plague of hers.

"She was mad," Jasha whispered to himself, thinking that this should make him feel better somehow.

But it didn't. And he lay awake.

Chapter 10

❖‒I‒❖

Long after Jasha left them, Torgan remained apart from the Qirsi. He didn't wander far—the Fal'Borna wouldn't let him—but he kept his distance, watching the sky darken, wondering if this would be his last night alive.

Let him go, Q'Daer had said, speaking of Jasha. *And when he doesn't return, we can kill Torgan and be done with this folly.*

He had no doubt that the Fal'Borna meant what he said, and though he didn't think that the Forelander would let Q'Daer follow through on the threat, there was always the chance that Grinsa would be powerless to stop the younger man. The larger question looming in Torgan's mind was whether or not Jasha would return. If Jasha had asked for his advice, he would have told him to ride eastward as fast as he could until he crossed into Eandi land. Yes, he'd be condemning Torgan to his death, but better one of them should get away.

Jasha didn't think that way, though. He was young. He still thought that kindness and generosity could win out over centuries of hatred and war. He truly believed that if they helped the Fal'Borna find the Mettai woman and end her plague, the white-hairs would let them go. So he'd go and speak with the merchants they'd seen, he'd find out what he could, and then he'd come back, thinking that they actually had a chance to succeed in this foolish venture.

Jasha was an idiot, and because of that Torgan would probably live to see another sunset.

Or would he? On more than one occasion the young merchant had surprised Torgan with his cunning. He'd done his part to keep them alive when they first spoke with E'Menua. And, in fact, he'd been so sly about it that at first Torgan believed Jasha had betrayed him, and he tried to strangle the younger man. Jasha had also turned conversations so as to keep Grinsa and Q'Daer at odds with each other, convinced that so long as the Forelander believed he had more in common with the two merchants, he was more likely to protect them from the Fal'Borna.

Jasha might well have come to the same conclusion that Torgan had reached: The Fal'Borna were likely to execute them no matter the outcome of their search for the Mettai witch. In which case, Torgan would never see the young merchant again.

Sitting on a boulder, staring at the clouds that scudded past, vaguely conscious of the two Qirsi nearby, Torgan pondered these possibilities, assessing the reasoning behind each, examining them for flaws as if they were goods in a marketplace. A part of him wondered at how calm he felt contemplating the possibility that he would be killed in a few hours. He knew better than to think that he had suddenly found courage. More likely this endless ordeal with the Fal'Borna had left him numb.

Or perhaps there was another explanation. Perhaps the knowledge that he wasn't entirely powerless had made him bold. Could it be that he had drawn strength from that scrap of cursed Mettai basket that he carried at the bottom of his travel sack?

He had told himself that he would use it against the Qirsi only as a last resort. Already he carried too many dead with him, and he was loath to add to that burden. Yes, the deaths he had caused in C'Bijor's Neck and S'Plaed's sept had been inadvertent, but that didn't make the wraiths hovering at his shoulder any less unsettling. If he were to use the scrap he had found in the ruined sept to expose Grinsa and Q'Daer to the witch's plague it would be murder, plain and simple.

Some murders are justified, said a voice in his head. *And is it really murder if it's the only way to save yourself?*

The question itself was enough to start Torgan shaking, and he thrust his hands into his pockets, though the Qirsi weren't close enough to notice.

It was the timing that made his decision so difficult. He wouldn't know until morning if his life was in imminent danger. Either Jasha would return or he wouldn't; if he didn't Q'Daer might well have his way, and Torgan would be killed. But from what he knew of the witch's pestilence, it took several hours to take effect, which meant that if Torgan waited for morning to use the basket scrap, he wouldn't be able to save himself; he'd merely be assuring that the Qirsi died several hours after killing him. Not that Torgan was above such vengeance, but it struck him as a thoroughly empty gesture. Better he should expose them to the plague tonight. Quite likely the Qirsi would be dead by morning and regardless of whether Jasha returned, Torgan would be able to escape.

By the time darkness fell and Grinsa kindled a small fire in a circle of stones, Torgan had made up his mind to kill his captors this night. He wasn't sure yet how he would do it—how close did the Qirsi need to be to the basket in order for the plague to take them? Would he need to put it near them somehow? Could he put it near their food, or their sleeping rolls?

Nor did his decision rest easy on his heart. The shaking that had started with his hands had spread to his entire body, so that he quaked as if from a fever, and barely trusted himself to walk. He tried to imagine himself riding away come morning, freed from his captivity, but the distance from where he was now—a coward with a daring plan and no idea as to how he might effect it—to where he hoped to be come daybreak seemed too great.

He heard a footfall nearby and looked up sharply. The Forelander stood a short distance off, the campfire at his back and his powerful frame in shadow.

"We're eating," he said, "if you want to join us."

Torgan nodded, afraid that if he spoke his voice would give him away. Grinsa stood there another moment, as if waiting for more of a response. Receiving none, he turned and walked back toward the firelight.

"Damn," Torgan muttered. At this rate he was going to raise the white-hairs' suspicions before he had the chance to do anything at all. He'd be lucky to survive the night himself.

Forcing himself up, the merchant walked after Grinsa. He thought about walking to his mount right away and retrieving the scrap of charred basket, but he couldn't bring himself to do it. *Not yet*, he told himself. *After they've eaten, when it's time for sleep.* It made sense. Still, Torgan cursed his cowardice.

As he drew near the fire, he caught the aroma of roasting meat riding the light wind. At first he thought the scent came from the camp of the Eandi merchants. A moment later, though, he saw that the white-hairs had set a spit over the fire and were cooking what looked to be a rabbit. Despite his nerves, Torgan realized that he was famished.

Grinsa and Q'Daer were already eating. As Torgan stepped into the firelight, the Forelander gestured toward the fire.

"Help yourself," he said, his mouth full. "There isn't much, but we've had our share."

Q'Daer cast him an icy look but said nothing. It seemed he was less inclined than Grinsa to share the food.

Torgan took some of the meat, sat down, and began to eat.

"Looks like your friend is still with the merchants, dark-eye," Q'Daer said after a while. "At least he was the last time we checked."

Torgan was in the middle of chewing and now he paused, looking first at the Fal'Borna and then at Grinsa. "So what does that mean?" he asked, after swallowing.

"It means Jasha's doing what we asked of him," Grinsa said.

"Or," Q'Daer threw in, "it means that he and the other merchants are planning to attack."

"He wouldn't do that," Torgan said without thinking.

Grinsa nodded once. "I agree."

Q'Daer looked at Grinsa disapprovingly, but kept silent.

"So then . . ." Torgan hesitated, eyeing them both. "Then you're not going to . . . to do anything to me?"

"No," Grinsa said. "We're not."

"The other one hasn't come back yet," Q'Daer said. "We know nothing for certain."

Grinsa frowned briefly before looking at Torgan again. "He'll be back come morning, and then we'll go on with our search. I'm hoping that he'll learn something that will tell us where to go next."

Torgan said nothing. He just stared at the half-eaten leg of rabbit he held in his hand. But it was all he could do to keep from weeping. Relief, hatred, frustration: all of them warred within him.

He wanted to rail at the white-hairs—at the Fal'Borna in particular—for their threats, for making Torgan believe that he had only hours to live. Yes, he was relieved to know that they wouldn't kill him. He might even have been relieved knowing that he didn't have to kill the men tonight if he didn't want to. But that was also the source of his greatest frustration. He *did* want to. He wanted desperately to be free of these Qirsi, and also to exact some measure of vengeance for all to which they had subjected him for the past turn and more. He knew, though, that he wouldn't, that without the imminent threat of his execution, he would never find the nerve to kill them. In that moment, sitting before the white-hairs' fire, eating their food, acquiescing to their continued control over him, Torgan realized that he had come to loathe himself.

"Are you all right?" Grinsa asked him.

"Fine," he said, his voice thick. "I'm fine."

He took another bite, but barely managed to choke it down.

"I'm not hungry anymore," he said, forcing himself to his feet. "Either of you want this?"

Q'Daer shrugged and held out his hand.

Torgan handed it to him and then left the small circle of light cast by the fire. He walked to where his horse was tied, found his saddle and travel sack lying in a pile on the ground, and opened the sack. The piece of burned basket was at the bottom, beneath his spare clothes, a coil of rope, and a few pouches of food.

"Just take it out," he whispered through clenched teeth. "Take it out and carry it back to the fire."

But he knew that he wouldn't. He'd started shaking again, sweat running down his temples despite the cold.

After several moments, he tied the sack closed once more and grabbed his sleeping roll.

He could hear the Qirsi talking as he walked back to the fire to sleep, but they fell silent before he could make out what they'd been saying. No doubt they'd been talking about him, maybe arguing over what they should do if by some chance Jasha didn't return with the dawn. Torgan didn't care anymore. Let them execute him if that's what they wanted. If this was the life that was left to him, he didn't care. If this was the man he'd become, he wasn't worth saving. He just ignored them, spread out his sleeping roll by the fire and lay down. Before long he'd fallen into a deep, dreamless slumber.

Torgan awoke to the sound of voices. Opening his eyes to another grey, chilly dawn, he saw that Jasha had returned already and was speaking with the white-hairs. The young merchant looked genuinely excited and both Grinsa and Q'Daer were listening intently as he spoke.

He rose and stumbled over to where they were standing, rubbing the sleep from his eyes as he walked.

". . . With so many out there, I'm not even certain where we'd begin to look for them," Jasha was saying as Torgan approached.

"What did he say about the woman?" Grinsa asked.

"The last he saw of her, she was in the ruins of a village near N'Kiel's Span." Jasha's eyes flicked toward Torgan. "He said she was mad, that she went on and on about how the baskets would bring death and ruin."

"Doesn't sound mad to me," Q'Daer said. "They did just that."

"He thinks that she had intended them for the Y'Qatt."

The Fal'Borna frowned. "The Y'Qatt? Why would she want to kill them?"

"Who are the Y'Qatt?" Grinsa asked.

"They're idiots," Torgan said, barely glancing at the man. "White-hairs who refuse to do magic—they say your god didn't intend it. Who are you talking about?" he demanded, looking at Jasha.

"The Mettai woman."

"No," he said, shaking his head. "No, I mean who was it who told you all this about the woman?"

"A merchant—Tordjanni from the sound of him. He said he knew you. His name was Brint HedFarren."

"HedFarren," Torgan said, whispering the name, staring at the ground, his brow creased in concentration. "HedFarren." It came to him abruptly. "Big fellow?" he asked, looking up again. "Red hair?"

"Yes, that's him."

"Why would someone want to kill these people—the Y'Qatt?" Grinsa asked.

Jasha raised his eyebrows. "That's a good question. Brint had no idea, and neither do I."

Grinsa turned to Q'Daer, who merely shrugged.

"They both live in the Companion Lakes region," Torgan said. "The Mettai and the Y'Qatt, I mean. There's no history of warfare between them but there could be old rivalries that the rest of us don't know about. Or it may be that this woman and her people had a feud with them."

The others regarded him with surprise.

"What?" Torgan asked, looking at each of them, until his gaze came to rest on Jasha.

"Nothing," the younger man said. "It's a good point."

"And that surprises you?"

None of them answered, but Grinsa and Jasha shared a look and after a moment both of them began to laugh.

"You think I got to be as successful as I did without knowing a thing or two about the people of this land? I can tell you about every sovereignty, and about every clan in the white-hair lands. I know this land better than any of you."

"I'm sure you do, Torgan," Jasha said, still grinning. "You're just not always that insightful about . . . about the feelings of other people."

Torgan dismissed the remark with a wave. "Feelings have nothing to do with it. We're talking about the Mettai and the Y'Qatt. They're strange, all of them. Eandi sorcerers? White-hairs who refuse to do magic? It's a miracle that they never went to war. It shouldn't surprise any of us that they're the ones behind all this madness."

"Now, that sounds more like Torgan," Jasha said, drawing another laugh from Grinsa.

Torgan glared at them a moment longer before stalking off toward his horse. "Forget it," he called over his shoulder. "I try to help you people and I just get ridiculed." His horse, a mount given to him for this journey by the Fal'Borna, snorted a greeting as Torgan drew near. Torgan stroked the beast's nose, then reached into his travel sack intending to pull out a pouch of food. As he did this, though, his hand brushed the frayed, blackened osiers of the basket scrap he'd been carrying. He hesitated, looking over at Jasha and the Qirsi. The merchant was deep in conversation with Grinsa, but at that moment Q'Daer happened to look Torgan's way. Torgan froze, staring back at him, like a boy caught stealing gold from his father's purse.

Their eyes remained locked for what seemed an eternity to Torgan, until finally one of the others said something that caught the Fal'Borna's attention, making him look away.

Torgan began to breathe again. Taking hold of the food pouch he'd been after in the first place, he pulled it from the sack with a trembling hand and opened it. It was only as he was raising a piece of hard cheese to his mouth that he noticed the black smudge on his hand. It was on the heel of his palm, just below the thumb; three faint streaks of black, as if some dark bird from the Underrealm had brushed his hand with the tips of its wings.

Again his gaze darted in the direction of the others, and again he found that the Fal'Borna was watching him. He put the cheese in his mouth and quickly wiped his hand on his breeches. Glancing down, he saw that the stain was still there and he wiped his hand again, harder this time. He looked back toward his companions.

Q'Daer was walking in his direction.

Torgan took another piece of cheese and shoved it in his mouth, taking care to wipe his hand once more. At last it looked clean. He closed the food pouch, shoved it back into the sack, and closed that as well. Then he began walking in Q'Daer's direction, wanting to put some distance between his sack, with its lethal scrap of basket, and the Fal'Borna.

"What are you up to, Torgan?" Q'Daer asked as they approached each other.

"Nothing. I'm eating."

The white-hair looked past Torgan toward his horse. "What is it you're hiding over there?"

"I'm not hiding anything." He gestured at his mouth which was still full of cheese. "See? I'm eating. That's all."

For a moment he feared that the Fal'Borna wouldn't believe him, that he intended to go over and search Torgan's travel sack. Instead, after peering over Torgan's shoulder a moment longer, he looked the merchant in the eye.

"They have more questions for you," he said. "Seems there are several merchants selling those cursed baskets on the plain, and they think maybe you'll have some idea where to look for them."

"All right."

Again the Fal'Borna hesitated, his eyes narrowing briefly. After a moment, though, he led Torgan back to the others.

"Do you know Stam Corfej, Torgan?" Jasha asked as Torgan reached them.

"Stam? Yes, of course. Good man. Aelean. Partial to pipeweed from Naqbae."

Grinsa smiled. "You truly are a merchant, aren't you?"

Torgan regarded him mildly. "You doubted it?"

"Where would he be right now?" Q'Daer asked.

He frowned. "That I'm less certain of." He removed his hat and scratched his head. "This late in the Harvest? He could be in any number of places. He might have returned to Aelea—if he planned to spend the Snows there, he'd cross the mountains before the weather turned too harsh. But he might also have headed south to the Ofirean, or west to the Horn, or into the southern sovereignties. Qosantia or Tordjanne," he added, for Grinsa's benefit. "Maybe even Naqbae."

Jasha looked troubled. "That doesn't help us much."

"Try one of the other names," Q'Daer said.

Jasha nodded once. "All right. What about Lark?"

"Lariqenne?" Torgan said, smiling. "Lovely woman, and what a singing voice. This time of year she'll probably be near the Horn, or heading toward the sea."

"And Grijed?"

Torgan frowned. "Semlor, you mean?" He shook his head. "He'd definitely be on his way south by now. He doesn't have the stomach for grey skies and cold nights."

"You don't like him," Grinsa said.

"Not much, no," Torgan admitted. "His goods are poor and he asks far too much for them. Men like him give men like me a bad reputation."

Q'Daer gave him a sour look. "I'd have thought you took care of that yourself."

Torgan ignored the comment, as did the others. Jasha named two other men, neither of whom Torgan knew.

"I'd never heard of them either," the younger man said. "They must be new to the plain."

"I agree."

"So then where should we go?" Grinsa asked. "We know of several merchants who might be headed toward the Ofirean or the Horn, and we have a crazed Mettai witch who we know is east of here."

"We go after the witch," Torgan said immediately. "That's the deal we made with E'Menua. We find the woman, he lets us live."

Grinsa looked at Q'Daer. "My conversation with the a'laq went much the same way, but knowing those baskets are out there changes everything. We'll save more lives going after the merchants. If that's what you want to do, we'll do it."

Torgan could hardly believe what he was hearing. "Are you mad? You're throwing away everything! Our lives! Your freedom!"

Grinsa hardly looked at him. "What do you think?" he asked the Fal'Borna.

"It's not his decision! The Fal'Borna are the enemy! Don't you get that?"

The Forelander whirled on him, stepping so close that Torgan had to back away. He hadn't realized until that moment just how big the white-hair was. "Keep quiet, Torgan! Q'Daer and I are going to make this decision, and you'll live with whatever we decide! Do I make myself clear?"

Torgan tried to hold the man's gaze, but failed. After a moment he nodded.

"You'd do this?" Q'Daer asked.

"If you think it makes sense to try. Torgan's right: We had an agreement with your a'laq, and eventually we have to find the woman. But if you think we can save lives, then that's what we should do."

The Fal'Borna was looking at Grinsa as if seeing the Forelander for the first time.

"The Horn," he finally said. "Finding the merchants on the shores of the sea would be next to impossible. It's a long coastline, and there are cities scattered throughout. But the Horn is a different matter. It's a small area, with a lot of people. The merchants will be easier to find there. And if those baskets reach S'Vralna or worse, D'Raqor, the effects would be . . ." He shook his head. "The dead would number in the thousands."

Grinsa's expression had turned grim, leading Torgan to believe that he, too, wanted to go after the Mettai woman. But he simply nodded. "All right, then. We'll go to the Horn."

"Damn you both," Torgan said. "You've just killed us."

Grinsa eyed him briefly before turning to Jasha. "If you're hungry you should eat now. I want to be moving before long."

"Right," the young merchant said.

Once more, Grinsa looked Torgan in the eye. "The sooner we find these merchants, the sooner we'll be heading east again, toward the Mettai woman. So I'd suggest you make peace with this decision and help us in any way you can." He didn't wait for a reply. He turned and walked to where his mount waited for him, leaving Torgan standing alone.

Torgan wanted to scream at the man. He wanted to pick up a rock and crush the white-hair's skull. And once more he thought of the burned osiers in his sack, and the decision he'd failed to make the previous night. He followed Jasha to where the younger man's horse stood and watched as he took out some smoked meat.

"Do you want some?" Jasha asked.

"You shouldn't have come back."

Jasha smiled and shook his head. "Right. I should have let them kill you."

"Yes, if that's what it came to, you should have let them." Torgan looked away, his eyes straying to his own mount, and to the travel sack resting beside the beast. "But it might not have come to that."

"Meaning what?"

"Nothing. Just that I can take care of myself. You might not think so, but I did pretty well for myself for a lot of years before all this foolishness began." He exhaled heavily, wondering how he had ever allowed all this to happen. He'd been the most successful merchant on the plain, perhaps in all the Southlands. He'd had enough gold to last the rest of his life, and he'd been carrying wares that could easily have doubled his fortune. Now he had nothing and spent every moment at the mercy of the Fal'Borna. And it had all happened in the span of maybe a turn, perhaps a bit more. It was enough to make his head spin. "The point is," he said, "you should have gotten away when you had the chance."

"No, Torgan. Maybe that's what you would have done, but not me."

He shook his head. "You're an idiot."

"You're welcome."

Torgan glowered at him. "Tell me about the merchants you met."

"There's not much to tell," Jasha said with a shrug. "HedFarren was reluctant to tell me anything at first, but I think in the end he realized how much was at stake, and his fear got the better of him. Actually, he reminded me of you." He said this last with his gaze lowered.

Torgan made a point of ignoring the remark. "What about the rest?"

"I didn't speak to all of them. The leader was an older man named Tegg. He was wary of me at first, but he did his best to help once he convinced himself that I didn't mean his friends any harm. And there was a woman named Ghella. She was the one who saw baskets in Lark's cart."

Torgan nodded. "I know Tegg, and Ghella, too. Tegg Lonsher, that's his name. Crusty old goat. Good enough wares, but a stubborn negotiator. I usually try to avoid doing business with him. I always liked Ghella, but she was just the opposite of Lonsher: too easy, too willing to close the deal. I always knew that I could get a good price from her, whether I was selling or buying. You don't want to do that," he said. "People always used to tell me that I was disliked, as if that was supposed to hurt my feelings or something. But the fact is, as a merchant, being liked is secondary. Chances are if you're liked it's because you're too easy. I didn't make all that gold by being friends with everyone. I did it by setting a price and sticking to it."

"Right," Jasha said.

The young merchant was merely saying it to humor him. Torgan should have been angry, but he understood. Both of them had lost their carts, their wares, and all their gold. Chances were they'd be dead before long, victims of the Fal'Borna's twisted sense of justice. And here was Torgan, dispensing advice on the finer points of trading as if they were in some Eandi market-place. But for just that moment, thinking like a merchant again, instead of like . . . whatever it was he had become, he remembered what it had meant to be Torgan Plye. He felt strong and smart and wealthy, and all the other things he once had been and wasn't anymore.

"You understand," Torgan said a moment later, "that by taking us to the Horn rather than east toward N'Kiel's Span, they're condemning us. We might find Lark and Stam, but we'll never find the Mettai woman, and they'll have all the reason they need to kill us."

"We don't know that for certain."

Torgan just stared back at him, saying nothing, waiting. It didn't take the lad long.

"Maybe you're right, but I can't blame them for the choice they made. If we were in Eandi lands, and our situations were reversed, we'd do the same thing. We'd gladly let them die in order to save Eandi lives."

He couldn't argue, but that only made him angrier. "We should be able to fight them," he said. "We're just letting them do this to us. It would be one thing if we'd fought them and lost, but we haven't fought at all. We've just surrendered."

Jasha's expression hardened. "I choose to see it differently. Yes, they've threatened to execute us, but they're trying to defend their people. We don't have to think of this as a war against the Fal'Borna. We're fighting with them against this plague. We're allies in an effort to save lives."

Torgan laughed mirthlessly. "Allies? You really are an idiot, aren't you?"

"And you're an ass. I imagine you always have been. I'd hoped to convince myself that there was more to you than greed and selfishness, but I was wrong." He took hold of his horse's reins and began to lead the animal away. "Fine then, Torgan. Fight your war. It's not one you can win, and it's certainly not one I intend to fight with you."

Torgan watched him go, his anger still building. *Yes,* he thought, *I'll fight my war. And I don't need your help, because I've got a weapon that even you don't know about. You don't think I can win? Just watch me.*

Less than a day before, that weapon meant nothing; he'd been too weak to use it, too afraid. But now they had abandoned their search for the witch and Jasha had left him to stand alone against the white-hairs. He still trembled at the thought of killing these Qirsi, but he no longer shied from it. And that was a start.

Grinsa walked to where his sleeping roll still lay on the ground and began to gather it up. He knew that Q'Daer would have more to say about all that had just transpired, but he wasn't certain that he was ready to explain himself quite yet.

The truth was he already regretted what he had done. He had no desire to see the Fal'Borna suffer. He wanted only to find the Mettai witch, return to Cresenne and Bryntelle, and leave E'Menua's sept for good. Now he was further than ever from making that happen, and he had only himself to blame. How could he explain to Cresenne that he would be gone for another turn or perhaps longer? How could he tell her that this had been his choice, that he had volunteered to go west, after the merchants, rather than east, toward the Mettai?

And what choice did he have? The baskets were out there, and though a'laqs on the plain had managed to warn one another about the danger facing them, that hadn't saved the sept they had found a few days before. Grinsa and his companions might be the only people on the plain who even knew enough to be looking for these merchants. If they did nothing, thousands would surely die, and their wraiths would haunt Grinsa for the rest of his life; they would follow him to Bian's realm. He had to do this. He knew it with the certainty of a condemned man.

So why did he feel that he had just betrayed Cresenne and Bryntelle, the only two people in this entire land who truly mattered to him?

He carried his sleeping roll to his bay and secured it to the saddle. He sensed that Q'Daer was watching him. The Fal'Borna would no doubt start asking him questions as soon as he had the opportunity. Glancing in the man's direction, Grinsa saw that he already had his sleeping roll and was striding toward his own horse, which was grazing near Grinsa's.

Grinsa hurried to secure the saddle. Finishing just as Q'Daer reached him he nodded to the man and then led his horse away, forestalling their conversation, at least for the moment.

"I'm going to check on the Eandi," he said, looking back at Q'Daer. "We'll leave as soon as they're ready."

The Fal'Borna stared after him, a slight frown on his youthful face. "You were right about the merchant," he called. "I didn't think he'd come back, but you were right."

Grinsa faltered in midstride, nodded without looking back, and continued walking.

He was surprised to find that the two merchants weren't together. He found Jasha standing near what was left of their fire, gazing at the ground and looking troubled. Torgan was standing by his horse still, watching the younger man from a distance.

"Are you ready to ride?" Grinsa asked.

Jasha looked up, seeming to rouse himself, as if from a slumber. "Yes."

"What about Torgan?"

"You'll have to ask him yourself."

Grinsa frowned. "What happened?"

That of all things drew a laugh from the merchant. "What do you think happened? Torgan's an ass."

Grinsa smiled. "Forgive me, Jasha, but Torgan's been an ass for a long time. What's changed?"

Jasha shook his head and stared off to the east, his smile gone, his brow furrowed. "I don't know. Maybe I'm just now starting to see how bad he is. Or maybe I've changed, and I don't tolerate it as well."

"You have to."

"What?"

"I know he's difficult," Grinsa said. "But you're the only one of us he'll talk to, and we need him if we're going to find these merchants. We need both of you. All three of us are risking a good deal by turning west instead of continuing to the east. We have to find the merchants as quickly as possible so that we can get back to hunting down this Mettai woman. So we need to work together."

Jasha didn't look pleased, but he nodded. "All right. Later, though. Please? I just need some time away from him."

Grinsa grinned and patted his shoulder. "Of course. I understand." He let his gaze slide toward Q'Daer before looking at Jasha again. "Better than you think."

The young merchant smiled.

A short while later, they were riding again, cutting northwestward across the plain. Torgan rode at the rear, as usual, with Jasha a short distance ahead of him. Grinsa led them, and Q'Daer followed just behind. Once more, Grinsa sensed that the Fal'Borna wanted to speak with him, but had hesitated to start a conversation.

For the first hour or so, that suited Grinsa. He couldn't avoid the man forever, though, and so eventually he slowed his mount, allowing Q'Daer to pull abreast of him.

"You have things you want to say to me," Grinsa said, staring straight ahead.

For a long time the young Weaver didn't answer, until finally Grinsa chanced a look at him. His expression was similar to the one Grinsa had seen on Jasha's face just a short time before. Q'Daer appeared young and puzzled and perhaps even weary. It occurred to Grinsa that as anxious as he was to rejoin his family, Q'Daer must have been just as eager to return to his home. He knew he should have realized this sooner, and he was chagrined that he hadn't.

"I'm trying to understand you," the Fal'Borna finally said. "On the one hand you fight me at every turn. You refuse to submit to the a'laq's authority. You make it clear that you don't respect Fal'Borna ways. And you make it equally clear that you wish to leave our sept as soon as you can. But then you turn around and abandon our mission—this one chance you have to win your way free of us—in order to save the lives of Fal'Borna who you haven't even met."

"Yes," Grinsa said dryly, "I've been trying to figure that out, as well."

"You're either the stupidest man I've ever met, or the most selfless."

He had to grin. "Couldn't it be both?" He glanced at Q'Daer and they shared a rare smile.

"Yes, perhaps it could. But that only confuses me more."

"It's not that hard to understand, Q'Daer. I've never hated your people, or your a'laq, or even you, despite what you might think. I just want to find a place where Cresenne and I can live and raise our daughter as we see fit. And yet, as much as I want that, I can't just let your people be killed when there's a chance that we can stop it from happening." He turned to face the man. "Doesn't that make sense? Is it really so hard to believe that I could be torn between my love of my family and my desire to save these lives?"

The Fal'Borna's eyes narrowed and he faced forward again. "You're a most unusual man, Forelander. The answer is, yes, it does make sense and yes, it is that hard to believe. In my land, clan is everything. Right now, you are the leader of a clan of three. For the moment at least, you've chosen to help my clan at the expense of your own. To a Fal'Borna—or, for that matter, a J'Balanar or a Talm'Orast or any other Southlands Qirsi—that's a strange choice to make. But it strikes me as being . . . noble, as well." He shook his head slowly. "I need to think about this more."

Grinsa nodded. "Of course." He started to ride ahead again, then fell back once more. "Thank you, Q'Daer."

"For what?"

"I didn't want to talk about this, but I'm glad we did."

Q'Daer started to say something, but then stopped himself, his eyes fixed on something to the north. Grinsa turned to look that way as well, and at first saw nothing.

"What is it?" he asked.

"I thought I saw a cart on the horizon."

They both slowed to a halt, still gazing northward. After some time Grinsa began to wonder if Q'Daer had imagined it. But then the Fal'Borna pointed.

"There." He stood in his stirrups. "They've turned. I think they're trying to avoid us."

Grinsa stood as well, and after scanning the plain for several moments finally spotted what the Fal'Borna had seen. It was little more than a dark speck in the distance and he was amazed that Q'Daer had noticed it at all, much less known what it was. But the form was definitely creeping along the horizon, angling away from them.

"A merchant?" Grinsa asked.

"Quite likely. But we should find out for certain."

Looking back at the two Eandi, Q'Daer signaled to them that they should turn to the north. And the four of them rode toward that distant dark form.

Chapter 11

Since the day Cresenne ja Terba had arrived in this settlement with Grinsa and little Bryntelle she had known that she had no standing of her own among the Fal'Borna. They were a patriarchal clan who judged men by the magics they wielded and their skills in battle. As a Weaver, Grinsa had been welcomed immediately. The Fal'Borna saw in him a man who could make them stronger in the eyes of friend and foe alike.

But though Cresenne wielded three magics of her own—fire, healing, and gleaning—and back in the Forelands had been viewed as a powerful sorcerer in her own right, here she was seen as little more than a companion for Grinsa, and a poor one at that. Among the Fal'Borna, Weavers were expected to be joined to Weavers. Since she was just an ordinary Qirsi, the men and women of E'Menua's sept did not recognize her as Grinsa's wife. When first they arrived, everyone referred to her as his "concubine." Grinsa and she took exception, and by and large the Fal'Borna stopped calling her this, but that was still how they treated her. And she never doubted that most of the Fal'Borna considered Bryntelle Grinsa's bastard child.

Cresenne had made peace with all of this; at least she had tried. Occasionally she still overheard people speaking of her as "the concubine" and speculating on who Grinsa might eventually marry, and it made her blood boil. But for now at least she and Bryntelle were stuck here, and Cresenne knew she had little choice but to endure these slights as best she could.

Only with Grinsa's departure, however, had she begun realize just how much their family had come to depend on the kindnesses shown by the sept to a new Weaver. Upon their arrival, they had been given a z'kal, one of the light but sturdy Fal'Borna shelters; each night food had been provided for them—Cresenne wasn't even certain where it came from; every morning fresh wood had been placed outside their z'kal so that they might build a fire and keep warm.

The shelter was still theirs. But once Grinsa left, the food vanished, as did the wood. Gathering wood wasn't much of a problem, though she had to borrow a hatchet from her new friend F'Solya, and, because the other families of the sept had already gathered wood for the coming Snows, she had to range farther from the settlement in order to find enough to see them through. Still, she could hardly complain.

Food, however, proved to be a much more difficult problem. Unlike the rest of the Fal'Borna, Grinsa and Cresenne hadn't been there to plant crops earlier in the year, nor to hunt rilda earlier in the Harvest. Beyond the meager supplies they'd had when they arrived, they had no food stores on which to rely during the colder turns.

They still carried ample amounts of gold, most of which Grinsa had left with Cresenne. Gold only helped so much, though, when there was so little to buy in the sept's small marketplace. Cresenne went every morning, hoping to find peddlers from whom she could buy food, but on many days the marketplace was virtually empty, and even on those days when it wasn't, she found little food for sale.

Bryntelle was still nursing, and Cresenne was able to make do with what little she had each morning and at midday, but by the evening Cresenne was famished, and she knew that if she didn't eat well, her child would suffer as well.

By the fifth day after Grinsa left, Cresenne was already growing weak from not eating enough. She slept poorly and woke later than she had intended. She went to tan rilda skins as she usually did, but arrived well after most of the other women, including F'Solya.

Her friend looked over at her as Cresenne sat in her usual spot and reached for her first hide and the foul tannins the Fal'Borna used to soften the skins.

"Trouble waking up this morning?" F'Solya asked, a smile on her round face, her bright golden eyes shining in the morning light.

Cresenne nodded. "A bit, yes."

F'Solya's smile faded. "You don't look well." She leaned toward Cresenne and laid the back of her hand against Cresenne's cheek. "You don't have a fever. Are you feeling all right?"

Cresenne made herself smile. "I'm fine. Just . . . just tired."

The Fal'Borna woman frowned. "I don't believe you. Is your little one sick?"

"No, Bryntelle's perfectly well." She smiled again, and this time it was genuine. She longed for Grinsa's return, but there could be no denying that she had at least one friend who cared about her. "I promise you, F'Solya: I'm fine."

"You miss your man, don't you?"

"Very much."

F'Solya nodded knowingly. "That can be an illness of a sort."

For a long time they simply worked, saying nothing. After a while, F'Solya began to tell her stories about her family and other people she'd known in the sept. It was something she did often and Cresenne had come to enjoy the tales quite a lot. She knew only a few of the people F'Solya mentioned, but hearing the stories taught her a good deal about the history of E'Menua's sept, and even about the ways of the Fal'Borna clan. That, she thought, may have been why F'Solya told them in the first place.

Near midday, they paused in their work for a meal. As usual, two of the younger girls who cared for the children while the mothers worked brought Bryntelle and F'Solya's twin boys so that the infants could be fed. After the young ones had been nursed, the girls took them away again, leaving the mothers to eat. Cresenne had only a few pieces of dried fruit and a small block of cheese, which she ate in just moments. When she had finished, she reached for her skins again. F'Solya was still eating.

"That's all you brought for today?" the woman asked between mouthfuls. F'Solya had a huge amount of food in front of her. Fruit, cheese, bread, dried rilda meat; a veritable feast. At least it seemed so to Cresenne.

"I'm not very hungry," Cresenne said, intent on the hide she was holding.

F'Solya shook her head. "I couldn't live on the crumbs you eat. Not with those boys crying for milk a hundred times a day. It's amazing to me that . . ." She trailed off, her eyes fixed on the food before her. She even stopped chewing. At last, she swallowed and looked at Cresenne. "Where have you been getting your food?"

Cresenne shrugged, not meeting her gaze. "We had some with us while we were journeying, and I've bought some in the marketplace."

"They were feeding you before, weren't they?"

A faint smile crossed Cresenne's lips and was gone. "They were feeding Grinsa. I just happened to eat some of what they gave him."

"And now that he's gone, they've stopped."

"It's all right, F'Solya."

"No, it's not. I realize now, you don't look ill, you look half starved."

"It's not that bad."

"You and your daughter will have your evening meal with us tonight."

"That's really not—"

"Don't argue with me," F'Solya said, sounding more like a stern parent than a friend.

She smiled to soften the words, but Cresenne could tell that she was serious, and also that she was concerned. And thinking about it, Cresenne decided that she had cause to be. How long could Cresenne expect to go on eating as she had been before she did become ill? There were times when pride mattered more than other considerations, but this, she realized, wasn't one of them.

"All right," she said, smiling. "Thank you."

It wouldn't solve their problem beyond this one night, but at least for this day she would be able to enjoy some adult conversation with her supper. At least on this night, she wouldn't feel that she was so utterly alone in the sept. The thought of it should have been enough to raise her spirits. It wasn't.

The more she considered the matter, the more she realized how dire her situation had grown. It must have been her imagination, but she could actually feel the air growing colder, as if the Snows were determined to begin today. Where was she going to get food? She was as capable as anyone—before Grinsa entered her life she had never needed a man to keep her fed and clothed and sheltered.

Any other time of year, she would have gladly planted her own crops, or even learned how to hunt, if only the Fal'Borna allowed their women to do so. Now, though, there was nothing she could do. Would F'Solya feed her every night? She dismissed the idea immediately. It was too much to ask of anyone, and Cresenne didn't want to become a burden on her friend and her family. Already, just because of this one invitation, she felt as though she had become a beggar and made one of her daughter. She knew that F'Solya would scoff at her for feeling this way, and that she was being foolish. Still, she couldn't help herself.

"Perhaps I can bring something," she said after a lengthy silence. "The cheese we've been eating is quite good, and so is—"

"Stop it," F'Solya said, a kind smile on her face. "The idea isn't for us to eat what little food you have left. It's to give you a decent meal so that you can take care of your little girl."

Cresenne relented with a nod, and she said nothing more about the supper until they had finished working. After they put their skins and tannins away for the evening, they retrieved their children from the care of the younger girls and made their way to F'Solya's z'kal.

Their shelter was somewhat larger than Grinsa and Cresenne's and within, a bit more cluttered, but in most ways the z'kal felt familiar. Cresenne marveled that it should be so. She and Grinsa had only been with the Fal'Borna for a short while, and she still remembered how alien everything about the sept had felt for the first few days.

F'Solya picked some roots from her stores and placed them in a cooking pot, which she took back outside. Cresenne followed her, feeling useless.

"I should be helping you," she said.

The woman shook her head. "I do this every day. If you want to help, you can keep an eye on my boys, particularly I'Jeq." She pointed as she spoke so that Cresenne would know which of the twins she meant. It seemed amazing to her that F'Solya could tell them apart, they looked so alike.

Cresenne sat on a low stone, and quickly came to understand why F'Solya wanted the boy watched. Unlike his brother, I'Jeq had learned to crawl, and he seemed to delight in careering from one danger to the next. If he wasn't reaching for F'Solya's knife, he was crawling toward the hatchet that leaned against their woodpile, or toward the fire that his mother had just kindled. Bryntelle, who wasn't crawling yet either, watched him with fascination and delight, clapping her hands and squealing each time Cresenne had to scramble after him.

"He moves so fast," Cresenne said after rescuing him from the hatchet a second time. "How do you ever get anything done?"

"Wait until they both can get around like that," F'Solya said, a rueful smile on her face. "I swear I don't know if they're most likely to kill each other or themselves or me. But no good will come of it."

Cresenne smiled, then stopped the boy from diving headlong into the fire. "I suppose I'll be putting up with this before long."

"Girls are easier," F'Solya said, sounding sure of herself. "At least at this age."

F'Solya didn't have daughters of her own, but it occurred to Cresenne that in a settlement this small she would have watched parents raising their children since she was old enough to walk. Cresenne, on the other hand, had spent her early years traveling with the festival in Wethyrn, back in the Forelands. There hadn't been many families in the festival, and she'd had few friends her own age, much less opportunities to watch mothers and fathers bringing up their children. She'd always counted herself fortunate to have grown up with the festival, traveling the land with her mother. Until this moment, she had never stopped to consider that she might have missed out by not living in some quiet village in a remote corner of the Wethy Crown. But listening to her friend speak, she found herself wishing that she understood the ways of children so well.

F'Solya retreated into the z'kal for several moments and emerged again bearing several small pouches. "Herbs," she said, seeing Cresenne's puzzled look. "Some we grow here. Others I trade for. Most Fal'Borna think that silverroot and rilda have enough flavor on their own." She wrinkled her nose. "I don't. I was bored with the taste of rilda before the end of my second four." She opened each of the pouches in turn and dropped small amounts of the herbs into her stew. In moments, the air around the z'kal was redolent with the aromas of thyme, watermint, and several other herbs that Cresenne had never smelled before.

"What did you put in there?" she asked.

F'Solya appeared surprised. "Surely you have herbs in the Forelands."

"Some, yes. The thyme and watermint I know. But the rest . . ." She shook her head.

"We call it rivermint here, but I'm sure it's the same thing. I also put in rildagreen, which grows here on the plain, and Qosantian sage."

"Can I smell them?"

F'Solya handed her the pouches and Cresenne sniffed lightly at each one. The Qosantian sage reminded her of sages she'd had in the Forelands, but it was sweeter, more pungent. "They're lovely," she said, handing the pouches back to F'Solya.

"The next time we're in the marketplace together I'll show you where you can find them."

F'Solya took the herbs back into her z'kal. Cresenne steered I'Jeq away from the knife once more.

As F'Solya reemerged from the shelter she smiled and waved her hand over her head. "Here comes I'Joled."

Cresenne's eyes snapped up, first to her friend, and then to the burly man approaching the z'kal. Until that moment, despite playing with the twin boys, she had forgotten completely about F'Solya's husband. Now she felt a rush of fear, though she wasn't certain why. I'Joled had no reason to dislike her; the fact that F'Solya had befriended her should have made him more inclined to accept her as a guest. But she knew that people in the sept had been speaking of her and of Grinsa since their arrival, and that to many she was nothing more than the woman who shared the new Weaver's bed.

I'Joled slowed when he spotted her, the smile fading from his face. He was a handsome man, like so many of the Fal'Borna warriors, with his golden skin, long white hair, and pale yellow eyes. He wasn't much taller than F'Solya—Grinsa would have towered over him—but he was barrel-chested and broad in the shoulders.

"Who's this?" he asked in a deep voice, his eyes straying to F'Solya's face for just an instant before studying Cresenne once more.

But Cresenne was sure that he knew already. How could he not?

"This is Cresenne," F'Solya said evenly. She pointed at Bryntelle with the end of her stirring spoon. "And that's her daughter, Bryntelle. A beauty, isn't she?"

F'Solya must have heard the wariness in her husband's voice. Cresenne had never met the man, and she heard it. But her friend seemed to ignore it, and so Cresenne made herself to do the same.

She stood and forced a smile. "It's nice to meet you, I'Joled. Thank you for allowing me to sup with your family tonight."

He looked at F'Solya, who just stared back at him. Finally, he faced Cresenne again. "Of course." After a moment he added, "You're welcome."

He entered the z'kal, pausing at the entrance to glance at F'Solya.

The Fal'Borna woman smiled thinly. "Excuse me for just a moment," she said before entering the shelter as well.

Cresenne heard I'Joled say something, though she couldn't make out the words.

"She has no food," F'Solya answered. "The a'laq had food brought to them while her man was still here, but now they have nothing."

I'Joled said something else.

"Oh, we have plenty, and you know it. In fact I've been thinking that we ought to let her come here every night until her man comes back."

This time she heard I'Joled's response clearly. "And what if he doesn't come back? What then?"

"Shhh!"

Cresenne couldn't make out anything more after that, but a few moments later F'Solya came out of the shelter, paused briefly in front of Cresenne, and then crossed to her pot of boiling stew.

"I'm sorry about that," she said quietly.

Cresenne feared that she might weep. Loneliness, fear for Grinsa, embarrassment; she couldn't say which lay heaviest on her heart at that moment. Probably all three. "Maybe we should go," she said, walking to where Bryntelle still sat, playing with the grass and dirt around her and watching the crawling boy.

"No need for that." F'Solya wrapped a cloth around the handle of her pot and lifted it from the fire. "Let's get these children inside. The food's ready."

It took some time to arrange the children and serve out the food, but soon enough they were all seated around a small fire in the z'kal, eating the stew, which was wonderful. Cresenne made quick work of one bowl and shyly asked for a second. F'Solya grinned and spooned her more. Cresenne sensed that I'Joled was watching her and she assumed that he disapproved, but she didn't look his way, and he said nothing. In fact, for a long time no one spoke, though Bryntelle and the boys made enough noise for all of them. Eventually F'Solya and I'Joled shared a look and the man put his bowl down on the floor, threw another stick of wood on the fire, and looked Cresenne in the eye.

"F'Solya says you've had a hard time of it since . . . since your man left."

Cresenne chanced a quick look at F'Solya, but she was staring at her bowl of stew. "Yes," she said, meeting the man's gaze. "To be honest, it hadn't even occurred to me to wonder where our food was coming from until Grinsa was gone."

"I suppose in the Forelands you were given food all the time."

Cresenne frowned, not sure whether to laugh or be angry, but knowing that he'd take offense if she did either. "No, not at all," she said, willing herself to keep calm. "We bought our food or got it for ourselves, just like everyone else. Why would you think it was given to us?"

"Well," he began, suddenly seeming unsure of himself, "I've heard Weavers are rare in the North. I thought he'd be honored there."

"Weavers are put to death there. So are their families. The Eandi are terrified of them, and the courts decreed centuries ago that all Weavers were to be executed. Grinsa only revealed the extent of his powers to his most trusted friends."

"Is that why you left?"

Cresenne hesitated. They'd had numerous reasons for leaving, not least of which was the fact that Cresenne had once been part of a failed Qirsi conspiracy to overthrow the courts. She had turned against the plot eventually and had helped the Eandi defeat it, but many still viewed her as a traitor. Grinsa had been instrumental in defeating the Weaver who led the renegades and had revealed himself as a Weaver, leading some to call for his execution, despite all he had done on behalf of the Eandi. And since Grinsa was a Weaver, it seemed possible that Bryntelle would grow to be one as well. In short, none of them had much future in the Forelands. That was why they left.

"In part, that was why," she said. "We needed to start over, and that didn't seem possible in the Forelands."

I'Joled nodded. "I'd heard something about that. There's been some talk."

F'Solya frowned. "That's enough," she said, her voice low.

Cresenne ate some of her stew, refusing to look at either of the Fal'Borna. This had been a bad idea. Yes, she needed to eat. But even F'Solya's friendship couldn't protect her from the tales about her past and Grinsa's that had made their way through the sept since their arrival. She wished only that Grinsa would return so that they could leave this place for good. And just thinking this made her eyes sting. *Don't cry,* she told herself sternly. *Not in front of this man.*

For a long time, none of them spoke, and when at last F'Solya broke the painful silence, she did so to talk about the storms that had passed over them recently, and how cold it would soon be on the plain. She asked Cresenne questions about the Forelands, most of them relating to the terrain and the weather. Cresenne answered, doing her best to keep her tone light, steadfastly avoiding I'Joled's gaze.

Eventually Cresenne excused herself, saying that it was late and that she needed to get Bryntelle to bed. She thanked them both and stood up to leave. I'Joled grunted a response to her thanks, but said nothing more. F'Solya, on the other hand, followed her out of the z'kal into the cold night air.

"Thank you," Cresenne said again, holding Bryntelle in her arms and adjusting her wrap to keep the child warm.

"You're welcome. I think you should come back again tomorrow."

This time Cresenne couldn't keep herself from laughing. "I think that's a bad idea. It's very kind of you, but I'm pretty certain that I'Joled wouldn't like it very much."

"I'll talk to him. It'll be fine."

"No, F'Solya." She laid her hand on the woman's arm. "I don't want you to think that I'm ungrateful. But I don't . . . people in this sept think poorly of me already. I don't want them thinking that I'm a . . ." She stopped herself, fearing that to say more was to risk ruining the one friendship she'd built here.

F'Solya nodded and looked down, a small smile on her lips. "I think I understand."

"Do you? I want you to. You've been so kind to me and the last thing I want to do is give offense."

She looked up at that, grinning broadly. "No chance of that. I'm not easy to offend." Her smile faded slowly, leaving her looking concerned. "What will you do, then?"

Cresenne shrugged. "I can try to buy more food in the marketplace."

"That'll only work for so long. When the Snows begin in earnest, the peddlers will stop coming."

"Would anyone here sell me food?"

F'Solya's eyebrows went up. "That's a good question. You should speak of it with the a'laq."

"No," Cresenne said, shaking her head. "The a'laq and I don't really get along."

"Nonsense. He's a difficult man—all a'laqs are like that. That's how they get to be a'laqs. But he can help you. I'm certain of it."

Cresenne ran a hand through her hair and exhaled through her teeth. If it had been just her own life at stake she might well have starved herself rather than face the man. That's how much she wanted to avoid any interaction with E'Menua. But she had to think of Bryntelle, too.

"How would I approach him?" she asked finally. She understood Fal'Borna ways well enough to know that a woman didn't simply march into the a'laq's shelter and ask to be fed.

"Actually, I'd suggest you start with D'Pera."

Cresenne shook her head. "D'Pera?"

"Yes, the n'qlae, E'Menua's wife."

"What would I tell her?"

"The truth. She's a mother, too. She won't let you starve."

"All right," Cresenne said. "I'll think about it."

"No, you'll do it. First thing tomorrow morning. I'll come with you if you'd like."

"Yes," she said immediately. "That would make this easier."

F'Solya smiled. "Very well. Go, put your little one to bed."

Cresenne started to go. Then she stopped and gave the woman a quick hug. She hadn't seen other Fal'Borna do this, and she felt F'Solya tense momentarily. But then her friend returned the embrace before quickly releasing her.

Cresenne offered a small, self-conscious smile and walked back to her z'kal.

The following morning, she took Bryntelle to the girls who usually cared for the Fal'Borna children, and then made her way to the fire circle where she tanned each day. F'Solya was waiting for her. Seeing her friend, Cresenne had to resist an urge to flee. She'd had the night to think about it, and she'd decided that her first instinct had been the correct one: she wanted nothing to do with E'Menua. Since Grinsa had left she'd done all she could to avoid the man, thinking that she'd be best off staying away from the a'laq until Grinsa's return. She knew though that F'Solya would insist, and she had to admit that her friend was probably right to do so. Still, at that moment it was hard to tell if the hollow feeling in her gut was hunger or fear.

As Cresenne drew near F'Solya asked, "Are you ready?"

"I suppose."

The woman merely smiled and patted Cresenne's shoulder.

They found D'Pera weaving blankets with several of the younger women, and instructing them in the finer points of the craft. Cresenne had never actually been introduced to the a'laq's wife, though she'd seen the woman from afar. She was strikingly attractive, with long, thick hair that she wore unbound, and a bright, piercing gaze from which Cresenne had found herself flinching away the few times the woman turned it on her. She had small lines around her eyes and mouth, but otherwise had surrendered nothing to age.

Seeing F'Solya and Cresenne approach, she frowned, got up from her work, and strode in their direction.

"What is it?" she asked. "What's happened?"

"This is a bad idea," Cresenne whispered.

F'Solya shot her a disapproving look, but quickly faced the n'qlae once more. "Forgive us for disturbing you, N'Qlae. We come seeking a favor."

Cresenne saw the woman relax, though her eyes narrowed as she looked from one of them to the other. "What kind of favor?"

F'Solya turned to Cresenne. It seemed there was only so much help her friend could give her.

"I . . . I wish to speak with the a'laq, N'Qlae."

D'Pera eyed her warily. "What for?"

"I . . . since . . . since Grinsa left, I've had very little food. We came too late to plant crops and Grinsa never hunted. We had some stores that we'd traveled with, but not enough to last me through the Snows. And I have a child—"

"The Snows take their toll on all of us," the n'qlae said, her tone betraying little sympathy. "We can't just give food away."

"I realize that," Cresenne said, her voice hardening as well. The woman could probably have her banished or killed with a word, but back in the Forelands Cresenne had been victimized repeatedly by the renegade Weaver and his servants; she had promised herself that she'd never allow herself to be bullied again. "I have gold. I can pay for what I get. But I can't eat coins, and I can't survive on wind and grass."

The n'qlae continued to regard her with mistrust. "The a'laq and I have been together for more than three fours," she said. "In all that time he's never taken another woman into his bed. He has no interest in concubines and bastard children."

Living in this alien culture, Cresenne often found herself unsure of how to respond to things said to her. But never in her life had she been at such a complete loss for words. A part of her wanted to laugh in the woman's face: She had no desire to share E'Menua's bed! Another part of her wanted to slap D'Pera as hard as she could for thinking her little more than a whore. Mostly, though, she feared she'd weep. This was how she was thought of here in the Southlands. She'd fled the Forelands because, in part, she didn't want to spend the rest of her days as a traitor in the eyes of all she met. Instead, they thought her the type of woman who was always looking for the next bed to sleep in, the next man she could steal from his wife.

"I've no interest in being anyone's concubine, N'Qlae," she said, struggling to keep her voice even, "or in bearing anyone's bastard child. Grinsa is my husband; Bryntelle is our daughter. The Fal'Borna may not see it that way, but to be honest I don't give a damn." She realized that her hands were shaking, and though she was trying to keep her temper in check, she knew she wouldn't be able to manage it much longer. "I can't do this," she said, turning to F'Solya. "I'm sorry, but I'd rather starve than put up with . . ." She clamped her mouth shut, to keep herself from saying more. She turned on her heel and began to walk away.

"Wait."

Cresenne would have liked to ignore the n'qlae's command, but she could only imagine what the Fal'Borna punishment for such a thing might be. She stopped and sighed. A moment later she faced the woman once more.

"I shouldn't have spoken to you so," D'Pera said, surprising her. "The a'laq promised your man that we would keep you safe while he was gone. It was a vow I encouraged him to give."

"Thank you for that," Cresenne said grudgingly.

"I'm not certain what he can do for you, but I'll take you to him. I expect he'll think of something."

"That would be . . . I'd be most grateful." She continued to stand there, wondering whether the n'qlae meant to do this now.

D'Pera gave her a curious smile and gestured in the direction of her z'kal. "Shall we, then?"

Cresenne nodded, feeling somewhat foolish. "Yes, of course."

She walked back to where the n'qlae stood and the three women began walking toward the a'laq's shelter.

After just a few steps, D'Pera stopped and looked archly at F'Solya. "Are you starving as well?"

"Uh . . . no, N'Qlae. We're fine."

"Then, I'd suggest you get back to work."

F'Solya looked back and forth between D'Pera and Cresenne. "But . . . Cresenne asked—"

"She'll be fine with me, F'Solya." The n'qlae smiled kindly. "Your concern for her speaks well of you, but I assure you she'll come to no harm."

"Of course, N'Qlae." F'Solya cast one last look at Cresenne, who smiled in return. Then she began to make her way back to the tanning circle.

"It seems you and F'Solya have forged a deep bond," D'Pera said, as they started toward the shelter again.

"She's been very kind to me."

"Do you have other friends here as well?"

The question made Cresenne uncomfortable, although she couldn't say why. "Not really, no."

"It must be difficult for you, being here without your . . . your husband, alone in a strange land."

"Grinsa and I have been apart before," she said, choosing her words carefully. "As long as I can feed myself and our child, I'll be fine."

"Of course."

They walked the rest of the way in silence. Upon reaching the z'kal, D'Pera instructed Cresenne to wait outside while she went in to speak with her husband. She emerged several moments later and nodded once. "He'll speak with you."

"Thank you, N'Qlae."

Cresenne entered the z'kal and was greeted immediately by the pungent smells of sweat, smoke, and roasted meat. It took her eyes a moment to adjust to the darkness of the shelter. A fire burned in the middle of the floor, and she could make out E'Menua's form on the far side, but at first she couldn't see his face.

"Sit," E'Menua commanded, his open hand, illuminated by the fire, seeming to materialize from the darkness.

"Thank you, A'Laq." She sat opposite him. She could see his eyes now, gleaming in the firelight.

"D'Pera tells me there's a problem with your food."

Cresenne frowned. It was an odd way to describe her problem, one that made it sound like she was complaining. "In a sense, I suppose you could say that. While Grinsa was here, we were fed each night."

"Of course. He's a Weaver and a stranger to our sept."

"Yes. And if he were here, I'm certain he'd join me in thanking you for your generosity. But since he left, my daughter and I have been without food."

The a'laq appeared to shrug. "You're not a Weaver."

Cresenne took a breath, trying to keep her patience, certain that he was doing all he could to provoke her. "I realize that, A'Laq. But I also know that you pledged to keep us safe in Grinsa's absence."

E'Menua bristled. "Do you imply that I've gone back on my word?"

"I'm sure it's no more than an oversight. You have an entire sept to look after. You couldn't remember that we weren't here when the others planted their crops or hunted rilda. None of this is anyone's fault. But the fact remains that we haven't enough food to get us through the Snows."

"And what is it you suggest I do about this?" he said in a tone that could have frozen the warmest waters of the Western Sea.

"We do have gold. We can buy what we need from the sept. You can set the price and whatever . . ." She trailed off.

E'Menua was shaking his head. She could make out his face now, and though he didn't appear to be enjoying her plight, he didn't look particularly concerned about it either.

"We have no need of your gold," he said. "The Fal'Borna are traders; we don't accumulate coins as the Eandi do. We trade skins for baskets, rilda meat for smoked fish. Besides, the food that we have in our stores is there to get our people through the Snows, should the colder turns prove more difficult than we anticipate. We can't simply sell it."

Cresenne felt panic rising in her chest. "Then what are we going to do? Bryntelle and I . . . before long we'll have nothing left. We'll starve."

He shook his head and offered what should have been a kind smile. But there was something predatory in those large, catlike eyes. "We won't let you starve. As you say, I made a promise to your man."

"Then what—?"

"You'll have to find another to provide for you."

"F'Solya and I'Joled offered," she said, knowing that she was giving her friend's husband more credit than he deserved. "But they have their boys to think about."

"I didn't mean them."

She stared at him, knowing they had come to the crux of their conversation. "Then who?" she asked.

"L'Norr. He's a Weaver, just like Grinsa. And he doesn't have a family to feed."

Cresenne knew just what he was doing and why. "I won't be . . . Grinsa is my husband. I won't share another man's bed."

"That's between you and L'Norr."

"But he'll expect something for his food, won't he?"

"He'll share his meals with you. I'll see to it. As I say, anything else is up to the two of you."

"There won't be anything else."

E'Menua regarded her placidly, a small grin on his narrow, tapered face. "You can go," he said, after a brief silence.

She wanted to say more, to tell him that despite all his efforts, there was nothing he could do to tear her and Grinsa apart. But she couldn't think of any way to say it that didn't sound weak and childish. At last, she simply stood and walked out of the shelter.

After the warmth of the z'kal, the harvest air made her shiver. Or was she trembling again?

Cresenne returned to the tanning circle and took her usual spot beside F'Solya. Her friend eyed her as she sat, but she said nothing, and Cresenne was just as glad.

After some time though, F'Solya's curiosity seemed to get the better of her.

"Is he going to help you?" she asked.

Help me? she wanted to say. *He has no interest in helping me. He wants only to destroy my life.* But however close she and F'Solya might have been, she couldn't be that honest.

"He's not going to let us starve," she said, which was true.

The woman smiled, looking so relieved it made Cresenne's heart ache. "Oh, good," she said. "I knew he wouldn't."

Chapter 12

Poljyn Rudd. Kherlay Swylton.

Those were their names.

Tirnya could picture both of them: Poljyn, tall and lanky, with a broad, open smile that made him look about twelve years old; and Kherlay—Kherry, the other men called him—also tall and rail-thin, but dark and serious, determined to be a lead rider by the time he was twenty.

Her father assured her that every leader lamented the loss of soldiers under his or her command, and he made it clear that it never got easier.

"The day it becomes routine to lose even a single man," he told her, two mornings after her skirmish with the brigands, "I want you to quit, because it'll mean that you're no longer fit for command."

No doubt he thought this would help her feel better. And perhaps in some small way it did. She wasn't the first commander to lead men to their deaths, she knew, and she certainly wouldn't be the last. But grief clung to her like the scent of blood, and even as the days passed and her wounds healed and her strength returned, still her sorrow lingered.

Poljyn's family lived in the countryside, a good twenty leagues from the city. But Kherry had been born and raised here in Qalsyn, and on the fourth day after the fight, Tirnya felt well enough to make her way to the west end of the city, where his parents lived. She dreaded this task, but she remembered her father making similar trips to the families of lost men; it was one of the responsibilities of command.

She was still sore and a bit unsteady on her feet. Oliban offered to ride with her, and even to let her share his mount, but Tirnya felt that she needed to do this alone. She rode Thirus, holding him to a gentle walk. Word of her victory over the brigands and her wounds had spread through all of Qalsyn, and people in the streets called greetings to her the entire way. She waved in return, but said little.

Qagan, who had been Kherry's lead rider, had described for her how to find the Swylton home. It was a modest house on the back of a farrier shop near the end of a narrow, dusty lane. On the other side of the road there was an overgrown paddock where a few horses grazed. Otherwise, all was still.

Tirnya dismounted gingerly, walked to the door, and knocked. She had no idea what she was going to say to them. She might have asked for advice on that from her father, but she chose not to. She leaned on him for enough. This she'd do on her own.

No one responded to her knock, and she began to wonder if she ought to leave. But then she heard footsteps inside and at last the door opened, revealing a plain-looking woman in a worn shift. Her hair was black, just as Kherry's had been, and Tirnya saw hints of Kherry's features in the woman's bony face. Kherry had never spoken of a sister, but this woman appeared too young to be his mother.

The woman stared at Tirnya for an instant. "Captain Onjaef!" She took a step back and then called over her shoulder, "Chran! Come quickly!"

"Are you Kherry's mother?" Tirnya asked.

The woman offered an awkward curtsy. "I am, Captain. I'm Sholi Swylton."

A man appeared beside her, also dark-haired and dark-eyed. He was tall and thin, and he looked so much like his son that it took Tirnya's breath away just to see him.

"Captain," he said. "I'm glad t' see ya up an' about. When we heard ya'd been hurt . . . well, we feared fer ya."

"Thank you."

"Please," the woman said, stepping aside and gesturing for Tirnya to enter the house.

After a moment's hesitation, Tirnya walked inside. The house looked larger within than it had from the street, though it was still tiny compared to her parents' home. It was clean and tidy, and it smelled of fresh bread.

"Would ya like t' sit?" Kherry's father asked her.

"No, thank you. I can only stay for a moment. But I wanted . . ." She took a breath, her throat suddenly tight. "I wanted to say how sorry I am."

"Ya's nothin' t' be sorry far, Captain. It were an honor far 'im t' serve under yar command. Said so hisself, he did." The man smiled, though there appeared to be tears in his eyes. "I don' know if'n he told ya, but I served under yar pa." He pointed to a scar on his arm. "An' ya see this?"

She nodded.

"Yar pa give me tha' in th' tournament one year. Sixth round." He nodded, looking proud, and wiped at his eyes. "We shared that, Kherry an' I did. We both fought in th' service o' th' Onjaefs. Men like us could do far worse."

"Kherry was a fine man," Tirnya said. "The others all liked him, and I think he would have made a fine lead rider in another year or so. He was brave and smart."

"Yar very kind t' say that," Kherry's mother said, crying as well.

Tirnya shrugged. "It's the truth."

They said nothing. As the silence grew, Kherry's parents looked at her, smiling through their tears.

"Well," Tirnya said, feeling uncomfortable, "I should probably be going."

"Course," Chran said, nodding once. "Ya've got things t' do. But we's grateful t' ya far comin' by."

"Oh, I almost forgot." She reached into her pocket and pulled out a small pouch of coins. "This is Kherry's share of His Lordship's reward for capturing the brigands. The men and I wanted you to have it. It's not much: about three sovereigns. But it's yours." She handed the pouch to Sholi, who merely stared at it.

"Tha's kind o' ya," Chran said. "An' th' men, too. Ya'll thank 'em far us?"

"Of course."

They walked her back to the door and Kherry's mother pulled it open.

"We was hopin' ya'd win th' tournament this year, Captain," Chran said. He winked at her. "We even had a bit o' coin on ya."

"Thank you," Tirnya said, smiling. It still bothered her to hear people speak of her match against Enly, but somehow she didn't mind this time.

"Ya'll win it next year. Ya wait an' see. Them Tolms can' keep it forever."

"Chran!" Kherry's mother said. "Ya watch yarself!"

"It's a'right, Sholi. Th' captain knows. We Swyltons, we came from th' Horn too, ya know," he said, nodding to Tirnya. "Came with yar family. We'd follow th' Onjaefs wherever ya led us."

Tirnya made herself smile, but she was a bit unsettled by the turn their conversation had taken.

"There's them tha' get wha' they deserve, and them tha' don't. An' tha' cuts both ways. Both th' Onjaef an' th' Tolm, they's them tha' don't, if ya understand me. Them Tolms has go' their city. Th' Onjaefs deserve th' same."

"Ya've said enough, Chran!"

He frowned at his wife, but then nodded. "Yeh, I have." He held out a hand, which Tirnya took. His hands were rough, callused, and very large, and when he covered her hand with his other one, it seemed that his hands had swallowed hers. "Thank ya, Captain. An' may th' gods bless ya."

"We're grateful t' ya far comin' t' see us," Sholi added.

"It was my pleasure." Tirnya winced. "I'm sorry. I didn't mean . . ."

Sholi shook her head, a sad smile on her lips. "We understan', Captain. Bless ya, an' go in peace." The woman took Tirnya's hand in hers for just a moment.

Tirnya nodded to them both before walking back to where Thirus was tethered. She knew they were still watching her and she had to make an effort not to seem to be in too much of a hurry.

She untied her mount, climbed slowly into the saddle, and nodded once more to Kherry's parents. Then she started back toward home.

Before she was halfway there, she realized that the only person waiting for her at the house was Zira. She turned and went in search of her men, who were training under Oliban's direction just outside the city walls. When the men saw her coming, they let out a cheer and stopped their training to gather around her.

"How're ya feelin', Captain?" Oliban called, as Tirnya dismounted.

"I'm fine," she said. And for the moment, away from Kherry's parents, away from her mother, surrounded by her soldiers, she truly was. "A bit sore still, but I'm better than I was." She looked around at all the smiling faces. "I owe you boys a bit of thanks, from what I hear."

"We was just afraid another captain would work us harder," Crow said with a grin. "They say Stri is pretty tough on his boys."

Tirnya laughed. "You just earned yourself an extra couple of hours out here, Crow. And your men, too."

The men in Crow's company groaned.

"That is, unless Crow cares to use the gold he got from His Lordship to buy me some ales."

"Gladly," Crow said with a laugh, as the men cheered again.

"All right, youse," Oliban said. "Back at it with ya."

The men grumbled a bit, but not for long.

"It's good to see ya, Captain," Dyn told her.

And Qagan said, "Welcome back."

Tirnya thanked them and watched the soldiers get back to work. Oliban stood beside her and for a long time neither of them said anything. But once all the men were working again, he asked in a low voice, "How was it with Kherry's parents?"

She shrugged. "About like you'd expect."

He nodded, but said nothing.

Tirnya hesitated, wanting to say more, but unsure as to whether she should.

"Her father said something strange."

Oliban glanced at her. "Oh?"

She started to tell him more, but then stopped herself. "It was nothing really. He's . . . he must be having a hard time."

Her lead rider was watching her, looking curious.

Tirnya shook her head and looked away. "I shouldn't have said anything. Please forget that I did."

"Course, Captain."

They watched the men for a time.

"Has there been any more word on the pestilence in Qirsi lands?" she asked.

"The pestilence? Not that I know of, Captain. But I can have someone ask for ya. Perhaps someone in th' marketplace might know."

"No, that's all right. Thank you."

She watched her soldiers for another few moments and then turned to Oliban. "I'm getting tired. I should get back home."

"Yes, Captain. We're glad t' see ya."

Tirnya left them there. She wasn't really tired, but she realized that she needed to speak with her father. No one else would know what to make of what Kherry's father had said to her. And probably no one else would understand why she was so consumed with tidings of the white-hair plague that the merchant had told her about the day of her battle with the brigands.

At home, she looked for her father, but Zira said that she hadn't seen Jenoe in hours. She then looked outside the eastern gate, where Stri often trained his soldiers. He wasn't there either. She finally found her father in the marketplace, of all places. He was speaking with a Qirsi trader, who was selling baubles and blades, but he left the man when she called to him.

Tirnya approached him, her questions about Kherry's father and the pestilence forgotten for the moment.

"What are you doing here, Father?"

He shrugged, looking uneasy. "Nothing, really. Just . . . just looking around." He frowned. "Can't a man come to the marketplace now and again?"

She'd rarely heard her father lie. He wasn't very good at it. "Are you buying me a gift?" she asked, smiling coyly.

"No," he said, seeming to dismiss the notion as foolish.

"Mother, then?"

He shook his head.

Tirnya's poor relationship with Zira notwithstanding, she felt a sudden rush of outrage. His discomfort, his transparent lies. Could it be?

"Father! Are you keeping a mistress?"

"Absolutely not!" he said, his outrage a match for hers. "How dare you even think it! I would never betray your mother!"

"Then why are you here?" she demanded.

Jenoe started to answer but then stopped himself, looking around the marketplace. Tirnya glanced about as well. People were watching them. Too late, it occurred to her that they'd been speaking in raised voices here in the most crowded part of the city.

He pulled her aside to a narrow lane just off the market.

"I would have preferred that no one hear that," he said, his brows knitted, his deep blue eyes searching the marketplace.

"I'm sorry," Tirnya said. "But I want you to answer me. What are you doing here? Why are you lying to me?"

"I haven't lied!"

She gave him a doubtful look. "You want me to believe that you're just here looking around?"

He avoided her gaze, running a hand over his dark beard, and for a long time, he said nothing.

"Father?"

"It's your fault," he told her, still staring off toward the market.

"Mine?"

"You got me thinking the other night." He looked at her. "The night you were wounded. You probably don't even remember all that you said."

Actually, she did. She recalled every word of it. "You mean about Deraqor? About my dream?"

"In part, yes. I was thinking more about the pestilence." He nodded toward the stalls and carts in the marketplace. "That's why I came here. I wanted to hear more about what's been happening on the plain."

"What have you learned?" she asked, trying to mask her eagerness.

"Not a lot. Though there are rumors that there was an outbreak in S'Vralna."

"S'Vralna!"

"It's just rumors."

"But if it's true," Tirnya said. She faltered, not certain what she had intended to say next.

Her father eyed her, a slight frown on his face. "If it's true, what?"

"Why are you so interested in this?" she asked, not ready yet to answer his question.

Jenoe shook his head and exhaled heavily. "I don't even know. Our family hasn't had any claim to that land in generations. This is all . . . idle curiosity."

"Is it?"

"What else could it be?" her father asked pointedly.

She looked around again, then pulled him farther down the lane. "I don't have to tell you, Father. You know already. That's why you're asking questions of merchants. That's why you're still thinking about the ramblings of a wounded soldier, even if she is your daughter."

"What else did you say that night? Something about a dream."

"Deraqor."

Jenoe nodded. "Right, Deraqor."

"You've heard what this pestilence does?" Tirnya asked. "It kills whitehairs. It attacks their magic and drives them to destroy themselves and their homes."

Her father looked troubled. "It's not right to revel in the suffering of others, even white-hairs."

"No," Tirnya said, "it's not. But they're the enemy. Yes, there's been peace for more than a century, but you know as well as I that the Qirsi will never be anything more or less than our enemy."

"So the fact that they're dying like this—"

"That they're dying like this is a tragedy. Make no mistake." She leaned closer to him. "But perhaps it's also an opportunity."

He shook his head. "I know where you're going with this, and I think you're mad."

"Am I? Is it wrong of me to want to take back Deraqor?"

"Deraqor is lost, Tirnya. It's been lost for a long time now."

"And you think we should give up on it forever?"

Jenoe looked hurt, as if insulted that she would suggest such a thing. "I never said that. Of course we shouldn't give up on it forever. It's our ancestral home. Someday we'll take it back. I want that every bit as much as you do."

"Then let me ask you this, Father," she said. "When will we have a better chance?"

He didn't answer and Tirnya pressed her advantage.

"Qirsi are dying. Their cities are being destroyed. They must be terrified. This may be the best opportunity we'll ever have to take back not only Deraqor, but all the lands between here and the Horn."

"You're talking about starting the Blood Wars again. People here aren't ready for that."

"They never will be. It's up to us to convince them that this is the time."

Jenoe didn't say anything, and Tirnya wondered if he'd had enough of this conversation. But a moment later he surprised her.

"Actually, it's not up to us. It's up to the sovereign. And it's up to His Lordship to present the idea to him. We'd just have to convince Maisaak."

"Do you think we can?"

"I don't know, Tirnya." He shook his head again, his lips pressed thin. "You haven't convinced me yet, and there's no one in Qalsyn who wants to take back Deraqor more than I do. My grandfather used to tell me stories about the city that his grandfather told him. I've dreamed of leading an army back into Deraqor since I was a child." He looked at her and smiled. "Just as you did the other night."

"We could do it, Father. We could do it together. I know that my men would follow us all the way to the Thraedes, and I'm sure Stri's would, too. With you leading us, I don't think there's a man in this city who wouldn't fight beside us."

"I need to think about this more," Jenoe said. "The Fal'Borna won't give up Deraqor easily, and even if we take it, they'll just turn around and try to take it back. There's a good chance we'd be starting down the road to another hundred years of war. It'll start with Deraqor, but before long they might well be fighting in Naqbae, and down along the Ofirean shores. This could spread through all the land. Are we really going to risk that? The sovereign would be mad to let us."

Tirnya wanted to say that she was willing to risk it, that she'd ride to Ofirean City herself to convince the sovereign. At that moment she would have done nearly anything to make her dream come true. Now that she knew her father was even considering this she was ready to ride to war immediately, never mind her healing wounds. But she knew that her father had a point, and that a mature leader had to look beyond warlust to examine the possible consequences of every battle. And she knew as well that he was watching her now, gauging her response to what he'd said, measuring her abilities as a commander.

"I'm aware of the risks," she said. "And to be honest I don't know if they're worth the reward. It may be that I can't think about this with an open mind. I'm an Onjaef. I want Deraqor back and I'd lead an army across the Silverwater tomorrow if the sovereign and His Lordship gave me leave to do so, regardless of the consequences."

He smiled at her, looking proud. "That's a more candid answer than I'd expected."

Tirnya arched an eyebrow. "I'm not certain how I should take that."

Jenoe laughed, but then quickly grew serious once more. "His Lordship will think this is folly."

"What about the sovereign?"

He shook his head. "Over the years, the Kasathas have usually deferred to their lord governors in such matters. And Ankyr is still new to his power. I think if we can convince Maisaak, the sovereign will follow his recommendation. Even in this. But I'd be very surprised if His Lordship entertained the idea at all. He'll see it as a waste of men in pursuit of our family's ambition and desire for vengeance." He grimaced slightly. "He probably wouldn't be far off the mark."

"I'm a soldier, Father," she said. "I don't claim to know as much about such matters as you or Maisaak. But there's more to this than our ambition. We'd be taking back lands that ought to be held by the sovereignties. And not just any land. The plain around the Horn and along the banks of the Thraedes is some of the most fertile, valuable land in all the Southlands."

"True."

"And I think we might also consider how long this peace will last even if we do nothing."

"It's lasted a long time, Tirnya. More than a century."

"Yes," Tirnya said. "But you know as well as I that this has always been a truce of convenience and not a true peace. The Blood Wars went on as long as they did because the hatred between the clans and the sovereignties runs deep. They ended because neither side had the stomach for more war."

Her father shook his head. "You're not helping your cause arguing so. What you say may well be true, but that only serves to convince me that this attack we're talking about would lead to an ever-widening war. This is a dangerous idea."

"You're missing my point," she told him. "This peace will only last until one side or the other sees some advantage in attacking again. If we wait—if we let this opportunity pass by—then the next advantage might be theirs."

Jenoe seemed to ponder this.

"The Qirsi have always been stronger than we have, Father. We have the greater numbers, but their magic is more than a match for our armies. I'm sure that others would be offended to hear me say that aloud, but you know it's true. We won our share of battles, we had our moments of glory.

But the fact is the Fal'Borna pushed us back steadily for the better part of five hundred years before the final truce. They took the land on the far side of the K'Sahd, they took the Horn, they pushed us farther and farther from the Thraedes, and finally they gave us no choice but to flee across the Silverwater. Next time, if we give them the chance, they might push us back to Ravens Wash." She smiled. "But right now, we're the stronger ones. Just this once, wouldn't you like to beat them? Wouldn't it be a boon to every Eandi in the Southlands if we could take land from the Qirsi?"

Even before her father opened his mouth, Tirnya knew that she had won. She could see the surrender in his eyes.

"I'll arrange an audience with His Lordship," he said.

Tirnya was so pleased she nearly shouted like a child, and in a corner of her mind she wondered when she had grown so eager for war. "Thank you, Father," she said, keeping her tone measured.

He raised a finger in warning. "I make no promises. I won't speak in favor of this to Maisaak. You'll do the talking yourself. And if he refuses, that's the end. Do you understand?"

"He won't refuse," she said.

Jenoe started to walk out of the lane. "I'm less certain of that than you are," he said, glancing back at her. "But we'll see soon enough."

Enly was training with his men, working up a good sweat despite the cool air and light rain, when the summons came.

As soon as he'd seen the man—a young soldier wearing a white baldric over his blue and green uniform—he'd known. Immediately he'd felt his mood souring. This had been a good day. His men were training well; it seemed the sting of having lost out on so much gold to Tirnya's company had finally started to ease for them. And Enly had received word that Tirnya was recovering well and would bear no lasting injury from her encounter with the brigands. He couldn't have been in finer spirits.

The summons changed everything. He could only assume that any of the other captains in Qalsyn would have found it unsettling to be called before the lord governor. They were soldiers; His Lordship was their commander. To be summoned thus was rarely a good thing.

That he was Maisaak's son only made matters worse. He often wondered if Berris would have felt the same way, if his older brother had lived long enough to be made a captain in Maisaak's army. Berris had gotten along with their father better than Enly ever did. Not that Berris and Maisaak had been close; no one was close to Maisaak, except maybe their mother. But Berris understood how to make the old goat happy. He knew the right things to say, he fought in his tournament matches with tactical precision, he rarely disagreed with their father's decisions, and if he did he kept his thoughts to himself. In short, he was boring, and Maisaak liked boring.

Enly's sense of humor, his willingness to flout convention, his daring technique in the ring, all of which made him so popular with his men, and with many of the court women, served only to irritate his father.

Perhaps that was why being summoned to the palace irked him so. More often than not it meant he had done something—who knew what?—to anger his father. Again.

So, though he saw the palace soldier approaching, Enly ignored him and continued to train, throwing himself into his swordplay with such abandon that the man he'd been working with was suddenly forced to retreat several steps. His father's guard stopped a few strides away and just stood there, waiting for Enly to notice him. Enly pretended not to.

"Captain Tolm?" the man said after a few moments.

Still Enly didn't look at him.

"Beg pardon," the soldier started again, speaking more loudly this time. "Captain Tolm? Sir?"

The man he was training kept glancing toward the guard, looking confused, not to mention tired. At last Enly relented. He broke off his attack, raised his sword in salute to his soldier, and turned to his father's man.

"Yes, what do you want?" he demanded. Before the man could reply he went on. "My father wishes to see me, is that right?"

The guard nodded. "Aye, sir."

"And did he tell you anything beyond that?"

"Only tha' he wanted ya right off, sir. He weren' in a mood t' wait."

Enly sighed. "Of course he wasn't." He wiped his brow on his sleeve. "Fine then. Tell him I'll be along just as soon as I can."

"Aye, sir." The man turned smartly and hurried back toward the palace.

He sheathed his blade, watching the man walk away. Then he turned to look at his men, who were eyeing him now. "The rest of you . . ." He shook his head. "The rest of you can do as you please until patrols begin."

The men cheered, making him smile in spite of himself.

He waited until his soldiers had dispersed before making his way back to the palace, not because he had to, but rather because he didn't want to give his father the satisfaction of thinking he'd been in any rush to obey the summons.

He thought briefly about changing his clothes, but his father had wanted him there without delay, so he'd have him as he was now, sweat and all.

The guards at the palace gates bowed to him as he passed. Among his own men he tried to be nothing more or less than their captain. Surely none of them forgot that he was a Tolm, the lord heir at that. But with time he had managed to build a rapport with his soldiers that was similar in most respects to that of other captains with their companies.

The soldiers of the palace guard, however, were another matter. Here there could be no doubt but that he was Maisaak's son and eventual successor. Probably that was as it should be, but after all these years, it still bothered him.

Reaching the door to his father's presence chamber, he stopped and waited while one of the guards there announced him to Maisaak. A moment later, the door opened and the guard bowed, gesturing for him to enter.

"You're late," Maisaak said, before the door had closed behind Enly, before Enly had even spotted him by his writing table. "I sent for you before market bells."

Enly bit back the first words that came to him. "I'm sorry," he said instead. "I was working the men, and had one last drill to finish."

"Well, we haven't much time. They'll be here shortly."

"They?"

Maisaak frowned, making his square face look even more severe than it usually did. "That fool of a guard didn't tell you?"

"He said only that you wanted to see me."

"Jenoe and Tirnya have requested an audience."

"She's well enough to come here?" This time Enly had been unable to keep from saying the first thing that came to him.

His father's frown deepened and he shook his head. "Either marry her or have done with it already. But either way, I need you to think clearly for a moment, not as her suitor, but as lord heir."

"What is it they want to discuss?" he asked, ignoring the rebuke, and refusing to admit that Tirnya had no desire to marry him.

"I was hoping you might know," his father said.

"I don't. I've barely seen her since . . ." Since the tournament, he'd been about to say. But he didn't want to bring that up again either. Talking to his father was like stepping through a briar patch: for every thorn avoided four others drew blood. "It's been some time now," he said.

"Well, nevertheless, I'd like you here when they arrive. I know Jenoe well enough, but your insights with respect to the girl might be of some use."

All he could say was "Of course."

For a time, as they waited for the marshal and his daughter to arrive, neither of them spoke. Maisaak went back to perusing the scrolls on his writing table. Enly wandered the chamber, looking idly at the baubles on his father's mantel and the ever-growing collection of daggers his father kept in a glass case in the corner of the great room.

Eventually his father looked up at him again, his brow creased. "You must be hungry."

"Thirsty, actually."

"Of course." Maisaak picked up the small bell on his table and rang it.

Almost instantly, a young servant appeared in the doorway and bowed.

"My son desires water," said the lord governor. "And with our guests arriving soon, I'd like food and wine brought as well."

The boy bowed a second time and withdrew, having said nothing. Maisaak had well-trained servants.

"How goes it with your company?" his father asked, sounding oddly formal.

"Very well, thank you."

"And their spirits?"

Enly had to laugh. "Their spirits would have been much improved if we had been the ones to earn your gold for killing all those brigands."

"Yes, well," Maisaak said sourly, clearly not seeing the humor in this matter, "I think the less said about that the better, don't you?"

"Yes, Father."

They fell silent once more until Enly's water arrived, and with it the food and wine. A few moments after, someone knocked, and at Maisaak's invitation, one of the guards stepped into the chamber.

"Yar Lordship, Marshal an' Captain Onjaef," the man said.

"Send them in," Maisaak said, sounding desperate for any new guests, even the one man in Qalsyn he hated most.

Tirnya entered the chamber followed by her father. She looked pale—the cut he had dealt her in the tournament had healed over, but the scar stood out starkly against her skin—and she moved slowly, without her usual grace. And yet, even while still recovering from wounds that had nearly killed her, she remained lovely. Her hair was tied back, though a few strands fell over her brow. Her eyes, blue-grey, the color of smoke from smoldering embers, found him immediately. She gave him a puzzled look, as if to ask why he was there.

Enly shrugged, then looked away.

As usual, Jenoe cut an imposing figure. He was a good deal taller than Maisaak and he still had the trim muscular build of a champion swordsman. He caught Enly's eye a moment after his daughter had and nodded in greeting.

The two of them, father and daughter, halted in front of Maisaak's writing table and bowed to him.

"Thank you for agreeing to see us, Your Lordship," Tirnya said.

Enly and Maisaak shared a quick look. Usually the marshal would have spoken for them, not his daughter.

"It's my pleasure, as always, Captain," Enly's father said, a smile fixed on his lips. "I take it you're recovering well."

"I am. Thank you, Your Lordship."

"I'm glad to hear it. You're to be commended for the performance of your company. They handled themselves quite well, even after you were wounded."

"You honor us, Your Lordship."

Maisaak turned to Jenoe, his smile growing ever more brittle. "You must be very proud of her, Marshal."

"Yes, I am. Your Lordship is most kind."

The servants had placed the food on the large table in the center of the chamber. Maisaak took his place there now, gesturing for the others to join him.

"Come, have something to eat."

"Thank you, Your Lordship," Tirnya said as she and Jenoe sat on opposite sides of the table. Enly sat at the end across from his father. A servant poured wine for them all, and Maisaak took some greens and fowl for himself before passing the platter to Jenoe.

"Well," Maisaak said, after a brief lull in their conversation, "I'm sure you didn't request an audience just so that I could feed you. Why are you here?"

Again it was Tirnya who answered, though not before she glanced uncertainly at her father. Jenoe merely gazed back at her, his expression revealing nothing.

"Perhaps Your Lordship has received word of the pestilence outbreak in the Fal'Borna clan lands."

Maisaak did nothing to mask his puzzlement. "Yes. Yes, I've heard something of it. Not much, but from what I've been told it seems the outbreak began west of the Silverwater and has spread westward across the plain." A hint of fear appeared in his eyes. "Is it headed this way now?"

"No, Your Lordship," she said. "Not as far as we know."

"Gods be praised for that," Enly said.

Jenoe nodded his agreement. "Indeed."

"From what we've heard, Your Lordship," Tirnya went on, "this is a strain of the disease that strikes only at white-hairs. It makes them ill, it robs them of control over their magic, and in the end it kills them."

The lord governor's eyes widened. "I knew of course that it was sickening the Qirsi. But you're saying that it has no effect on our people? You're certain?"

"Quite, Your Lordship. Several peddlers, Qirsi and Eandi alike, have said much the same thing. It seems we're immune, and the white-hairs are not."

"Interesting," Maisaak said, sounding genuinely intrigued. "But why bring this to my attention?"

Again Tirnya glanced at her father, and again Jenoe did nothing more than return the look.

"Because, Your Lordship," she replied, facing Maisaak again, "I believe this white-hair plague, as the merchants are calling it, offers us a unique opportunity."

Maisaak's eyebrows went up.

And as Tirnya began to describe for them just what it was she had in mind, Enly's must have as well. Her proposal struck him as audacious, perilous, and foolhardy. After a time, Enly stopped staring at her and turned his gaze to her father, watching for Jenoe's reaction to what she was saying. Surely the marshal, a man Enly had always respected despite the rivalry that existed between their two houses, couldn't approve of this folly. He had to see the danger.

But Jenoe made no effort to stop her. Could it be that both of them were blinded by their desire to reclaim the Onjaef ancestral home and their need to avenge the defeat of their forebears?

Tirnya spoke passionately for this invasion of hers. Her cheeks, which had been ashen when they entered the chamber, now were flushed, and there was a look in her eyes that Enly had seen there previously only in the tournament ring, and on two memorable nights in his own bed. What frightened him most, as he continued to listen to her, was that she made a certain amount of sense. If one managed to ignore the fact that she was talking about restarting the Blood Wars, it would have been easy to be persuaded by her reasoning.

At first, after she finally finished, no one said anything. The four of them had even stopped eating, though Tirnya took a quick sip of wine, her hand trembling slightly as she raised the goblet to her lips. As the silence stretched on, she looked at her father and then at Enly. Her cheeks were red still, but it seemed that this was now more a product of discomfort than ardor.

"What do you think of all this, Jenoe?" Enly's father finally asked, turning to his rival.

"This is Tirnya's idea," the marshal said. "I told her I'd accompany her to your palace, but that's all."

"Yes, I gathered as much. But now I'm asking your opinion as a marshal in the Qalsyn army and the man who would probably lead this assault. What do you think of this?"

Jenoe shrugged, taking a bite of fowl. "I'm not sure what to think of it," he said, after swallowing his mouthful.

"Come now," Maisaak said, frowning. "I should have added a moment ago that you're also the person with the most to gain should this campaign succeed. And you want me to believe that you have no thoughts whatsoever on the matter?"

"With all respect, Your Lordship, that's not what I said. Precisely because I have the most to gain, I'm not sure what to think of it. It strikes me as terribly dangerous. And yet, I'd be lying if I told you I wasn't intrigued by the possibilities of such a gambit."

"How many men do you think it would take?" the lord governor asked.

Jenoe narrowed his eyes in thought, as he played idly with his wine goblet. "Probably every man under my command, and then some. But a lot of that will depend on how hard this pestilence has struck at the Fal'Borna. If only a few of the septs have been hit, we'll have a hard time of it. If the damage is more extensive, we may meet with little resistance until we reach the Thraedes."

Enly couldn't keep still any longer. "Pardon me for speaking out of turn, Father. And, Tirnya, forgive me for saying this, but what you're suggesting is madness, pure and simple. The Blood Wars are a blot on the history of the Southlands. They did unspeakable damage to both the clans and the sovereignties; especially to the sovereignties. To start them again . . ." He shook his head. "It's madness. There's no other word for it. I find it hard to believe that you'd support this, Marshal. And I'm shocked, Father, that you haven't dismissed the idea already."

Maisaak took a breath and nodded. "Well, Enly, I appreciate your candor, and I'll consider what you've said." He looked at Tirnya. "Captain Onjaef, what do you say to that?"

She regarded Enly coolly for just an instant before facing Maisaak again. "Nothing, Your Lordship. I've made my case. I'll stand by it."

The lord governor nodded and grinned. "Very good." He stood, forcing the others to do the same. "Thank you for bringing this to my attention. Both of you," he added, with a glance at Jenoe. "Obviously I'll need to give this a good deal of thought before I send any messages on to Ofirean City. And we can do nothing, of course, without Ankyr's approval. And if he does allow us to go forward, I'll want to send missives to the other lord governors to see if we can put together a larger force. If we're going to do this, I don't want to be undermanned. I'll let you know what I've decided. In the meantime, speak of this with no one."

Tirnya was practically beaming. "Yes, Your Lordship. Thank you." She bowed, as did Jenoe, and then left the chamber, her father hurrying to keep up with her.

As soon as the door closed, Enly whirled toward Maisaak. "Father—!"

The lord governor raised a finger, silencing him. He had his head cocked to the side, as if he were listening for the Onjaefs' footsteps. After some time, he lowered his hand and nodded. "All right, go ahead."

"You can't be considering this!" Enly said. "She's blind with battle lust!"

"And Jenoe? What about him?"

Enly shrugged. "You said it yourself: He has the most to gain should they somehow manage to succeed."

Maisaak smiled. "So it might seem."

"I don't understand."

The lord governor sat back down and resumed his meal. "I agree with you," he said between mouthfuls. "It is madness. Even if this plague has weakened the Fal'Borna, they still have their magic, and they remain fearsome warriors. I doubt the entire Qalsyn army could defeat them, even with the great Jenoe Onjaef riding at the fore."

"Then why didn't you say so?"

Maisaak stared at him as if he were simple. "Do I really have to explain it to you?"

It hit him like a fist in the chest, stealing his breath and making his entire body sag.

"You want them to fail. You'd send ten thousand soldiers to die if it would rid you of the Onjaefs."

"I don't like your tone," Maisaak said, his expression hardening. "And to be honest with you, it wouldn't matter to me if they succeeded or failed. If her idea works, Jenoe takes back Deraqor, and he can spend the rest of his days defending it from Fal'Borna raiders. If they fail, Jenoe will die, or at best return here disgraced and broken. Either way I'd be rid of him."

"The sovereign will never allow this."

Maisaak laughed. "You have much to learn about House Kasatha. They're fools, the whole lot of them. I suppose at some point in the past they must have been somewhat more, or they'd never have managed to become Stelpana's ruling family, but Joska was greedy and small-minded and ambitious to a fault, and Ankyr is no better. If I tell him the invasion is a hopeless waste of men, then yes, he'll reject the idea. But if I tell him about this plague, and the opportunity it presents, and if I remind him of the wealth of the Horn and the lands around Deraqor, he'll give his approval. He might even send us gold to help pay for the war."

"You want to be rid of them that badly?" Enly asked, appalled by what he was hearing.

"I wouldn't expect you to understand. You're so besotted with the girl that you don't see the Onjaefs for what they are."

There was nothing Enly could do here. "I'll talk Tirnya out of it," he said, starting for the door. "I don't care if you give me a direct order never to speak to her again."

Maisaak laughed. "No wonder you couldn't keep her in your bed. You don't understand that girl at all. You could no more talk her out of this than you could teach her to fly. She's made up her mind, and the more you try to dissuade her, the more determined she'll be to prove you wrong."

Enly wanted desperately to fire back a retort, something that would silence his father and wipe that smirk off his face. But he could think of nothing to say, and in the end he simply left the chamber.

Chapter 13

❖❖❖

In the days following her audience with His Lordship, Tirnya's mind was so filled with thoughts of taking back Deraqor and the Horn that she could barely sleep or eat. Her wounds continued to heal, and five days after meeting with Maisaak, she began to train with her men once more. She worked them hard—so hard that her lead riders seemed puzzled. Oliban went so far as to ask her if the men had angered her in some way. She assured him that they hadn't.

"I just want them ready," she said.

Oliban had given her an odd look. "Ready for what?"

"For anything. Look around you, Oliban. I'm not the only commander pushing her soldiers."

This much she knew was true. Her father wasn't as eager to fight the Fal'Borna as she was, but he was warming to the idea. To her surprise, Stri Balkett hadn't dismissed the notion out of hand.

"It could work," he said over dinner in the Onjaef house two nights after the audience. "But I'm not convinced the sovereign will allow it."

Jenoe also remained skeptical about their chances of convincing the sovereign. Still, both Stri and Tirnya's father were pushing their men harder than they had in years, just in case.

Aside from Stri, Tirnya and Jenoe had told no one about their conversation with the lord governor and lord heir. Even if Maisaak hadn't ordered them to keep the matter to themselves, they knew better than to discuss the invasion with anyone. If they were to succeed in this venture, they would have to take the white-hairs utterly by surprise.

Tirnya knew, though, that even surprise would not be enough to overcome Qirsi magic, and for days after their audience with Maisaak, she racked her brain, trying to develop a workable strategy for their attack. She wondered, if the lord governor had known how formless her plans were for this invasion, whether he would even have considered her proposal. She had, of course, never led an invasion before; neither had her father, though he did have far more battle experience than she. In the first several days after the

audience, however, Tirnya was afraid to admit even to Jenoe how formless
her plans were. Surely, she thought, with a little time she would come up
with something. She avoided him, and she wasn't terribly subtle about it,
though if Jenoe noticed he kept his thoughts to himself. Finally, after several
days of trying to think of a way to defeat the white-hairs and coming up
with nothing, of feeling overwhelmed and fearing that the audience had
been a terrible mistake, she raised the matter over the evening meal at
home.

"How does one plan something like this?" Tirnya asked abruptly as her
father poured her a cup of dark wine. "I wouldn't even know where to begin."

Jenoe grinned. "I was wondering when you'd ask me."

She felt her face redden. "You knew? And you didn't say anything to me?"

"It seemed clear that you didn't want to talk to me about it, at least not
yet."

She stared at the roasted meat and boiled greens that sat in front of her.
"I thought you'd think me foolish for having suggested an attack without
having any strategy for one."

He shook his head and took a sip of wine. "If you, or any commander
your age, had come up with a workable plan on your own I would have been
very much surprised." He eyed her over the rim of his cup. "This isn't going
to be easy."

"I know that."

Jenoe nodded. "Good."

"So," she said, relieved to be talking about it. "How do we begin?"

"You start with your soldiers," Jenoe answered, sounding so calm that it
reassured her. "Always. How many? How do you get them where they need
to be? How do you arm them and clothe them and feed them and shelter
them?"

She nodded. It made perfect sense. "Right. Of course."

He raised an eyebrow. "So? How many?"

Tirnya ran a hand through her hair. "Well, you said the other day it
would take every soldier under your command, and then some."

"Yes, I did. But I'm asking you what you think."

"I don't know, Father. We'll need far more men to take the city than
they'll need to defend it."

"True. We'll probably need siege engines as well, and they'll need to be
assembled quickly. The longer we take to build them, the more opportunities the white-hair shapers will have to destroy them."

"Will siege engines even work against sorcerers?"

Jenoe tipped his head to the side, considering this. "The sovereignties had some success with them during the Blood Wars, though mostly in the early years." A grim smile touched his face and was gone. "Later on, we were usually the ones defending against sieges rather than the other way around."

Tirnya thought about it briefly and then shook her head. "Siege engines won't work," she said. "They're too predictable, too slow, too much like what Eandi armies have done in the past. We need to try things that have never been done before. That's the only way we can win."

Her father grinned. "Now you sound like a commander. What do you have in mind?"

"Nothing yet," Tirnya said. "But we'll come up with something. The two of us, together."

Jenoe nodded. "All right."

They traded ideas for the rest of that evening, coming up with little that might actually work against the Qirsi, but irritating Zira, who would have liked to enjoy what she referred to repeatedly as "a normal conversation."

The following day, as Tirnya made her way to the training grounds, she found her path blocked by Enly, whom she also had been avoiding, and who clearly had been waiting for her.

"We need to talk," he said, indicating that she should follow him so that they could speak in private.

Tirnya stayed just where she was. "Why?"

"You know perfectly well why."

She arched an eyebrow. "I see. So, you want me to come along so that you can tell me what a fool I am for wanting to . . ." She glanced around and lowered her voice slightly. "For wanting to do this."

Enly sighed. "Just come with me for a moment. Please."

Tirnya held up a hand and shook her head. "As much as I enjoy it when you tell me I'm reckless and stupid, I think I'll pass this time." She started to walk away.

"I don't care about this at all," he called after her. "I'd just as soon see your plans ruined, so if you think I won't speak of it openly, you're wrong."

She spun to face him. The road they were on wasn't crowded, but there were enough people around—most of them now staring at the two of them—to undermine any effort she and her father might make to keep the invasion plans secret. She strode back toward him, her fists clenched. She had half a mind to punch him right in the mouth.

"Are you mad?" she said, her teeth clenched, but her voice low.

"You're the mad one as far as I'm concerned."

She stopped just in front of him, glaring at him, wishing she had kept walking away. At last, feeling that she was surrendering, she indicated with an open hand that he should lead her wherever it was he wanted to go. He started down a narrow lane that led between two buildings and then into an open pasture where a couple of old plow horses grazed. When they reached the middle of the pasture, Enly turned to face her.

"You can't go through with these plans you're making," he said.

"Why can't I? Because it'll keep us from ever being together? Because it will bring my family and me more glory than any Tolm will ever know?"

"Because you'll fail," he told her, an earnest look on his handsome face. She knew in her heart that he was wrong about this, but there could be no denying that he cared about her. "Because you'll probably be killed. And you may well plunge all the Southlands back into war."

"I have no control over the other armies of the Southlands. I can only do what's best for Qalsyn and Stelpana, and, yes, for Deraqor as well."

"That's a load of dung," he said. "You know as well as I that a battle between the clans and the sovereignties anywhere in the land will bring war to every corner of the Southlands."

"Do you honestly believe that the peace between Eandi and Qirsi can last forever?" she asked, returning to the argument that had swayed her father days before.

"It's already lasted more than a century."

"Only because neither side has seen an opportunity to attack."

"And now we have that opportunity," Enly said derisively. "Is that it?"

"Yes, Enly," she said. "It's as simple as that. We have an opportunity. We can take it, or we can let it slip away. But if next time it's the white-hairs who see a chance to attack us, I guarantee you they'll take it, and we'll wonder why we let them."

"How very convenient for you. You declare the peace illusory, and then justify destroying it."

"It's not illusory," she said, glowering at him. "But it is temporary. Surely you must understand that. You said yourself that our attack on the Fal'Borna would spread war through all the land. If the peace is that fragile, it's just a matter of time before someone else does what we're considering. Or do you really believe that we and the white-hairs just suddenly stopped hating each other?"

"Of course not. But both sides did finally realize that the wars were destroying the land and benefiting no one. Finally, after centuries of combat and blood and suffering, they somehow managed to say 'enough.' One act of sanity in a thousand years of madness, and you want to destroy it."

He was calling her reckless, a fool, playing on doubts that lay so deep within her that she'd barely even acknowledged them. Worse, he was getting in the way of her greatest ambition, trying to keep the Onjaefs from reclaiming their rightful place among the great families of the sovereignties. So what she said next was meant to wound, though she regretted the words as soon as they crossed her lips.

"I think it's fortunate for all in Qalsyn that your father still rules. He, at least, is a man of vision, of courage. Berris would have been, too, had he lived. For all the years of rivalry between our houses, I've never known any Tolm except you to be a coward."

She knew from the hurt look in his pale grey eyes that her barb had found its mark, and in that instant she nearly apologized. Then it was too late. He'd hidden the pain behind a brittle smile. "My father," he said, his voice flat.

"Yes, your father. He thinks this a fine idea. He understands why we want to make the attempt."

"You're right, he does. Don't you find that odd? Doesn't it give you pause to find that he should be so eager for the Onjaefs to reclaim the glory of their past?"

Tirnya hesitated. "Not really. He probably likes the idea of it. Once we take back Deraqor we won't be here in his city. He won't have to compete with my father anymore."

"That's right," Enly said. "Think about what that means for a moment. He doesn't think this is a good idea; he doesn't even think you're likely to succeed. He sees this as a way to get rid of both you and your father, pure and simple. He told me so himself. 'If they succeed, Jenoe can spend the rest of his days defending Deraqor from Fal'Borna attacks; and if they fail, they'll return here disgraced and broken.' Those might not be his exact words, but they're close enough."

She opened her mouth, closed it again, not knowing how to respond. Enly could have been making this up, but she didn't think so. The truth was, that sounded just like Maisaak. After a few moments, though, she realized that it didn't matter to her what His Lordship thought, just as long as he gave them enough men to make the attempt.

"We're not going to fail," she finally said.

He shook his head impatiently. "You're not listening," he told her, his voice rising. "There is no victory here. Even if you take back the city, you're dooming yourselves and your children and their children after them to life-times of warfare. The Qirsi won't give up. You might beat them this time, assuming that the plague we've been hearing about is real. But they'll just turn around immediately and lay siege to Deraqor themselves."

"Then we'll fight them off."

He stared at her, disbelief plain on his face. "You really are mad. You and my father both. He'd send ten thousand men to die just so that he could be rid of your father, and you'd plunge all the land into war just so that you might reclaim for your family a city you've never even seen."

She straightened. "I wouldn't expect you to understand."

"Have you spoken of this to your men yet? Do Oliban and Qagan and Crow know what you have in mind?"

"Of course not. You heard your father. He told us not to mention our plans to anyone."

"What do you think they'd say if they knew?"

She leveled a finger at his heart as if it were a dagger. "Don't you dare say a word to them, Enly. If you want to spread word of this invasion through taverns and inns be my guest. But they're my men, and you'd better not—"

"I didn't mean it as a threat," he said, holding up his hands. "I'm asking you what they would say if they knew."

She looked away. "I have no idea."

"Don't you?"

"Clearly you think you do," she said, her anger flaring once more. "Are you so arrogant that you'd presume to know my soldiers better than I know them myself?"

"I know men," he said. "I know my own soldiers. Like yours they're loyal, good men, who would follow their commander wherever I told them to go. But they don't want to die in a useless, futile quest, nor do they wish to be remembered as the army that led the Southlands down the path to its own destruction."

She pushed past him, starting back toward the main road. "I'm not listening to any more of this!"

"You're throwing their lives away!" he called after her. "You're throwing your own life away! Can't you see that?"

Tirnya stopped, turning to face him again. "You must really think me an idiot."

"What?" he said.

"You just assume I'm going to fail, that I'm leading my soldiers to their deaths. Do you really think I'm that poor a commander?"

He shook his head. "That's not—"

"You wouldn't be saying these things to a man. You'd never question Stri's abilities as a leader or tell him he was leading his soldiers to their deaths. But because I'm a woman, you think you can speak to me as if I'm simple."

"That's ridiculous!"

"Is it, Enly?" she demanded. "You mean to tell me that you'd be having this conversation with anyone but me?"

He took a breath and walked to where she stood, stopping just in front of her.

"You're right," he told her, his voice low. "There's no one else I'd say these things to. I wouldn't tell Stri or your father, or even my father, not to lead this invasion of yours. Because as much as I respect them—again, even my father—as much as I might believe that they were endangering the land by doing this, I'd know that I could live with the consequences of their failure. I could bear to see them carried home on a bier. But not you."

He held her gaze for a moment longer. Tirnya tried to think of something clever and biting to say in return, but she had no answer for what she saw in those pale eyes.

Then, without another word, Enly walked away.

She watched him go, saw him turn back toward the city marketplace at the end of the narrow lane. Only then did she follow him out of the alley, turning in the opposite direction when she reached the main road.

Damn him! she thought as she walked. Who was he to speak to her so? Whatever there had been between them ended long ago. Hadn't she made that clear again and again? And still he spoke as if he had some claim on her. If ever she had loved him—and she wasn't certain that she had—she didn't anymore. And next to her desire to take back Deraqor and its surrounding lands, the one true home the Onjaef family had ever known, her feelings for Enly Tolm were nothing.

Tirnya was still in a rage when she reached the training grounds, but she did her best to mask her anger as her soldiers greeted her. Oliban and the other lead riders had already arranged the men in training groups and were awaiting her first instructions.

Seeing them now, though, she realized that Enly had made at least one valid point. These soldiers would be going with her to Deraqor, risking their lives, so that she and her father could realize their dream of taking back the city. It would be up to her lead riders, as well as Stri's and those of Jenoe's other captains, to carry out whatever plan she and her father decided on. Didn't she owe it to them to reveal at least some of what they were planning?

"Is there somethin' wrong, Captain?" Crow asked, watching her closely as she pondered all of this.

"No," she said, shaking her head and making her decision. "But I would like a word with the eight of you."

She turned to walk off a short distance, though not before she saw her lead riders exchange glances. She heard Oliban shout to the men that they should relax. A moment later her lead riders joined her.

"I wasn't entirely honest with you the other day," she began, speaking to Oliban. "I haven't been training the men harder because I'm angry with any of you, but there is some purpose behind it."

The men waited, saying nothing, but eyeing her keenly. Now that she had them there she wasn't entirely certain how to tell them. She couldn't bring herself just to come out and admit that she and Jenoe intended to attack the Fal'Borna, and once more she found herself thinking of Enly and all that he had said.

"Captain?" Oliban finally said, the frown on his face mirrored on the faces of his fellow riders.

"How many of you have heard about the plague currently striking at the Fal'Borna?"

Oliban glanced at the others once more. "We all 'ave, Captain."

"So you know that it seems to strike only at white-hairs; not at our kind."

"Hadn' heard tha'," Crow said

"Well, it's true. It strikes at their magic and it leaves their cities in ruins. Most recently it struck at S'Vralna."

She took a breath before continuing. "The marshal and I have been to see His Lordship. We believe—all of us do—that this white-hair plague presents us with an opportunity. We've already begun to form a plan to take back Deraqor and the lands around the Horn."

Silence. None of the men so much as moved.

At last, Crow narrowed his dark eyes. "Ya mean t' say tha' ya're considerin' an attack on th' Fal'Borna?"

"That's right."

Tirnya sensed Crow's incredulity, but to the man's credit he merely nodded at this. "When?" he asked a few moments later.

"We don't know yet. Soon, but not before our strategy is ready."

"Can ya tell us wha' tha' strategy is?" Qagan asked.

She shook her head. "Not yet. My father and I have been working on it for days," she added quickly, ashamed of herself for misleading them, but even more ashamed to admit how little they'd come up with thus far. "But we don't want to reveal any of it until we can reveal all of it."

Qagan nodded. "Tha' makes sense."

If anything, this made her feel worse.

"I'm sorry I can't tell you more," she said. "But I thought I should at least prepare you, let you know . . . what we've been talking about and why we've been training so hard in recent days."

They nodded, and after a moment Oliban said, "Yes, Captain." He sounded subdued, though.

"How can we help, Captain?" Dyn asked. Of all of them, he seemed the least daunted by what she had said. He and a few of the others, including Crow, were from families that had come to Qalsyn from Deraqor with the Onjaefs. It might take them time, but they'd come to support this idea soon enough.

"I'm not sure you can right now," she said. "You must not mention this to anyone else, not even your men. Not yet at least. The fewer people who know what we have in mind, the better our chances of catching the white-hairs unaware."

"O' course," Dyn said, clearly expecting more.

"And the training of the men must be kept at the level we've established in the last few days."

"We'll see t' it," Oliban said crisply. He seemed to have recovered from his initial shock.

She nodded, forced a smile. "Very good."

They stood there a few seconds more, the eight men still watching her as if waiting for her to say more. When they realized that she had nothing else to tell them, they shared looks again.

"Well, then," Oliban said. "We'll get back t' th' men."

"Thank you," Tirnya said.

The lead riders started to walk away. After only a few strides, however, Oliban paused, turned, and walked back to where she stood.

"Forgive me, Captain," he said, sounding unsure of himself. "I was born an' raised here in Qalsyn. I've never seen Deraqor or th' Horn."

She smiled nervously. "Neither have I."

"No, o' course not. But I realize it's yar homeland, th' city o' yar family. There's lots o' families here tha' can trace their lines back there. Bu' no' mine."

"I know," Tirnya said.

"Is tha' . . ." He frowned and shook his head. "I'm tryin' t' understand. This is a . . . a huge undertakin'. We'd be riskin' a great deal."

"Are you trying to ask me why we're doing this?" she said.

He stared down at his feet. "In a sense, I suppose I am. It's been over a hundred years since yar family . . . since th' Onjaefs and the others were driven from Deraqor. As ya say, ya've never even seen th' city. Do ya . . . do ya hate Qalsyn tha' much?"

Tirnya winced at the question. "No," she said quickly. "This is the only home I've ever known. How could I hate it?"

"But then—"

"You have to understand, Oliban. My family was once like the Tolms. We ruled Deraqor. My father would be lord governor for all the lands between the Thraedes and the K'Sahd were it not for the white-hairs. But instead of being one of the leading families of Stelpana, we're a family in exile. We live with the constant shame of having lost our ancestral home."

"I don' think anyone in Qalsyn thinks of ya or th' marshal tha' way," he said.

Her first thought was that Maisaak certainly did. She kept this to herself, though, saying instead, "I appreciate that. But in a way it doesn't matter how others think of us. This is how we think of ourselves. The loss of Deraqor is a stain on our family's past, and now we have an opportunity to win it back, for ourselves, for Stelpana, for all the sovereignties. My feelings about Qalsyn are beside the point. This is about redeeming my ancestors and also about giving something wondrous to my children and my grandchildren."

Oliban appeared to consider this for some time. "From all tha' I've heard," he finally said, "Deraqor was a glorious city."

Tirnya smiled. "I've heard that, too. I can't wait to see it." She started walking back toward the soldiers and the other riders. "Come on," she said, gesturing for him to walk with her. "We have work to do."

He followed, though reluctantly, his eyes still fixed on the ground, his brow creased in thought. "If ya succeed," he said after a few moments, his voice lower now, as they approached the men, "will ya expect all o' us t' stay with ya in Deraqor?"

Tirnya stopped, taken aback by the question. Her distress must have shown on her face.

"Don' get me wrong, Captain. Servin' under ya has been an honor, and I'll do all I can t' help ya win back those Onjaef lands. But then . . ." He shrugged, looking embarrassed. "As I told ya before. Qalsyn's th' only home I've ever known. I wouldn' want t' leave it forever."

"No, of course you wouldn't," Tirnya said, finding her voice again.

"That's a long way off still, but I'm sure we'll work out something." She tried to smile. "If this works, His Lordship will need new captains. I can't think of anyone better suited to taking my place than you."

Oliban smiled at that. "Thank ya, Captain."

She nodded, then turned and walked on.

Tirnya and her soldiers spent the rest of the morning training. After the ringing of the midday bells, they resumed their patrols along the lanes outside the city walls. With her company's victory over the brigands, the attacks on merchants and travelers had fallen off greatly, but even in the best of times, road thieves remained a problem. On this day, her soldiers captured three men they spotted loitering along one of the side paths and then chased into the forest. There wouldn't be any reward this time, but as they returned to the city her men were in high spirits anyway. They were gaining a reputation as the best company in Qalsyn; this day's success would only enhance their status.

Tirnya tried to share in their good humor all the way back, but she was preoccupied with her conversation with the lead riders, and, she had to admit, her exchange with Enly as well. All of her men had seemed over-awed by what she told them, though just as Enly had expected, not one of them expressed any reluctance to follow her. In a way, though, their faith in her and Enly's doubts led her to the same place: She needed to think of something—anything—that would work against the white-hairs. She had no intention of failing in this and giving Enly the chance to gloat. But more to the point, she refused to throw away the lives of the brave men under her command, the men who had saved her life and who would march into Fal'Borna lands risking their lives, simply because she and her father asked it of them.

Enly might well be right: His Lordship probably was expecting them to fail. Tirnya's own father had questioned the wisdom of taking on the Fal'Borna just as had Enly. Why were they all so afraid?

Yes, the Fal'Borna had won most of the battles late in the Blood Wars. They had pushed the sovereignties back across the Thraedes and the Central Plain, and finally across the Silverwater. But in her long history Stelpana had also fought battles against the Aeleans and the Tordjannis, winning some and losing others. No one in Qalsyn was afraid of them.

It all came down to magic, then. Yes, the Fal'Borna were said to be fearsome warriors, but it was their magic that made them such a formidable enemy. Obviously.

So, how could an Eandi army overcome Qirsi magic and prevail in a

war? Surely it had happened. The Blood Wars had gone badly for the sovereignties at the end, but for a time the Eandi clans had more than held their
own against the white-hairs. What changed? What had happened to turn
the tide of the war so strongly against her people?

The question occupied her mind for the rest of the day and into the
night, when their patrols finally ended. Rather than heading directly back
to her home, Tirnya went to the Swift Water for an ale.

She should have known better. Enly was there, and he sought her out
immediately.

"I've come to apologize," he said, stopping just in front of her and sway-
ing slightly. His breath stank of whiskey, and he spoke with too much precision, as if trying to avoid slurring his words.

As angry as she had been with him earlier, she couldn't help but be
amused. "Apology accepted," she said. "Now go home and get some sleep."

But he shook his head and stepped up to the bar, blocking her way. "Another whiskey for me." He glanced back at her. "And an ale for the lovely
captain."

The barkeep grinned, then winked at her. A moment later Enly had
both drinks in hand and was leading her to a table at the back of the tavern.

"Come here and sit," he said, beckoning to her with the hand that still
held her cup, and sloshing ale onto the table. He stared down at the stain for
just an instant. "Sorry 'bout that."

She took the cup from him and sat. "Why don't you just sit, before you
hurt yourself?"

"Good idea." He lowered himself into his seat, sipping his whiskey as he
did. "Now then," he said. "How can I help?"

"What?"

"Well, obviously talking you out of this didn't work. So, if I want you to
live and bear my children, I'll have to find some way to keep you alive, won't
I?" He raised his cup to her, as if toasting, and then took another sip.

She laughed. "You arrogant bastard! I thought you were a horse's ass
when you're sober, but give you a few whiskeys . . ." She shook her head.

He blinked, clearly surprised by her response. "What did I say?"

Tirnya laughed again. "Never mind," she said sipping her ale. "You
don't really want to help. This is just another feeble attempt to get me to
change my mind."

He put down his cup and smacked the table with his open hand, the
sound echoing loudly through the tavern. He started at the noise, glancing
around self-consciously. "Not true," he said a moment later. "Not true at all."

"So now you think it's a good idea?"

"No," he said, frowning. "It's a terrible idea. Worst I've ever heard. But like I said, you'll never listen to reason, particularly if it comes from me. So, I want to help. I don't want you to die, Tirnya." He looked away briefly and took a long breath. "Yes, I'm drunk," he said, facing her again. "But I really . . . I care about you. Surely you've figured that out by now. I don't want to lose you. But if you're going to leave me, I at least want to know that you're safe and living happily in your precious Deraqor."

"Shhh!" she said sharply.

He looked around again, nodded, and took a quick drink. "Right. Sorry."

Tirnya ran a hand through her hair, shaking her head once more. No one appeared to have noticed what he said. And, for all his tortured logic and drunken nonsense, he had managed to touch her heart just a bit. "Fine," she said. "You want to help me? You can help me."

He patted her arm. "There you go! Good girl. I knew you'd come around." He leaned closer. "How?" he asked in a conspiratorial whisper.

"I haven't any idea."

Enly scowled at her and she laughed.

"You enjoyed that," he said.

"Yes, I did."

He turned away and took another drink, looking hurt.

"I'm sorry, Enly. But I really don't . . . ." She trailed off, thinking again of her conversations from earlier in the day. "What do you know about the Blood Wars?" she asked after a brief silence.

He gave a short high laugh. "What do I know about the wars? Everything. My father wanted both of us—" His smile faded. "Berris, I mean. Berris and me." He drained his cup. "Father wanted us to know everything about the wars," he went on, grim-faced now. "Like you, he didn't believe this peace could last, and he wanted us to be ready when the fighting started again." He looked at her. "Why?"

"There was a time when the sovereignties enjoyed some success, wasn't there?"

Enly shrugged. "I suppose you could say that. It wasn't the sovereignties back then. We were still fighting as clans. But if you mean the Eandi, yes, we won our share of victories early on."

This time she was the one who leaned closer. "How, Enly? How did we beat them?"

He smiled and nodded. "Ah, yes. That's the question, isn't it? If we knew that . . . ." He opened his hands. "Anything would be possible."

"You don't know then?" she asked, sitting back and frowning.

"No one does. The secret's been lost to the ages."

She took a pull of ale. "Damn," she muttered.

"It could have been anything," he went on, paying little attention to her. "It might not have been anything the Eandi did. The Qirsi might have been weaker then, or their leaders might have been less clever. They might have had fewer Weavers. Or maybe our leaders were smarter." He looked at her, narrowing his eyes. "Do you think that's it? Do you think we're just not as good as the people who came before us? Not the soldiers, but the captains and marshals and lords. I'd wager my father doesn't like that idea very much." He chuckled.

"No," Tirnya said, not liking it either. "I don't suppose he does." She sat staring at the table for several moments, while Enly tried to catch the eye of the barkeep so that he could order another whiskey. "What did it mean that we weren't fighting as the sovereignties?" She looked up again meeting his gaze. "I understand that the various nations hadn't been created yet. But I'm asking what that meant in terms of how we fought."

Enly's eyebrows went up. "I'm not really certain. I'd imagine that it meant we were more unified. We hadn't split off into separate armies yet." He shrugged. "Then again, some of the clan rivalries were pretty bitter, so that might not be the case. I don't know."

"Did all the clans fight in those early battles?"

"I think so. The old histories list the names. It's been a while since I read them, and even then there were some I didn't recognize. But they were there, fighting the white-hairs. I don't think our kind were ever so united as we were in the early years of the wars."

Tirnya nodded thoughtfully. "Perhaps. Certainly that would help when it came to waging war. But could that kind of unity make enough difference to . . . ?"

The realization came to her with such force that for several moments she could hardly breathe, much less speak.

"Tirnya?" Enly said, eyeing her with concern.

"Could it be that simple?" she whispered.

"Could what be that simple?"

"You just said that we fought not as sovereignties, but as clans, that our people had never been so united."

He nodded, his forehead furrowing in concentration. "Yes."

"And do you think it's likely that all of our people fought the white-hairs?"

"Well, that's—"

"All of them, Enly. *All of them!*"

He shook his head. "I don't understand."

"Think for a moment!" Tirnya said, her voice rising. She noticed that others in the tavern had started to look at her. She leaned closer to him, and when she spoke again it was in a whisper. "What is it that we fear most about the white-hairs?"

"Their magic, of course."

"Yes!" she said, her eyes wide with excitement. "What if you're right and we were more united than we've been at any time since? What if the Eandi of that time were so united that they were even willing to fight alongside the Mettai?"

He stared at her. "The Mettai," he said, the word coming out as softly as a breath.

Tirnya nodded. "The Mettai. What if we succeeded in those early days of the wars because like the white-hairs we didn't only carry weapons into battle, we carried magic as well?"

She didn't wait for his answer. She stood, drained her cup, and spun away from the table.

"Where are you going?" Enly called after her.

"Home," she said over her shoulder. "I need to speak with my father."

Chapter 14

❧

Jenoe's reaction was not quite what Tirnya had expected. The breathless, wide-eyed whisper she had drawn from Enly, the quickened pulse and rush of excitement she had felt herself—these, or some variation, were what she also expected from her father.

Instead, he merely stared back at her, looking perplexed, and said, "The Mettai?"

"Don't you see it, Father? We don't have to fight this war without magic. It doesn't have to be Eandi might against white-hair sorcery anymore. We can ride into battle and challenge their greatest strength."

Her father shook his head, clearly still skeptical. "I think you're overly taken with the idea, Tirnya."

"'Overly taken'!" she repeated, sitting back in her chair beside the hearth and shaking her head in amazement. "I can't believe I'm hearing this."

"First of all, Mettai magic is no match for the power that Qirsi sorcerers wield. They have no Weavers to coordinate their attacks. Every conjuring requires blood. It's not like the magic of a white-hair at all."

"But still," she said, "it's something. It's more than we have without them."

Jenoe shrugged, conceding the point with obvious reluctance. "Perhaps, but that's the other matter. Over the past several centuries, our kind have had few dealings with the Mettai. We've shunned them, and they've kept to themselves in the northern reaches near the Companion Lakes. What makes you think they'd want to help us?"

"Their eyes are as dark as ours, Father. And I doubt very much that they have any affection for the Qirsi. As I understand it, the Mettai have been shunned by both races."

"Yes, they have. But after all these years that's hardly the basis for an alliance."

"Maybe they don't want to be shunned anymore," Tirnya said. She sensed that the Mettai were the key to all of this, and she refused to give up on the idea. "Maybe they're ready to reconcile with the sovereignties. For all we know, they have been for years, but none have approached them."

"You're thinking with your heart, and not your mind. The Mettai are a proud people. There would have been no need for them to wait for us. If they wanted to reconcile, they could have approached one of the sovereignties long ago." He shook his head. "Whatever their history, at this point they keep to themselves because they want to. No one bothers them, which I assume is just how they like it. I can't imagine them suddenly wanting to fight in a new round of Blood Wars."

"Fine then," Tirnya said. "We can offer them gold or land, or whatever it is they want. If they help us take back Deraqor and the Horn they can have the entire Central Plain, for all I care."

"I'm not sure that will work, either."

She propelled herself out of the chair and began to pace the chamber, struggling to control her frustration. She felt her father watching her, but she didn't look at him.

"I'm just trying to make you see this plainly, Tirnya. It's not going to be nearly as easy to make an ally of the Mettai as you seem to think it is."

Tirnya halted just in front of him. "Put that aside for a moment, and answer this: Do you think it would help us to have them fighting on our side?"

"If it were possi—"

"No!" she said. "Never mind the difficulties of getting them to join us. I'm just asking you if you think it would help."

He seemed to weigh this for several moments before nodding. "All other considerations aside, I'd have to say that it would. Their magic might not be as potent as that of the Qirsi, but it's formidable in its own way."

"Not only that," Tirnya said, "but if we could approach them quietly and add them to our army without the white-hairs knowing it, their magic would come as a complete surprise to the Fal'Borna." She squatted down in front of him, looking into his dark eyes. "Imagine that, Father! Think of what it would be like for the Qirsi to find themselves confronted not only with a great army, but one that somehow could attack them with magic. By the time they recovered and figured out what was happening . . ." She stopped herself, afraid to say the words aloud. "Well, it would give us a tremendous advantage."

"It might at that," Jenoe said soberly. And she knew what was coming next. "But that brings us back to the point I was making earlier. It's fine to speculate about all of this. But I don't believe we can convince the Mettai to fight with us."

"As the man leading this army, what would you be willing to give them in order to have them wielding their magic on our behalf?"

Jenoe frowned. "What would I give them?"

"We're hoping to win back our homeland, to take back Deraqor. We have gold, we'll have land. What would you give the Mettai?"

"I really don't know," he said, shaking his head.

"Well, think about it," Tirnya told him. "We've been trying to come up with a plan that will give us a chance against the Qirsi. And we can't wait much longer. The Snows are coming, and the effects of this plague won't last forever. In my opinion, this is the best chance we have, and I intend to tell His Lordship as much as soon as he'll see me."

Jenoe regarded her for a long time, saying nothing. At last he shook his head. "I'm not sure that's a good idea, Tirnya. I've been thinking . . ." He faltered and looked away. "I don't think this is such a good idea."

"Going to the Mettai, you mean?" she asked. But she had the feeling that he meant much more.

"No. I'm not sure about that either. But I mean this whole plan: attacking the Fal'Borna, trying to take back Deraqor."

His words struck at her heart. It was bad enough arguing with Enly and hearing the doubt in Oliban's voice. But to learn now that her own father doubted her! She wasn't usually given to tears, but for just an instant she thought that she might cry. A moment later she had managed to master her emotions. Jenoe gave no indication that he understood how much he had hurt her, and that was fine with Tirnya.

"There's nothing wrong with the idea," she said evenly. "The last time we spoke you were all for it. We can do this, Father. You know we can. The white-hairs are suffering; the Mettai might well be willing to join us. But really it's up to you. If you speak against the idea, Maisaak won't allow us to go forward."

"Then I should speak against it," he said quietly, staring at the fire.

"Just the other day you agreed that the Horn and Deraqor were worth fighting for. You were the one who arranged for us to see His Lordship."

His eyes flicked toward hers. "I was wrong."

"No, you weren't. Now, what happened?"

Jenoe shifted uncomfortably in his seat.

"It was Mother, wasn't it?" Tirnya said, knowing as she spoke that it was true. "She talked you out of it."

"You'd talked me into it," he said, sounding sullen. "I've been caught between the two of you before, and I don't like it one bit. There are times when you're right, but this isn't one of them. I'm too old to be marching off to war so late in the year. And I have no desire to die in a hopeless battle, even if it is for Deraqor."

"It's not—" She stopped, shaking her head. Enly, her father, and now her mother as well. Her lead riders hadn't spoken against the idea of attacking the Fal'Borna, but they wouldn't have. They were good soldiers, all of them. They understood that it wasn't their place to gainsay their captain. It seemed clear from Oliban's questions, though, that he had his doubts, too.

It appeared that the only people who agreed with her were Stri and the lord governor, and having Maisaak on her side made her uncomfortable. What if Enly was right? What if Maisaak only encouraged her because he saw her idea as an easy way to rid himself of the Onjaefs? The truth was, until she'd thought of approaching the Mettai, Tirnya herself had harbored doubts as to their ability to defeat the Fal'Borna.

Still, she wasn't ready to give up her dream so easily.

"I have a compromise to offer," she said, pacing once more.

Her father looked up at her. "What kind of compromise?"

"I still think that this can work, that we have a chance to take back the Horn and Deraqor. You think I'm being reckless and that we're doomed to fail."

Jenoe winced. "Tirnya—"

"It's all right, Father. I'm just about the only one who believes that we can succeed at this, so maybe I am being a bit reckless."

"What's your idea?"

"We lead an army westward to the Silverwater, and then we seek out the Mettai. If we can convince them to join us, we march on to Deraqor and fight for our family's lands. If we can't we return to Qalsyn."

He looked genuinely surprised. "You'd do this?"

"I'm not certain I have any choice."

"What if Maisaak won't agree?"

Tirnya shrugged. "Then there's really not very much we can do, is there?"

Jenoe gazed into the fire again. After a few moments, he began to nod slowly. "Very well. We'll seek an audience with His Lordship tomorrow."

"All right," Tirnya said, nodding in turn. It wasn't ideal; it wasn't as much as she had hoped. But it was something. Her dream was alive still. Considering all those who were arrayed against her, that was as much as she could have expected.

Every sound was too loud, as if some evil sorcerer from the west had made his ears five times their normal size. The least light stabbed into his eyes like sparkling shards of glass, and there was a taste in his mouth that had him wondering if he'd snacked on ashes from the floor of his hearth before stumbling into bed the night before. This last he didn't dwell on for long, because the very thought of eating anything—anything at all—nearly made him retch.

All Enly wanted to do was sleep. A day or two ought to have done it. But once more his father had summoned him to his chambers, and though Enly's memories of the night before could generously be called sketchy, he did recall something of his conversation with Tirnya. He could only assume that once more the Onjaefs had requested an audience with the lord governor, and once more, rather than face Jenoe and Tirnya alone, Maisaak had called for him. He might have found it amusing, but the mere thought of laughter served only to redouble the pain in his head.

The guards outside his father's chamber were, of course, unfailingly courteous, except for the fact that they kept yelling at him, and when they knocked on His Lordship's door they seemed to be using a smith's sledge.

They opened the door at his father's reply and gestured for him to enter.

"Thank you," he whispered as he stepped past them.

He thought he heard one of the men snicker at his back.

"You look awful," Maisaak said as Enly stumbled in.

Enly shaded his eyes with an open hand and searched the chamber for his father, who was by his writing table. "Thank you," he muttered. "Would you mind closing the shutters on those windows? It's blinding in here."

Maisaak actually laughed. "Sit down. I'll have the healer bring you a tonic."

Enly dropped himself into a chair that faced toward one of the walls and closed his eyes. "I take it that's a no."

His father didn't answer. Instead he stepped to the door, opened it, and spoke briefly with one of his guards.

"Late night, eh?" Maisaak asked a moment later.

"So it seems."

"What was the occasion?"

Enly shook his head, both hands raised to his temples. "I haven't any idea."

That much was a lie, but after all these years, telling his father that he was still drinking himself senseless over Tirnya Onjaef struck him as unwise.

"I suppose you know why I called for you."

"There's no need to shout. And yes, I assume this is about Jenoe and Tirnya."

"Good. I'm glad to know that you still have your wits about you, such as they are."

A thin smile flitted across Enly's face, but he didn't respond or open his eyes.

"Do you have any idea what the Onjaefs might want this time?" his father asked.

"Tirnya's been making plans for their new war. I suppose they've come up with something."

"Perhaps," Maisaak said. "Would this have anything to do with your present condition?"

"You think their plans include getting me drunk?"

"You know what I . . . Never mind."

His father went back to the parchments on his desk, leaving Enly to wallow in his misery. When she'd left him the night before Tirnya had been saying something about the Mettai, but that was really the extent of what he could recall. In truth, he didn't want to remember more. When he first spotted her in the Swift Water, she'd still been angry about their argument earlier in the day. But she'd seemed pleased as she left, and it occurred to him that whatever plan she and Jenoe had concocted might well have originated with him. The thought made him feel even sicker, which he hadn't believed was possible.

He might have dozed off, because the next thing he knew his father was shaking him none too gently.

"What?" he complained.

Maisaak forced a warm cup into his hand. "Here's your tonic."

Enly managed to open his eyes. "Oh. Thank you."

His father didn't answer.

He lifted the cup to his lips, then hesitated. The brew smelled strongly of mint, ginger, and dittany, and he wondered if he could keep it down.

"Drink it," Maisaak said. "You'll feel better."

"And if it has the opposite effect?"

His father's mouth twisted sourly. "If it comes to that, there's a chamber pot in the next room."

Enly nodded and took a small sip. When that did nothing to make him feel worse, he took another, and then a third. Soon he was drinking the brew more freely, and by the time another knock on the door signaled the arrival of Tirnya and her father, he was starting to feel just a bit more like himself.

He stood to greet the marshal and his daughter, his head spinning slightly as he did.

Jenoe grinned and nodded toward the cup. "I'd know that scent anywhere. Late night?"

Enly glanced at his father. "Why is it that men of a certain age always assume that a hangover indicates a late night? I'm perfectly capable of drinking myself into a stupor before midnight bells."

"'Men of a certain age,'" Jenoe repeated, raising an eyebrow and glancing at Maisaak. "I think, Your Lordship, that we've just been insulted."

Maisaak smiled thinly. "Pay no attention to him, Marshal. I've learned that's the best way to handle his little barbs." He indicated a pair of chairs near his writing table. "Please sit," he said.

"Thank you, Your Lordship," Tirnya said.

They took their seats, as did the lord governor. Enly returned to his chair near the hearth. Two servants appeared, laden with platters of cheese, fruits, and a flask of honey wine. He tried to ignore the food and the wine.

"So," Maisaak began, once the servants had withdrawn, "you have matters to discuss with me?"

Jenoe and Tirnya shared a look. After a moment the marshal nodded to her, as if in encouragement.

"Yes, Your Lordship," she said. "Since speaking with you last, we've come to see that any assault on the Fal'Borna would be . . . well, it would be very difficult." She cleared her throat. "More so, I fear, than I had originally thought."

Enly's father nodded. "No doubt. A siege is always difficult. And against the Qirsi . . ." He shrugged, leaving the thought unfinished.

"Yes," Tirnya said. "We'd be risking a great many lives and destroying a peace that's lasted more than a century. And, of course, we have no guarantee of success."

"There are no guarantees in warfare, Captain," Maisaak said. He narrowed his eyes. "Are you telling me that you've reconsidered, that you no longer want to take back your ancestral homeland?"

"No, Your Lordship."

Maisaak frowned. "Then, I'm afraid I'm confused."

"Forgive me," Tirnya said. "I'm not explaining this well. We've come to the conclusion that we have but one path to success. It carries some risks, and you may not approve. If you give us your pemission, and it works, we'll continue on into Fal'Borna lands and take back Deraqor. If it doesn't, we'd choose to return here, without facing the Fal'Borna."

She had Maisaak's attention. Enly could see that much. He had a look on his face that was both wary and amused.

"And what is it you propose?" the lord governor asked.

Tirnya hesitated, casting another glance at her father. Again the marshal nodded.

"We'd like to approach the Mettai, Your Lordship. We'd like to propose an alliance with them."

For a moment, Maisaak didn't so much as blink. It appeared to Enly that this was the very last thing he had expected her to say.

"The Mettai," he whispered. He looked at Jenoe. "Was this your idea?"

"No," Jenoe said. "Tirnya came up with this all on her own."

Through the haze of whiskey and ale came a sudden burst of memories. In the instant before Tirnya opened her mouth Enly knew what she would say and more than anything he wanted to silence her. But his reactions were slow. And really, what could he have said even if he had been quicker? In the next moment it was too late.

"Actually, Your Lordship," she said, "without Enly I never would have thought of it."

Maisaak's eyebrow went up and he glanced Enly's way once more, his expression unreadable. "Is that so?"

Tirnya appeared to realize what she had done. "He was merely answering my questions about the old Blood Wars, Your Lordship. I was curious as to how Eandi armies had managed to win as many early battles as they did, and I knew that you had encouraged him to learn as much as possible about the history of the wars."

Enly's father frowned. "And he said that our ancestors fought alongside the Mettai?"

"No, Your Lordship. He merely mentioned that the Eandi clans were more united in the early years, which made me wonder if perhaps they had been so united as to ally themselves with the Eandi sorcerers."

Maisaak still did not look satisfied. But he nodded once, his familiar thin smile fixed on his lips again. "I see. That's quite a leap, Captain. Some might even call it inspired." The words were kind enough, but he didn't sound admiring so much as annoyed.

"Thank you, Your Lordship."

He turned to Jenoe again. "And you believe this will work?"

"Actually," Jenoe said, "I don't. I doubt very much that the Mettai want anything to do with a new war against the Qirsi. But as Tirnya says, our other options are poor at best. And to her credit, I do think she's hit on the one tactic that the white-hairs won't be expecting. If by some chance we had the magic of the Mettai at our disposal, it might give us an advantage."

"What would you offer them?" Maisaak asked.

"We could offer them gold or we could offer them land," Tirnya answered.

Enly's father shook his head. "I won't empty Qalsyn's treasury for this."

"You wouldn't have to," Jenoe said, his voice hardening just a bit. After a moment he added, somewhat peremptorily, "Your Lordship."

Maisaak glared at him. "No?"

"House Onjaef is not without its resources, Your Lordship," Jenoe said. He paused briefly, seeming to gather himself. When he began again, it was in a lower, more respectful tone. "Since this is our fight, and since you have already—most generously I might add—offered to provision us and let us use your armies, we wouldn't presume to ask for more." He glanced at Tirnya. "Besides, I think the Mettai are far more likely to want land. We can offer them some of the territory near the Horn. They're farmers, most of them; they'll appreciate the value of those lands."

"And if they refuse?"

"If they refuse, Your Lordship," Tirnya said, "we'll return here, somewhat chastened, but your loyal subjects as always."

Enly had to smile. It was deftly handled. On this morning at least, she seemed more skilled than both their fathers in the art of statecraft.

"What are you grinning at?" Maisaak demanded.

Enly looked at him, his smile fading just a bit. "Nothing, Father."

"I suppose you have an opinion on this?"

His eyes met Tirnya's for just an instant. Then she looked away. "Not really, no," Enly answered. "I believe that the Mettai would be a valuable ally in any fight against the white-hairs, but like the marshal, I'm skeptical about our chances of winning them over."

"I see," Enly's father said dryly. "Well, I have to admit to being skeptical myself, about this entire endeavor." He stood and walked back to his writing table and began to peruse some of the scrolls there.

Enly and the Onjaefs stood as well.

"I'll have to give it some more thought before sending a message to the sovereign," Maisaak said. He glanced up at them all. "Thank you."

Tirnya looked at Jenoe, appearing confused. Her father gestured toward the door, and started to walk toward it.

"We haven't much time, Your Lordship," she said, facing Maisaak again.

"Tirnya," Jenoe said, a warning in his voice.

Maisaak had looked up from his parchments. "What did you say?" he asked.

Enly wanted to tell her to let it go, to leave now, before she said something she'd regret. Clearly her father wanted to do the same. But as always, she kept her own counsel. She didn't so much as look at her father or at Enly.

"Forgive me, Your Lordship. But time is our enemy in this matter. The Snows are coming, and we don't know how long the effects of the white-hair plague will last. You need to send a message to Ofirean City, and then you'll have to wait for the sovereign's reply. That could take an entire turn. If we're to attack, we need to do it soon."

Maisaak stared back at her, his eyes glittering in the light from the windows. "You would presume—"

"She didn't mean anything by it, Father," Enly said. "She's merely stating what you and I both know to be true. We haven't much time, and if we delay much longer, we'll have no choice but to wait for the thaw."

Maisaak opened his mouth to fire back a reply, but then he stopped himself, his gaze drifting toward Jenoe and Tirnya. "Leave us," he said.

"Your Lordship," Jenoe said, sketching a quick bow. He pulled the door open. "Come, Tirnya."

Her eyes flicked toward Enly again, and he thought he read an apology in the frightened expression on her lovely face. Then she turned and strode quickly toward the door.

"Captain," Maisaak said.

She halted, turned toward him, though she kept her gaze lowered. "Your Lordship?"

"Don't ever presume to tell me how much or how little time I have to make a decision. Ever. Do I make myself clear?"

She bowed, still keeping her eyes lowered. "Yes, Your Lordship."

Enly had never heard her sound so meek, and he found himself hating his father for making her grovel so.

A moment later the Onjaefs had gone, and Maisaak turned his rage on Enly, which he actually preferred.

"How dare you intercede when I'm disciplining an officer under my command! When you're lord governor you can coddle her as much as you please! But that won't be for some time now, and until then you keep your mouth shut!"

"Yes, Father," he said mildly.

Maisaak stepped out from behind his writing table and crossed to where Enly stood. For a moment, Enly thought his father might strike him and he readied himself for the blow. But Maisaak didn't touch him. He merely regarded him for several moments, before turning away once more and walking to the window.

"You sound like a fool when you defend her that way." He glanced back at Enly. "You know that, don't you?"

He usually had little trouble enduring his father's criticism; he'd certainly had enough practice over the years. But when Maisaak spoke to him this way about Tirnya, it stung, perhaps because Enly knew that he had handled his relationship with her so poorly.

"Is that so?" he answered, trying to sound composed.

"She's stronger than you are. She should be defending you, not the other way around."

"Is there a point to this, Father?"

Maisaak turned. "Yes, there is. When did you become an Onjaef?"

"What?"

"You should hear yourself," his father said with disgust. "'I'm skeptical about *our* chances of winning over the Mettai.' '*We* haven't much time. *We* can't delay much longer.'" He sneered, shaking his head. "You're more eager for this fight than Jenoe. Does she really find that kind of fawning attractive, or are you just so desperate that you don't care anymore?"

"I don't have to listen to this." Enly spun on his heel and took a step toward the door.

"What were you thinking?" Maisaak demanded. "The Mettai? Are you really that great a fool?"

"You heard Tirnya," Enly said, reaching for the door handle. "It was her idea. I just told her a bit about the Blood Wars."

"While you were drunk?"

He turned. "Yes, Father. While I was drunk. Earlier in the day I'd tried to talk her out of this attack on the Fal'Borna. That didn't work, so I took comfort in a flask or two of Qosantian whiskey."

"And you led her straight to the Mettai." Maisaak shook his head. "You're an ass."

"I don't think so, Father. I think it actually might work."

"*Idiot!*" He swept the parchments off his writing table in a single, violent motion. "I don't want it to work! Don't you understand that?" He ran a hand over his face. "You're so concerned with saving her life so that another man can have her, that you've lost sight of who and what you are."

"Who and what I am?" Enly repeated. "You think you have any idea of who I am?"

"You're a Tolm. One day you'll be lord governor yourself, and contrary to what you want to believe, she'll never marry you. You'll have to live with a second ruling family here in Qalsyn, just as I have." He laughed harshly, shaking his head. "It's remarkable really. The Onjaefs have done nothing for the last century except win a few tournaments and fight a few skirmishes with road brigands. Their last moment of historical significance ended in failure and disgrace. And yet they're adored by the oafs who followed them to this city, while those of us who see to it that those same oafs remain safe and prosperous . . ." He trailed off, his face coloring slightly. "Someday that will be your burden as well, and you'll understand what I do: that the Onjaefs threaten everything House Tolm has sought to build here since the earliest days of Stelpana's history."

"Then let them go," Enly said. "A few days ago you saw Tirnya's invasion as a way of ridding yourself of them. There's a chance now that the Mettai will refuse to join them, and that they'll return here. But there's also a chance that their plan will actually work. They'll take back Deraqor and you'll be rid of them for good."

Maisaak merely stood there, saying nothing, his cheeks still red, the muscles in his jaw bunched.

"But you don't want that, do you, Father? The calculation has changed because now they might actually succeed. You never wanted them simply to leave. You wanted them dead, or at least defeated and humiliated. The idea of them taking back Deraqor galls you."

Still, his father didn't answer.

Enly grinned. "You know, I believe that's all the more reason to see that they succeed."

He pulled the door open.

"Where are you going?" Maisaak asked, stopping him once more.

"To train my men. If they're going to ride with the Onjaefs to Deraqor, they'll need to be prepared."

"You will not be riding to Deraqor!"

Enly's smile broadened. "Try and stop me."

"I can stop you!" Maisaak told him. "I can stop all of you from going anywhere! You heard Jenoe! He knows that he can't do a thing without permission from me, without men and weapons and horses from me, without provisions from me! If I decide they won't be going then . . . then they . . ."

Maisaak gave a small laugh and hung his head briefly before looking up at Enly, a bitter smile on his lips.

"You almost had me," the lord governor said. "I have to give you credit for being clever."

Enly shrugged and pushed the door closed again, doing what he could to mask his disappointment. "It was worth a try."

Maisaak shook his head, and laughed again. "Very clever, indeed."

"Are you going to let them go?" Enly asked.

His father eyed him briefly, the way a swordsman might regard a foe with whom he had done battle once, and might have to again. "I don't know. Was there any truth to what you were saying a moment ago? Would you consider riding with them?"

Once more Enly shrugged, averting his gaze. Talking to his father about Tinrya was never easy.

"Do you think they can lure the Mettai into an alliance?" Maisaak asked. "Because I'm not certain that I do. But it may be the most . . . audacious idea I've ever heard. She really is a remarkable girl, isn't she?"

"Is she?" Enly said. "I hadn't noticed."

Maisaak stared at him for an instant and then burst out laughing, a full-throated laugh of a kind Enly had only ever heard from him once or twice before.

After a few moments the lord governor's laughter subsided. He opened his mouth to say something, but appeared to think better of it. They stood in silence for a few moments. Finally Enly reached for the door handle again.

"I suppose I should go."

"You were right before," Maisaak said. "Not about all of it. But I do find it hard to accept the idea that Jenoe might succeed at this, that he might reclaim his ancestral home and that the Onjaefs might reclaim their place among Stelpana's great families."

"And I find it hard to accept the idea that Tirnya might leave here for good."

"We could work together, you and I. Perhaps, for once, our interests are similar enough to warrant . . . an alliance."

Enly shook his head. "I don't think so, Father. Not unless you're willing to help them and truly give them a chance to succeed."

Maisaak frowned. "One moment you want her to stay, the next you speak of her succeeding. I don't think you know your own mind."

"I don't want her to leave. But I don't want her to be hurt or disgraced either. And I don't think you want them to remain here as they've been. Which would leave us with two alternatives. Either I go with them, and do everything I can to make certain that they take back Deraqor. Or we let them go and do nothing to influence their fortunes one way or the other."

For a long time Maisaak said nothing. The stark light from the windows and the shadows of the chamber made the lines on his face appear deeper and darker than they usually did. Abruptly, perhaps for the first time, it occurred to Enly that his father was getting old.

"Contrary to what you said the other day," Maisaak finally told him, "I'm not indifferent to the loss of life. And no matter my feelings about Jenoe, I don't wish ill any of the men under his command." He looked at Enly and took a breath. "Do you want to go?"

The question came as something of a surprise, and he hesitated briefly. "That depends," he said. "If you intend to recommend to Ankyr that they be allowed to do this, then yes, I do." He narrowed his eyes. "You'd be willing to send me?"

"They'll have a better chance of succeeding with you there. And if Jenoe is to become a lord governor, I'd best do what I can to improve our rapport. The last thing I need is another enemy at the sovereign's table."

"You're convincing yourself," Enly said.

"Well, yes. As you remember, I wasn't very fond of the idea a few moments ago." He returned to his writing table and sat, looking weary. "I want to be rid of them. And while I'd enjoy seeing Jenoe bloodied and humiliated, if they fail, the sovereign will look upon it as my failure."

"Then don't let them do it."

"Perhaps if you go with them, she'll marry you," Maisaak said, as if he hadn't heard. "That might force Jenoe and me to put aside this feud of ours."

Enly shook his head. "No. If they retake Deraqor, she'll be the heir to a ruling house, just as I am. She could no more leave Deraqor to live here than I could leave Qalsyn to live the rest of my days in the Horn." He smiled, though his heart ached. "No, Father. One of us—you or me—will get his wish, and one of us won't. Either they'll remain here and I'll still have a chance to win her, or they'll leave and you'll be rid of Jenoe for good."

His father nodded slowly. At last, he looked at Enly again. "Train your men, and begin preparing to ride westward. I intend to send my message to the sovereign before day's end."

Chapter 15

FAL'BORNA LAND, THE CENTRAL PLAIN

F'Ghara made good on his promise to feed Besh and Sirj and to sell them as much food as they needed for the next stage of their journey. Even more, for that one night, as Besh recovered from his wounds and tried to make peace with the fact that he had killed Lici, he and Sirj were treated as esteemed guests in F'Ghara's sept. The irony was that while the Fal'Borna were honoring them, Besh was nearly overwhelmed with shame and grief.

He knew he'd had no choice. Lici had been torturing him; she'd made it clear that she had every intention of killing him before the day was out; and she'd been speaking of doing to her own people—Besh's people—what she had done already to the Y'Qatt. Killing her had been an act of desperation and of necessity. There wasn't a person in the sept who would have considered it murder, nor would any of the people he'd left behind in his own village of Kirayde. Sirj had said nothing to indicate that he found fault with what he'd done. It seemed that Besh himself was the only person who objected.

He'd never killed before. He hoped never to kill again. But he could hardly claim that he hadn't meant to do it, or even that he'd meant her no harm. He'd threatened to kill her; he'd as much as promised Pyav, Kirayde's village eldest, that he would do so if he couldn't stop her any other way. All of which begged the question, if her death hadn't been murder, what in Bian's name had it been?

These questions plagued him that first night when, as guests of the a'laq, he and Sirj ate and took their rest among the Fal'Borna. Besh lay awake for hours that night. Ema's voice in his mind assured him that he'd had no choice, that he'd done what was necessary. He didn't hear Sylpa's voice, which had become nearly as familiar to his thoughts as that of his dead wife, nor did he expect that he ever would again. She had been like a mother to Lici. Was it so surprising that she should forsake him now?

When at last he did sleep, he was haunted by dreams of Lici. In one, she appeared to him as a young girl, newly orphaned by the pestilence that had ravaged her village. She looked emaciated and she was crying, her face burned by the sun, her limbs scored by brambles and covered with insect bites. He went to her, intending to comfort her. But when he drew near, she reached out with a talon-like hand and took hold of his throat. Then she cut the back of the hand that held him, wiped dirt on the wound, and began to chant the words a spell.

"Blood to earth, life to power, power to thought, plague to old man!"

Instantly Besh felt the pestilence flowing through her hand into his throat, the fever spreading through his body, his stomach souring until he gagged.

He woke up, sweating and breathless, addled, not quite certain of where he was. After a few moments though, he recognized the sound of Sirj's muffled breathing, and realized that the faint reddish glow came from the coals of the fire that had warmed their shelter.

He lay back, and immediately fell back into the dream. Lici had been transformed into the old woman he'd killed earlier that day, but otherwise nothing had changed. She had her hand wrapped around his neck, her bloodied nails digging into his flesh, her hot, sour breath on his face.

"I'm not finished with you," she said coldly. "I'll never be finished with you."

Again she started to chant a curse, and again he awoke. The glow of the coals had grown faint, and Sirj was snoring loudly. Besh tried to rouse himself, but soon found himself in the dream again. On and on this went. Sometimes he encountered Lici as the old, crazed Mettai witch, other times as the pretty young girl he'd known in his youth. But always she was strangling the life out of him; always she had the words of a curse on her lips.

When, mercifully, morning came and Sirj woke him, he felt wearier than he had when he first had lain down for the night, and he despaired of ever sleeping again.

Under F'Ghara's direction, the Fal'Borna sold them a good deal of food, including lots of dried rilda meat, which might have been the best smoked meat Besh had ever tasted. He had expected that they would have to pay dearly for the food—the Fal'Borna were known as stubborn negotiators. But F'Ghara charged them about what Besh might have expected to pay in the Kirayde marketplace. When they thanked the a'laq, he nodded, looking grave, and then drew the two of them aside, so that the others in his sept wouldn't hear.

"Where will you go from here?" he asked.

"With your leave, A'Laq," Besh said, "we'd continue west, farther into

Fal'Borna lands. We know the name of the merchant who has the woman's baskets. We want to find him and keep him from doing more damage."

The a'laq regarded them both. "You have my permission to cross the clan lands. And you have my thanks as well. Your people . . ." He grimaced, shaking his head.

"The Mettai are hated by Qirsi and Eandi alike," Besh said. "It's no great secret."

F'Ghara smiled. "Perhaps not. But it does seem undeserved. You've made a friend today, not only for yourselves, but for all the Mettai." He reached behind his neck and untied the necklace bearing the small white stone. "Take this," he said, handing it to Besh. "It's a token of my gratitude for killing that woman, and if you encounter other Fal'Borna it will serve as proof that I've named you both friends of my people."

"Thank you, A'Laq," Besh said, closing his hand over the necklace.

F'Ghara placed one powerful hand on Besh's shoulder and the other on Sirj's. "Go in peace."

A few moments later, they steered Lici's cart out of the sept and started westward toward the Thraedes. Lici's few personal belongings were still in the cart—her clothes, several small blades that she might have used for making her baskets, some rope, and a small skin she'd used for water. Besh piled these things in a corner of the cart, and tried to ignore them as he rode beside Sirj in front. But he was aware of them constantly; he felt as though she were still there, watching them, silently accusing him. At last he told Sirj to stop.

"Why? Are you all right?"

"Just stop. Please."

Sirj tugged on the reins until the horse halted. Besh climbed down off the cart, grabbed her things, and threw them on the ground. Then he pulled his knife free, cut himself, and conjured a fire that quickly engulfed the pile he'd made. He watched it burn for a few moments before climbing back onto the cart.

"You can go now," he said.

"What about the horse and the cart?"

He looked sharply at Sirj, but the younger man was grinning. Besh smiled reluctantly.

"I suppose I can live with those," he said.

"Are you sure?" Sirj asked him, growing serious. "I'm certain the Fal'Borna would take them, particularly the horse."

"No, it's all right. And I don't feel much like walking to the Horn."

Sirj nodded and flicked the reins. "Good," he said, as the nag started forward again. "I don't either."

They traveled west for several days, covering more distance by far than they ever had with Lici. Besh still dreamed of the woman, though with each night that passed, the visions grew less disturbing, until Lici was little more than a distant, silent presence in dreams of other people and places. But she was always there, on the fringe of Besh's consciousness, and he wondered if she'd ever leave him.

During the waking hours he and Sirj talked but little, not because of any lingering discomfort between them, but simply because there seemed to be little to say. Sirj had some idea of what had happened between Besh and Lici that last terrible day, and it wouldn't take much imagination to piece together those details that hadn't been so apparent. Still, had Besh been in the younger man's position he would have been curious to know more, and he was grateful to Sirj for sparing him all the obvious questions.

Yet, he asked himself the same questions again and again. Could he have defeated Lici without killing her? Would he have wanted to? Had Lici, in some small way, been hoping that he would kill her? Was that why she had done and said all those things at the end? Even if she had been hoping to die, Besh knew better than to think that absolved him in some way. If anything, it made him wonder if he had been so transparent in wanting her dead that she'd seen fit to use him to achieve this dark end.

By their fourth morning out from F'Ghara's sept, Besh had grown weary of thinking about the old witch day and night. As they rode through yet another desolate stretch of plain, caught between the monotony of the grasses and another grey sky, it occurred to him that whatever else he might have accomplished by killing the woman, he certainly hadn't rid himself of her. For some reason, this thought struck him as funny and he chuckled.

"What are you laughing at?" Sirj asked him.

Besh shook his head. "It was nothing."

Sirj just shrugged.

"I've been thinking about Lici," Besh admitted, flexing his wounded hand, which still felt stiff and a bit sore. "Dreaming about her as well. And it just came to me that she's troubling me nearly as much now as she did when she was alive."

Sirj didn't laugh, nor did he say anything, at least at first. Besh could see, though, that he was considering what Besh had told him.

"You saved my life the other day," the younger man finally said. "And not just in the obvious way."

"What do you mean?"

Sirj didn't look at him, but Besh could see the muscles in the man's jaw bunching. "When I was riding to the sept to speak with the Fal'Borna, I wished that you'd gone instead of me. I assumed I'd make a mess of talking to them." He laughed. "Actually, I did make a mess of it."

"It seemed to me that you did just fine," Besh said. Even as he said the words though, he realized that he'd heard little about Sirj's encounter with the white-hairs.

"No, I didn't." He described for Besh his conversation with the warriors and his offer to submit to the a'laq's mind-bending magic. "They learned about Lici. They were ready to kill all three of us."

"I doubt I would have done any better."

"Yes, you would have," Sirj said. Then he shook his head. "That's not important, though. But I think that if you'd left me with Lici, I'd be dead now, and she'd have escaped."

Besh frowned. "I don't think—"

"Please." Sirj's smile was pained. "I know myself pretty well. I'm not being modest, or paying you idle compliments. I have my strengths, but using magic as you did isn't one of them." He glanced at Besh, looking almost shy. "Elica told me that you vowed to keep me safe, and I just wanted to say that you've done that and more." He shrugged again. "Anyway, I don't know what you're thinking about Lici, or what thoughts are troubling your sleep, but I wanted you to know that."

"Thank you," Besh said.

They rode in silence for a short while, the cart bouncing along through the grass, the wheels squeaking occasionally.

"Have you ever killed anyone?" Besh finally asked.

Sirj shook his head.

"I never had, either. I know I made the blood oath to Pyav, and I threatened Lici, but I never really thought I would. That's why I'm having these dreams, I think. I'd never killed a person, and I'm not entirely sure that I had to kill Lici."

"You think you had a choice?" Sirj asked, sounding incredulous.

"There might have been—"

"No," the younger man said. "Don't even say it. I saw you, Besh. You were bleeding all over. Your hand . . ." He shook his head, swallowing. "I don't know how you managed to fight her in that condition, but you were lucky to survive at all. If you hadn't killed her when you did, you would have died."

Besh shook his head slowly. "We could have learned more from her. She told me that there was no way to defeat her plague, but I have to believe there is, and that we might have learned something from her, given the time. Just as we finally learned about that merchant who bought her baskets."

"You're assuming that what she told us was true," Sirj said. "We don't even know that anymore."

Besh had never even considered this, and the idea of it hit him like a fist. "If she lied to us . . ." Abruptly he found himself blinking back tears. "That would mean we had nothing, that it was all for nothing."

"We stopped her," Sirj said. "Or, rather, you did. That's hardly nothing."

Besh started to argue the point, but at that moment, Sirj suddenly stood up from his seat in the cart, balancing precariously as the wagon continued to rock and shudder.

"Do you see that?" the younger man asked, pointing to the southwest.

Besh scanned the horizon, and half stood himself before being thrown back onto his seat by the motion of the cart. "I don't see anything," he said. But he knew better than to think this meant much. Sirj's eyes were keener by far than his own. "What is it?"

"Riders, I think."

Hope blossomed in his heart. "A merchant?"

Sirj shook his head, looking grim. "No cart. Just riders. White-hairs, I think."

"The Fal'Borna."

"They'd have to be, out here," Sirj said.

"The a'laq named us a friend of the Fal'Borna."

Sirj was already turning the cart northward, as if hoping to avoid the strangers. "Yes, he did. But I'd just as soon not put too much faith in the hospitality of the Fal'Borna."

Besh could hardly argue.

Sirj pushed Lici's old horse harder than Besh would have, always steering to the north, his eyes constantly flicking in the direction of the riders.

"Are they coming this way?" Besh asked after a time.

For several moments Sirj didn't answer. Finally, though, he exhaled through his teeth and whispered, "Damn." He glanced at Besh. "I didn't turn soon enough. I'm sorry."

"It was going to happen eventually."

"We can't outrun them," Sirj said, sounding desperate.

"We don't have to. We've done nothing wrong."

The younger man took a long breath. "Right," he said.

Still he drove the nag on, until Besh finally laid a hand gently on his arm. "You'll kill the beast," he said. "Let her rest."

"But the Fal'Borna—"

"We're not trusting in the . . . what was it you said? The hospitality of the Fal'Borna? But we can have some faith in ourselves, I think." Besh raised his eyebrows. "We've earned that, haven't we?"

Sirj smiled, though he looked nervous. "Yes, I suppose we have."

Reluctantly, he slowed the cart until they halted. Besh could now see the riders approaching, though he couldn't make out what they looked like. There appeared to be four of them, and as they drew nearer he saw that the two in front were definitely Qirsi. But the other two . . .

"What would two Eandi be doing out here, riding with white-hairs?" Sirj asked, speaking as much to himself as to Besh.

"Do they look like marauders?" Besh asked, suddenly fearful. "I may have just killed us by telling you to stop."

Sirj said nothing, but he pulled free his knife. Besh did the same. With all that had happened in the past few turns, and especially in the last several days, Besh didn't need anyone to tell him how potent Mettai magic could be. If these were marauders, thinking they had stumbled upon some easy prey in the form of Eandi merchants, they were in for a surprise.

Sirj went so far as to jump down from the cart, grab a handful of earth and cut the back of his hand. Besh, after just a moment's hesitation, did the same.

To his great surprise, though, the riders halted a short distance from them, the Eandi still remaining behind the two white-hairs.

"Drop your knives!" one of the Qirsi called to them. He was a young man, powerfully built with golden skin like that of the Fal'Borna. "And drop the dirt you're holding, too!"

"And leave ourselves defenseless against your magic?" Besh answered. "You must think we're fools!"

The white nag reared suddenly, kicking out violently and straining against her harness.

"That was language of beasts, Mettai," the young Qirsi said. "I also have shaping and fire. You're already defenseless against our magic. Now drop the dirt and blade!"

"If we're defenseless already, then it shouldn't matter to you that we hold on to them."

The Fal'Borna glared at him for several moments. Besh could see frustration written on his face. His companion said something to him that Besh couldn't hear, but the younger man didn't appear to pay any attention.

"I can shatter your blades, you know!" he said. "But at this distance, I might shatter your hands instead. Or your arms. Or maybe even your necks."

"Yes, well perhaps you'd like to see what Mettai magic can do!" Sirj shouted back at him.

Again the other Qirsi said something, and this time the Fal'Borna looked at him, though he didn't respond otherwise.

"They have seen what it can do," Besh whispered, knowing as he spoke the words that it was true. "They know about Lici."

"How can you tell?" Sirj asked.

Before Besh could answer, he felt a strange sensation in his hand. He knew instantly that it was magic—white-hair magic—and he actually cried out, thinking that they were under attack.

A moment later, though, another realization came to him. This wasn't shaping magic, or fire, or any of the other Qirsi magics that he'd learned to fear over the course of his life. This was healing. One of the white-hairs was healing the cut he'd made in the back of his hand.

"What is it?" Sirj asked him, his eyes wide with alarm.

Besh shook his head. "It's . . . it's all right. I'm all right."

The other white-hair said something to his mount and rode forward a short distance, his pale eyes fixed on Besh. He appeared older than the Fal'Borna. He clearly belonged to another clan. His skin was ghostly white. But unlike so many of the white-hairs Besh had met over the years, this man didn't look sickly or frail. He was as powerfully built as any Fal'Borna, and a good deal taller. He also had a kind face. He smiled now as he stopped in front of Besh.

"You did that," Besh said.

"Yes. I didn't mean to startle you, but it seemed the best way to get your attention, and to deny you access to your magic, at least for the moment."

He had a strange accent, one that Besh had never heard before.

"What did he do?" Sirj demanded. "What's going on?"

Besh raised a hand, signaling to Sirj that he should keep quiet for a moment.

"What clan are you from?" he asked the stranger. "I've never heard that accent before, and I thought I'd met Qirsi from every clan in the Southlands."

"I'm not from any clan that you know. I'm from the Forelands. My name is Grinsa jal Arriet."

The Forelands! It certainly explained the accent. And for some reason listening to the man speak and hearing where he was from put Besh's mind at ease. That, and the fact that the stranger had chosen to prove his might by healing him rather than attacking him.

"I'm called Besh," he said. "This is Sirj; he's my daughter's husband."

The two men exchanged nods.

"I need to ask you what you're carrying in your cart, Besh. It's important that you answer me honestly. Lives may be at stake."

Besh glanced at Sirj, an eyebrow raised. After a brief hesitation, Sirj nodded.

"We're carrying no baskets," Besh said, facing the Forelander again. "In fact, we're looking for a merchant who might have them."

The Fal'Borna kicked at the flanks of his mount, and in a moment was just beside Grinsa. "You know of the witch who made them?"

Besh took a breath, suddenly ashamed, though he knew he had no reason to be. "She was from our village."

The Forelander's eyes narrowed. "You speak of her as if she's dead."

"She is," Besh said. "I killed her."

The reaction to this from the two Qirsi, indeed, from all four of the strangers, was not at all what Besh had expected. Grinsa winced. The two Eandi, a large, heavy man with one good eye, and a slight man with a youthful face, both responded much the same way. The Fal'Borna, on the other hand, merely frowned.

"How long ago?" Grinsa finally asked in a thick voice.

"Just a few days. She attacked me, and she threatened to do to my people what she had done to the Y'Qatt."

"It's not just the Y'Qatt," the Fal'Borna said, glowering at him.

"Forgive me. I know that. But she intended it for the Y'Qatt. It was to be retribution for an old injury they did her."

The younger of the two Eandi steered his mount closer to those of the Qirsi. "You say you're looking for a merchant. Did the woman tell you his name?"

Sirj glanced Besh's way and shook his head.

"I'll answer your questions in good time," Besh said, understanding immediately. "But first I want to know what you intend to do to us." He nodded at his hand. "You've shown me what your magic can do; you know what Mettai magic is capable of. I don't want to fight you, and I'm not sure that we can prevail if you force the matter. But I'm not going to tell you all we know so that you can turn around and kill us." His gaze flicked toward the younger Qirsi. "I know how the Fal'Borna deal with those they consider enemies. I know as well that the last a'laq we encountered named us friends of the Fal'Borna after I killed Lici. But I don't expect you to take my word on that." He pulled from his pocket the necklace F'Ghara had given him and held it up for the Qirsi to see. "He gave us this."

The Fal'Borna glanced at the stone and nodded. "What was the a'laq's name?" he asked.

"F'Ghara."

The man looked at Grinsa. "I know him. He leads a small sept. He has few Weavers, if he has any at all."

"But if he's named them as friends of your people . . . ?" Grinsa asked.

"Then we have no choice but to honor his decision."

Grinsa looked at Besh again and opened his hands. "There's your answer."

Still Besh hesitated.

The Forelander smiled. "I haven't been among the Fal'Borna for long, and I don't pretend to understand all their customs. But I can tell you that they take naming someone a friend or enemy quite seriously. If this a'laq has declared his friendship, you're safe on the plain."

Besh considered this for several moments. "Very well." He looked at the young Eandi. "To answer your question, the merchant's name was Brint HedFarren. At least that's what Lici told me."

The Eandi nodded grimly. "That's the right name. I've met HedFarren. He doesn't have the baskets anymore. He sold them to other merchants."

The elation Besh felt upon learning that Lici hadn't lied to him vanished as quickly as it had come. "Damn. How many other merchants?"

"Several."

"We were about to turn toward the Horn to look for some of them when we saw you," Grinsa said. "You're welcome to travel with us if you'd like."

"They should go to the Ofirean," the Fal'Borna said with quiet intensity. "Some of the merchants are headed there."

The two Qirsi eyed each other, but said nothing

"We're far from our home already," Sirj finally told them. "We can go as far as the Horn, but we're not going all the way down to the sea. That's too much to ask of . . ." He broke off, his face reddening.

Besh grinned. "What he was going to say, before he thought better of it, is that it's too much to ask of an old man like me." Glancing at Sirj he saw that the man's cheeks were still red, but a small grin was playing at the corners of his mouth. "As much as I'm loath to admit it," he went on, "he's right."

Grinsa spoke to the Fal'Borna again, lowering his voice so that none of the rest of them could hear. Besh couldn't hear the Fal'Borna's response, either, but after a few more words from Grinsa it seemed that the two of them came to some sort of understanding.

"All right then," the Fal'Borna said brusquely to Besh and Sirj. "You can ride with us. Try to keep up."

He wheeled his horse away from them and started westward, giving the rest of them little choice but to follow. Grinsa remained where he was for a few moments, eyeing Besh and Sirj. But in the end, he rode ahead with the Fal'Borna.

Besh and Sirj started after them, as did the two Eandi. The younger one trailed behind the Qirsi, but the old one, with his scarred face and single dark eye, pulled abreast of the cart.

"You're fools to cast your lot with us," he said. "You should have gone your own way when you had the chance. You still can if you handle it right. Tell them you'll go to the Ofirean after all, and then, once we're far enough away, turn back home."

"We want to find those merchants," Besh said.

The man shook his head. "As I said, you're fools. But I suppose I should have expected no less from Mettai."

Besh sensed that Sirj was bristling. "How is it you came to be traveling with them, friend?" he asked quickly, hoping to keep the younger man from saying something they'd both regret.

"I'm their prisoner," the Eandi said. "I sold some of those crazy woman's baskets to a sept north of here, and the Fal'Borna hunted me down. Me and the lad there," he added, nodding toward the young Eandi. "Our one hope of winning our freedom was helping them kill the witch. But now you've done that for us, and I don't know what that means. Maybe they'll let us go; maybe they'll execute us. In either case, you should get away while you can. I don't care what the Forelander says: you can't trust the Fal'Borna."

He spurred his mount angrily and rode ahead of them.

"Do you believe him?" Sirj asked once the man was out of earshot.

Besh considered this as he eyed their new companions. "Yes," he said. "I suppose I do."

"But he claims they're prisoners. What's to keep them . . . ?" He trailed off. Besh could see him working it out. "Magic," he finally whispered. "Language of beasts, the threat of fire or shaping. That would be enough."

Besh nodded. "I should think so."

"Maybe he's right, then," Sirj said. "Maybe we should get away while we can."

"I think we're past that point already." Besh watched Grinsa briefly, noting that while he and the Fal'Borna rode together, they didn't speak. "Besides, I'm intrigued by the Forelander, by this entire company, actually. How did they all come to be journeying together? Even if we believe what the Eandi said, that doesn't explain why the Forelander is with them. It's all very odd."

"It's not our problem," Sirj said.

Besh shrugged. "No, it's not. But they seem intent on finding Lici's baskets, and that is our problem. If we're going to find a way to undo her curse, it might be helpful to have access to Qirsi magic, as well as our own."

Sirj regarded him briefly, then shook his head. "You have a better mind for these matters than I do. I hadn't thought of that."

"You would have soon enough."

Sirj smiled, and they rode on, following their new companions.

They rested a few times, seeking out the rills that flowed through this part of the plain, so that their horses could graze and drink, while they themselves ate a bit. The others said little during these respites, and Besh thought it best to follow their example. The two Eandi avoided one another, which surprised him, though their relationship seemed no more or less strained than that between the two Qirsi. The more Besh watched these four the more curious he grew.

Eventually, later in the day, his curiosity getting the better of him, he had Sirj steer their cart closer to the younger of the two Eandi.

"My pardon, friend," he called to the man. "I was wondering if I might ask you a question or two."

The young man eyed him briefly, then nodded.

"I'm Besh," he said, knowing that the man had already heard this, but wanting him to introduce himself. "This is Sirj."

"I remember. I'm Jasha Ziffel."

"It's nice to meet you, Jasha. I was curious as to how you came to be riding with the white-hairs."

Jasha pressed his lips thin, looking pale and very young. His eyes strayed to the other Eandi. "That's a difficult story."

"Your companion—the other Eandi—he says that you're both prisoners of the Fal'Borna."

"That's true, as far as it goes."

Besh frowned. "As far as it goes?"

Jasha shifted uncomfortably in his saddle. "Torgan . . . that's his name. Torgan Plye. He's a merchant; both of us are, actually. In any case, Torgan managed to buy some of the baskets your witch made, and then he sold them to a Fal'Borna sept. I don't think he knew what he was doing, but the Fal'Borna blame him for what happened afterward. He fled, and I went with him. I'm still not certain why. I thought that together we might find the woman before she could kill again. But I also didn't entirely believe Torgan's story, and, just in case he was lying, I wanted to keep him from spreading any more of the disease."

"So you and he aren't actually friends," Sirj said.

A bitter smile touched his lips and then vanished. "Torgan doesn't have friends, at least not that I know of." He faced Besh again. "I suppose you'd say that we're prisoners. But they allowed me to leave the camp in order to get information from other merchants."

"And you returned."

Besh kept his voice even as he said this, but Jasha seemed to hear a challenge in the words. He straightened and nodded once.

"Yes, I did. I could have run away, but they would have killed Torgan—at least that's what they said. And I want to find these merchants. I wanted to find the witch, too. I'm . . . I'm glad to know that she's dead."

"What can you tell me about the Qirsi?" Besh asked, eager to change the subject.

The young merchant shrugged. "Not much, really."

"Do you know how Grinsa came to be living among the Fal'Borna?"

Jasha shook his head. "No, though I gather that it wasn't by choice. He and Q'Daer—that's the Fal'Borna—they don't get along very well."

That much Besh had gathered for himself.

He had other questions, but he didn't want to push Jasha too far. Building a friendship under these circumstances was, he decided, a bit like tending his garden back in Kirayde. Patience was the key. He'd established a bit of trust with the man, and no doubt Jasha would be able to tell him more in the days to come. Better then to let their rapport grow slowly.

"Thank you, Jasha," he said, smiling. "You've been most helpful."

The Eandi nodded, but he didn't ride off, nor did he return Besh's smile.

"Why did she do it?" he finally asked. "You knew the woman, right?"

Besh felt the color drain from his face. "Lici, you mean?"

"Was that her name? Lici? I thought I heard you say it before, but I wasn't certain."

"Yes," Besh said, his mouth suddenly dry. "Her name was Lici."

Jasha shook his head slowly. "It's a nice name. Friendly. I suppose names don't mean as much as we think they do." He shook his head again. "You said before that she wanted to avenge some old injury done her by the Y'Qatt. Can you tell me more?"

At first, Besh was reluctant to answer. It was a Mettai matter and all his life he'd been wary of Eandi and Qirsi alike. In the end, however, he decided that he owed Jasha the truth. The young merchant had been forthcoming with him; Besh could hardly refuse to answer his questions.

"As a young girl Lici lost her entire village to the pestilence. She tried to find Qirsi who could heal her family, but she found the Y'Qatt instead of the Fal'Borna and they refused to help her."

"The Y'Qatt wouldn't use magic to heal themselves much less strangers from another village."

"You and I know that," Besh said. "But Lici was a child at the time. She'd never even heard of the Y'Qatt."

"And now there are Y'Qatt children and Fal'Borna children who will grow up hating the Mettai." Jasha looked like he might weep. "We saw a village—a Fal'Borna sept—that had been destroyed by her plague. They'll hate her forever, and because of that they'll hate all of you. This is how wars begin. I don't know how the first of the Blood Wars started, and I'm sure it didn't involve a plague like this one. But that's beside the point. People on this plain will hate the Mettai for generations. Y'Qatt and Fal'Borna children will be taught that your magic is . . . evil."

Besh smiled sadly. "Aren't they taught that already?"

"You know what I mean."

"Yes, I do," Besh said. "That's why Sirj and I are out here, looking for the baskets. That's why we went after Lici. You might even say that's the reason she's dead."

Jasha looked away again, his face coloring. "You're right, of course. I shouldn't have said all that. I know it's not your fault."

"No," Besh said. "It's not. But that's beside the point, too, isn't it?"

The young merchant met his gaze again and nodded. "Yes. I'm afraid it is."

Chapter 16

They made camp for the night by a wide, slow stream that carved through the grasses like the curved blade of an Uulranni horseman. The stream was swollen from the recent rains, its waters black in the dying light.

While Grinsa hunted for scraps of wood to burn and Q'Daer pulled food from their sack of stores, the merchants gathered stones from the streambed to make a fire ring. The Fal'Borna had said nothing for hours, but Grinsa sensed that Q'Daer remained uncomfortable with their new companions and unhappy with him for asking the Mettai to join them. Perhaps he should have been concerned by this—the two of them had reached something of an understanding in recent days, but it wouldn't take much to undo the small bit of progress they'd made.

Just now, though, Grinsa couldn't bring himself to care. He and the Fal'Borna were never going to be true allies. Grinsa only wanted to get away from E'Menua's sept; Q'Daer could only take this as an affront.

The two Mettai, though, struck Grinsa as well-meaning and sincere. He was eager to speak with them beyond the hearing of Q'Daer and the two merchants, but this proved difficult to arrange. As soon as the company had finished eating their modest meal of dried meat, hard bread, and cheese provided by the Mettai, Q'Daer pulled him aside.

"We need to be more vigilant now," the Fal'Borna said, his gaze straying toward the merchants. "We need to watch them all the time. You know this, right?"

Grinsa frowned. "You think they'll try to escape?"

Q'Daer shook his head. "They no longer need to escape. They have magic now."

He shook his head. "I'm confused. Are you talking about Jasha and Torgan, or the Mettai?"

"All of them, of course."

"I thought that most Eandi hated the Mettai."

Q'Daer raked a hand through his hair, looking exasperated. "They're dark-eyes," he said, as if Grinsa were the biggest fool in the Southlands. "There's no separating them now. Already I've seen both merchants speaking with the new ones. It's only a matter of time before they try to get away."

Grinsa wondered if they wouldn't be better off allowing Torgan to go, but he kept this to himself.

"I don't think we have anything to fear from Besh and Sirj," he said instead. "Or from the merchants, for that matter."

"You're wrong. We need to keep watch at night. Do you want the first shift or the second?"

"Neither," Grinsa said, shaking his head, knowing that he was only going to make the Fal'Borna angry. "If you want to stay awake all night you can, but I intend to sleep."

Q'Daer glowered at him.

"If it would make you feel better," Grinsa went on a moment later, sensing an opportunity, "I can speak with the Mettai. Afterwards, if they say anything that seems alarming, I'll keep watch with you."

"You're too trusting, Forelander. You may have had Eandi friends in the Forelands, but dark-eyes are different here."

Grinsa merely shrugged. Q'Daer waited, as if expecting Grinsa to say more. When he didn't, the young Weaver stalked off angrily.

He watched Q'Daer walk away and then started off himself in the opposite direction, intending to find the Mettai. Instead, he found himself face-to-face with Torgan.

"They killed the witch," the man said, his scarred face livid in the pale pink glow of the rising moons.

"Yes," Grinsa said, exhaling, wanting no part of this conversation. "It seems they did."

"What does that mean for us?"

Grinsa shook his head. "I don't know, Torgan. It'll prove to E'Menua that the woman was real, and that you were telling the truth. On the other hand, the a'laq made it clear that he wanted us to kill the woman and bring glory to his sept. We didn't do that."

"So he might still execute us."

"He might. He might also refuse to let my family and me leave the sept. I just don't know. I'm sorry."

He tried to walk past the merchant, but Torgan blocked his way.

"You have to let us get away," he said, dropping his voice, and glancing around, as if afraid that Q'Daer might be nearby. "Maybe you needed us before to help you find the woman and her baskets. But she's dead, and now you have the Mettai to help you. Jasha and me—we can't do any more. Surely you see that."

"Torgan—"

"They'll kill us. That's what E'Menua wanted to do all along, and now there's nothing to stop him."

"I can't let you go, Torgan."

The man glared at him. "Why not?"

"Because if I do, E'Menua will never let us leave."

Grinsa half expected the merchant to hit him.

"You white-hair bastard! You'd trade my life for your freedom."

"Not if I don't have to, no. I'll do what I can to keep you and Jasha alive. But if I let you go now, my wife and I have no chance at all. We'll go back to the sept—all of us. And we'll win our freedom together."

Once more Grinsa tried to walk past, and again Torgan stopped him, this time putting a hand to Grinsa's chest.

Grinsa glanced down at the man's hand before meeting his gaze again.

"You want me to shatter that?" he demanded, his voice level.

Torgan blinked once. Then he dropped his hand to his side. "You're killing us," he said bitterly.

"Not if I can help it," Grinsa told him. "But let's be honest, Torgan. If our positions were reversed, you'd do exactly the same thing. Actually you'd do far less for me than I've done for you."

He didn't wait for a reply; he simply walked away. This time, Torgan didn't try to stop him. But Grinsa heard him mutter "White-hair bastard" under his breath.

Grinsa paused, but then walked on, knowing that nothing good would come of prolonging their confrontation.

It was late enough that he feared the Mettai might already have gone to sleep. But both men were sitting beside their cart in the light of the moons. They weren't speaking to each other, nor did they appear to be doing anything in particular. It almost seemed that they had been waiting for him to join them. As Grinsa approached, the older one whispered something to his companion that sounded like, "At last."

"May I join you?" Grinsa asked, pretending that he hadn't heard.

Besh nodded. "Please."

He sat in front of them, eyeing them both.

"It seems that all in your company bring their troubles to you," Besh said. "How is it that a Forelander has won the trust not only of two Eandi merchants, but also a Fal'Borna warrior?"

Grinsa laughed. "Is that what you think is going on?"

"Isn't it?" the old man asked. A small smile tugged at the corners of his mouth, leading Grinsa to wonder if the Mettai was mocking him. The man's tone, though, was gentle, and he didn't strike Grinsa as the type of person who would go out of his way to make an enemy of a stranger. He had a kind look to him, a smile that appeared open and sincere. His face was round and friendly, with deep creases in the skin around his mouth and a web of wrinkles at the corners of his eyes. He had a dark complexion and eyes that looked black in the dim light. His white hair was cut short. Like the younger man, he wasn't particularly tall or broad, but he was lean despite his years, and there was a quiet strength to him.

"The truth is I don't think any of them trust me. But they trust one another even less."

"Sounds like we've joined a fun group," the young Mettai said quietly.

Grinsa's laughter seemed to surprise him. He smiled briefly, but looked uncomfortable.

"You didn't answer my question," Besh said.

"Didn't I?"

"Not really. How is it that you're here, journeying with these men who don't trust you or each other?"

Grinsa smiled wearily and glanced up at the sky. A few stars shone brightly through the moonglow and small white clouds drifted past. It was as lovely a night as he'd seen in the Southlands. Abruptly his longing for Cresenne and Bryntelle was like a knife in his heart.

"It's a long tale to begin so late in the evening."

Besh said nothing. He just stared back at Grinsa, as if daring the gleaner not to explain himself.

"We were forced by circumstance to leave the Forelands," he said at last.

"We?" Besh asked.

Grinsa smiled, though once more he felt a twisting in his heart at the thought of Cresenne and Bryntelle. It had been too long since last he reached for Cresenne's thoughts and walked in her dreams, as a Weaver could. Tonight perhaps, later before he slept.

"Yes. My wife and our daughter made the journey with me."

"How old is your daughter?"

"Not even a year."

Besh's eyes widened. "She must be strong to have traveled so far at such a tender age."

"Yes, she is, like her mother."

Besh nodded approvingly before gesturing for Grinsa to continue.

Grinsa began to tell the Mettai about all that had befallen him and his family since their arrival in the Southlands, starting with their trek across the Eandi sovereignties. He described how they had come to be living among the Fal'Borna, explaining as best he could the bargain he had struck with E'Menua in order to save the lives of the Eandi merchants. At first he was reluctant to reveal all of this to men he barely knew, but as he continued to talk the words came easier. He sensed that Besh and Sirj merely wished to understand what he was doing out here on the plain, riding with Q'Daer and the merchants, and he felt relieved to be telling his tale to people who had no cause to judge him or doubt his word.

For a long time after he finished speaking, neither Besh nor Sirj said anything. He could tell, though, what they were thinking, and so he wasn't surprised when Besh finally gave voice to his thoughts.

"You've risked a great deal for men you barely know."

"I suppose," Grinsa said, shrugging. "From what I've heard of the Mettai, you're not well thought of by either the Eandi or the Qirsi. And yet the two of you have left your home and family in order to save strangers from the curse of a madwoman."

Besh grinned. "Only a fool would choose to justify himself by likening his actions to those of a bigger fool."

Grinsa laughed. "Well said." His smile faded slowly. "The Fal'Borna thought me foolish as well. Maybe I was. Torgan and Jasha meant nothing to me at the time, and I've since come to question whether Torgan was worth saving. But back in the Forelands I met a man who was falsely accused of a crime, and if I hadn't helped him prove his innocence he would have been executed and our land would have suffered greatly for the loss. I don't know if either of the merchants will someday justify whatever sacrifice I've made. But, like the rest of us, they deserve the chance to prove their worth."

"I don't pretend to know much about your land," Besh said. "But I can't imagine that many men there think as you do. Is that why you left?"

"No," Grinsa said. "We left for a number of reasons, and some aren't mine to tell. But I'm a Weaver, and in the Forelands my kind are feared. By law Weavers and their families are supposed to be put to death. I fought in a war on behalf of the Eandi courts and because of this, my king, rather than following the law of the land, allowed us to leave."

"Another noble man," Besh said. "I wish I'd had the chance to see the Forelands when I was younger. It sounds like an extraordinary place."

Sirj hadn't said much since Grinsa's arrival, but now he looked at the gleaner, his brow creased. "Before, when you were telling us about your bargain with the a'laq, you said that he expected you to find Lici and kill her yourself, or perhaps return her to his sept. By killing her ourselves, we've . . . we've made matters more difficult for you."

Grinsa shrugged again, conceding the point. "I don't get the feeling that you had much choice." He nodded toward Besh. "You were hurt, your hand especially."

"How can you know that?" Sirj asked.

"I sense a residue of the magic used to heal him. I thought I could feel only Qirsi magic, but apparently Mettai magic isn't all that different."

"Sirj healed some of my wounds," Besh said, "but the Fal'Borna healed me as well. That might be what you're sensing."

"Perhaps. But you acted out of necessity. I can hardly blame you for killing a woman we ourselves were hunting."

"And now you're hunting these merchants who have Lici's baskets."

Grinsa nodded, looking grave. "Yes."

"Do you think you can find them?" Besh asked, sounding doubtful himself.

"I don't know," Grinsa said. "Probably not." It was a more honest answer then he would have given the others in his company, but already he found himself trusting these men. "But I'm not even certain how much difference it will make if we can."

"I don't understand," Sirj said, frowning deeply. "I thought finding those baskets was the most important thing left for us to do."

Grinsa rubbed a hand over his face. "It probably is, though that isn't saying much. The point is, even if we find some of the baskets, we don't know what to do with them. I suppose we can try burning them, but we can't be certain even that will be safe." He eyed both men closely. "What we really need is a way to defeat the plague."

"We don't know how to do that," Besh told him. "I'm not even certain that Lici did."

"Did you ask her?"

The Mettai nodded. "Yes, I did."

Grinsa nodded knowingly. "And she refused to help you."

"Worse," Besh said. "She said there was no way to undo her curse. 'It can't be undone,' she told me. And then she said, 'There's no spell you could make that would defeat it.'"

"She could have been lying to you," Grinsa said.

"She had no reason to lie. It was the day I killed her, and at the time she thought that she had me fully under her control." Besh shook his head. "I think she was trying to break my spirit, but I also think she was using the truth to do so."

"'There's no spell you could make . . .'" Grinsa repeated. "It seems an odd way to say it, don't you think?"

"I don't follow," Besh said.

"She said it can't be undone, and that there was no spell *you* could make that would stop it. So Mettai magic alone can't do it. But what if there's another way, one that uses Qirsi magic as well?"

Besh nodded. "I've thought of that, though it never occurred to me that Lici might be hinting at the possibility. But even if there is a way, I have no idea where to begin. Do you?"

Grinsa actually laughed. "Not at all. A turn or two ago I didn't even know that your people still existed. Beyond knowing that you need blood to conjure, I have no idea how your magic works."

"You make us sound like ghouls," Sirj said. "We can't conjure with just any blood. It has to be our own. And we don't need much. Just enough to mix with earth."

Grinsa held up his hands in a placating gesture. "I meant no offense."

"It's not blood magic," Sirj went on, as if he hadn't heard. "That's what others call it, Qirsi and Eandi alike. It's earth magic; that's what they should call it. 'Blood magic' makes it sound . . . evil."

Besh laid a hand on Sirj's arm. The younger man glanced at him and then looked away, his lips pressed thin.

"It's not easy being a Mettai in the Southlands," Besh said quietly.

"You may find this hard to believe, but that's something we have in common. Being a Qirsi in the Forelands can be trying at times as well, and being a Weaver is worst of all."

"So you told us. It must be a great relief for you to be here in the Southlands." Besh said this with a wry smile on his wizened face.

"Given the chance, would you give up being Mettai in order to be accepted by the Qirsi or the Eandi?"

"No," Besh said quickly. "I'm proud of my ancestry. Sirj is, too. As you say, this is something we have in common."

"Can you explain to me how your magic works?"

Besh shrugged. "There's not much to it, really." He held up his hand so that the back of it faced Grinsa. Even in the soft glow of the moons, Grinsa could see dozens of thin white scars, stark against the old man's brown skin.

"I cut myself here, blend my blood with a handful of dirt and . . ." He trailed off. "Actually it's probably easiest just to show you."

He drew his knife from its sheath and pulled the blade across the back of his hand. Grinsa noticed that he didn't wince at all, as if he felt no pain.

"Does that hurt you?" he asked.

Besh smiled, though he didn't take his eyes off his hand. "A bit. I hardly notice it anymore." His looked up for just an instant, his gaze meeting Grinsa's. "I've been doing this for a long time."

Blood had welled from the wound and now Besh caught it deftly on the flat of his knife. Balancing it there, he reached down with his cut hand, picked up a handful of earth, and tipped his blade so that the blood poured into the same hand, making a small dark pool in the soil. An instant later, the blood and dirt swirled together as if stirred by some unseen force.

Besh glanced at Sirj. "What should I do?"

The younger man shrugged.

"Blood to earth," Besh said in a low voice. "Life to power, power to thought, earth to fox." As he finished the incantation, he opened his hand with a quick motion, so that the ball of dark mud flew from his fingers. Before it hit the ground it took the form of a fox, which landed nimbly in an alert crouch and stared up at Grinsa, its eyes shining with moonlight.

Grinsa stared back at it for several moments, afraid even to breathe. At last he chanced a question. "Is it r—"

The animal bolted at the sound of his voice, bounding into the grasses and vanishing from view.

"Is it real?" Besh said. "Is that what you were going to ask?"

Grinsa gazed after the creature, shaking his head. "That's the most remarkable thing I've ever seen!" He faced Besh again. "You created a living creature out of nothing!"

"No," Besh said. "That's not what I did at all. I created a living creature out of life—my blood, Elined's earth."

Grinsa eyed him briefly, then nodded. It made sense when he put it that way.

"That litany you recited; must you do that each time you conjure?"

"Yes," Besh said. "I've met some Mettai who recite the words in near silence, but they're necessary for the magic to work." He licked the blood from the back of his hand, and then licked the blade clean before returning it to its sheath. Seeing that Grinsa was watching him he said, "A Mettai never wastes blood. What we don't use, we return to our bodies."

Grinsa nodded again. That made sense, too. Q'Daer had said much the same thing to him the day he and Cresenne first arrived in E'Menua's sept. *A Fal'Borna wastes nothing.* Laws of survival in a hard land. He looked off into the grasses again, hoping for another glimpse of Besh's fox.

"Qirsi magic can't do anything like that," he said.

Besh smiled once more. "No, I don't suppose it can."

"That's how she was able to do it."

The old man's smile faded. "Lici, you mean."

Grinsa nodded. "Qirsi magic couldn't have done that, either. Don't get me wrong," he was quick to add. "My people are capable of doing terrible things with their powers, but a Qirsi couldn't have conjured a plague as she did, any more than one of us could have created that fox."

"Had you asked me a year ago," Besh said, "I wouldn't have thought a Mettai could do such a thing either. Lici surprised us all."

"You and she fought before she died, is that right?" Grinsa asked.

Besh's mouth twitched slightly. "Yes."

"How does that work?"

"What do you mean?"

Grinsa took a breath, wishing immediately that he hadn't asked the question. He was curious, and he thought perhaps that if he learned enough about Mettai magic, he might think of a way to counter the witch's plague. But he didn't see a way to explain what he meant without revealing more of his own past than he would have liked.

"I did battle with another Weaver," he explained. "Both of us commanded armies of Qirsi." He didn't mention that he and his allies had been hopelessly outnumbered or that in the end his victory was bought by the sacrifice of another. "When I fought him, I sensed what magic he was using and countered it by drawing on the same magic. If he attacked with shaping power, I defended our ranks with shaping. If he sent fire at us, I sent fire back at him." He shook his head. "But I don't see how a Mettai could fight the same way."

"We don't. When I fought Lici, I just had to guess what spell she intended to cast at me, and then respond accordingly. Sometimes I guessed correctly, sometimes I didn't. And in the end, I had no defense against her attacks except to kill her."

Sirj was watching him, as if he hadn't heard the entire tale of Besh's fight with Lici. For his part, Besh looked more uncomfortable than he had at any point in their conversation.

"In any case," the man said, staring at the ground. "That's how it happened for me. I think Mettai magic isn't intended for combat."

Grinsa smiled, drawing a curious look from Besh.

"Forgive me," Grinsa said. "But many of us in the Forelands have long said the same thing about Qirsi magic."

"But throughout the history of the Southlands—"

"I know." Grinsa shrugged. "Perhaps we're all inclined to understate the extent of our powers. Or maybe this just proves that anything can be made into a weapon if we're desperate enough."

They fell silent for several moments, the two Mettai looking thoughtful, Grinsa watching them. He had assumed for so long that he would find no allies in this land, that his struggle to defeat the curse and win freedom for himself and his family was his alone. Meeting these two men, he was no longer so certain of this. But he was also wary of trusting them too quickly. He sensed how eager he was to claim them as friends, and he feared that he was being rash.

Grinsa stood, intending to return to the fire where Q'Daer and the Eandi merchants were sleeping.

"Thank you for speaking with me," he said.

Besh smiled, though it looked forced. "Of course."

Grinsa started to leave, but the old man called him back.

"The older merchant—I've forgotten his name."

"Torgan. Torgan Plye."

"Yes," Besh said, "Torgan. He told us that he and the younger Eandi were your prisoners."

"They're not my prisoners. But they are prisoners of the Fal'Borna."

The man nodded once. "I see. He made it sound as though we were making ourselves prisoners by agreeing to journey with you."

"You told me yourself that a Fal'Borna a'laq had named you a friend of the clan. You have nothing to fear from Q'Daer. He's a difficult man, and he has little use for Torgan. But he'll honor a declaration of friendship from another a'laq, no matter how small the sept he leads."

"So you don't believe that we've placed ourselves in peril."

"No," Grinsa told him. "I don't." He hesitated, but only for a moment. He didn't like the idea of having to trust all to instinct, but he felt certain that he had nothing to fear from Besh or Sirj. "And I make you this promise," he went on a moment later. "If Q'Daer or any other Fal'Borna threatens either of you without cause, I'll do everything in my power to protect you." He grinned. "Though given what I've seen of the magic you wield, I can't imagine you'd really need my help."

This time Besh's smile appeared genuine. "And I make you this oath in return, Grinsa of the Forelands. If we can do anything to stop Lici's plague from spreading and help you and your family win your freedom, we'll do it."

Grinsa inclined his head, acknowledging the offer. "Thank you for that."

He turned and started back toward the dim light of the fire, feeling happier than he had at any time since the company left E'Menua's sept. It wasn't just that he now had allies in his fight for freedom, though certainly that gave him more hope than he'd had in what seemed like ages. He also felt that he'd found a friend in Besh.

It was late, and he was deeply weary. But it had been too long since last he spoke with Cresenne. So before lying down to rest, he walked a short distance from the camp, sat down among the grasses, which shone faintly with the pink and white glow of the moons, and reached with his mind southward to where his beloved slept.

Chapter 17

For several days after she spoke with E'Menua, Cresenne refused to go to L'Norr's z'kal at mealtime. She knew that the young Weaver would be expecting her, that E'Menua would have wasted no time in making arrangements for the man to feed her and Bryntelle. She knew as well that her refusal to go was pointless. She didn't manage to find any new sources of food in the intervening days, nor did she magically inure herself to hunger and its effects.

It was pride that kept her away. She didn't want to feel like a beggar again, as she had the night she ate with F'Solya and I'Joled, and she certainly didn't want to be made to feel like a whore. So she kept to her z'kal, carefully rationing what few scraps of food remained from the journey she and Grinsa had made across the sovereignties. She nursed Bryntelle as she usually did, but by the end of the third day, she realized from her daughter's cries that she was no longer making enough milk to satisfy her.

That was what finally broke her. Starving herself was one thing; starving Bryntelle was another entirely.

On the fourth evening, after leaving the tanning circle, she went not to her z'kal, but to that of L'Norr, which was located near the center of the sept, not far from E'Menua and D'Pera's shelter. She slowed as she drew near L'Norr's home, trying desperately to think of any other way she might survive without having to do this. But her stomach hurt, and her mind felt dull, and Bryntelle was crying again, having fussed for much of the day. Cresenne glanced around and realized that several people were watching her, no doubt wondering what she was doing so far from her own z'kal. They would see her knock on the outside of the young Weaver's shelter, and they would assume the worst, but there was little she could do about that. For all she knew, that too had been part of E'Menua's plan: anything to drive a wedge between her and Grinsa. Maybe he hoped that if Cresenne grew unhappy enough she would simply take Bryntelle and leave the sept.

Several days ago, this thought would have been enough to send her back to her own z'kal without a bite to eat. It was a measure of how wretched she had become that she straightened, stepped forward, and, heedless of the stares, tapped on the flap that covered the entrance to the shelter.

For a moment her knock was greeted only by silence, and Cresenne wondered if L'Norr was elsewhere.

Then she heard a voice call out quietly, "Enter."

She hesitated before pushing the flap aside and stepping into the z'kal.

It was dark within, and like all the z'kals she had been in, it smelled like sweat and smoke and food. Her stomach rumbled loudly.

L'Norr sat on the far side of a small fire, stirring a pot of stew. He glanced up at her, but then quickly looked away.

"Sit," he said, waving vaguely at the ground in front of her. "I wasn't certain whether your child eats this food yet, but I made extra, in case he does."

"She's a girl," Cresenne said, still standing.

He looked up at that, meeting her gaze. "Forgive me. She."

He turned his attention back to the stew, stirring it again and crumbling into it some dried leaves that looked much like the rildagreen F'Solya had used. L'Norr looked much like the other Fal'Borna men Cresenne had encountered. Broad in the shoulders and chest, with long white hair that he wore loose to his shoulders and bright yellow eyes that glittered like gold coins in the firelight. His face was rounder than that of the a'laq or F'Solya's husband, which made him look barely old enough to be living away from his parents.

The man glanced up at her again. "Please, sit," he said. "You have nothing to fear from me."

"You know that I'm Grinsa's wife," she said, not moving. "I don't consider myself his concubine, and I'm not looking to be anyone else's. Not even for food."

A slight smile touched his lips. "I have a concubine."

Cresenne felt her face reddening. "Oh."

"The a'laq told me you needed food." He shrugged. "I have more than I can eat. So sit down, and have something."

Still uncomfortable, she lowered herself to the ground on the opposite side of the fire. Bryntelle was looking around the z'kal, chattering nonsense, her pale eyes wide. Eventually, her gaze came to rest on a small pile of items that sat along the edge of the shelter: a small hide-covered drum, a shield and spear, what looked to be a ceremonial mask. The child let out a small squeal and then tried to wrench herself out of Cresenne's grasp so that she could go investigate. Not that she could crawl or walk yet, but she seemed determined nevertheless, and she began to fuss again when Cresenne didn't put her down.

"Is she all right?" L'Norr asked, a slight frown on his face.

"Yes. She's just curious."

"About what?"

Cresenne laughed in spite of herself. "About everything."

He nodded, but said nothing more, stirring the pot again. Cresenne felt that she ought to say something, but nothing came to her and as their silence lengthened she grew increasingly uncomfortable. Before she could break the lull in their conversation, however, there was a quick tap on the flap covering the entrance to the z'kal. L'Norr glanced up, looking alarmed, but before he could say anything, the flap was pushed aside and a young woman stepped into the shelter.

"T'Lisha!" the Weaver said.

She didn't answer him. Instead, she stared down at Cresenne a hard expression on her pretty oval face.

"So, it's true," she said after some time. Her gaze flicked toward L'Norr briefly, then quickly back to Cresenne, as if she expected her to attack at any moment. "They said that she was here, but I didn't believe them."

Coltish. That was the one word that came to Cresenne's mind as she looked at the girl. She was tall for a Fal'Borna—nearly as tall as Cresenne herself. And unlike F'Solya and so many of the other women of the sept, she was lanky, her body showing only the first faint signs of maturing to womanhood. Her skin was smooth and colored golden brown like that of the other Fal'Borna, and her eyes were so pale they almost looked white. She was exceedingly pretty, but Cresenne couldn't help thinking that she was far too young to be any man's concubine.

She didn't give voice to this, of course. Rather she extended a hand in greeting. She would have preferred to stand, if for no other reason than to put herself on equal footing with the girl. But she still held Bryntelle in her lap, and without being certain how T'Lisha was going to respond to the situation, she didn't want her child anywhere but in her arms.

"My name's Cresenne," she said, making herself smile.

"I know who you are," the girl shot back.

Cresenne kept the smile fixed on her lips. "Good! Then you understand that I'm already married and that you have nothing to fear from me."

The girl narrowed her eyes, but didn't respond immediately.

Cresenne pressed on. "With Grinsa gone, my daughter and I have no food, and at the a'laq's suggestion we've come to L'Norr for our evening meal. He's generously offered to share his stew with us. Will you be joining us as well?"

The girl eyed her for another moment, still looking confused.

"He's mine," she finally said, her expression hardening once more. "You claim the Forelander as your husband, but you're no Weaver."

"No," Cresenne said, still wishing she could stand, "I'm not. But where we come from that doesn't matter."

"Well, it does here. And with Q'Daer gone, and your man with him, L'Norr is the only Weaver left who doesn't have a wife."

"That's enough, T'Lisha," the young man said quietly.

"You think I'm too young to understand why you're really here?"

"I said that's enough." He had raised his voice this time, drawing the girl's gaze.

He stood, stepped around the fire, and took her by the arm, though not roughly. "Come with me," he said, his voice low again.

She glared back at Cresenne, but she allowed L'Norr to lead her out of the z'kal.

They started arguing almost at once, and though Cresenne could hear their voices clearly, she made a point of not listening, choosing instead to sing to Bryntelle.

Eventually the flap opened again, and L'Norr reentered the shelter. He faltered for an instant, glancing down at Cresenne, but then returned to his place on the far side of the fire and sat. He stirred the stew once again, before reaching for bowls.

"She won't have any?" he asked, indicating Bryntelle with a curt nod.

"No, thank you."

He spooned some stew into a bowl and handed it to Cresenne along with a second, smaller spoon. He served himself and immediately began to eat, seemingly doing his best to ignore both Cresenne and Bryntelle. After a moment, Cresenne began to eat, too. The stew wasn't nearly as flavorful as F'Solya's had been, but it was warm and Cresenne was ravenous.

"It's very good," she said between mouthfuls. "Thank you for sharing it with us."

L'Norr grunted something that might have been a "thank you" or a "you're welcome"; it was hard to say for certain. Before long, Cresenne had emptied her bowl, and despite the awkwardness of the situation, she held it up for him to see.

"May I?" she asked.

He nodded, barely bothering to look at her.

She refilled her bowl and sat back again, eating this second helping almost as quickly as she had eaten the first.

"I'm sorry if our being here has created problems for you," she finally said. Her bowl was empty again, but she decided to wait before asking for more.

L'Norr shrugged.

"You could have invited her to join us."

"This is my z'kal," he said, casting a quick, dark look her way. "I don't need you telling me what I can and can't do."

"No, of course you don't," she said. "That's not—"

"You're here because the a'laq has commanded me to share my meals with you. You have no claim on me or on my shelter or even on my food. Were I to decide to give you nothing more than rancid meat and stale bread, I would still be living up to the a'laq's expectations. I share this food out of kindness. So I'll thank you to leave me alone while I'm eating and to say nothing about matters that don't concern you."

She felt as though she'd been slapped. She had to bite her tongue to keep from railing at the man. She didn't deserve to be talked to in that way—she'd done nothing wrong, nothing to give offense. Since her arrival in the sept she'd done all she could to make herself invisible. She wanted only to survive until Grinsa returned, so that they might find a way to get away from this settlement and out of Fal'Borna lands. And yet it seemed that at every turn, someone was yelling at her or insulting her or accusing her of things she hadn't done and had no intention of doing. It was enough to make her want to scream.

But of course she couldn't, any more than she could yell back at him. She couldn't get up and leave, either. She was utterly powerless here. She'd never truly felt this way before. Even when she was still living in the Forelands, a prisoner in the castle of the king of Eibithar, victimized again and again by the renegade Weaver and his assassins, she hadn't been this helpless. She'd been able to fight back, to use her magics and her wits to protect herself. Here, even that comfort was denied her. She could only sit, enduring the sting of this man's ire, willing herself not to cry in front of him.

She put down the bowl, her hands trembling slightly, what was left of her appetite gone.

"May I have some water?" she asked, her voice barely more than a whisper.

He stared at her for a moment, then reached for a full skin and handed it to her. She took a drink and gave it back to him.

"Thank you."

L'Norr took it back, drank a bit himself, and placed it on the ground beside him. His jaw muscles were clenched and he refused to look her in the eye.

"A Fal'Borna Weaver has to marry another Weaver," he finally said, his voice so low that Cresenne had to lean closer just to hear him. "You know this. But there aren't any Weavers among the women of E'Menua's sept, except for D'Pera, of course. U'Vara, the a'laq's daughter, shows signs of being a Weaver. But she can only marry one man, and eventually the a'laq's sons will come of age, and they will be given wives before any of the rest of us."

He looked up. "That's why concubines are so important. T'Lisha is young, and she shouldn't have spoken to you as she did, but she's all I have. She may be all I ever have, unless I'm willing to leave here or marry a woman from another sept."

It was more explanation than she had expected, and no doubt he felt that it was more than she deserved. Yet, Cresenne could muster little sympathy for him. Her life had come to a point where she had no choice but to think first of herself and her child.

"Are you saying that you don't want me to come back?"

L'Norr smiled thinly. "If I could tell you such a thing, I would. I have no reason to wish you ill, and I'm sorry for you. But if I could send you away to make T'Lisha happy, I'd do it in an instant." He shook his head. "But E'Menua has made it clear to me that I'm to feed you until your man returns."

Her relief was immediate and profound, making it much easier for her to be generous.

"Then what can I do to make things better between you and T'Lisha?"

The question seemed to surprise him. "What can you do?"

"She's not going to like the fact that I'm here every evening. But perhaps there are ways in which I can convince her that she has nothing to fear from me."

L'Norr shook his head, looking terribly young, his eyes fixed on hers. "I don't know. I'll have to think about this."

"Would you like me to speak with her?"

"No!" L'Norr said quickly. "That would be a bad idea. She's made up her mind about you already. She considers you a rival, an enemy even. You'd be best off staying away from her."

The relief Cresenne had felt a moment before vanished, leaving her feeling cold. It was bad enough that everyone in the sept thought of her as Grinsa's concubine and as someone who was intent on luring every Weaver in the settlement to her bed. But to have an enemy, someone who actually wished her ill . . . This was precisely why she had wanted to go unnoticed. She knew what it meant when the Fal'Borna declared someone an enemy, and though she couldn't imagine that the enmity of one girl meant the same thing as that of the entire clan, she had no desire to find out what it did mean.

"You have to tell her that I'm not a rival!" she said. "I don't want her for an enemy, L'Norr. You have to tell her that!"

He looked taken aback. "I . . . I can try to tell her, but I'm not sure she'll listen. If I defend you, she'll only hate you more."

Of course he was right. She once had a jealous lover, and there had been no reasoning with him. Every reassurance she offered him he managed to twist into further proof of her infidelity.

"The last thing I need is for someone else in this sept to have a reason to hate me," she said, trying to sound reasonable. Bryntelle had started to fuss again, perhaps sensing Cresenne's distress, as she so often did. Cresenne kissed her brow and began to rock her gently. "And the last thing you need," she went on, "is for T'Lisha to think you're betraying her every time I come to your shelter for a meal. I understand that you don't want me speaking to her, but then you need to convince her that she has no reason to fear me."

"And I'm telling you I don't know how to do that," L'Norr said.

"Have her eat her meals with us. Let her be here whenever I am. That way she can see that there's nothing more to these meals than there appears."

He shook his head, looking uncertain. "I don't know if she'll agree. And even if she does, it may not satisfy her."

"Then think of something else," she said, her patience waning. "As you said, E'Menua expects you to feed me. So unless you want to lose her, you'll find a way to fix this."

The young Weaver didn't look happy, but after a moment he nodded.

They sat without speaking for several moments.

"Thank you for the meal," she finally said. "Do you need help cleaning up?"

He shook his head. "No. You can leave."

Cresenne hesitated. She had hoped that her meals with L'Norr might lead to some sort of friendship. She certainly hadn't wanted this night's meal to end with such bitterness. But she didn't see any way to make matters better; it seemed more likely that the longer she stayed, and the more she said, the worse it would be.

She stood, still holding Bryntelle in her arms, and looked down at him. "Good night, then."

"Good night."

She turned and left the shelter. Glancing around as she emerged from the z'kal, she saw that a few people were looking her way, all of them young women. None of them said anything, and she did her best to ignore their stares as she walked back to her shelter. But she felt their eyes boring into her back, and she expected at any moment to hear them start calling her a whore, or worse. By the time she reached her z'kal she was shaking with anger, her cheeks burning, her eyes brimming with tears. She'd done nothing wrong. *Nothing.* So why did she feel so ashamed?

As much as she wanted to cry, she refused. Since arriving in E'Menua's sept, she had been treated with contempt by nearly everyone except F'Solya. She had been dismissed as being an unworthy mate for Grinsa, she had been ignored and insulted, and she had been forced to endure all of this in near total isolation. And she'd had enough.

She had no way of fighting back, of course. Most of the Fal'Borna had made up their minds about her long ago; Cresenne had little hope that she could convince any of them that she was anything more or less than they already thought her to be. But she wasn't helpless, and she didn't need anyone else to tell her what she already knew to be true: Grinsa loved her. No matter what they had been through—and the gods knew that they had been through a lot—he had chosen to spend his life with her, and she with him. The Fal'Borna could not take that away from them.

"We don't care what they think, do we, Bryntelle?" she said, blinking the tears from her eyes as she looked down at her child. "They can call me whatever they want, but we don't care, right?"

Bryntelle grinned at her and then laughed.

Cresenne smiled. "That's right."

She put Bryntelle to bed and then lay down herself. It took her a long time to fall asleep, though, and even after she did, she slept fitfully, troubled by strange, disturbing dreams that made no sense to her when she awoke in the morning. She sensed that she had slept too long and she dressed hurriedly, feeling disoriented.

Once more, as she made her way to the tanning circle, she felt that people were watching her, speaking of her behind her back. Even the younger girls who took Bryntelle for the day behaved strangely around her, some of them suppressing grins as if amused by some ill-mannered joke, others staring at her with open hostility. Despite having resolved the night before not to let all of this bother her, she had to grit her teeth to keep from screaming at all of them that she'd done nothing wrong. But it was only when she reached the tanning circle that she realized how serious matters had become. F'Solya was there, and her space beside the woman was open, but her friend said nothing to her as she sat. Worse, when Cresenne said "Good morning," F'Solya didn't reply.

Cresenne felt herself growing cold, though the sun was shining and the air was warmer than it had been in days.

For a long time neither of them spoke, until finally Cresenne couldn't endure the silence any longer.

"You have something you want to say to me?" she asked, keeping her eyes fixed on the skin she was tanning.

At first F'Solya said nothing, though Cresenne could tell that she had stopped working and was staring at her. "Why would you do it?" she demanded at last. "After all we've done for you, why would you do such a thing?"

Cresenne turned to face her. "What is it you think I've done?"

"T'Lisha said that she found you in L'Norr's z'kal last night."

"And did she tell you why I was there?"

The question seem to catch her friend off guard; the reason would have seemed so obvious that probably none of the people T'Lisha told—the entire sept by now, no doubt—even thought to ask.

"No," F'Solya said, her voice softening. "She just . . . she just said . . ."

"She told all of you I was there, and allowed your imaginations to do the rest." Cresenne shook her head. "I expect that from the rest of them, F'Solya. But I thought you and I were friends."

"We are," F'Solya said. She took a breath. "Tell me why you were there. Please."

"I was there for food."

The woman frowned. "Food?"

"Yes. That's all."

"But the a'laq—"

"The a'laq refused to sell me food," Cresenne said. "And he said he wouldn't give me any, either. But he said he'd arrange for L'Norr to share his meals with me. E'Menua said that since he didn't have a wife or children, he'd have plenty to spare."

F'Solya shook her head, looking utterly confused. "But that makes no sense."

"I know," Cresenne told her. "But it's the truth."

"Why would the a'laq make feeding you so complicated when it could have been so simple?"

"Because he's intent on destroying my marriage to Grinsa. He wants us to stay here, and he wants Grinsa to marry a Weaver, be it a woman from your sept or someone from a neighboring one. He doesn't care. Either way he gets what he wants: more Weavers. He knew how T'Lisha would respond to this; he might have thought that this would drive her away from L'Norr so that he would try to make a concubine of me. And E'Menua is probably hoping that Grinsa will react the same way T'Lisha did. Anything to drive us apart. He's like this old spider spinning webs all around him, trying to catch as many flies as he can before he dies."

"You're speaking of my a'laq," F'Solya said, an edge to her voice.

Cresenne winced, realizing that she had gone too far on the one day when she could least afford to do so. "I'm sorry," she said. "It's just . . . he doesn't like me very much, and he seems intent on forcing Grinsa to marry a Weaver."

They lapsed into another lengthy silence. Cresenne tried to keep her mind on her work, but her hands were trembling again. She wasn't certain what she would do without F'Solya's friendship. It was bad enough longing for Grinsa day and night, but to be friendless as well would drive her mad.

"T'Lisha is telling anyone who'll listen to her that you're trying to steal her man," F'Solya finally said.

Cresenne wanted to ask if F'Solya believed the girl, but she was afraid of her friend's answer. So she simply said "I'm not."

"I believe you," F'Solya said.

Cresenne lowered the skin she was working on and looked at the woman. "Do you really? It didn't seem that way before."

F'Solya met her gaze. "I was wrong to speak to you the way I did. I'm sorry."

She smiled, feeling so relieved that tears came to her eyes. "Thank you."

"The others . . ." F'Solya trailed off, her brow furrowing.

"I know. The others believe T'Lisha. Why shouldn't they? They know nothing about me, and I was in L'Norr's shelter last night. I will be again tonight and tomorrow, and every day until Grinsa returns."

The woman frowned again. "It does seem an odd way to get you food," she said. "Do you really believe that E'Menua wishes you ill?"

Cresenne looked away. "I suppose there might be another explanation."

"Look at me," F'Solya said, as if Cresenne were but a child.

She faced her friend once more.

"Do you really believe all those things you said before about the a'laq?"

Cresenne nodded. "I do. I'm sorry."

F'Solya shook her head, looking troubled. "It's all right. I was . . . troubled by the way D'Pera spoke to you the day we went to see her. She as much as accused you of trying to . . ." Her face colored. "Well, anyway, she shouldn't have spoken to you the way she did."

"They need Grinsa," Cresenne said. "At least they think they do. And because of who I am, they feel that the only way to get him, to convince him to stay, is to drive me away." She shrugged, not quite certain why she was justifying the way they had treated her. "I'm sure it makes a great deal of sense to them."

F'Solya seemed to consider this for several moments. Cresenne went back to working on the rilda hide she was holding, feeling a bit better. Let T'Lisha spread rumors about her. As long as F'Solya didn't believe them, Cresenne didn't care, at least not much.

"What will you do?" the woman asked her eventually.

"About T'Lisha, you mean?"

Her friend nodded.

"I've told L'Norr to have her join us for the evening meal each night, so that she can see for herself that she has no reason to be jealous."

F'Solya's expression brightened. "That seems like a fine idea."

"L'Norr didn't think so. He wasn't certain that T'Lisha would agree, and even if she did, he didn't think it would satisfy her."

"Then she's a fool."

Cresenne smiled. "That thought had crossed my mind."

"I can try speaking to her for you. I've known her for a long time. She's headstrong—girls her age often are—but she's a good child at heart. She might listen to me."

"I don't know, F'Solya," she said, shaking her head slowly. "Don't get me wrong: I'm grateful for the offer. But you've done a good deal for me already. At this point you might not want to make it so clear to everyone that we're friends."

"Nonsense," F'Solya said.

Again, Cresenne smiled.

"But you may be right about talking to T'Lisha. I'd be better off speaking with T'Resse, her mother."

"Her mother?" Cresenne repeated. "That sounds like a very bad idea."

"Not at all," F'Solya said, sounding quite sure of herself. "T'Resse and I have known each other for years." She nodded, clearly convinced by the soundness of her choice. "She'll be able to help."

She stood.

"You're going to talk to her now?" Cresenne asked.

"Of course. She'll be grinding grain—that's what she does most days. I'll be back in just a bit."

Cresenne watched her walk off, hoping that her confidence would be rewarded. She had her doubts, though, and as she turned her attention back to the rilda hide, she began to consider once more the possibility of speaking to T'Lisha directly. L'Norr had thought it a bad idea, but Cresenne wasn't certain that they had many choices.

Before long, she looked up from her work to see F'Solya returning. Her friend didn't look at all pleased, and Cresenne was glad that she hadn't allowed herself to share in F'Solya's earlier optimism.

F'Solya sat down heavily and took up her hide once more, a deep frown on her pretty face.

"I've never known her to be so unreasonable," she said. "Or so stubborn." She looked at Cresenne. "When my boys misbehave I'm the first to admit it. But T'Resse sounded as if T'Lisha had never done an ill deed her entire life. And I *know* that's not true."

"I'm sorry, F'Solya. I shouldn't have gotten you involved in this."

The woman waved a hand dismissively. "You didn't. I wanted to help. And I do now more than before." She frowned again and shook her head. "I just can't believe that T'Resse could be so foolish."

They worked a while longer, then paused for their midday meal. Cresenne's meal was meager as usual, but F'Solya had packed extra food for her, so she ate well. It was her second ample meal in as many days, and already she could feel herself growing stronger. After they ate, they worked some more, until Cresenne couldn't sit still any longer.

"Where does T'Lisha work?" she asked abruptly.

F'Solya regarded her for several moments before responding. "Are you certain that's a good idea?" she asked.

"No. But doing nothing isn't helping matters either."

The woman shrugged, as if conceding the point. "She's often with the younger ones, caring for the children."

Cresenne's blood ran cold and she felt her face go white. "She wouldn't hurt Bryntelle, would she?"

F'Solya shook her head. "No. She's many things, but a brute isn't one of them. I assure you, your daughter is safe."

Cresenne exhaled, then nodded and climbed to her feet. "All right then. Wish me luck."

She started off toward the area where the older girls cared for the children, ignoring the stares of the other women. She'd been an object of curiosity during her imprisonment in Eibithar's great castle back in the Forelands, when she had actually done something wrong. This was easy by comparison. And the fact that T'Lisha was near Bryntelle gave her an excuse to approach the girl that she wouldn't have had otherwise. She needed to feed her daughter anyway.

As she drew near, Cresenne suddenly wondered if she'd recognize the girl when she saw her. They'd only spoken briefly, and the z'kal had been dim. As it turned out, she needn't have worried. She spotted the girl immediately, and T'Lisha saw her almost as quickly, stiffening noticeably, her eyes growing wide.

Cresenne didn't approach her at first. She found Bryntelle and once she had assured herself that her daughter was fine, she fed her. Only after she had returned Bryntelle to the girls who had been caring for her did she go to T'Lisha.

Even as she walked up to the girl, T'Lisha didn't look at her. She was standing with several other girls who appeared to be her age, but none of them said anything to Cresenne or to each other.

"I wanted to let you know that I'd be eating my evening meal with L'Norr again tonight. It's not by choice; the a'laq is making me do it. But I'm hoping that you'll be there, too, so that you can see that there's nothing more to it than a simple meal."

T'Lisha let out a short, disbelieving laugh, but still refused to say anything.

"I have a husband, T'Lisha. I love him, and only him. And L'Norr cares only about you. He doesn't want me."

T'Lisha glanced her way. "How do you know that? Did he refuse you when you tried to climb into his bed?"

Cresenne actually smiled. Had she ever been this young?

"No. I told you, I've a husband whom I love. But I've had other lovers in the past, and I know something of men and the way they behave when they're in love."

She didn't wait for a reply. She simply turned and started back toward the tanning circle.

T'Lisha didn't call for her to stop or come after her. She could only hope that the girl would give some thought to what she had said.

"What happened?" F'Solya asked as soon as Cresenne took her place beside her once more.

"Nothing, really. I asked her to eat with L'Norr and me. We'll see if she does."

That evening, though, she and Bryntelle found L'Norr alone in his z'kal, roasting rilda meat over his fire.

"Did you speak with T'Lisha today?" he asked, as Cresenne sat across the fire from him. He sounded angry.

"Yes, I did," she said mildly.

"I warned you against doing that."

"Yes, I remember. I did it anyway."

"You had no right! I told you not to speak with her."

"Did you speak with her?" she demanded.

He hesitated.

"Did you plan to any time in the near future?"

"Of course!" he said.

"I'm not certain I believe you. I didn't want her spreading any more rumors about me than she had already, so I did something about it. If that bothers you . . . well, too bad. Someone had to do something, so I did."

"You had no right," he said again, sounding sullen this time, like a chastised boy.

"What did she say to you? Was she angry with me?"

"She was . . ." He shook his head. "Just what did you say to her?"

"I said several things. Nothing that should have disturbed her. I told her that I have a husband, and that I love him, and that I'm not interested in any other man. I also told her that you weren't looking for another concubine."

His face turned bright red. "Did you tell her . . . did you make it sound like . . . ?"

She suppressed a grin. "What's the matter, L'Norr?"

"She seems to think now that I'm in love with her."

Cresenne widened her eyes in mock surprise. "Really?"

The young Weaver scowled at her.

"Did you tell her that you're not?"

"Of course I didn't."

"Are you in love with her?" she asked.

His face colored again. "That's not . . . I'm not going to answer that."

Seeing him so flustered, she nearly laughed aloud. "Would you have preferred that she remained angry with you?"

He twisted his mouth sourly. "No."

"Then you have no cause to complain." She leaned closer to the fire and peered at the cooking meat. "That looks nearly done. Unless you were planning to burn it."

He took the meat off the fire, cut several slices for her, and handed her a shallow bowl that held the meat and some boiled root.

"Thank you," she said, starting to eat. The rilda was excellent and the root, which she'd never tasted before, was tender and slightly sweet. "This is good," she told him after several bites. "Thank you for sharing your meal with me."

He nodded, avoiding her eyes. He no longer seemed angry with her, merely embarrassed. They spoke little for the rest of the meal, and when it came time for her to leave, he said "good night," but nothing more.

Emerging from his shelter with Bryntelle in her arms, Cresenne saw that several people were watching her, including T'Lisha. Their eyes met briefly and then the girl looked away. But the hostility Cresenne had sensed in her earlier in the day and the night before seemed to have vanished, or at least abated.

No doubt most of the people to whom T'Lisha had spoken the night before still thought the worst of her; it would take a few days before they realized that the girl had been mistaken. But it seemed that T'Lisha herself no longer wished her ill. Perhaps the notion that L'Norr truly loved her had been enough to make her forget her jealousy.

Cresenne made her way back to her z'kal, put Bryntelle to bed, and then went to sleep herself. Her slumber this night was far more restful than it had been the night before. And at one point Grinsa came to her, as a Weaver could, to walk in her dreams and speak with her and hold her. He looked tired and pale, but he was well, and he told her of his travels and of the Mettai men his company had encountered.

"They killed her?" she said, when he informed her of the witch's fate.

"Yes."

"But E'Menua wanted you to kill her."

"I know," Grinsa said, holding her hand and brushing a strand of hair from her forehead. "There's nothing to be done about it now. We're going to try to keep the baskets she sold from reaching any more villages, and then we'll return to the sept."

"He won't be happy," she said. "The a'laq, I mean."

He shook his head. "I don't care anymore. He can try to keep us there, but it won't work. We're leaving Fal'Borna lands as soon as we can. You have my word."

She rested her head against his chest, feeling his heartbeat. "Good," she whispered.

"Are you and Bryntelle all right?" he asked, sounding concerned. "You look thin. Have you been eating?"

"We're fine," she said. She looked up into his eyes and kissed him. "Really. We had a bit of trouble, but it's all right now."

"What kind of trouble?"

"It doesn't matter. Nothing serious." She smiled. "I can handle it."

And she meant it. Before he left she'd told Grinsa to do what he had to do and return to her. She'd told him that she and Bryntelle would get along without him. Brave words. But at the time that was all they'd been. Now, though, finally, she actually believed them.

"You're certain?" he asked her, still looking worried.

"Yes. I'm not sure the Fal'Borna will ever accept me as one of their own, but I think I'm starting to figure out how to live among them."

He smiled, though he looked puzzled. "Someday you'll have to explain what you mean."

"I'll try." She grinned. "It might take a while."

Chapter 18

S'Vralna, Memory Moon waxing

On the seventh day of the new waxing, they came within sight of a great walled city. Its towers and battlements were made of pale stone that gleamed like bone in the late-morning sunlight, and great columns of black smoke rose from within its walls. Though Grinsa had been in the South-lands for only a few turns, and had been living among the Qirsi clans for only part of that time, he had already come to think of all Fal'Borna settlements as being like E'Menua's. Fortifications like the one in front of him belonged in the Eandi sovereignties. This city seemed to have much more in common with Yorl, along the Aelean coast, where he and Cresenne had first set foot in the Southlands, than it did with the z'kals and open pad-docks of E'Menua's sept.

He had to remind himself that this city—S'Vralna, Q'Daer called it—and the lands around it had once belonged to the Eandi of Stelpana. The night before the young Weaver had been in an uncharacteristically expan-sive mood, and had spoken at length of the Blood Wars and the battles for control of the Central Plain.

"The Fal'Borna took it from the dark-eyes during the Blood Wars," he had said, sounding so proud that one might have thought he'd had a hand in winning the city during those battles a century and a half ago. "The Eandi once held all this land, everything west to the K'Sahd. Now all of it is ours, and they hide on the far banks of the Silverwater."

The two Eandi merchants, as well as Besh and Sirj, had kept their thoughts to themselves, and before long Torgan and Jasha wandered off to sleep. Grinsa had tried to turn the conversation in a different direction, ask-ing Besh about the history of the Mettai. But Q'Daer had interrupted, and soon after Besh and Sirj left them as well.

On this morning, though, the young Weaver kept silent, his expression grim as he eyed those clouds of smoke. Grinsa continued to gaze at the city, keeping his thoughts to himself. Even after the city came into view, the dis-tance to the gates remained great, and it was some time before he began to notice that the walls were not as uniform as they first appeared. They had been broken in places; parts of them were blackened as if by fire; at least one of the corner towers had collapsed in on itself. It had to have been the pestilence, unless the Southlands were at war again.

"How many people live in S'Vralna," he asked, his voice low.

Q'Daer shook his head. "I don't know for certain. Three thousand perhaps. Maybe more. It's one of our bigger cities, though not as big as D'Raqor or Thamia." He raised himself up on his mount, squinting in the sun. "Damn," he muttered. He'd been chafing at their slow pace all morning, and now he glanced back at the rest of their company. "Faster!" he shouted at them, before kicking his mount to a gallop.

Grinsa stayed with him, but he glanced back repeatedly to see that the others were following, particularly Torgan. The one-eyed merchant had been behaving strangely in recent days, even more so than usual. On the best of days Torgan was belligerent and selfish, but more recently he had retreated into a dark, brooding silence. He spoke to no one, not even Jasha, though at times he appeared to mumble to himself. Grinsa had tried to speak with the man a few times, hoping at least to find some sign of the argumentative arrogance he recalled from their earliest encounters. But the merchant said little to him, and when he did speak he was unfailingly polite, which in many ways alarmed Grinsa even more than did his silence.

At the moment, however, Grinsa was concerned more with the fate of S'Vralna and its denizens than with Torgan. The closer they drew to the city walls, the more severe the damage appeared to be. Many of the buildings within the city were made of the same white stone as the outer wall, so that closer inspection revealed breaches in many parts of the wall that had appeared whole from a distance. Vultures, crows, and kites circled over the city and occasionally great flocks of dark birds rose into the sky from within the walls, crying plaintively at whatever had driven them from their scavenging. Wild dogs prowled a short distance from the gates, eyeing the city warily.

The riders were still a good distance from the city walls when the stench reached them: the acrid smell of smoke and the sickening fetor of rotting corpses. Grinsa had feared that they would find no one alive in the city, but now he saw that there were soldiers at the gates, their weapons glittering in the sun.

"There are guards," he called to Q'Daer.

The young Weaver didn't even look at him. "I see them."

"They won't let us pass."

That drew a frown from Q'Daer, who then glanced back at the rest of their company.

"I think they will," he said after a moment. "I'm Fal'Borna; we're both Weavers. They'll be wary of the dark-eyes, but they'll let us through. And if they won't let the Eandi in, we can leave them at the gate, under their watch."

Grinsa didn't believe that it would be quite so easy, but he kept this to himself.

They slowed their mounts as they drew near the gate and then dismounted, leading their horses on foot the rest of the way. There were two men guarding the gate, both of them young. Their uniforms were stained with soot and dirt and blood, and one of them bore a dark, angry scar on his cheek that appeared to have been healed only in the last day or so.

"Who are you?" the scarred man demanded as Grinsa and Q'Daer walked toward them.

Both men had drawn their swords.

"My name is Q'Daer. I am a Weaver in the sept of E'Menua, son of E'Sedt. This is Grinsa of the Forelands. He, too, is a Weaver."

The guard looked past them to the Eandi, who had halted a short distance off. "And them?"

"Our companions," Q'Daer said. "We've been looking for merchants who are selling the cursed Mettai baskets."

The man shifted his gaze back to Q'Daer. "You're too late."

"How long ago did this happen?" Grinsa asked.

The guard eyed him briefly, but didn't answer. Eventually he faced the Fal'Borna again. "Our n'qlae, who leads us now—she instructed us to turn away strangers. She didn't say anything about answering questions."

"You're led by your n'qlae?" Q'Daer asked.

"She's . . . she's the only Weaver we have left."

Q'Daer exhaled through his teeth. "I would speak to her," he said. After a brief pause he added, "If I may."

The two guards exchanged a look. Finally, the scarred man nodded, and the other soldier retreated through the gate.

"What are you doing traveling with dark-eyes, Q'Daer?"

Q'Daer opened his mouth to reply, but Grinsa answered before he could speak.

"That tale is best saved for your n'qlae," he said.

The guard frowned, but he didn't argue the point. Grinsa might have been a stranger to these lands, but Q'Daer had told the guard that he was a Weaver. No doubt a soldier in a Fal'Borna army was expected to defer to Weavers at all times.

For a time none of them spoke, until Q'Daer said softly, "Here she comes."

Grinsa saw her, too, leading the young guard back through the gate. She was a small woman, with pale golden eyes, long white hair that looked windblown and matted, and deep lines around her eyes and mouth. Once, perhaps not so long ago, she might have been beautiful. Now she looked careworn and slightly mad.

"Who are you?" she demanded, walking toward them. "You're both Weavers. What do you want here?"

"We're searching for the merchants who are selling cursed Mettai baskets, N'Qlae," Q'Daer said.

"Yes, so I've been told. The merchant who sold us the baskets is dead. My husband took her life before he died."

"Who was your a'laq, N'Qlae?" Q'Daer asked. "What was his name?"

She stared at him briefly, and Grinsa wondered if the young Weaver had erred in asking.

But then she said, "His name was P'Crath. I lost my daughter as well. I should be dead myself. I haven't any idea why I'm not."

"We're sorry we didn't get here sooner," Grinsa said, drawing her gaze. "But is there some way we can help you now?"

She narrowed her eyes. "Your accent is strange."

"I'm from the Forelands. I've only been in your land for a short time."

She looked at the Eandi, not bothering to mask her hostility. "And them?" she asked with contempt. "What are they doing here?"

Q'Daer caught Grinsa's eye and shook his head. A warning. Under different circumstances, Grinsa would have ignored him and told the woman the truth, but not here, not on this day.

"They're merchants, N'Qlae," Grinsa said, gesturing vaguely at all four of the Eandi. "They've been helping us track those who may have been selling baskets."

"Were they selling them, too?" she demanded.

"One of them was," Q'Daer said. "But he claims he didn't understand the danger until it was too late."

"The woman said the same thing. P'Crath didn't think it mattered."

"What was her name?" came a voice from behind them.

Grinsa and Q'Daer both turned. Torgan had steered his mount a few paces closer to where they stood.

"The woman—the merchant your husband killed. What was her name?"

"I never knew," the n'qlae said, ice in her voice. "Some called her by the name of a bird."

Jasha inhaled sharply, the color draining from his cheeks.

"Lark," Torgan whispered, closing his eyes. "Lariqenne Glyse. You bastards killed Lark."

"Torgan!" Grinsa said sharply.

"Torgan Plye?" the woman said, her voice rising.

The merchant stared back at her, unflinching. "That's right."

"You've been declared an enemy of the Fal'Borna."

"So I've been told," Torgan said, his tone bitter.

"My a'laq has taken his goods and his cart, N'Qlae," Q'Daer told her quickly. "And upon our return to the sept, he's to be executed. For now, he's helping us."

Torgan's face paled, though it seemed to Grinsa that he didn't look frightened so much as enraged.

"You lament the killing of this woman you knew, dark-eye?" the n'qlae asked, still glowering at the merchant. "You think her death an injustice?"

"Yes, I do."

"Do you know how many people used to live in this city?" When Torgan didn't answer, she asked again, "Do you?"

"I have some idea," Torgan admitted. "I used to pass through here from time to time."

"There were more than four thousand," she said, her chin quivering. "Four thousand! Fewer than eight hundred survived the pestilence that your friend brought to us."

"She wouldn't have meant for it to happen," Torgan said quietly. "She wouldn't have hurt even one of you on purpose."

"I don't give a damn about what she meant to do! And neither did my husband! Three thousand of my people are dead! Someone had to pay for that! She had to pay!"

None of them spoke. Grinsa didn't so much as look at the n'qlae, and he silently begged Torgan to say nothing more. Her city had been devastated, its army no doubt destroyed, but still she held their lives in her hand. If she decided that all of them should die, there was little he and Q'Daer could do to save them. And there was no telling what she might do if she learned that Besh and Sirj were Mettai.

Which was why his heart nearly stopped beating when he heard the old man call out to her.

"My pardon, N'Qlae," he said. "But it may comfort you to know that the woman who created this curse also is dead. I . . . I killed her."

Q'Daer had turned his glare on the man, his blazing eyes seeming to ask, *Are you mad?*

But Besh kept his eyes on the n'qlae, and she took a step toward him.

"What is your name?" she asked, her voice more subdued now.

"I am called Besh, N'Qlae."

"And where is your home?"

Grinsa held his breath, but Besh seemed to understand that the truth could do only so much good.

"I live to the north, in Aelea, N'Qlae."

"And you say that you killed this woman?"

"I did. She meant to kill me, and I had no choice in the matter."

She stared at him for a long time. Then, "You're Mettai, aren't you?"

"He's been named a friend of all the Fal'Borna for what he did," Grinsa told her before Besh could answer. "An a'laq to the east named him so. What was the a'laq's name, Besh?"

The n'qlae held up a hand to silence them both. "It's all right, Forelander. I have no desire to kill him. If what he says is true, we owe him a great debt."

Grinsa exhaled and closed his eyes briefly. He had taken hold of his magic, expecting that he would need it to save Besh's life. He relaxed his hold on it now, though he didn't let down his guard entirely. The n'qlae's reassurances notwithstanding, the two soldiers had exchanged looks when they heard that Besh was Mettai, and they continued to eye him darkly now.

"You offered to help us earlier," the n'qlae said. "Was your offer sincere?"

"Of course, N'Qlae," Grinsa said. "What can we do?"

"We have bodies to burn," she said. "And our city is in ruins. A few more able hands would be welcome, even if just for a few hours."

Grinsa glanced at Q'Daer, who nodded.

"Lead the way," he said, facing the woman again.

She turned and started back through the gate. Grinsa, the young Weaver, and their company followed. Besh and Sirj left their cart by the gate, after being assured by the n'qlae that it would be safe.

"How is it that a Forelander speaks for your company, Weaver?" the n'qlae asked Q'Daer, as they walked beneath the portcullises.

The young Weaver's face colored and he eyed Grinsa with obvious resentment. "He doesn't," the man said.

She nodded. "I see. Forgive me."

Emerging from the gateway into the sunlight, Grinsa faltered. Nothing he had seen from beyond the city walls could have prepared him for the amount of damage he now saw within. It seemed no building had been spared. Homes and shops lay in ruins, piles of shattered stone and wood lined the lane, the charred remains of people's lives were strewn everywhere. It appeared that some great beast had rampaged through the city streets, destroying anything and everything in sight.

The smell of rotting flesh was far stronger here than it had been outside the city, and the scavenger birds circled overhead, their shadows slipping across the roads and mounds of debris like dark, elusive wraiths. The bodies had been cleared from this lane, but Grinsa could smell the great pyres burning farther in, toward the city's marketplace.

Here and there Fal'Borna moved among the ruins, picking through the rubble for lost items, or perhaps for those dead who had yet to be found. Hearing Grinsa and the others approach, many of them looked up and watched the company pass, the expressions in their yellow eyes bleak and haunted. A great number of them appeared to be children, too young yet to have come into their power.

"So many young ones," Grinsa heard Besh say behind him.

"Yes," the n'qlae said over her shoulder. "More than half of those who survived were children, and nearly all of them lost at least one parent. Many— too many—are now orphans."

"Do you know why so many children were spared?" Grinsa asked her.

"My husband believed that the disease struck at our magic. Those who hadn't come into their power were immune. My daughter had only been wielding her magics for a few turns. If the pestilence had come to us in the Planting, rather than the Harvest, she would still be alive."

The n'qlae faced forward again, still walking, and Grinsa followed her, wanting to ask more questions, but mindful of treading on emotions that obviously remained raw.

Before they reached the marketplace, they passed a great structure of white stone that looked to be less damaged than the rest of the buildings, though perhaps only because it had been more sturdily constructed. Again, Grinsa wanted to ask what it was, but didn't want to press the n'qlae.

To his surprise, though, she gestured at the building as they walked past, and said simply, "This was our home."

Grinsa chanced a quick look at Q'Daer, who was walking beside him.

The young Weaver looked much as he had the day they found the small sept that had been devastated by Lici's curse. His face was pale, and his eyes burned with fury and grief and maybe even a touch of dread, as if he were imagining what this pestilence might do if it struck at E'Menua's sept.

Past the marketplace, they turned to the west, where the destruction seemed to have been more severe and less work had been done to clean up the streets. Again, there were Fal'Borna here, young and old, many of them with cloths wrapped around their mouths and noses to protect them from the stench of the dead.

"We need help here, to find and pile the bodies," the n'qlae said. "And we also need help farther to the north."

"How long ago did all this happen?" Torgan asked, surveying the lane with obvious disgust.

"It's been more than half a turn," the n'qlae told him.

"And you're only cleaning it up now?"

"We fled the city the night . . . the night all this happened. My husband told us to." She turned to Grinsa and Q'Daer, eager, it seemed, to make them understand. "I had to leave him. I had to leave my daughter. I didn't—" She stopped and shook her head. For several moments she stared at the ruined buildings. "He was very wise, my husband. He told us to separate. He said we should stay apart for ten days. Only then could we risk returning to the city." She appeared to shudder. Then she shook her head, as if rousing herself from a dream. "We spent several days searching for survivors, and when we were convinced we'd found everyone, we returned here to reclaim our home."

Jasha approached Grinsa. "We shouldn't help them," he said, keeping his voice low. "At least you and Q'Daer shouldn't. You remember the village we found. There were pieces of the baskets there. Even if these people aren't carrying the disease anymore, those baskets will be. You can't go digging around in this mess. You'll kill yourselves."

"The Fal'Borna are doing it," Grinsa answered, lowering his voice as well.

Jasha hesitated. "They have no choice," he finally said.

Grinsa looked at Q'Daer, who was watching them both. "You heard what he said?"

The young Weaver nodded.

"And what do you think?"

He expected Q'Daer to dismiss the merchant's concerns and insist that they help the n'qlae and her people. But the man surprised him. "I don't know," he said. "I want to help, but he makes a good point."

"Why don't you and Jasha work together," Grinsa said. "Jasha, you do the digging. Q'Daer can clean up and carry what you've already checked through. I'll take Torgan."

"Do you trust him?" Q'Daer asked.

"I'll take the Mettai as well. I trust them."

The n'qlae had waited patiently while they spoke, but now she cleared her throat.

"Forgive us, N'Qlae," Q'Daer said. "The young merchant and I will remain here. The rest will go on with you."

"I didn't agree to that," Torgan said, sounding petulant.

Q'Daer shot him a look that should have made the man quail. "You weren't asked."

The Fal'Borna woman walked on, and Grinsa followed her with Torgan beside him and the Mettai just behind.

"What is it we're doing here?" Torgan asked, far too loudly. "And what were the three of you talking about back there?"

"We're helping these people for a short while," Grinsa whispered. "And Jasha pointed out that there might still be remnants of the baskets here, just as there were at the village we found."

The merchant's face blanched. "The Mettai baskets?" he said.

"Yes. So I need for you to go through the rubble and make certain there are none there before I handle anything."

A look of purest malice flashed in the man's eyes so suddenly and vanished again so quickly that Grinsa could easily have convinced himself it wasn't real. But he knew better. He shuddered in spite of himself.

"Sirj," he called.

Both of the Mettai men hurried forward to join them.

"Yes?" the younger man said.

"I need you to dig through the rubble for me. I can't risk finding the remnant of one of Lici's baskets."

Sirj nodded. "Of course."

"You don't trust me," Torgan said.

Grinsa shook his head. "No, I don't."

Torgan looked away for several moments. His color had returned, and he was scowling, which gave his scarred face a fearsome look. "Well, why should I be concerned for you?" he asked with quiet intensity after a few moments. "You heard what the Fal'Borna said. They're going to execute me when we get back to the sept."

"He had to say that," Grinsa whispered, eyeing the n'qlae to make certain that she hadn't heard. "You saw the way she reacted to hearing your name. Everyone here knows that you were named an enemy of the Fal'Borna, and after what's happened to them, they're probably eager for your blood themselves. Q'Daer said that to mollify her."

"I don't believe you," Torgan said. He stopped, grabbing hold of Grinsa's arm so that he had to stop, too. "You have to let me escape. You know you do. They'll kill me otherwise."

Grinsa wrenched his arm out of the man's grip. "We've been through this. I'll do what I can to keep you alive—to keep all of us alive—but you're not leaving."

A strange look came into the man's eye once more, and then was gone just as quickly. "Then maybe you're right not to trust me."

Grinsa just stared back at him, not certain what to make of his behavior.

"Here," the n'qlae said, as they stepped into yet another lane of collapsed and charred houses. A pile of bodies burned at the end of the road, feeding a great column of rank, black smoke. A few Fal'Borna worked nearby, watching the strangers with guarded expressions.

"We'll do what we can, N'Qlae," Grinsa said. "We can't stay here long. We're still hoping to find other merchants who have these evil baskets among their wares. But we'll help you as long as we can."

She merely nodded and started away.

"Besh," Grinsa said, turning to the older Mettai. "I want you to watch Torgan for me. If he does anything that seems . . . unusual, anything at all, let me know. And if you need to use magic against him, you have my permission."

"I understand," Besh told him.

Torgan glared at each of them in turn. "Damn you all to Bian's demons."

Ignoring him, Grinsa turned to Sirj and nodded. Sirj began to dig through the rubble, pulling out broken wooden beams, half-burned blankets and pieces of furniture, and occasionally pots or pans. Grinsa sorted these things into piles, and tried to clear away some of the stone that littered the road. After only a few moments, Sirj pulled from the ruins the body of what might have been an old man. The smell was so bad that the Mettai turned away and gagged, though he managed to keep from being ill. Grinsa reached into his carry sack and pulled out an old shirt, which he tore into wide strips. He handed one to each of his companions, and they tied them around their faces. Then they went back to work.

"This is pointless," Torgan said, his voice carrying through the ruins.

Several of the Fal'Borna looked up from their work.

Grinsa barely even glanced his way. "Keep quiet, Torgan."

"At least let us work, too," the merchant said. "Sitting here doing nothing . . . I might as well help."

"Not here," Grinsa said. "Not near me."

"Fine then. Let us go down the street." He waved a hand in Besh's direction. "Your friend here will keep an eye on me, won't you, Besh?"

Grinsa turned to the old man. "Are you willing to do that?"

Besh nodded. "Yes. I'd rather be helping, too. And I won't let him get away. I killed Lici with magic. I can kill this one, too."

Clearly he said this more for Torgan than for Grinsa. Grinsa didn't really believe the old man would kill Torgan. But the merchant scowled again and began to walk away.

"Be careful," Grinsa said, lowering his voice. "I really don't know what he's capable of doing."

"All right." Besh walked after the merchant toward the pyre.

Grinsa and Sirj returned to their grim work, and for a long time neither of them spoke other than to ask for help with a heavy object or warn each other of a splintered end of wood or a stray nail.

At midday, the bells in some of the gates rang, though not all of them. One of the Fal'Borna children working nearby explained that the other gates had been been so badly damaged that their bells didn't work anymore. Q'Daer and Jasha joined them, both of them looking weary and somber.

"We should be going soon," Q'Daer said.

Grinsa had stopped working for the moment, but Sirj did not.

"They need our help," the Mettai said.

"I know they do," Q'Daer told him, his voice hard. "But it's more important that we find the other merchants and keep this from happening again."

Sirj had pulled out a long, charred piece of wood. He paused now, holding it as he stared at the young Weaver. Then he threw it on the pile of beams and nodded, exhaling heavily. "You're right."

"Where's Torgan?" Jasha asked, looking around for the other merchant.

Grinsa indicated the end of the lane with a nod. "He's down there, with Besh."

Jasha scanned the street, shading his eyes with an open hand. "Where?"

Grinsa turned to look. "They were just . . . Damn." He started down the lane. "Come on," he called to the others. "This might take all of us."

Chapter 19

✦╍╍✦

Besh didn't relish the idea of keeping watch on the one-eyed merchant, but with Grinsa and the others, including Sirj, busy helping with the bodies and the wreckage, he could hardly refuse. As he followed the Eandi to the end of the lane, he scanned the ground surreptitiously. With stone and dust and debris scattered everywhere, it wouldn't be easy for him to grab a handful of earth. He'd spoken bravely of using magic to control the merchant if the need arose, but if he couldn't find dirt, he wouldn't be able to do anything at all.

Torgan walked a few paces ahead of him, his head down and his shoulders hunched. He seemed to be muttering to himself, no doubt still put out by Besh's threats. The old man barely recognized himself. Only a season before he'd been in his home village of Kirayde, playing with his grandchildren and tending his garden. Now, for the second time in less than half a turn, he'd threatened someone's life. The last time he'd done it, he'd made good on his threat. Would it come to that again? Was he a killer now?

Look what you've done to me, Lici. Look what I've become.

"Is it magic that does it?" Torgan asked suddenly, his voice so low that Besh wasn't certain he'd heard him correctly.

"What?" Besh said, walking quickly to catch up with the man.

"It's like you're one of them now. You act like the Fal'Borna and like that Forelander. You said you'd kill me if you had to."

"I was only—"

"I know what you were doing. And I'm asking you if it's the magic that makes all of you like that. You have power over people, is that it? You're stronger than the rest of us, because you can conjure and the rest of us can't. Is that what makes you threaten and bully?"

Besh would have laughed had Torgan not sounded so earnest and so hurt. He had never thought of himself as a bully; he still didn't. But here was this great brute of a man—Torgan was a full head taller than Besh and he probably weighed half again as much—claiming that Besh had browbeaten him.

"Have you ever used your size to intimidate others?" Besh asked him. "Perhaps to get your way in a negotiation?"

Torgan glanced his way, though only for an instant. "Maybe. I don't know."

"We use what weapons we have," Besh said. "I'm not a big man, Torgan. And I'm probably older than you are by four fours, perhaps more. But I wield powerful magic. That's my strength. I'd be mad not to use it, wouldn't I?"

The merchant shrugged. "I suppose."

Reaching the end of the lane, they found three young Fal'Borna men digging through the rubble. All of them bore cuts and scrapes on their arms, and one of them had a nasty burn on the side of his face that he must have gotten the night the pestilence struck. It had healed somewhat, as if treated by magic. But it looked as if it still hurt, and Besh thought it likely that the man would bear the scar for the rest of his life. The three men stopped working as Besh and Torgan approached.

Off to the side, the pyre smoldered, its dark smoke still staining the sky overhead.

"We've come to help if we can," Besh said.

The men stared back at him, saying nothing.

"We can do whatever you need us to do. We can dig. We can pile the things you find."

"We're searching for the dead," one of the men said, his voice flat.

"We can search as well. Or we can place the bodies you find on the pyre. As I say, we've come to help."

"We don't want you touching them," said the burned man.

Torgan bristled. "Well, then—"

Besh laid a hand on the merchant's arm, silencing him.

"I understand," Besh said. "If I was in your position, and two Eandi men came offering help, I'd probably send them away, too. But we're here, and you've a grim, difficult task to complete. So perhaps we can help in some other way."

The third Fal'Borna looked at the other two, a question in his bright yellow eyes. After several moments, the scarred man shrugged.

"Fine then," he said. "You can dig over there. Call us if you find anything. Or anyone."

"We will, of course," Besh said. He started toward the ruins the man had indicated.

Torgan was close behind him. "Ungrateful bastards," he whispered. "We should have just left them to do it alone."

Besh said nothing, and soon they were fighting their way through the massive pile of shattered stone and twisted wooden beams. Almost as soon as they began to pull away some of the rubble, Besh caught the foul scent of rotting flesh. There was at least one body beneath the wreckage.

"Damn," he muttered.

"I smell it, too," Torgan said. "We should tell them."

"Not yet," Besh said. "We'll clear away what we can, but we'll honor their wishes. When it comes time to pull out the dead, we'll call them."

They continued to move away the wood and stone, saying little. Torgan, not surprisingly, was a poor worker. He rested often, pausing after every scrap of wood and every chunk of rock, and even when he did work, he did so slowly, as if refusing to exert himself. Besh kept these thoughts to himself. He didn't expect Torgan would take criticism well.

The stench from the rubble grew steadily worse as they worked. The scrap of cloth that Besh had wrapped around his face helped a bit, but his eyes were watering, and he felt ill. It took all his will to keep working, particularly with Torgan doing so much less than his share of the labor.

So it was that Torgan's whispered words caught him completely by surprise.

"This can't be good," the merchant said.

Looking up, Besh saw the two soldiers from the gate approaching from the far side of the pyre. It almost seemed to Besh that they had taken a route that would keep them away from Grinsa and the others.

"Mettai!" the scarred soldier called. He had a predatory grin on his face, as did his companion.

The three Fal'Borna looked up at that, and then turned toward Torgan and Besh.

"That's right," the soldier said, looking at the other Qirsi. "That one, the old man. He's Mettai. Didn't they tell you?"

"Mettai?" asked the young Fal'Borna with the scar. "You're Mettai?"

Besh was bent over, and he straightened now, though not before he took a handful of dirt from the lane. There was a good deal of dust from the stone walls mixed in, but he thought that he could conjure with it, provided he could get his knife out. None of the Fal'Borna appeared to notice what he had done.

"Yes," Besh said. "I'm Mettai. I'm also the person who killed the woman responsible for the pestilence."

The young Fal'Borna's eyes widened. "You killed her?"

"He's Mettai!" the soldier said, drawing the man's gaze. "Never mind the rest of it. Our people are under attack, and his people are the enemy."

"Your n'qlae didn't see it that way," Besh said.

The soldier shook his head. "No, but the a'laq would have. She's not our leader, not really."

"And you are?" Besh asked. "I've been declared a friend of all Fal'Borna by an a'laq on the plain. You would put yourself above that man as well?"

"Keep quiet, Mettai!" the man said. He looked down the lane back toward where Grinsa and Sirj were working. Then he pulled his sword free and waved it at a small alley off the lane. "In there. Now." He pointed his blade at Torgan. "You, too, dark-eye."

The alley appeared to be cluttered with broken stone, but it was open enough for a small group of men; a perfect place for the soldier to kill them both. But Besh noticed that the Fal'Borna was relying on his weapon, rather than on his power, and he wondered what magics the man wielded. He was tempted to pull his knife free right away, but quickly thought better of it. His best hope was to catch the Fal'Borna unaware.

He started walking slowly toward the alley. Torgan fell in step beside him.

The guard and his companion followed. "The three of you stay out here," the soldier said. "Watch for their friends."

"What are you going to do to him?" the young Fal'Borna asked.

The soldier looked at him, as if trying to decide whether or not to answer. "This is war," he finally said. "And like I told you, these men are our enemies."

"Aren't you going to do something?" Torgan asked, his voice low. "You can do magic, right?"

"Yes, I can. Get directly behind me as we walk into the alley."

"What?" Torgan asked. "Why?"

"I need my knife. If you can block me from view for a moment, I can get it free without anyone noticing."

Torgan nodded. "All right."

"Once I have it out, you'll need to get out of my way so that I can throw my conjuring at him. I'll tell you when."

"Right."

They neared the mouth of the alleyway, and Torgan fell in step behind Besh.

"Now," Torgan whispered.

Besh pulled his knife from its sheath on his belt, quickly cut the back of his hand, and gathered the blood on the flat of the blade, no small feat while walking over the wreckage of the buildings.

"After the third element in the spell, you need to get down," Besh said.

"What? The third what?"

Besh didn't wait; Torgan would just have to figure it out. "Blood to earth," he said. "Life to power, power to thought." He spun around. Torgan's eyes widened and he dropped to the ground.

Too late, the Fal'Borna soldier realized the danger.

"Earth to fire!" Besh shouted. And as he said this, he threw the blood and earth at the man. Instantly, the clump of dirt changed to a ball of flame that soared toward the Fal'Borna's chest. The soldier lunged down and to the side, avoiding the attack, but his companion was not so fortunate. The fire crashed into his shoulder, the force of it knocking him to the ground.

Besh stooped quickly to grab another fistful of dirt, but before he could do anything more, the Fal'Borna's magic hit him. It was also fire, and Besh had no warning at all. Suddenly his shirt was burning, searing his arms and chest. He fell over and writhed on the ground, trying to extinguish the flames, though it was difficult to do with the debris all around him. By the time he'd managed to put the fire out, the soldier was standing over him, the tip of his sword hovering over Besh's heart. Torgan merely sat where he was, doing nothing, seemingly afraid of alerting the man to the fact that he was there. But the merchant's clothing bore burn marks as well, mostly on his left arm and shoulder. Apparently the fire magic had been directed at both of them.

"Mettai scum!" the Fal'Borna said to Besh, still menacing the old man with his blade. "Drop that knife."

Besh took a breath and said, "No," as bravely as he could, knowing what the man would do, hoping that the blow wouldn't be enough to sever his arm.

Just as Besh had expected, the soldier slashed at his forearm. Besh cried out in pain and grabbed at the wound with his other hand, which already held a fresh handful of dirt.

"I told you to drop the blade!" the soldier said.

Besh did as the man commanded, but already he was speaking the spell under his breath. He'd used this one on Lici during their first encounter and it had distracted her without killing her, which was just what Besh hoped it would do now. "Blood to earth, life to power, power to thought, earth to swarm."

He flung the dirt at the soldier, and as it flew from his hand it became a cloud of yellow and black hornets. Beset by the insects, the soldier dropped his sword to swat at them. He backed away, then turned and ran, the hornets following him.

"That was remarkable!" Torgan said, staring at Besh as if the old man had transformed himself into a god. "I'd heard people speak of Mettai magic, but I'd never seen anyone actually do it until now. Very impressive."

"Thank you," Besh said, still clutching his injured arm.

The merchant climbed to his feet, and helped Besh up. But the old man hadn't been standing for more than a heartbeat when pain exploded in his right leg and he collapsed to the ground again, crying out as he fell. Only after he had fallen did he realize that he'd heard the bone in his leg snap.

"I'll do the same to you, dark-eye," came a voice. "Back down on the ground. Now!"

Looking up through a haze of agony, Besh saw the other soldier approaching, the one he had burned with his fire spell, the one who, it seemed, possessed shaping magic.

Besh reached for another handful of dirt.

"Stop, Mettai! Unless you want that arm shattered, too!"

He'd been willing to risk a cut from the other man's sword. But whatever this soldier had done to his leg hurt nearly as much as what Lici had done to his hand. He stopped moving.

The soldier grinned. "That's right. Your magic might be able to do us some harm, but it's nothing compared with the power of a Qirsi." He walked to where Besh lay sprawled on the ground and kicked his injured leg. The wave of anguish that broke over Besh in that moment almost made him pass out.

"How should I kill you, Mettai? I'll give you the choice. Magic or steel?"

"Just make it quick," Besh said, staring at the ground, trying to keep from being ill.

The soldier placed the tip of his sword under Besh's chin and forced the man to look up at him. "I don't think so."

This was another way his life had changed in the last few turns, Besh thought. Not only was he threatening to kill people, but others always seemed to be looking for reasons to hurt him, to make him suffer. *I'll make you a deal,* he said within his mind, speaking now to the gods. *Stop the torture and I'll stop the threats.*

With a flick of his sword, the soldier cut his cheek, this newest pain making Besh gasp. *So much for prayers,* he thought.

"Who says I need to choose?" the man said. "Magic and steel will do nicely."

Besh expected at any moment to have another bone explode within him, and so at the next snapping sound he winced and shuddered. An instant later, though, he realized that this sound had been different. There'd been a metallic ring to it. Opening his eyes, he saw that the soldier still stood over him. The man's sword, however, lay in fragments at his feet, and all the soldier held in his hand was the hilt of his weapon.

"Get away from him!"

The soldier spun. Besh looked toward the entrance to the alley. There stood Grinsa, Q'Daer, Sirj, and Jasha. It was the Forelander who had spoken.

For several seconds it seemed that nothing happened and no one spoke. Then the Fal'Borna roared in frustration, and Besh understood that something had indeed been happening, but it had been beyond his comprehension.

"That's right," Grinsa said. "I'm a Weaver. You won't be using any more magic against that man. And if you don't get away from him now, I'll shatter every bone in your body."

"He's Mettai!" the man shouted, grief and rage mingled in his voice. He held up his hands, gesturing at the ruins around them. "His kind did all this to us! Don't you understand that?"

"The woman who did this may have been Mettai, but that doesn't make her his kind. Now one last time, get away from him. Or I swear I'll kill you."

The man stared down at Besh for a moment, as if contemplating whether it was worth dying if he could take Besh with him. In the end, he seemed to decide that it wasn't. He started forward toward Grinsa and the others.

Grinsa said something to Q'Daer before hurrying past the man to kneel at Besh's side. Sirj was just behind him.

"What did he do to you?" Grinsa asked. "The cuts. It looks like you've been burned, too. Your chest and arms? What else?" Before Besh could answer the man said, "Your leg. He broke your leg, didn't he?"

Besh nodded.

Without another word, Grinsa laid his hands gently on Besh's shattered leg and closed his eyes. For a moment there was a cooling sensation, as if cold water were moving over his skin. Then the pain came back, hot and intense, and Besh inhaled sharply through his teeth. And then it began to diminish, slowly at first, but more quickly with each passing moment, until at last all that remained was a dull ache.

A fine sheen of sweat had appeared on Grinsa's brow, but when he finished with Besh's leg he turned his attention to the burns on Besh's torso and arms. Eventually Besh's burns stopped hurting, and Grinsa moved his hands to the cut on the old man's arm. Finally, he healed the cut on Besh's face and sat back on his heels.

"There," he said, sounding weary.

Besh smiled. "Thank you."

Grinsa stood. "You're welcome. You probably want to rest," he said. "Really you should. But you can't. We're not going to kill this soldier, and so it won't be long before he returns with enough of his friends to make more trouble for us."

"I understand," Besh said. "And I've already sent one of his friends off. He has some hornets to get rid of, but once he does, I imagine he'll be looking for us, too."

"Hornets?" Grinsa said. "I'll look forward to hearing about that." He held out a hand to Besh.

The old man took hold of it and pulled himself up. The pain in his leg increased some once he was standing and he didn't think he'd be able to walk without support from Sirj. But he felt so much better than he had a few moments before that he didn't complain.

"Come on, Torgan," Grinsa said.

The merchant got up slowly. "What about me?" he demanded, gesturing at his burnt arm. "I need healing, too."

"And you'll be healed," Grinsa said. "Later. But for now you can walk, and we need to get going."

Before Torgan could argue the matter, a cry went out from far off.

"What's that?" the merchant said, sounding frightened. "They're coming for us, aren't they?"

Grinsa frowned, looking back at Q'Daer. "I don't think—"

More cries went up. A strange sound overhead drew the gazes of all of them.

"What was that?" Jasha asked.

"Fire magic," Grinsa said.

"Why—?"

Grinsa spun toward Q'Daer. "It's another outbreak! We have to get out of here, now!"

"What do you mean 'another outbreak'?" the soldier asked.

"The pestilence has returned to your city," the Forelander said. "Go! Your people need you."

"You see?" the man said, pointing at Besh. "You see what he did? You claim he's different, but he brought the pestilence to our city again!"

"No, he didn't!" Grinsa said. "Most likely, someone came across the remains of one of the cursed baskets. That would have been enough to bring the illness back again. Besh had nothing to do with it. Now, go! Quickly!"

The soldier hesitated for just a moment, his eyes straying toward Besh. Then he turned and ran.

"This way!" Grinsa said, following the man toward the end of the alley.

The others fell in behind him, walking as quickly as they could, but clearly mindful of not leaving Besh and Sirj behind. Once clear of the alley, they paused long enough to help Besh onto one of the horses, so that he wouldn't have to walk. Then they retraced the route the n'qlae had taken through the city. Besh knew that there had to be a quicker way to the gate. That was the only way to explain the sudden appearance of the soldiers. But he didn't know the way, and he didn't want to become lost and lead them deeper into the city.

Before they reached the gate, they found their way blocked by the n'qlae and a small party of Fal'Borna soldiers. The woman looked pale and frightened, her eyes even wider than they had appeared when they first met her.

Now that they had been forced to stop walking, Besh could hear more cries echoing through the ruins. Behind them, great clouds of dark smoke billowed into the sky. Besh thought he could hear stone and wood breaking. He couldn't even begin to imagine what another full outbreak of Lici's plague would do to the city.

"Are you responsible for this?" the n'qlae demanded. She pointed at Besh and Sirj. "Did they do it?"

"No, N'Qlae," Grinsa said. "They've done nothing but protect themselves from the attacks of your men."

She looked at the Mettai again, seeming to notice for the first time the marks of Besh's face, the blood and burns on his shirt. "Then how did this happen?" she asked, looking once more at Grinsa and Q'Daer.

"We think some of your people must have come across the remains of the baskets while they were digging through the rubble."

The woman appeared stricken. "After all this time, they could still sicken us?"

"It would seem so," Grinsa told her. "We know nothing for certain. But that makes the most sense."

She shook her head. "P'Crath said that we should come back here after ten days. He wouldn't have told us to return if he'd thought we would get sick."

More screams reached them, more rending of wood and stone. The company's horses reared suddenly, including the one Besh was riding. He grabbed hold of the beast's mane, barely managing to keep himself from being thrown.

"It's coming closer, N'Qlae," Q'Daer said. "You and your men should get away from here while you can."

"That's what you're doing. You're running away."

There was a challenge in the words, and for a moment none of them answered. At last Grinsa nodded. "Yes, we are. I'm sorry for your city, N'Qlae. But I won't die here. I have a family on the plain, and I have every intention of seeing them again."

"We could keep you here."

Besh felt his blood turn cold.

Grinsa, though, merely shook his head. "You don't want to do that. You have no cause to want us dead. Q'Daer's right. Your only concern now should be getting yourself and as many of your people as possible away from here."

"No," the woman said. "I fled once. I won't do it again. It seems this is the fate of S'Vralna and her people. We are to perish here."

"That doesn't have to be true," Grinsa said, pleading with her. "Your city can still have a future. You might have to start over again. You might have to raze what remains of the city and rebuild it. But you don't all have to die here!"

The woman shook her head. "You're a stranger to the Southlands. You know nothing of the Fal'Borna. I wouldn't expect you to understand." She turned to Q'Daer. "But you do, don't you? You know that this is what I have to do."

"Yes, N'Qlae," the Fal'Borna said. "I understand."

She nodded, the ghost of a smile touching her thin, lined face. "You can go," she said. "May the gods keep you safe."

Grinsa bowed to her, as did Q'Daer. A moment later the others did as well.

"Thank you, N'Qlae," Grinsa said.

They hurried past her, the sounds of suffering and death and rampant magic at their backs. Once clear of the gates, Besh dismounted and joined Sirj on their cart, while the others took to their horses and started westward, away from the city and toward the banks of the Thraedes. They didn't speak, though all of them took turns glancing back over their shoulders at the walled city, where dark smoke belched into the sky. Occasionally Besh caught sight of a spear of fire soaring above the city, but he saw no people, and as they put more distance between themselves and S'Vralna, he heard no more cries.

They rode for a long time without stopping, until Grinsa finally raised a hand to call a halt. They were near a small rill, probably a tributary to the river, and they allowed the horses to drink and graze for some time. Besh found a small rock to sit on near the stream, and Sirj soon joined him there. The younger man said little other than to offer Besh some food, which he refused. In fact, the old man noticed that none of them ate. Not even Torgan.

Grinsa approached the one-eyed merchant. "I can heal you now, if you'd like."

"Yeah. Yeah, all right," Torgan said.

Grinsa had him sit on the grass, and then the Forelander knelt beside him and placed his hands on the merchant's shoulder. After some time, Grinsa moved his hands down Torgan's arm. Eventually, he sat back, much as he had when he finished with Besh, and nodded once to the Eandi.

"Thank you," Besh heard Torgan say.

It sounded grudging and Grinsa responded with a thin smile before standing and walking away. He started toward his horse but then turned and came to where Besh and Sirj were sitting.

"How are you feeling?" the Forelander asked as he drew near.

"Tired," Besh said. "And sore. But I'm far better than I was before you healed me."

"I would hope so."

Besh grinned. "Does it make you tired to heal so many wounds in such a short time?"

"A bit," Grinsa said. "I'm a Weaver, so I tire less quickly than other Qirsi. But it's a strain."

"I would think so." He hesitated. Then, "Thank you. You saved my life before."

Grinsa shrugged. "You would have done the same for me."

Besh held his gaze. "Yes, I would have. And I will, if the need arises."

The Forelander smiled, a genuine, open smile, free of the cares that usually seemed to weigh on the man. It was a good smile, and it made Besh wonder what Grinsa was like when he was untroubled and with his family.

A moment later it was gone and the Forelander looked up at the sky, seeming to gauge the position of the sun.

"We should be moving again soon," he said. "I'm not proud to say this, but I want to put another league or two between us and S'Vralna."

"Of course," Besh said. "We're ready whenever you are."

"Thank you," Grinsa said before walking away.

"He's a good man," Sirj murmured as they watched him leave.

"He is," Besh said. He turned to his daughter's husband. "I know you're eager to go home, to see Elica and your children again. I am, too. But I don't want to leave the plain until we're certain that Grinsa and his family will be safe."

Sirj looked at him, his wild dark hair stirring in the cool wind. He nodded. "Yes, all right. We owe him that much, don't we?"

Besh smiled and put his hand on Sirj's shoulder, something he probably had never done before. Theirs had never been an easy relationship, mostly because Besh had been slow to accept that Sirj was worthy of marrying his daughter. Earlier, during their search for Lici, he finally realized that he'd been a fool to doubt him, and to doubt Elica for that matter. He should have been able to say as much, to tell Sirj that he, like Grinsa, was also a good man. In that moment, though, this simple gesture seemed enough.

He probably should have been grateful. Yes, he'd had to wait, but the Forelander had healed him eventually. And it seemed the white-hair had done an adequate job.

Riding once more, Torgan moved his shoulder and looked at the skin on his lower arm. His shoulder felt much better, and though the skin was still discolored, it wasn't tender anymore.

No doubt the others in the company expected him to be thankful that Grinsa had healed him. Besh couldn't have walked with his injuries; Torgan could. They'd needed to get away from the city as quickly as possible. Torgan knew all this, and he told himself these things again and again.

But still, he'd had to wait. He'd had to endure his pain for a long time, far longer than Besh. The only injuries that kept Besh from being able to leave the city had been the broken bone in his leg and the deep gash on his arm. Yet Grinsa had healed all of his wounds right away.

It shouldn't have bothered him; that's what Jasha would say. But it did.

To be more precise, it pointed to something that disturbed him a great deal: None in this company seemed to care whether he lived or died. Grinsa did what he could to keep Torgan alive for the time being, probably because he thought that the merchant might still help them in some way with their search for the rest of the cursed baskets. But he could tell the man didn't like him. And the rest of them spoke with unnerving frequency of killing him. Grinsa might swear that the young Fal'Borna Weaver had just been trying to mollify the n'qlae when he said that Torgan was to be executed. Torgan wasn't so certain.

The Mettai promised to kill Torgan if he tried to escape, and Grinsa and Q'Daer had said similar things in the past. Jasha seemed to have reached some sort of accommodation with the Qirsi, and Torgan could tell that Grinsa liked the Mettai. Torgan alone remained a prisoner among a company of free men.

More than ever, he now believed that his only hope for survival was to escape before they returned to E'Menua's sept. And more than ever he knew that he would have to find a way to flee on his own, without help from any of the other Eandi.

So be it.

S'Vralna had been a waking nightmare. He hoped never to see or hear or smell such horrors again. But their brief time there had also shown him beyond any doubt that the scrap of basket he still carried in the bottom of his travel sack remained a potent weapon. If the baskets in S'Vralna could bring on a second outbreak of the Mettai woman's plague, so could his. If the Qirsi riding a few paces in front of him refused to rule out killing him, he would continue to guard his secret so that he might strike back at them. He would be a fool to do less.

And Torgan Plye had never been a fool.

Chapter 20

It all happened much faster than she'd had any right to expect. The day after her second audience with His Lordship, Tirnya received word that Maisaak had dispatched a messenger to Ofirean City. Within ten days of this man's departure the lord governor received a message back from the sovereign. She and her father had expected the exchange of missives to take close to a turn; instead they had taken less than half that time. By any measure, they had been remarkably fortunate.

And yet, for Tirnya, each day of waiting seemed an eternity. Whatever relief she had felt in learning that the lord governor had made his decision so quickly gave way to childlike impatience as she awaited the reply from Stelpana's royal city. She would go from being utterly certain one moment that the sovereign would approve their plan, to imagining in the next all sorts of reasons why Ankyr might say no. During this time she treated horribly everyone she knew. She knew it, and yet she could do nothing about it. She was far too rough on her men, pushing them so hard during their training sessions that afterward none of her lead riders would speak to her. At home, she was moody to the point of rudeness, speaking to her mother and father as if they were common servants. She avoided Enly entirely.

When at last His Lordship summoned Tirnya and her father to his palace to inform them of the sovereign's decision, Tirnya was so exhausted from the ordeal of waiting that she managed to convince herself she didn't care one way or another what Ankyr's message said. Of course, this didn't stop her from trembling with anticipation as she and Jenoe waited in the palace corridor to be admitted to Maisaak's chamber. She paced back and forth in front of Maisaak's door, muttering under her breath, reminding herself of all the reasons why the sovereign was bound to give his permission.

After some time, Jenoe said something to her, though Tirnya barely heard him.

She halted in front of him. "What?"

"I said, perhaps this time you should let me do the talking."

Tirnya frowned. "Why?"

Jenoe glanced at the two guards positioned on either side of the door. Both men were smirking.

"Because," he said, his voice dropping to a whisper, "I'm afraid of what you might say to His Lordship if this doesn't go the way you'd like it to."

She started to argue with him, then stopped herself. "I really have been dreadful, haven't I?"

Her father looked down at the floor, his lips pursed. After a moment he nodded. "Yes, you have."

"I'm sorry," she said. "By all means, speak for us. If His Lordship lets us go, you'll be in command anyway."

A moment later, the door opened, and the two of them were ushered into the chamber. Once again, Enly was already inside, and while Tirnya steadfastly avoided his gaze, she realized that she was glad to have him there, although she wasn't exactly certain why.

She and her father stopped just inside the doorway and bowed to the lord governor.

"Come in," Maisaak said. He wasn't smiling, but there was something in his voice that put Tirnya's mind at ease. He sounded pleased, and given his eagerness to be rid of her father, Tirnya assumed this meant that the sovereign had granted their request. "I'm sure you know why I summoned you here, so I won't waste your time or mine. The sovereign has granted me authority to send our armies west into Fal'Borna land, provided we succeed in forging an alliance with the Mettai."

Tirnya could barely contain her glee; she had to resist an urge to rush forward and throw her arms around His Lordship's neck. Just the idea of it made her giggle.

"Is something funny, Captain?" Maisaak asked.

"No, Your Lordship. I'm . . . I'm pleased."

"I imagine you are. I mentioned in my message to the sovereign that this was your idea, Captain," His Lordship went on. "He told me to commend you for your imaginative thinking. But he also wanted me to make clear that if the Mettai refuse your overtures, you're to return to Qalsyn. He doesn't want to risk this war without their aid."

"I understand, Your Lordship," Tirnya said.

"Good." Maisaak stepped behind his writing table and sat. "You'll take all the companies under your command, Jenoe. I'll be sending Enly and his soldiers with you, as well. And the sovereign has ordered sixteen companies from the north and a dozen from the south to meet you along the wash at Enka's Shallows."

Tirnya wasn't certain that she had heard him correctly. "But, Your Lordship—"

"Don't worry, Captain. The northern army comes out of Fairlea, the southern companies from Waterstone, and the sovereign has made clear to them that they'll be under your father's command."

She frowned. "Yes, Your Lordship, but—"

"She wasn't concerned about the other armies, Father," Enly said, watching her with a slight smile on his lips. "She's wondering why you'd send me along, when I've made it clear from the start that I don't approve of this venture."

His Lordship looked first at Enly and then at Tirnya. "Is that true, Captain?"

She hesitated. "Yes, Your Lordship."

"Do you want to explain?" Maisaak asked his son. "Or should I?"

"I volunteered for this," Enly said, not bothering to look at the lord governor. "I felt a bit responsible, since I was there when you first thought of approaching the Mettai. And I suppose I feel that I can be of some help."

Tirnya wasn't certain what to say. She couldn't even decide if she wanted him riding with them. It occurred to her that this might have been Maisaak's idea, that His Lordship might have instructed Enly to do whatever he could to see that the invasion failed. As quickly as this notion came to her, she dismissed it. Enly and his father hardly spoke to one another unless they had to. Maisaak wouldn't trust Enly with such a task, and Enly wouldn't take it on if he did. Forced to choose between Tirnya and his father, Enly would have chosen her. Everyone in the chamber knew it.

"We'll be glad to have you with us, my lord," Jenoe said, after a brief silence.

Enly inclined his head slightly. "Thank you, Marshal."

"You'll be leading them, Jenoe," His Lordship said. "Even with my son there, this is your army to command."

"You honor me, Your Lordship. With such fine captains riding at my side, we're sure to prevail."

Maisaak's smile this time was thin and clearly forced. "Indeed," he said. He turned his attention back to the scrolls on his writing table. "You all have much to do in the next few days. Enly, tell the quartermaster to gather and prepare provisions for two thousand men. Jenoe, I'd suggest you send some of your men to the armory. You'll want to have at least five hundred bows with you, and I'm not certain we have that many ready right now." He looked at Tirnya. "Captain, I'd like you to speak with the stablemaster. Obviously most of your soldiers will be on foot. But all told you'll have close to forty commanders and lead riders. The stablemaster may need a few days to equip that many beasts."

"Yes, Your Lordship. I'll see to it immediately."

"Good. Keep me apprised of your progress."

"Forgive me, Your Lordship," Jenoe said. "But when last we spoke, I told you that I could pay for provisions out of my family's treasury. I fully intend—"

"No need, Jenoe," Maisaak said. "The sovereign has pledged to pay the costs of this war. We don't need your gold."

Jenoe eyed the man for just a moment. "Yes, Your Lordship."

Maisaak nodded once. "That's all."

Tirnya, Jenoe, and Enly left the chamber together, none of them saying a thing as they made their way through the palace corridors. Only when they reached the city lanes did Enly stop and face them.

"I just want to repeat what my father told you in there," he said. "I have no desire to lead this army, Marshal, and I won't do anything to challenge your authority."

"Thank you, my lord," Jenoe said.

"I'd suggest you get used to calling me captain. We don't want to give the men any reason to question who's in command."

Jenoe smiled. "You're right. Captain."

Enly smiled in turn, nodded once to Tirnya, and walked away.

"I'm not sure I trust him," Tirnya said, gazing after him.

"I don't trust him at all," Jenoe answered, surprising her. "I say that not as his commander—I trust him entirely in that regard." He glanced at her, his eyes twinkling. "It's as your father that I have my doubts."

Over the next several days, all of Qalsyn seemed to come to life, like a bees' nest that's been prodded with a stick. Now that it was no longer a secret, word of the impending attack on the Fal'Borna spread swiftly to every corner of the city. Suddenly, every man, woman, and child was working with a single purpose: to provision and arm Jenoe's army. Though many of the soldiers under Tinrya's command might have had their doubts about the wisdom of her plan, they all trained with a passion and purpose she had never seen in them before. And knowing now what had been concealed from them previously, they seemed to forgive Tirnya for how hard she had pushed them.

It was another six days after their meeting with Maisaak before all was ready for Jenoe's army to march from the city gates. On that seventh morning, with a fine, cold mist falling on the city, all the people of Qalsyn turned out to see the soldiers off. Zira stood at the front of the crowd with Tirnya's twin brothers, Galdry and Laeris. The boys were still a year shy of their fourth four, but they had argued with Jenoe late into the night, begging him to let them march to war. Zira had said little to Tirnya over the past few days. But Tirnya had heard her speaking with Jenoe as well, pleading with him not to go. On this morning, her face looked puffy and her eyes were red-rimmed. She wouldn't meet Tirnya's gaze.

Maisaak was there as well, standing beside Riyette, Her Ladyship, whose golden hair seemed to shimmer in the grey light.

"Gods keep you safe," the lord governor said, his voice barely carrying in the still, damp air. His pale blue eyes flicked ever so briefly toward his son. "All of you. We'll await word of your success."

"Thank you, Your Lordship," Jenoe said. He pulled his sword free and held it to his forehead in salute. The rest of the commanders and soldiers did the same.

His blade still in hand, Jenoe steered his mount through the city gate and out into the rolling hills that surrounded Qalsyn. His captains, including Tirnya and Enly, followed, and behind them came a long column of soldiers, their helms and weapons gleaming. Some in the crowd that had gathered to watch them leave cheered and called out the names of their friends and loved ones. Most remained silent. In all, it struck Tirnya as a solemn affair, and she feared there was an ill omen in the grave aspect of those who had lined the city lanes.

They marched northwestward, toward the Companion Lakes. By late in the day, the skies had cleared, and the wind had freshened from the west. With the dreary weather behind them, Tirnya's mood improved. Though Jenoe chose not to push the men too hard that first day, they still managed to cover more than two leagues before stopping for the night. As they made camp under a darkening sky of indigo, she decided that she'd been foolish that morning, and that omens were for children and superstitious fools. She was a soldier, helping to lead a fine army. Their success or failure would be determined by their training and the soundness of their strategy, not by gloomy skies and the facial expressions of wet, tired cityfolk.

Over the next several days, Jenoe gradually increased the length of their marches. Tirnya and her father had estimated the distance between Qalsyn and the southernmost Mettai villages in the Companion Lakes region at just over forty leagues, and with the good weather holding, and the moons offering some light after nightfall, they expected that they could cover that distance in twelve days or so, fewer if they were lucky.

For the most part, the soldiers remained in good spirits throughout the march. Occasionally, at the end of a particularly long day, they began to grouse a bit. But usually a meal and a good night's sleep mollified them, and by the next morning, they were ready to resume their journey northward.

Riding with her father and the other captains, Tirnya could hardly fault the soldiers for their complaints. It was a far more arduous journey for them than it was for her. Still she couldn't help but take pride in the fact that it was men from other companies who grumbled most loudly. Her soldiers comported themselves well, and if on some days they felt that the marshal drove them too hard, they kept silent about it.

Enly rode with the commanders, of course. But he spoke little, and he always made camp with his soldiers, slightly apart from the rest of Jenoe's army. He and Tirnya avoided each other, which suited her just fine. She spent most of her time with her father and Stri Balkett, or with her own lead riders. This was her first major military expedition, and despite the uncertainties and the dangers, she couldn't help but be excited.

As they approached the Companion Lakes region, the terrain began to change, and so did the weather. The plain gave way to rolling hills; the open land was replaced by thick forests of cedar, spruce, and pine. At the same time, the air grew colder, though the skies remained clear. Ravens Wash, which they had followed all the way from Qalsyn, flowed more swiftly here, its waters roiled and frothy. Before them, though still a good distance off, loomed the jagged, white-capped peaks of the Border Range. Tirnya had grown up within sight of the Aelind Mountains, but never before had she seen summits as high and imposing as these.

On the tenth day out from Qalsyn, the wind shifted so that it blew directly from the north and seemed to carry with it the cold of those distant snowy ridges. That night, the camp glowed bright orange with all the fires lit by Jenoe's army. Tirnya huddled in her sleeping roll throughout the night, sleeping poorly, and thinking, despite her better judgment, of the warm nights she had passed in Enly's bed. When she awoke the following morning, the ground and her sleeping roll both were coated with a thin white frost.

They broke camp quickly. For once every soldier under her father's command seemed eager to be marching.

As they started out, Enly rode past her, a small smile on his lips. "I thought of you last night," he said, his voice pitched just loud enough for her to hear.

She didn't answer, but she felt her face turn red.

They came to their first Mettai village later that morning. They had encountered several towns and villages along the banks of the wash as they made their way north, but during the previous two days had seen none at all. It almost seemed that over the years a boundary had formed between the Eandi villages and those of the Mettai.

There was little in the village itself to mark it as being Mettai. The houses and lanes looked much like those in other settlements. The homes might have been a bit smaller here, a bit more ragged in appearance. But Tirnya saw nothing that told her definitively that this was a Mettai village. Still, she knew it immediately, and so, it seemed, did her father.

They'd passed by all the towns they'd seen previously; this time they stopped a short distance from the settlement. Jenoe surveyed the village and then the surrounding woodlands, as if searching for signs of a trap.

"Have your men remain here," he told his captains. "Tirnya, Enly, and I will ride in and speak with the leaders."

Tirnya and the other captains rode back to inform their lead riders of what they were doing. Then Enly and Tirnya rejoined the marshal and the three of them steered their mounts toward the village.

Black-haired children playing in the lanes and yards stopped to stare at the riders as they went past. Their eyes were wide and dark, their skin still brown from the Growing sun. Men and women appeared in doorways or stepped around from in back of houses to look at the strangers.

"They certainly look like Mettai," Jenoe said quietly. "Every Mettai I've ever seen was dark like these people."

They came to a small marketplace and halted, wondering where to seek out the village's leaders. They needn't have wondered. After only a moment or two, a woman approached them. Her hair was white and her face bore deep lines, but she stood straight and she regarded them with shining black eyes that seemed to have surrendered nothing to age.

"Who are you?" she asked in a gravelly voice. "What is this army that you've brought to my village?"

Jenoe dismounted and nodded once to Tirnya and Enly, indicating that they should do the same.

"My name is Jenoe Onjaef, good woman," the marshal said. "This is my daughter, Tirnya, and with us is Enly Tolm, lord heir of Qalsyn."

The woman glanced at the younger riders, appearing unimpressed. Then she faced Jenoe again. "All right," she said. "That's who you are. What about the rest of it? Why are you here?"

Jenoe favored her with his most disarming smile. "May I ask where we are, gentle woman? What is the name of his village?"

She frowned, and for a moment Tirnya wondered if she would answer. "This is Shaldir," she finally said. "You're near the Companion Lakes. Or did you know that already?"

Tirnya's father chuckled. "Yes, that much we knew. And your name?"

Again the woman hesitated, clearly not pleased by the way he was evading her questions. "I'm Kenitha. I'm eldest of this village."

"And you're Mettai, aren't you, Eldest?"

"What are you doing here?" she demanded, her voice rising.

"Are you Mettai?"

She pressed her lips in a thin line, but then held up her left hand so that they could see the back of it. Her brown skin was scored with dozens of thin white scars and several more cuts that were darker, fresher. "Now, answer me. What do you want with us? We've done nothing that would displease the lord governor."

"No, you haven't," Jenoe said. "Please forgive us if our presence here has unnerved you or the people of your village." He glanced around. "Is there somewhere we might speak to you in private?"

Her expression darkening even more, Kenitha stared at them briefly before turning on her heel and walking away. Jenoe glanced at Tirnya, an eyebrow raised. Then he followed the woman, as did Tirnya and Enly.

She led them to a small house just south of the marketplace, but she didn't take them inside. Instead, she sat on the steps outside the door.

"Now, for the last time, what are you doing here?"

Jenoe looked around. There was no one else in sight. This was as much privacy as they were likely to get.

"Have you heard talk of the pestilence recently?" the marshal asked.

Clearly Kenitha hadn't been expecting this. "Yes, I have. The outbreaks have been west of here, in the Y'Qatt villages on the Silverwater, and on the Central Plain."

Jenoe nodded. "That's right. Apparently this is a peculiar strain of the disease. It only strikes at Qirsi. As far as we know, not a single Eandi village has seen an outbreak."

The woman frowned again. "That I hadn't heard, but now that you say it, I think you're right. All the villages that have been struck have been west of the Silverwater." She shook her head. "But what does this have to do with your army being here?"

"You know the history of the Central Plain, don't you?" Jenoe said. "That it was once held by the Eandi. The Horn, Silvralna, Deraqor—all of it was ours." He indicated Tirnya with an open hand. "And my family—mine and Tirnya's—once ruled in Deraqor."

"Onjaef," she whispered, comprehension lighting her eyes. "I knew I'd heard the name."

Jenoe smiled. "Yes."

"You're marching to war," Kenitha said. "That's why you've come this way. It's not enough that the white-hairs are dying from the pestilence; you want to slaughter them on a battlefield as well."

Tirnya felt as though she'd been slapped. "That's not—!"

Her father held up a hand, silencing her. "You're right. That's essentially what we're doing. But you have to understand that they took our ancestral lands from us. We've been exiles for more than a century. And now we have an opportunity to take back those lands."

"The Blood Wars have been over for a long time," the woman said, a gust of wind making her hair dance around her face. "And yet the tales of them that my grandfather told me—tales his grandfather told him—are still enough to keep me awake on a cold, dark night. You're stepping back into horrors you don't even understand."

Jenoe cast another quick look at Tirnya, his expression bleak. Clearly this wasn't going to work, at least not with these Mettai. But her father made the effort anyway.

"I'm sorry to hear you say that," he told the eldest. "We came here hoping that you and your people might join us in our fight. We could offer you land on the Central Plain, or perhaps even in the Horn. You wouldn't have to take up arms, but your magic . . ."

He trailed off. The woman was laughing and shaking her head.

"Remarkable," she said. "You actually came here hoping to lure us into this folly. The Mettai have been ignored by your kind for centuries. On those few occasions when you do take notice of us, it's to push us off our land or something of the sort. And now, suddenly, you want us to be allies in your war? You must be joking."

Jenoe straightened. "I assure you, Eldest, we're utterly serious about this."

"Well, you'll have to get your magic elsewhere," she said, standing, and starting up the stairs toward the door. "Because we want nothing to do with you or your battles." She entered the house and shut the door behind her, leaving the three of them standing there.

Jenoe clicked his tongue once and started to lead his horse away from the house, back to where the army was waiting. Tirnya followed, leading Thirus, her sorrel, and Enly fell in step beside her. After a moment, Jenoe slowed down, allowing them to catch up with him.

"So what do we do now?" the lord heir asked.

"This isn't the only Mettai village around here," Tirnya said quickly.

"No," her father agreed, "it's not. But I'm afraid that Kenitha's attitude may be more typical than you'd like to believe."

"I'm not ready to give up yet," Tirnya said, looking at both men in turn, as if challenging them to argue the point.

"Neither am I." Her father kept his tone mild, no doubt as determined to avoid a fight as she was to keep trying. "I'm just saying that we may run out of villages before long."

Tirnya felt certain that Enly was thinking much the same thing, but he kept his thoughts to himself.

They rejoined the army a short time later and turned northward once more. The following day they came to a second settlement, this one somewhat larger than the first. As before, Tirnya, Jenoe, and Enly rode into the village to speak with the leaders there.

The town, it turned out, was called Kirayde. The eldest this time was a blacksmith by the name of Pyav, who spoke to them in the middle of the marketplace and appeared wary of them from the start. Despite her certainty that their plan could work and her resolve to keep trying, Tirnya knew immediately that this man would refuse them as well.

Her father began by saying much the same thing to Pyav that he had to Kenitha. As soon as he mentioned the pestilence, however, Pyav's face turned ashen.

"You're certain that it's only Qirsi who are getting sick?" the man asked.

Jenoe nodded. "Yes."

"But all Qirsi. Not just the Y'Qatt?"

Tirnya's father narrowed his eyes slightly. "No, it's not just the Y'Qatt. We'd heard that it started in some of the Y'Qatt settlements, but it's spread westward into Fal'Borna land since then."

"May the gods save us all," Pyav muttered, looking ill himself.

"Well, as I say, it only strikes at Qirsi. I don't think you need to fear for your people. That's not why I came."

"What?" the man said, as if rousing himself from a dark dream.

"I said we didn't come here to warn you about the pestilence. I don't think it poses any threat to you."

Pyav rubbed a hand over his face. "Well, she's not here anymore," he said. "She lived here once, but she's gone now. I don't know where she's gone."

For several moments Jenoe said nothing, his expression so puzzled that it might have been comical had Tirnya not been certain that hers looked just the same.

"I'm sorry," Jenoe said. "I don't know who or what you're talking about."

Pyav stared back at him. "No," he said. "I don't suppose you do. I'm sorry. I . . . I was confused for a moment. Please, why is it you've come?"

As he had in Shaldir, the marshal spoke briefly of the history of the Central Plain and the Onjaef family. He still seemed puzzled by the eldest's behavior, and he rambled on a bit, but eventually came to the crux of the matter.

"So you mean to attack the Fal'Borna while they're weakened."

"Yes, we do," Jenoe told him. "And we'd like to enlist the Mettai as allies in this venture. We can offer you land, and we can promise that it will be yours for as long as we hold the plain."

Pyav shook his head slowly. "First a plague," he whispered, "and now a war."

"Your magic would be a great boon to us."

"No," Pyav said, shaking his head more vehemently this time. "Our magic has done enough damage already. We want no part of a new Blood War." He turned and started to walk away. "Take your men and go, Marshal. We can't help you."

"He's a strange man," Enly said, watching the eldest hurry away from them.

Jenoe furrowed his brow. "Possibly. Certainly there was something odd in the things he said to us. 'Our magic has done enough damage already'? I have no idea what he meant by that." He looked at Tirnya. "Regardless of his reasons, though, that's twice now we've been turned away. How many more villages do you think we ought to visit before we accept that this isn't going to work?"

She felt Enly watching her. "I don't know," she said, her voice flat. "A couple."

Her father nodded. "All right. Two more, then. After that, if we still haven't convinced any Mettai to join us, we'll turn back."

"No," she said. "That's too few."

"You're the one—"

"Yes, Father, I know. And now I'm telling you that it's too few. We've been in Mettai territory for two days. That's all. Rather than limiting ourselves to two more villages, we should give this a set amount of time. Five more days, let's say. After that we can go back."

Jenoe looked past her to Enly. "What do you think?"

Enly exhaled, chancing a quick glance at Tirnya. "I think you could take an entire turn, visit twenty more villages, and it wouldn't change a thing. The Mettai have been shunned by both the clans and the sovereignties for hundreds of years. And while they might not have wanted to be ignored, they have managed to survive and avoid the wars. None of them want anything to do with us or the white-hairs." He gave a small, dry chuckle. "I can't say that I blame them."

"Someone among them will want to join us," Tirnya said. "They're Eandi. I don't care what kind of magic they possess, nothing can change that. We're offering land, and a chance to rejoin Eandi society. There must be one leader among them who'll want that."

Enly shrugged. "Maybe. But you have to wonder . . ." He stopped, shaking his head.

"You have to wonder what?" Tirnya demanded.

"Nothing. You may be right. That person may be out there somewhere. But how long will it take us to find the right village?"

Chapter 21

LIFARSA, NEAR THE COMPANION LAKES, MEMORY MOON WANING

After leaving Kirayde, all of them still puzzled by the odd behavior of the village's eldest, Tirnya, Enly, and Jenoe led the Qalsyn army deeper into Mettai lands. They continued to follow the banks of Ravens Wash, believing that most Mettai settlements would be found within sight of the river. They found no more villages that day, however, and though they set out at first light the following morning, by midday they had yet to see any other settlements.

"They may be clustered nearer to the lakes," Jenoe said at one point. "In the years following the end of the Blood Wars the Mettai were pushed pretty far north."

Neither Tirnya nor Enly said anything, and they continued on.

By nightfall, they still had found nothing, and Tirnya's frustration mounted. She'd thought that by arguing for a set time period in which to search for potential allies, instead of agreeing to visit a certain number of villages, she was helping her cause, making it more likely that they would find Mettai who were willing to help them. Now it seemed that she might have miscalculated.

Clouds began to move in as the soldiers made camp and by the time Tirnya went to sleep it had begun to snow, further darkening her mood. If the weather turned against them, her father might insist that they start back toward Qalsyn, even if that meant visiting no more villages.

When they awoke the next morning, the first of the new waning, all the camp had been covered with a light dusting of snow. The skies, though, had already started to clear, and while Tirnya's father made jokes about how poorly Tirnya's mother would have fared under such circumstances, he said nothing about returning to the city.

Tirnya had also feared that the cold might dampen the spirits of the soldiers, but as the men broke camp that morning, they threw snowballs at one another, acting more like children on an outing than grown men marching to battle.

For the first few hours, the snow hindered their progress some. But by midday, the air had turned warm and much of the snow had melted, allowing the men who were on foot to walk faster. Still, they came upon no settlements. Tirnya kept her eyes fixed on the northern horizon, straining her eyes for any sign of the Mettai.

Finally, late in the day, she spotted a town ahead of them. At first, both Enly and her father thought she was imagining it, but eventually they saw it, too. This came as a great relief; for just a short time, she had started to fear that in her eagerness to find the Mettai she really had started to imagine things.

Once more Jenoe marched his army to the outskirts of the village before continuing on into the heart of the settlement with Tirnya and Enly. As they rode up the lane leading into the center of the settlement, Tiryna felt her hopes rising. This village was similar in size to Kirayde, but it didn't look nearly as prosperous as Pyav's village. Several of the houses were in disrepair, and the land around the village didn't appear as fertile. Many of the garden plots were filled with wispy grasses, and the few animals they passed looked underfed.

"This is the one," Tirnya said quietly.

Her father looked at her. "You think so?"

"Look at the homes. Look at the garden plots. They need us as much as we need them."

"I'm not sure that's reason enough to make them our allies," Enly said.

Tiryna looked at him sharply. "What's that supposed to mean?"

"Just that we're going to be counting on these people in battle. We need them, yes. But we should be able to trust them. If they're just doing this because they need more fertile land—"

"That's as good a reason as any," Tirnya said. "You're just looking for ways to keep us from succeeding. One day you say that the Mettai won't ally themselves with us because of how they've been treated. Now you're saying that if we can overcome their doubts by offering them a better place to live, we shouldn't trust them. So by your reckoning, the only Mettai worthy of being our allies are the ones who are too principled to join us."

"That's not . . ." Enly stopped and looked at Jenoe.

The marshal raised an eyebrow. "Actually, I agree with her. We came prepared to offer them land, because we knew that might be the best way to win their support. This is war, Enly. We're fighting for land ourselves. Yes, there's more than that at stake for Tirnya and me, but essentially, we're trying to win back the Horn and Deraqor. Why should we expect more of the Mettai?"

"I suppose," Enly said, not sounding convinced. He looked at Tirnya. "I'm not trying to keep you from succeeding. I just . . . I'm suspicious of magic, be it Mettai or white-hair. I don't like the idea of going into battle depending on sorcerers to save my life."

"Would you rather face an army of sorcerers without any magic on your side?"

Enly tipped his head, acknowledging the point. "No. I'd rather have nothing to do with magic at all."

"Then you shouldn't have come," Tirnya said, facing forward again.

As they approached the village marketplace, they saw that several people were standing in the middle of the lane, apparently waiting for them. One of them, an older woman with short white hair and a narrow face, raised a hand in greeting. But Tirnya noticed that most of the men and women standing behind her held axes, hoes, spades, and hammers. They looked like they were ready for a fight.

Jenoe raised a hand in return. "Greetings," he called to the woman.

She said nothing.

"Friendly place," Enly said under his breath.

The three riders dismounted a short distance from the villagers and covered the remaining distance on foot.

"I take it you're the eldest of this village," Jenoe said.

"I am," the woman answered warily. "My name is Fayonne. And you are?"

"Jenoe Onjaef, marshal under His Lordship Maisaak Tolm in Qalsyn. This is my daughter, Tirnya, and His Lordship's son, Enly. What village is this, Fayonne?"

"Lifarsa. We saw your army from a great distance. If it's supplies you need, you've come to the wrong place. We haven't food to spare, at least not enough to make a difference to so many."

Jenoe smiled. "No. We're well provisioned."

Fayonne had a sharp chin and large, wide eyes, which she narrowed now, making her face look feline. "Then why have you come?"

Jenoe asked her about the pestilence, of which she'd heard a good deal, and then spoke to her briefly of the history of house Onjaef. Like Kenitha, in Shaldir, Fayonne understood immediately what he had in mind.

"You intend to take back your land," she said. "You're going to fight the Fal'Borna."

"That's our intention," Jenoe said. "And we'd like to propose an alliance with the Mettai. We're going to fight against sorcerers, and we'd like to have magic wielded on our behalf as well."

"How much do you know about Mettai magic, Marshal Onjaef?" the woman asked.

"I'd be the first to admit that I know very little. I know that it's blood magic, that you need to cut yourself in order to wield it. Beyond that . . ." He opened his hands and shrugged.

"Our magic doesn't work the way Qirsi magic does. Some would say it's not as powerful, although we Mettai know better. But it is different. We have no Weavers; we can't combine our powers in any way."

Jenoe looked at Tirnya, a question in his eyes. She nodded.

"We understand all of that, Eldest. We still wish to discuss an alliance."

Fayonne, in turn, glanced back at those who were standing with her before facing the marshal again. "Very well," she said. "What would we get in return?"

Tirnya suppressed a smile. At long last, they'd found what they were seeking. Her eyes flicked toward Enly, who was already looking at her, the expression in his pale eyes unreadable.

"If we manage to take back Deraqor and the Horn," Jenoe said, "we can offer you land. I don't know where exactly." He looked around at the village. "I can promise you, though, that it will be more fertile than the land you have here."

The eldest eyed him for several moments, her tongue pressing her cheek outward. "I'd like for us to discuss this further, and I need to talk to my Council of Elders. You can remain here for the night?"

Jenoe nodded. "Of course."

"Good. Again, we can't feed all your men. But if the three of you will return at dusk, we'd be pleased to have you as our guests for the evening meal."

"You honor us, Eldest. We'll look forward to supping with you."

The woman nodded, her expression so grave one might have thought that she'd told Jenoe and his army to leave at once.

The three riders turned and started back down the lane toward the army, saying nothing until they were certain that the Mettai couldn't hear them.

"Seems you were right," Tirnya's father finally said.

Tirnya grinned. "Yes."

"They were very quick to agree," Enly said, not looking nearly as pleased as Tirnya felt. "They must be desperate to leave this land."

Jenoe glanced around, frowning slightly. "I can't say that I blame them."

"Neither can I," Enly said. "But still, there's something odd about this place. I can't see any reason why the land here should be any worse than it was in Kirayde or Shaldir. But clearly it is."

"Maybe the soil gets worse as one moves northward," Tirnya said.

Enly shook his head. "I've never heard that."

"And since when are you an expert on farming?"

"I've never heard it, either," her father said.

Tirnya wanted to tell them both that they were being foolish. They'd found allies for their war. The rest hardly mattered. But she could imagine what Enly would say to that. In the end she simply said, "Well, then perhaps they have some other reason for wanting to leave."

Even that wasn't enough to end their discussion.

"Exactly," Enly said pointedly. "And I, for one, would like to know what that reason is before we ride into battle with them."

"We'll learn what we can at supper," Jenoe said.

Enly nodded his agreement. "What will you promise them?"

"No more than I have to."

"Father!" Tinrya said.

Jenoe held up a hand. "I'm just saying that there's too much we don't know right now. How much land will we win back? Which parts of the territory will be easiest to take? I can't promise them much, because we don't know yet what we have to offer."

He had a point. Still, Tirnya had hoped that her father at least would join her in celebrating their good fortune. Instead, he sounded nearly as doubtful as Enly.

They reached the army a few moments later and immediately Enly and Tirnya informed their lead riders that they wouldn't be marching any farther this day and that the men should begin to make camp. As word of this spread, cheers went up from the soldiers. Not wishing to be near her father or Enly for now, Tirnya remained with her soldiers.

She hadn't spoken much with her lead riders in the last few days, and she missed their company. Oliban returned to her a short while after she'd given the order to make camp, trailed by several of his men.

"Th' men are askin' if they can hunt, Captain," he told her. "They'd like some game for their suppers."

Tirnya considered this for just a moment. "I don't see why not." She smiled at the soldiers. "Good hunting."

"Thank ya, Captain!" the men said, before hurrying off.

She and Oliban watched them go.

"So these are th' ones, eh?" Oliban asked after some time. "These Mettai I mean."

"It looks that way," she said. "Their leader wanted to speak with their Council of Elders, but she seemed eager to help us."

"So we'll be goin' t' war after all."

Tirnya eyed him a moment. He'd kept his tone light, but it seemed an odd way to phrase the question. "Were you hoping we wouldn't?"

"No, Captain," he said quickly. "We was jus' wonderin'. That's all."

She nodded, though she didn't quite believe him. "Well, as I say, we'll be speaking with their leader again this evening. I'll let you know what happens."

She turned away from him and began to walk among her men. Many of them shouted greetings to her that she acknowledged with a wave or a smile. But she spoke with no one.

At dusk, she joined her father and Enly, and the three of them rode back into the village. Once again, they found the eldest waiting for them in the marketplace. Several torches had been mounted on poles, which were arrayed around a long table. It seemed they were to eat right there, out in the open, despite the chill creeping into the night air. The eldest had been joined by perhaps ten men and women, most of them white-haired like Fayonne. They were already seated, leaving four spaces at the table's center. All of them stared at Tirnya and the others, but they didn't smile or say a word. They just watched.

"Welcome," Fayonne said. "Thank you for coming."

The words were kind enough, but once again there was something grim in the woman's manner. In spite of herself Tirnya wondered if Enly might be right about this village and its people.

Fayonne indicated the table. "Please, join us." She led them to the table and sat, clearly expecting them to do the same.

There were already loaves of bread on the table and a bowl of dark stew at each place. The eldest picked up her spoon, dipped it into the stew, and held it up, glancing at Jenoe, a thin smile on her lips.

"Again, welcome," she said. "Enjoy."

With that, she began to eat, as did the other Mettai.

Jenoe nodded to the two captains and picked up his spoon as well.

Tirnya followed his example, tasting the stew tentatively. It was awful. It had been heavily spiced with some herb that burned her tongue but didn't quite mask the sour taste of whatever meat had been used in the dish. What few vegetables there were had been badly overcooked, and the meat was tough and stringy. She reached for some bread at the same time Enly did.

Her father had taken one spoonful, and now he laid his spoon back down on the table and looked at the eldest.

"Have you and your council come to a decision?" he asked.

"We have," the eldest said, in between spoonfuls. One might have thought it was the most delicious meal she'd ever had. "We'll join you in your war against the Fal'Borna, and in return we want land, gold, and horses."

Jenoe raised an eyebrow. "I see."

"Surely you can offer us all of that and more," Fayonne said. She put down her spoon and took a sip of water, which was, Tirnya realized, the only thing there was to drink. "I see your army, your weapons, your horses, and I think to myself, 'Here are people with riches to spare.'"

Jenoe smiled faintly and toyed with his spoon. "Our wealth isn't as great as you might think. But as I said when we first spoke, we can offer you land. If you help us against the Fal'Borna, you'll share in the spoils of our victory."

"Horses and gold, too," the woman said.

"If those are among the spoils," the marshal said, after eyeing her briefly, "then perhaps we can offer them. But I make no promises."

The woman frowned, but after a moment she nodded once. "Very well. When do we leave?"

Tirnya's father opened his mouth, then closed it again. "Forgive me, Eldest. I'm certain that you're a skilled sorcerer. But we're marching to war, and right now we have no spare horses to offer you. I believe that you'd be best off sending some of your younger men and women with us. And then after—"

"No!" Fayonne said, shaking her head. "We're going with you. That's what you said before."

Jenoe glanced at Tirnya, looking doubtful. "If you feel that you need to accompany us, I suppose you can."

"Not just me," she said, her voice rising. "All of us! Everyone!"

The marshal's eyes widened. "Everyone?" He laughed nervously, though his forehead was creased deeply. "You can't be serious."

She started to answer, but stopped herself, glancing at the elders. Tirnya couldn't see many of their faces, but she thought she saw several of them shake their heads.

A moment later, the eldest gave a small breathless laugh that clearly was forced. "No, of course I'm not, Marshal. I'll come with you. As eldest it's my place. But other than that it will only be the youngest and strongest of us."

Jenoe looked around the table, much as Fayonne had done a moment before. "All right," he said, sounding unnerved.

"Why are you so anxious to leave this place?" Enly asked.

Fayonne looked at him sharply, torchlight shining in her dark eyes. "Wouldn't you be?" she demanded.

"Other Mettai have refused us."

"Enly!" Tirnya said, glaring at him.

"They have a right to know," he said. He faced the eldest again. "Other Mettai have told us they want nothing to do with our war, but you . . . You didn't hesitate at all."

Fayonne regarded him for several moments. "Are all the men of Qalsyn like you?" she asked. "Are all of you the same?"

Enly gave a sour look. "Of course not."

"Then why should you expect all Mettai to be?"

"I don't, but as I say, these other Mettai—"

"Their villages were more prosperous than ours, weren't they? Their land was more fertile?"

Enly conceded that point with a nod. "Yes, it was."

"There's your answer." The eldest picked up her spoon and took another mouthful of stew. "Please," she said. "Eat. There's plenty."

None of them ate much more, and before long they were riding back to their camp, trying to make out the lane as their eyes adjusted to the night.

"Something's not right here," Enly said quietly.

"I agree," Jenoe told him.

Tirnya couldn't bring herself to argue with them. Despite how eager she was to ride to war, she knew it as well.

"We could ride farther north," Enly said. "There may be other Mettai who'll agree to join us."

"And what if there aren't?" Tirnya asked. "We've struck a bargain with them. We asked them to ride to war with us and they agreed. Now you want us to break our word?"

"We could tell them that we want to find more Mettai to join us," Jenoe said.

She shook her head fiercely. "We're not going to find any others. You both know it's true. You're right, Enly: They are desperate. That's why they agreed. And before you argue that this makes them unfit in some way to march with us, I'll remind you that war often fosters alliances of convenience. How often did the Fal'Borna and J'Balanar fight together against the sovereignties?"

For a long time neither of the men spoke, until finally Tirnya's father said, "She makes a valid point."

"I know," Enly said. "I just hope their magic is worth all this."

"I just hope," Jenoe said, "that we're not forced to eat any more of their food."

Tirnya and Enly laughed.

"When we left earlier my men were on their way to hunt some game," Tirnya told them. "We can eat when we get back to camp."

As it turned out, though, Oliban and the others had found precious little to eat, and most of the men had been forced to cobble together an evening meal from the stores the army had carried from Qalsyn. Before going to sleep, Tirnya ate a bit of dried meat and cheese, but not enough to get the taste of the Mettai stew out of her mouth, and not enough to keep her stomach from growling as she lay down under the stars.

Tirnya slept poorly, plagued by hunger and vague, disturbing dreams of white-hairs and Mettai. She awoke well before dawn and spent the rest of the night staring up into a cloudless sky, wondering if they were making a mistake by trusting these strange, desperate people.

They broke camp with first light. As Jenoe and Fayonne had agreed, the Mettai appeared on the road just as the sun was rising. The eldest walked at the head of their company, and with her were at least fifty younger men and women, all of them carrying travel sacks on their backs, and many of them bearing axes and long daggers, as well as the knives they carried on their belts.

Tirnya stood with her father, watching the Mettai approach.

"Whatever else you might say about them," she remarked, "they look like they're ready to fight."

Jenoe nodded but said nothing. Many of the men around her had stopped what they were doing and were watching the Mettai approach. Some of them merely looked curious, but a good number were eyeing the villagers with suspicion, even fear.

Fayonne led her people directly to Tirnya's father, stopping just in front of him. "We're ready to march when you are, Marshal."

"Thank you, Eldest," he said. "My daughter was just saying that you and your people truly look like warriors."

The woman regarded him solemnly. "You honor us, Marshal." She glanced at the soldiers. "But your men don't seem happy to see us."

"It might take some time for them to get used to you," he said.

She nodded. "No doubt. We'll have to get used to them, too."

Jenoe took a long breath. "Yes, I suppose so." He forced a smile. "We'll be marching soon. You can take whatever place you'd like in our column."

"We'll walk behind you," Fayonne said immediately. She turned and spoke quietly to the Mettai man behind her. He nodded, and started leading the rest of the Mettai to the far end of the camp. "Thank you, Marshal," she said, facing Jenoe again. "We'll speak again at the end of the day." With that, she turned and left them.

Jenoe shook his head slowly, watching Fayonne walk away. "What was it Enly said last night? 'I hope their magic is worth all this'?"

"It will be," Tirnya said. "They may be strange, and they may be driven by needs we don't understand. But they're sorcerers. By the time the Fal'Borna realize what's happening to their armies, we'll have taken back Deraqor." She nodded, as if convinced by the logic of her own argument. "I'm certain of it," she said, her voice low.

"I think you may be right."

Tirnya looked at her father.

"I don't relish the idea of riding to war with these people," he went on. "But I can't imagine the Fal'Borna will be expecting this. It might just work."

She continued to stare at him, saying nothing.

"What?" her father asked, a slight grin on his face.

"I'm surprised. I thought you didn't like this idea."

"I thought so, too," he said. "But now that we're here, and the Mettai are with us, I'm starting to reconsider."

"Really?"

He nodded. "We're riding to Deraqor. I've dreamed of this since I was a child."

Tirnya smiled, feeling better than she had in days.

Let Enly doubt their plan. Let those Mettai who had refused them doubt it as well. Tirnya knew it would work. Yes, Fayonne and her people were strange. Their reasons for agreeing to this alliance clearly had far more to do with the desolate conditions in which they lived than with any affinity they felt for Jenoe's army and their cause. But the Mettai of Lifarsa were marching with them: fifty sorcerers added to an army of two thousand of Qalsyn's finest soldiers. Soon they would join forces with another two thousand men from northern and southern Stelpana, and together they would cross the Silverwater into Qirsi land.

Tirnya wasn't foolish enough to think that the coming battles would be won easily. But they would be won. Just as the early battles of the Blood Wars had been won by Eandi and Mettai fighting as allies.

Chapter 22

✦—✠—✦

"C ommerce cares nothing for the color of a man's eyes."

It was an old saying, one that explained how trade could continue in a land long riven by racial hatred, one that many peddlers used to justify their willingness to take gold from people who would, under other circumstances, just as soon kill them as buy from them.

R'Shev had been selling his wares in the sovereignties for nearly all of his adult life—more than four fours now. He was Nid'Qir by birth, but he had left his clan and the Iejony Peninsula as soon as he came of age, believing that there had to be a better life for him elsewhere. The Nid'Qir were to the Qirsi of the Southlands what Qosantians or Tordjannis were to the Eandi. His people were among the wealthiest of the clans, and they had never seemed to care much where their gold came from. Many of the clans specialized in one trade or another: The M'Saaren and A'Vahl were known for their woodcraft; the R'Troth were miners; the D'Krad were seafaring folk. The Nid'Qir did a little of everything. Mostly though, they accumulated gold.

R'Shev often told those who asked that he left Nid'Qir land because he would have had to work too hard there to become as rich as he wanted to be. The truth was, he wanted no part of his people's obsession with wealth, nor did he wish to associate himself with the obvious disdain the Nid'Qir harbored for the other clans. Qirsi in the Southlands often spoke of the arrogance of the Nid'Qir. R'Shev had grown up with it, and had freed himself from it as soon as he could.

He made a decent living in the sovereignties, selling those Qirsi-made goods that wealthy Eandi often coveted—wooden boxes from the Berylline Forest, silverwork from the I'Prael, wines from the H'Bel. But he hadn't gotten rich as a peddler; he hadn't even tried. He journeyed the land, he spent his evenings sitting around a fire with other Qirsi peddlers, trading stories, drinking good wine, and laughing. Occasionally he found a woman with whom to pass the night. All in all, his was a good life.

But though he never once had regretted his decision to leave the Nid'Qir, neither had he become one of those Qirsi who forgets who and what he is. He wielded two of the deeper magics—language of beasts and shaping—and in all the years he had spent among the Eandi, he hadn't ever shared a bed with a dark-eye woman. He had some Eandi friends and had come to respect many of the merchants he dealt with in the sovereignties. But his blood ran Qirsi.

A few turns before he had encountered on the plain a Qirsi couple and their young daughter who had come to this land from the Forelands. They had been on their way to Fal'Borna land and had come upon R'Shev and his friends on a stormy night, having been refused a room in an Eandi inn in Bred's Landing. R'Shev hadn't seen the man or woman since, but he thought of them occasionally, hoping that they had found a home among one of the clans.

Often when he thought of the young family he reflected on what a shock it had been to them to be treated so poorly by the Eandi of Stelpana. From all R'Shev had heard, the Forelands had seen its share of trouble between the races in recent years. Yet, apparently even their experience with the Eandi of the north had not prepared the man and woman for the hostility directed at them in Bred's Landing. All this made R'Shev wonder if the Eandi were worse here, or if the divide between the races was just wider and deeper in the Southlands. He knew for sure that there was nothing in the history of the Forelands to match the intensity, bitterness, and duration of the Blood Wars.

Whatever the reason, and notwithstanding the fact that he took gold from an Eandi as readily as he did from a Qirsi, there could be no doubt that R'Shev would never fully trust the people of the sovereignties. And he long had vowed that if ever war returned to the Southlands, he would leave the sovereignties immediately and do all that he could to aid his people.

That was why he now found himself steering his cart toward the Silverwater Wash and Fal'Borna land.

He'd been in Kirayde, trading with the Mettai—not something many merchants were doing these days, with rumors of cursed Mettai baskets scaring everyone so. But the pestilence, it seemed, had moved off to the west, having devastated the Y'Qatt settlements near the Companion Lakes, and since there'd been no reports of the disease striking east of the Silverwater, he assumed that it would be safe. Since many were avoiding the Mettai now, he had thought to find a few bargains and sell some of his goods. The Mettai were wary of him at first, as they often were of strange Qirsi, but by morning's end he'd managed to make some sales.

When he first saw the three Eandi riders he thought little of it. True, they were all wearing the blue and green uniforms of Stelpana's military, but that hardly seemed unusual. This might have been a Mettai village, but the sorcerers lived under the authority of Stelpana's sovereign. Still, he watched with interest as they spoke to the village's eldest, who seemed unnerved by their presence here.

An older man who had been looking at some silver blades from the I'Prael had paused over R'Shev's wares to watch the exchange as well.

"Do you know who they are?" R'Shev asked him.

The man looked at him and shook his head. "No idea," he said. "But the older one's a man of some importance. Got an army with him that could ring the entire village."

"What?" R'Shev said, not quite believing it.

" 'S true," the man told him. "You can look yourself. They're waiting on these three, just outside the village." He stooped and picked up one of the blades. "How much for this one?"

"Five sovereigns."

The man frowned and shook his head. "Too much." But he didn't put the blade back on the blanket.

"That's the price, my friend," R'Shev said, still watching the soldiers and the eldest out of the corner of his eye.

The man stared at the dagger, twisting his mouth.

Abruptly, the eldest turned away from the strangers and hurried down the lane out of the marketplace. The soldiers didn't follow, and a moment later they left in the opposite direction.

"I'll give you three and a half," the man said.

R'Shev looked at him. "The blade is silver, mined and forged by the I'Prael themselves. The hilt is black crystal, also from the I'Prael. If you don't want it, don't buy it. But if you want it, the price is five."

The Mettai man didn't look pleased, but after a moment he dug into his pocket and pulled out five sovereigns. Then he walked away, muttering to himself about white-hair merchants and their high prices.

R'Shev made a few more deals as the day went on, but mostly he sat on his cart wondering what an army so large would be doing so far north this close to the Snows. Late in the day, just as he was thinking it was time to pack up his cart, he spotted the eldest again, making his way through the marketplace. After a moment's hesitation, R'Shev called to him.

The man paused, checking the position of the sun in the sky before approaching R'Shev's cart. The eldest was a burly man, a smith or a wheelwright by the look of him, with dark eyes and steel grey hair. He had a kind face, and he smiled as he stopped in front of R'Shev, though there was a troubled look in his eyes.

R'Shev stood to greet him.

"What can I do for you, friend?" the eldest asked. "I hope business has been good today."

"It has been. Thank you, Eldest. But I was curious about those soldiers I saw you talking to earlier."

The eldest's smile vanished. "What about them?"

"I heard someone say they were leading an army. Is that true?"

He exhaled, then nodded. "Yes, it's true. It looked to be a large force. Nearly two thousand men, I'd say."

R'Shev shivered, though he wasn't cold. "Two thousand? Do you know what they're doing here?"

The eldest didn't answer at first. He looked down at the ground and kicked at the dirt with his foot. Finally, he looked R'Shev in the eye again. "I'm not sure I should say. I could . . . Stelpana's sovereigns have allowed us to remain here for generations, but they've never been happy about it."

"Did they threaten you?" R'Shev asked.

The eldest smiled wanly, though only for an instant. "No, nothing like that." He started to say something, stopped himself, licked his lips. "You might want to consider whether you wouldn't be better off west of the Silverwater," he finally said.

"West of the . . ." R'Shev stared at the man. "There's a war coming, then."

"I . . . I shouldn't be saying any of this, but after all that's happened . . ." He broke off again, shaking his head. "The Mettai have never had any dispute with either the clans or the sovereignties. I told him that—the marshal, I mean. But there may be others in my position who feel differently."

R'Shev frowned. "I don't understand."

The eldest shook his head again. "I know. The point is, it isn't safe for you here anymore. Or at least it won't be for long."

"Are you ordering me to leave your village, Eldest?"

The man shook his head, a pained expression on his face. "I'm urging you, as a friend, to leave Stelpana while you still can."

R'Shev nodded slowly, trying to make sense of what the man was telling him. "All right, Eldest. Thank you."

"I'm sorry," the eldest said. He hesitated again before turning and walking away, his shoulders hunched.

R'Shev began to pack up his wares, all the while thinking about what the eldest had said. Clearly those soldiers had been marching to war, which was alarming enough considering the Southlands' history. But he thought there was more to the man's words than just the obvious. He'd been trying to tell R'Shev something, and he'd been too circumspect—or R'Shev had been too dense—for the message to get through.

Still, R'Shev knew what he had to do. There was more at stake here than his safety. He might not have thought of himself as Nid'Qir anymore, but he was Qirsi, a brother to every man and woman west of the Silverwater. The Fal'Borna were a hard people, fearsome in battle and uncompromising in the marketplace. But their hair was white, their eyes as yellow as his own. They had to be warned.

He was on his way from the village well before sunset, and for the rest of that day, and over the next two days, he drove Ebbie, his old black cart horse, as hard as he dared. The distance between Kirayde and the Silverwater wasn't great—less than eight leagues. He was safely in Fal'Borna land just after midday the day after he left the Mettai. But even after he reached the river and crossed over it on a stone bridge just south of Turtle Lake, near what little remained of the Y'Qatt town of C'Bijor's Neck, he didn't stop. Instead he turned north and followed the shores of the lake and the wash above it toward Lowna, the closest Fal'Borna settlement.

As he traveled, he continued to reflect on his conversation with Kirayde's eldest, asking himself the same questions again and again. As a merchant, and particularly as a Qirsi in Eandi lands, he spent much of his time alone with his thoughts. He often had dialogues with himself, sometimes even speaking aloud so that Ebbie's ears would twitch, as if she were trying to listen in on his conversations with himself. He considered it a skill of sorts, a way of keeping his mind sharp, a way, at times, of staving off boredom.

Why would the Eandi risk war now? The answer to this question, the easiest of all, became clear to him as soon as he realized that his travels would take him so close to C'Bijor's Neck. The same pestilence that had ravaged that town was said to be decimating Fal'Borna villages on the Central Plain. What better time to strike?

But why would they speak to the Mettai? Would they have been asking permission to march through Mettai lands? Did they plan to attack from the north? That would surely be unexpected, and anyone who knew the history of the Blood Wars understood that the sovereignties needed every advantage they could get. But the Eandi had never shown any consideration for the Mettai in the past, and they'd long made it clear to the dark-eye sorcerers that the land on which they lived belonged to the sovereign, not to the Mettai. R'Shev could think of no reason why the sovereign's command-ers would suddenly see fit to ask permission to march an army through the Companion Lakes region.

All of which brought R'Shev back to the same question: Why would they speak to the Mettai?

"What was it the eldest said?" he asked aloud as he steered his cart along the lakeshore.

Ebbie snorted and shook her head, drawing a grin from the merchant.

"Weren't listening, eh? That'll teach you."

R'Shev had asked the man what the army's commander said, and the el-dest refused to tell him. But then he said, "Stelpana's sovereigns have allowed us to remain here for generations, but they've never been happy about it."

At the time, R'Shev had taken this to mean that the commander threat-ened the Mettai, but the eldest denied it. He said a bit more then, referring vaguely to things that had happened recently—R'Shev hadn't understood what he meant. And then the man said, "The Mettai have never had any dispute with either the clans or the sovereignties . . . but there may be oth-ers in my position who feel differently."

Again, R'Shev had been confused by this—the eldest had spoken in riddles throughout their conversation. But this was essentially the last thing the man said before warning R'Shev to leave Stelpana, and it struck the merchant as being at the crux of whatever he and the sovereign's marshal had discussed.

He considered the matter for nearly the entire day, repeating the el-dest's words to himself as if they were a litany. By the time the sun began to go down, he was well past Turtle Lake, once again following the course of the Silverwater. Eventually he made camp for the night, lit a small fire, and ate a modest meal of cheese and hard bread. He tried to sleep, but still his thoughts churned, keeping him up. Eventually he pulled out a sealed flask of H'Bel wine, one he could have sold, and opened it. He rarely drank alone, and was usually reluctant to treat himself to something that could have brought him gold, but he needed his sleep, and he knew that with his mind working so furiously he wouldn't get any without a bit of help.

Sleep still came grudgingly, and he was awakened repeatedly by strange, frightening dreams in which he was pursued by hordes of Eandi warriors. Still, he managed to sleep later than he had intended, waking to a high sun and a pounding headache. His stomach felt tight and sour, and all through the next morning, as the motion of the cart jostled him, he cursed himself for ever opening that flask.

Near the end of his third day out from Kirayde, R'Shev finally reached Owl Lake, turning slightly westward to follow its shoreline. Before long, he reached Lowna. He was no closer to figuring out what the eldest had been trying to tell him, but at least now he could warn the Fal'Borna. Perhaps they could glean something from the man's words that he could not.

He steered his cart to the center of the village, where most peddlers were just putting their wares back into their carts.

"A bit late, aren't you, old man?" one young Eandi trader called to him.

Another Eandi laughed, but R'Shev said nothing, searching instead for anyone who seemed to live in the village. The two men shook their heads and went back to packing their carts. For a moment R'Shev considered warning them to leave Fal'Borna land. With a war coming, they were no safer on this side of the Silverwater than he had been in Stelpana. But his first allegiance was to his people, and he feared that such a warning given to the dark-eyes might eventually get back to Stelpana's army. Best not to let the Eandi know that the Fal'borna would be readying themselves for an assault.

A moment later, he spotted a Qirsi woman and two young girls walking away from the marketplace. He flicked the reins, and Ebbie started after them.

"Hello there!" he called.

The three of them turned. The woman was older than he had expected her to be, given the age of her children. But she had a kind face, and she smiled at him, though she looked just a bit puzzled. The two girls eyed him warily.

"Hello," the woman said in return. "Can I help you?"

"I hope so," R'Shev said. "I'm searching for whoever governs your village. An eldest perhaps?"

"You mean our a'laq?" she asked.

"Of course," R'Shev said, shaking his head at his own foolishness. It hadn't been that long since last he was among the Fal'Borna. He should have remembered. "Your a'laq. Do you know where I might find him?"

The woman smiled, clearly amused. "Actually, our a'laq is a woman. Her name is U'Selle." She pointed at a small house just off the marketplace. "She lives there."

"Thank you." He always carried sweets with him to offer to children. He pulled some out now and held them out to the girls. "If it's all right with your mother, you're welcome to these."

The younger of the two girls, a beautiful, fine-featured child with brilliant yellow eyes, turned away, burying her face in her mother's dress. The older child, who was also very pretty, though with a look of deep sadness in her eyes, merely stared back at him and shook her head.

R'Shev frowned.

"Thank you anyway," the woman said, running her hand over the older girl's hair and patting the back of the younger one. "They're shy with strangers."

"Well, then perhaps I can give them to you, kind woman, and you can see that they have them later, after they've had their supper."

She smiled, and stepping forward, took the sweets from him. "Thank you."

They walked away, leaving R'Shev to steer his cart toward the house the woman had pointed out to him. Before he reached it he heard someone coughing, and he realized that there was an older woman sitting outside the house. He climbed down off his cart and covered the remaining distance on foot.

The woman was still coughing when he reached the house, her body racked by the paroxysm. She saw him approach, waved him forward even as she still struggled to draw breath. Once the spasm had passed, she sat back in her old chair and closed her eyes briefly.

"Forgive me," she said. "It gets worse with the colder air."

"Can I get you anything?" R'Shev asked. "Some water perhaps?"

She dismissed the offer with a wave of her hand. "I'm all right now. You're looking for me?"

"I am if you're the a'laq."

The woman nodded. "That I am, for the moment at least." She eyed him for a moment, her eyes narrowing. She was small, her face wizened, her body bent and frail-looking. But her eyes remained clear and her voice was strong, despite her coughing. "Have we met?"

"I don't think so, A'Laq, though I've traded in your village before."

"Ah," she said. "A peddler. I tend to avoid getting involved with disputes in the marketplace. Best you work things out on your own."

He grinned at that. "A wise policy, A'Laq. But that's not why I'm here."

"Then why?"

"I've come from Kirayde, a Mettai village south of Porcupine Lake. While I was there, an Eandi army, nearly two thousand men strong, stopped outside the village. The army's commander spoke briefly with the village eldest, seeking some boon from him, though I've yet to figure out what it might have been. The eldest refused him, but I gather from all he told me later that the commander intended to speak with other elders in other villages. And I gather as well that eventually this man and his army intend to cross the Silverwater and bring war to the Fal'Borna."

Her eyes didn't widen; her face didn't blanch. She didn't say anything or leap to her feet or otherwise betray any hint of fear. If the strength of a leader could be measured by her calm in the face of such tidings, U'Selle had to be very strong indeed.

"You're certain of this?" she asked after a brief silence, her voice even.

"I am, A'Laq."

"How many days has it been since you saw this commander and his army?"

"Three."

She raised an eyebrow. "You got here quickly."

"As quickly as I could, A'Laq." He grinned. "A younger man might have been here sooner."

The woman smiled at that. "Maybe. A younger man might not have known what to do with such news. I'm grateful to you. All of us will be before long."

He nodded.

"I'd like you to speak with the members of our clan council. Would you mind remaining here for the night? We can offer you food and perhaps even a place to sleep."

"I can sleep in my cart, A'Laq, but I'll gladly take the food. After a while a man tires of his own cooking."

"Very well." She stood and started to make her way down the lane. After taking only a couple of steps, though, she turned and faced him again. "What's your name, friend?"

"R'Shev, A'Laq."

"And what clan are you from?"

"I was born Nid'Qir."

That, of all things, made her eyebrows go up. "Nid'Qir? And here I thought you seemed so nice."

R'Shev laughed. "I left the peninsula a long time ago."

"Ah," she said, turning away and starting off again. "That must be it."

S'Doryn had just returned from the lakeshore with five beautiful trout when N'Tevva and the girls reached the house. He was outside still, preparing to clean the fish. At the sound of the two children calling to him, he straightened and waved to them.

Vettala reached him first. "Look what I got!" she said. She held out her hand, showing him a small sweet of some sort.

The girl had come such a long way since she, Jynna, and several other children first arrived in Lowna, their lives shattered by the plague that had killed their families and destroyed their home village of Tivston. Jynna had grieved for all she lost, as one would expect, but Vettala had been so devastated by all she'd seen that horrific night that she wouldn't even speak. Now, only a few turns later, she looked and acted like any normal child. Mostly. There were difficult days when she brooded in silence, nights when she couldn't sleep for the grisly visions that haunted her slumber. But even these were growing less frequent. She and Jynna called S'Doryn and N'Tevva by their names, but in all other ways they treated them as they would their parents. For their part, S'Doryn and his wife, who had despaired of ever having children of their own, were grateful beyond words for the chance to take care of these girls and raise them as their own.

"What is that?" S'Doryn asked the girl, staring at the treat she held as if he'd never seen such a thing before.

"A sweet! Jynna got one, too! A peddler game them to us!"

"A peddler. Is that so?" He looked at N'Tevva, his eyes narrowing. "And just how much did we give him before he gave us the sweets?"

His wife grinned. "Nothing. I promise," she added, in response to his skeptical look. "He just wanted to know where he could find U'Selle."

"You caught five of them?" Jynna said, seeing his catch. She sounded impressed.

S'Doryn looked at her. "Yes, I did. Even without your help." He glanced at N'Tevva again. "I think T'Noth and Etan are going to join us, so I wanted extras."

She nodded. "All right. The fish look lovely."

He smiled and then went back to cleaning them, while N'Tevva took the girls into the house and began to prepare the rest of their evening meal.

He had just finished with the second fish when he heard voices. Glancing up, he saw T'Noth approaching the house. He quickly looked up a second time. Etan was walking beside his friend, but so too was the a'laq. S'Doryn rinsed his hands in the bucket that held the three remaining fish, and then went to greet them.

"I don't mean to interrupt your supper, S'Doryn," U'Selle said. "As I told T'Noth and Etan, I was just out for a stroll, so I thought I'd join them."

"Of course, A'Laq," he said, though he wasn't certain he believed her. There was something strange in her voice, in the way she looked at him. "Etan," he said. "The girls are waiting for you inside."

"All right," the boy said, bounding into the house.

S'Doryn looked at the a'laq again. Her eyes flicked toward T'Noth.

"I think N'Tevva could use some help," he told his friend.

T'Noth eyed them both, a slight frown on his square, youthful face. "Of course she could," he said.

The a'laq chuckled. "Forgive us, T'Noth. I need a word with him."

"I understand, A'Laq." He looked at S'Doryn once more before following the boy into the house.

"No doubt you'll tell him everything once I'm gone," U'Selle remarked quietly, watching the man walk away.

"Only with your permission. You know that."

She nodded, taken by a fit of coughing. "I do know that," she said, when she could speak again. "I'm afraid I have to take you away from your supper, at least for a while. I need everyone on the clan council at my house immediately. I'd like you to summon the rest for me."

"Of course, A'Laq," S'Doryn said. "I just need to tell N'Tevva."

She nodded and he started toward the house. After a few strides he stopped and turned again. U'Selle had already begun to walk away.

"Can you tell me what this is about?" he asked.

She looked back at him and shook her head. "No, not yet."

Lowna was by no means the largest village in Fal'Borna land, but it wasn't the smallest either. It took S'Doryn some time to find all the other members of the clan council and direct them to the a'laq's house. By the time he and the last of his fellow members were able to join the rest, night had fallen.

A peddler's cart stood outside U'Selle's home and when they entered they found another man there with the a'laq, a stranger S'Doryn had never seen before. S'Doryn knew immediately that the man wasn't Fal'Borna; he was too tall, too narrow in the shoulders and chest, and his complexion was entirely too pale. He was an older man with a wispy white beard that made his face appear even thinner than it was. S'Doryn assumed from the man's appearance that he hailed from one of the western clans.

Seeing that all of them were there, U'Selle stood.

"I'm sorry to have summoned you on such short notice," she said. "If this could have waited even until the morning I wouldn't have disturbed you." She indicated the peddler with an open hand. "This is R'Shev," she said. "He's just come from the Companion Lakes, where he saw something that alarmed him enough to drive his cart all the way here in just three days. I'll let him tell his story in his own words."

She sat once more, looking expectantly at the stranger. R'Shev stood, his long legs unfolding as if he were a child's toy. On another occasion, S'Doryn might have found his appearance comical. But as soon as the man began to speak, in a clear voice that was nearly devoid of any accent, he realized that this was no laughing matter.

It was bad enough that so large an Eandi army had been seen within ten leagues of the Silverwater. But to have the leader of a Mettai village issue such a stark warning was truly frightening. Yet there was still more to the man's tale. Like R'Shev and the a'laq, S'Doryn wasn't sure what to make of what the eldest of the Mettai village had said, but the words sounded ominous.

"So war is coming," said Y'Bej, one of the other council members, when R'Shev had lowered himself into his chair once more.

"Yes," U'Selle said. "That much is clear. It seems that word of the plague sweeping across our lands has reached the dark-eyes. They think we've been weakened, and so they've chosen to attack us and exploit that weakness."

"Did the eldest say this?" Y'Bej asked the peddler.

"This is my thinking," U'Selle told him before R'Shev could respond. "Do you disagree?"

"No, A'Laq," Y'Bej said.

"What about the rest of you?"

No one spoke.

U'Selle nodded. "I'm wondering," she went on, "if any of you can make some sense of the rest of what Kirayde's eldest told our friend here."

"Perhaps the eldest knew of the baskets and their curse," S'Doryn said. "When he referred to all that had happened, perhaps that's what he meant. Could it be that the commander was thanking the Mettai for weakening us?"

"Or maybe he asked them to make more cursed baskets," said E'Vylia, the village herbmistress.

"Wait just a moment," R'Shev broke in, his eyes flicking back and forth between U'Selle and S'Doryn. "Are you telling me that the Mettai are responsible in some way for the pestilence that's been striking at septs on the plain?"

The a'laq nodded, her expression grim. "Yes, although we have no reason to believe that all the Mettai were behind this. But at least one woman made baskets for trade that she then cursed and sold. The Y'Qatt were the first to be affected, but the plague eventually spread to our people."

"Blood and bone," the peddler whispered. "Forgive me, A'Laq. Had I known, I wouldn't have set foot in their marketplace."

U'Selle reached over and patted the man's arm, a sad smile on her lips. "It's all right, R'Shev. You've proven your friendship to the Fal'Borna." She glanced around the room at the members of the council. "Our friend here is Nid'Qir," she told them. "Remember that the next time you have in ill word to say about his clan. In any case, we were talking about the Mettai and what the Eandi commander might have been asking of them."

"It could be that they were asking for more baskets," Y'Bej said.

S'Doryn shook his head. "At this point every a'laq in every sept on the plain has been warned against Mettai baskets. Besides, if there's a war coming, we're not going to be welcoming Eandi traders into our villages, at least not for a while. Baskets, blankets, woodwork—no matter how they might disguise the curse, it wouldn't work a second time. Not if we're at war."

"What if they used someone like me to get you the goods?" R'Shev asked.

S'Doryn grinned. "Unless the Nid'Qir have powers I don't know about, any curse that kills me will kill you, too."

The man's face colored. "Of course. I might be handsome, but I'm not very smart. Actually, I think that's why the women like me so much."

S'Doryn and a few of the others chuckled.

U'Selle, though, appeared still to be deep in thought. "An alliance then," she finally said.

S'Doryn felt himself grow cold. "What?"

She looked at the peddler. "What was it the eldest said? 'The Mettai have never had any dispute with the clans or the sovereignties, but others in my position might feel differently.'"

R'Shev nodded. "Yes, that's about right."

U'Selle passed a rigid hand through her hair. "They asked him to join their army, and he refused them. That's the explanation that makes the most sense."

"But if he refused—" Y'Bej began.

"The man was right," U'Selle said. "There may well be others who won't refuse, who'll take whatever the Eandi are offering and fight on their behalf."

"The Fal'Borna have fought the Eandi before and won," said another member of the council. "We can defeat them again."

Several of the others nodded.

After a moment U'Selle nodded as well. "That's true. But it's been many centuries since we had to fight both Eandi warriors and the Mettai. Of course we'll prevail," she added a moment later, offering a smile that clearly was forced. "I just don't want any of you thinking this will be easy, because it won't." She stood again. "That's all," she told them. "I intend to begin speaking with other a'laqs tonight. Whatever advantages the Eandi may think they have, surprise won't be one of them." She turned to the peddler. "Thank you for that, R'Shev."

The other members of the council stood as well and began to file out of the a'laq's house, all of them pausing to thank R'Shev. Eventually, only S'Doryn and the peddler were left with the a'laq.

"I have no heart for this fight," U'Selle said, looking at S'Doryn. "I always knew that the Blood Wars would begin again eventually, but I hoped and expected that I'd be long dead when they did."

"K'Pril was right, A'Laq. We've defeated them before."

"The Mettai didn't fight beside the Eandi during the last few hundred years of the wars. But when they did, earlier on, they were . . . a formidable enemy. We lost many more of those early battles than we did the later ones."

S'Doryn wasn't certain what to say.

She smiled at him, and this time the smile appeared genuine. "Go home, my friend. Your fish will be cold by now, that is if T'Noth left any for you."

"He better have." S'Doryn started toward the door, but then stopped in front of R'Shev and held out a hand, which the peddler took. The man had a strong grip. "Thank you," S'Doryn said. "You may well have saved our village."

R'Shev shrugged. "I'm Qirsi. We may be of different clans, but we both have yellow eyes; we both have white hair."

S'Doryn nodded and smiled.

"S'Doryn," U'Selle said, as he reached for the door handle. "You can tell N'Tevva, of course. And T'Noth as well. Tidings like these . . ." She shook her head. "Everyone in the village will know by sunrise."

"Yes, A'Laq. Thank you."

S'Doryn had to pass T'Noth's house in order to get back to his own. Walking past his friend's home, he saw a lamp burning in one of the windows. It wasn't surprising really; he'd been gone for a long time, and T'Noth would have needed to put Etan to sleep. After a moment's hesitation, he walked to his friend's door and knocked once.

T'Noth opened the door, a grin on his face. "I was hoping you'd stop by. Come in."

He shook his head. "I can't stay long."

"You'll be glad to know that we saved you some trout. It was very good, by the way."

"Good. Thanks for not eating it all."

T'Noth narrowed his eyes. "Something's troubling you. What's happened?"

"It's a longer story than I can tell you tonight, but the short answer is that the Eandi appear to be marching against us, and they may have at least some Mettai on their side."

His friend stared at him, looking as if he had just been punched in the gut. "Damn. You're certain about this?"

"There's no doubt that the Eandi are coming. The part about the Mettai . . ." He hesitated. The truth was they weren't certain. But S'Doryn had little doubt that U'Selle was right about why the Eandi had gone to Kirayde. "There's not much doubt about that either," he finally said.

"What are we going to do?" T'Noth asked.

"U'Selle will talk to other Weavers tonight. And tomorrow every Fal'Borna in the clan lands will begin preparing for war."

He gripped his friend's shoulder and then walked away, suddenly eager to be home with N'Tevva and his girls.

N'Tevva looked up and smiled when S'Doryn entered the house. As soon as she saw his expression, however, her face fell.

"What is it?" she asked.

He sat beside her and took her hand. And then he related all that had been said in the a'laq's home. After a time, as he continued to speak, he looked down at their hands because he couldn't bear to see the fear in her pale yellow eyes or the color draining from her cheeks.

For a long time after he had finished, she just sat there, shaking her head slowly. "They're mad," she whispered. "They must be. That's the only explanation that makes any sense. How else could they even consider such a thing?"

"They think we're weak," he said. "They think that the Mettai curse has left us vulnerable."

"Are they right?"

S'Doryn shrugged. "I don't know, N'Tevva. Truly I don't."

She laid her head on his shoulder. "I never thought I'd see this day."

"U'Selle said much the same thing," he told her. "And I feel the same way. But maybe we've all been foolish to think it couldn't happen. The clans and the sovereignties have spent most of the past thousand years fighting one another. The history of the Blood Wars is the history of the Southlands. This peace we've enjoyed—that's the aberration. Instead of being surprised, we should be grateful it didn't happen sooner."

She looked at him with an expression of both surprise and despair. "Do you really believe that?"

He met her gaze and saw in her eyes how desperately she wanted him to say that he didn't. He looked away, shrugged. "I don't know. I don't want to believe it." He started to say more, but stopped himself.

N'Tevva stood. "You need something to eat. We saved some supper for you."

"All right," S'Doryn said. "I'm going to check on the girls first."

"Oh, they're asleep by now."

"I know. I just want to see them."

The door to the room Jynna and Vettala shared stood slightly ajar; Vettala still didn't like the room too dark when she went to sleep. Peeking in, S'Doryn saw that Vettala was sprawled on her side of their bed, her arms stretched above her head and her eyes closed. Jynna was still awake, though. S'Doryn stepped into the room and sat on the bed beside her.

"You should be asleep," he whispered.

"I heard you come in."

S'Doryn felt his stomach tighten.

"I heard what you were talking about, too."

He closed his eyes for a moment, cursing himself for being so careless. "Jynna—"

"Just tell me we'll beat them," she said.

Almost since the moment she arrived in Lowna, Jynna had been closer to S'Doryn than to anyone else. She loved N'Tevva—he knew she did—but he was the one she trusted most. He'd been with her when she first told the a'laq and the clan council of the Mettai witch who brought the cursed baskets to her village. He'd been with her when they returned to her village and found her home destroyed, her family dead. And since she'd been living here they'd been nearly inseparable.

The only point of contention between them had been the Mettai. He had tried to make her understand that the woman who brought the plague to her village was insane, and that she couldn't hate all the Mettai for what this one madwoman had done to her.

But what could he tell her now? If the peddler was right, the Mettai really were their enemy, just as Jynna had been saying all this time. And he and his people would have little choice but to defeat the dark-eye sorcerers and the Eandi who marched with them.

S'Doryn brushed a strand of white hair from the girl's forehead and then bent to kiss her cheek.

"We will beat them," he said. "I swear it."

She nodded, her face so grim that she looked more like a seasoned warrior than a little girl. He saw no fear in her gaze, no hint of the terror that gripped his own heart. All he could see in those bright golden eyes was her resolve and her hatred of the Mettai and the confidence of a child who didn't know any better than to believe a parent's promise.

Chapter 23

Wake up, Forelander."

Grinsa felt himself being shaken and he tried to shrug off the hand gripping his bad shoulder.

"Forelander! Grinsa! Wake up! Now!"

He opened his eyes. The sky above him was still dark. A few bright stars shone through a thin layer of clouds, which glowed with a faint pink hue from the setting moons.

It took him a moment, but he recognized the shadowy figure beside him as Q'Daer.

"What is it?" he asked, blinking his eyes, trying to force himself awake. "What's happened?"

"I've just spoken with the a'laq," the young Weaver told him. "We have to turn back. We have to return to the sept."

"Why?" Abruptly he was very much awake. "Are Cresenne and Bryntelle all right?"

"They're fine. But an Eandi army is marching this way." He appeared to glance back over his shoulder. "And it seems there are Mettai with them. War is coming to the plain."

"Demons and fire," Grinsa muttered. "E'Menua is certain of this?"

"Yes. He was contacted by another a'laq, who had heard it directly from the a'laq in Lowna, a village to the east. We don't know if the dark-eyes have crossed the Silverwater yet, but it's only a matter of time. The a'laq wants us back in the sept before the invaders reach them. And I want to be there, too."

Grinsa nodded. He still didn't think of himself as Fal'Borna, but his family was living in E'Menua's sept, and he had every intention of protecting them. "All right." He sat up and rubbed a hand over his face.

"What should we do about the Mettai?" Q'Daer asked, looking back toward their cart again.

Grinsa hesitated. He trusted Besh and Sirj more than he did any of his other companions, including Q'Daer. But if there really was a war coming, and if the Mettai had allied themselves with the sovereignties, he might have to rethink that trust. Just as he was ready to fight alongside the Fal'Borna, Besh and Sirj would no doubt choose to fight with their people.

"Forelander?" the Fal'Borna said.

"I don't know, Q'Daer. Everything they've done so far tells me that we have nothing to fear from them. But if all this is true . . ."

"I . . . I didn't tell the a'laq that we were traveling with Mettai," Q'Daer told him, gazing off to the east, where the sky was beginning to lighten. "If I had, he would have insisted that I kill them, or at the very least take them as prisoners. But since I didn't . . ." He shrugged. "If you think it best to let them go, we can do that."

Grinsa stared at the man, not bothering to conceal his surprise. "Why did you do that?" he finally asked.

Q'Daer shrugged, clearly uncomfortable. "As you say, all that they've done to this point tells me that they're not our enemy. I thought it was . . . the right thing to do."

Grinsa nodded. "I believe it was."

He stood and together they woke the others. Torgan demanded to know why they had roused him so early, but Grinsa and Q'Daer refused to answer until the Mettai had joined them. Once all of them were together, the young Weaver repeated the tidings he had shared with Grinsa.

By now a faint grey light was touching their faces and brightening the sky above them, so Grinsa could see how Besh's face blanched at word that there were Mettai marching with the Eandi. Sirj merely stood beside the old man, staring at the ground, shaking his head slowly.

"So what does this mean?" Torgan demanded. "What are you going to do with us?"

"I told you," Q'Daer said. "We're going back to the sept, and you're coming with us. E'Menua wants all his Weavers with him before the dark-eye army reaches the plain."

Torgan looked at Grinsa, but the gleaner refused to meet his gaze. He knew what the merchant was thinking. He'd been begging Grinsa to let him escape almost since the moment they left the sept. Now he'd claim that with the Qirsi and Eandi going to war, E'Menua was sure to execute both him and Jasha. For his part, Grinsa thought it likely, too, at least in Torgan's case. But though he had sacrificed a good deal to keep the merchant alive all this time, he still wasn't willing to endanger his family or jeopardize his own effort to win their freedom from the Fal'Borna in order to save this man.

"It makes no sense to me," Besh finally said, his voice hardly loud enough for Grinsa to hear. He looked at Sirj. "Why would any Mettai agree to such a thing?"

"Your people are Eandi," Q'Daer said, as if that alone was enough to explain it.

Besh shook his head. "Not really. Our eyes may be dark, but in other ways we have more in common with your kind than we do with the people of Stelpana or Aelea. We wield magic, and for that reason alone we're feared, even hated."

"But you haven't been treated much better by the white-hairs," Jasha said. "Even I know that much."

"Exactly!" Besh answered, his voice rising. "Both races have wanted nothing to do with us, and so we've wanted nothing to do with you. We had nothing to do with the last of your wars and we hoped that the rest of you would just leave us alone. And now some among us have decided to fight in a new Blood War? It makes no sense! None at all!"

"The dark-eyes would have offered land, perhaps gold," Q'Daer said. "They'd pay handsomely to meet our magic with yours."

"I don't care what they offered," Besh said. "The cost is too high."

"I agree with you," Q'Daer said. "But the fact remains that your people and mine are going to war. We have to return to our sept, but you don't. You should leave here. You should return to your village. You'll be far safer there."

"Wait!" Torgan said, his one eye growing wide. "You're going to let them go, but not us?"

"They killed the woman who cursed those baskets," Q'Daer said. "And an a'laq has named them a friend of all Fal'Borna people. They've earned their freedom and then some."

"And I haven't. Is that what you're saying?"

Q'Daer regarded him briefly, his expression mild. "Yes, I suppose it is. Gather your belongings," he told both of the Eandi, "and eat something. We'll be leaving shortly."

The young Weaver walked back to his sleeping roll. After a moment Torgan and Jasha turned and walked away as well, leaving Grinsa with the two Mettai.

"It seems we'll be parting company," Grinsa said. "I'm sure you're eager to be returning to your home, but I'm sorry we won't have more time together. I've enjoyed our conversations."

"As have I, Forelander," Besh said. "Perhaps once you've left the Fal'Borna you'll come to see how the Mettai live."

"Perhaps," Grinsa said, knowing that it probably wouldn't happen. "If there's to be war it wouldn't be wise for us to cross back into Eandi land."

Besh shrugged, seeming to concede the point. "No, it probably wouldn't be." He shook his head again. "I meant what I said before: This isn't like my people. I can't imagine what would make any Mettai fight for either side."

Grinsa didn't know what to say.

"We never did find a way to defeat Lici's plague," the old man went on a moment later. He turned to Sirj. "I don't suppose there's anything to be done about that."

The younger man shook his head. "Not unless you want to risk staying in Fal'Borna land."

"Don't," Grinsa said. "I admire you both for even considering it, but the Fal'Borna aren't to be trifled with."

"No, they're not," Sirj said. "Never mind our people, I'm not even sure why the sovereignties would do this."

"Blood and bone," Besh whispered.

Sirj looked at him. "What?"

"They're attacking because of Lici, because of what her plague has done."

"You don't know that," Sirj said.

But Grinsa could hear doubt in the younger man's voice. For his part, the gleaner thought that Besh was right, though it hadn't even occurred to him to wonder about this until now.

"You know how the last of the wars ended," Besh said, his voice bleak. "The Eandi wouldn't dare attack unless they knew that the Fal'Borna had been weakened. It has to be because of this pestilence Lici conjured."

Grinsa sensed where Besh was going with this. "You still need to go back, Besh. You can't risk staying here."

"With all respect, Grinsa, it's not your place or the Fal'Borna's to tell us what we can and can't risk. I swore an oath to stop Lici from doing any more harm."

"And you did that!"

"I killed her," Besh said. "That's all. Her plague is still spreading, and now there's to be a war. Her war." He looked at Sirj. "You know I'm right, don't you? You know that we can't just leave, not now."

"I don't know that Q'Daer and I can keep you safe," Grinsa told him before Sirj could answer.

Besh frowned. "I don't recall asking you to. There's a reason why the Eandi sought an alliance with the Mettai. You've seen just a hint of what our magic can do. Believe me when I tell you that we're not to be trifled with either."

Grinsa had to smile. Besh was right: He and Sirj hadn't asked for any protection, and since another a'laq had declared them friends of the Fal'Borna, they didn't need anyone's permission to remain in the clan lands.

"Forgive me," he said. "I shouldn't have assumed that you'd need us to protect you. As your friend, I'd like you to go back to your home, where you'll be safer. But of course it's your choice to make."

Besh nodded. "Sirj and I will speak of this further. We'll let you know what we decide."

Grinsa still heard a touch of ice in the old man's voice, so he merely nodded in return and left them. One way or another, they'd be leaving soon and he wasn't ready yet.

Long before he reached his sleeping roll, however, he saw Torgan striding toward him. Grinsa knew just what the merchant was going to say and he had no desire to hear any of it. He kept walking, pretending that he hadn't noticed. After only a few moments of this, however, Torgan began calling to him. Heaving a sigh, Grinsa stopped and faced the man.

He'd been thinking about this for so long. More than once, he had thought he finally had the courage to do it. He'd gone to his carry sack fully intending to pull out the scrap of basket and take it to the white-hairs. But always something stopped him: lack of nerve, guilt, questions about whether it would even do any good.

These last, at least, had vanished in S'Vralna. The scrap of basket he carried would surely kill them. That much he now knew for certain. But the rest . . .

Guilt should have meant nothing to him. The Fal'Borna would kill him without hesitation; why should he feel any remorse for striking at them first? And though the Forelander had once argued for his life and for Jasha's, he had since shown himself to be much like the white-hairs of the South-lands. He seemed perfectly willing to trade Torgan's life for his freedom and that of his family. And why shouldn't he? Torgan was wise enough to know that he'd have done the same in the man's position. But then why should Torgan feel any pangs of conscience at taking the man's life in order to save his own?

That left his nerve, or rather, his lack thereof. This was not something he could overcome with logic, or by cataloging the ways in which the white-hairs had earned his enmity these past few turns. This cut to the very core of who and what he was. And for some time now Torgan had known that he was a coward. For years he had denied it to himself, citing as proof his refusal to flee Medqasse even when he knew that the coinmonger who eventually took out his eye was hunting him. Really, though, he had been more fool than hero at the time. He'd believed he could evade the man and his henchmen, and there was nothing courageous in the way he had cried and groveled, pleading for mercy when at last they caught up with him. But only recently, since that first night just outside of C'Bijor's Neck when he had watched the Y'Qatt city burn, had he known for certain.

He had long expected to die old and fat, happy and rich. Then he'd bought those damned baskets from Y'Farl in the Neck, and in a matter of days his world had crumbled. A wiser man—perhaps a braver man—would have embraced death in the face of all that had happened to him since then. He was fat still, but happy and rich were lost to him, possibly forever. And yet even now, he was terrified of dying.

He could start again, buy new wares, earn back the riches he'd lost. His desire to live reflected his belief that he could find wealth and happiness once more. That's what he told himself.

But he knew better. Fear controlled him, not hope. He didn't want to live so that he could overcome all he'd endured these past few harrowing turns. He wanted to live because the thought of dying unmanned him. It stole his breath and turned his innards to water. It wasn't so much that he wanted to live as that he simply didn't want to die.

Torgan would never accept that he was a killer. Whatever he did to get away from the Fal'Borna the white-hairs drove him to do. War was coming to the plain. An Eandi army was marching toward the Silverwater, and Torgan hoped that they would lay waste to every sept they encountered. Damn the white-hairs to the Deceiver's realm—let every last one of them burn in Bian's fires and be tortured by his demons. He hated them all, and, he knew, they hated him. If he returned to E'Menua's sept, he'd be killed, not because he had sold cursed baskets to the Y'Qatt or to Fal'Borna living in the small sept he'd visited in the north, but simply because he was Eandi. White-hairs and dark-eyes. It was simply the way of things.

He no longer had time for guilt or doubt. And knowing what was coming, understanding with the certainty of a condemned man that the remainder of his life could now be counted in days, hours, hoofbeats, he found his nerve.

"Gather your belongings," the Fal'Borna Weaver told them. "We'll be leaving shortly."

Torgan and Jasha had barely spoken in days. Up until now, the young merchant's hostility had bothered him a good deal. But this once Torgan was glad that the young merchant was nowhere near him when he reached into his sack and pulled out the scrap of burned basket. His hands were trembling violently. No doubt the color had drained from his face, leaving him ashen. It didn't matter. Jasha wasn't there to see any of it.

He'd give the white-hairs one last chance to let him go. They deserved—

"No," he said aloud. He wasn't going to lie to himself. He didn't believe that they deserved any consideration at all. But he remained too frightened of what he was about to do; he would give them this last opportunity because the only way he could do this was to convince himself that he had no other choice.

Gripping the burned osiers in his hand, he turned, searching for the two Qirsi.

He spotted the Forelander first.

"We're not going to talk about this now, Torgan," Grinsa said as the merchant drew near. The man's face was so white he actually looked Qirsi, and there was rage in his eyes. Grinsa half expected him to throw a punch, and indeed Torgan's right hand was balled in a fist, his knuckles white.

"And when do you propose that we do talk about it?" the merchant demanded. "You can't really believe that Jasha and I have any chance at all once we reach the sept."

"You have a chance so long as we're all alive and I can argue for your life. That's why we have to get out of the Horn and back to the plain. Once we're there, I'll talk to E'Menua."

"He won't listen, and you know it! He's a warrior; we're at war. He'll look at Jasha and me, and all he'll see are dark-eyes. Make us go back and you kill us."

Grinsa closed his eyes briefly and raked a hand through his hair. It was something Cresenne would have done, and he nearly laughed at himself.

"You see?" Torgan said. "You know I'm right."

How had he ended up in the middle of all this? Why hadn't he just let E'Menua have his way from the start? Yes, Torgan and Jasha would be dead by now, but maybe he, Cresenne, and Bryntelle would be away from here, living peacefully with another clan. "I don't know anything, Torgan. I'm not Fal'Borna. I'm not even from the Southlands. I'm just trying to keep myself and my family alive long enough for us to find a home."

"That's right," Torgan said, as if trying to wheedle him into buying some bauble that he didn't really want. "You're not from here. You're not like the Fal'Borna. You don't have any reason to hate Jasha or me. In fact, if it wasn't for you, we'd be dead already. You fought for our lives, at great cost to yourself. You don't want all that you've sacrificed to be for nothing. So let us go. If you allow it, Q'Daer will go along."

Grinsa shook his head. "I don't know that for sure. And I don't know if I can risk letting you go. It may not be fair, but for good or bad your fate and mine are linked. If I return to the sept without you, I might never be allowed to leave. I can't risk that." He started to turn away from the man. "I'm sorry, Torgan."

"Wait!" Torgan faltered, opened his mouth, then closed it again. A drop of sweat rolled down from his temple. He raised that fisted hand, but an instant later let it drop to his side again. It almost seemed that he was holding something, though Grinsa could see nothing but a faint shadow near the base of his thumb that might have been a trick of the light or a smear of black from the previous night's fire.

"We need to get ready, Torgan," Grinsa said, after waiting several moments for the man to speak. "The sooner we're on our way, the safer we'll be."

"No, I . . ." He shook his head, licked his lips. "I want to speak with Q'Daer about this. I want to hear from him that he won't let us go."

Grinsa exhaled, knowing that this was a waste of time, and knowing as well that it would only serve to anger the young Weaver. "Torgan, I promise that once we're back—"

"No!" the merchant said sharply. "I want to speak with both of you about this. I . . . I don't want the two of you to . . . to have a chance to discuss it alone. I want to be there." He nodded, as if convincing himself of this.

Clearly there was no reasoning with the man. "Fine," Grinsa said. "Come on then."

He started toward the Fal'Borna with Torgan just behind him. After just a few steps, he heard Jasha calling to the merchant. Torgan, though, either didn't hear the younger man or chose to ignore him.

Grinsa looked back at him. "Jasha—"

"I know," the merchant said irritably. He didn't stop or look back.

"Torgan!" the young merchant called again.

"Not now!" Torgan shouted over his shoulder, still not breaking stride.

Q'Daer was tying his sleeping roll onto his mount when they found him. He looked up at the sound of their approach and frowned.

"What's this?" he asked.

Grinsa turned to Torgan. "You wanted to talk to him. So talk."

The man licked his lips again. "You have to let us go," he said.

Q'Daer's frowned deepened. "What?"

"There's a war coming. If you take us back to your sept, the a'laq will kill us. You have to let us go."

Grinsa stared at the man, his eyes narrowing. Something wasn't right. Torgan's words made sense, but all the anger had drained from his voice. He seemed distracted, as if this conversation with Q'Daer was the last thing on his mind.

"We're not letting you go anywhere, dark-eye," Q'Daer said. "You still have to answer for your crimes, and the a'laq is the only one who can decide your fate. Even if I wanted to let you go—and I don't—it's not my place to do it." He turned his attention back to the sleeping roll. "Now, go ready your horse."

For several seconds, Torgan didn't move at all. Grinsa thought he might argue more, but he said nothing. He simply stood there, his chest rising and falling with each breath, as if he couldn't get enough air into his lungs. He glanced at Grinsa, and then looked at Q'Daer once more.

"We have nothing to do with this war," Torgan said, although still he sounded strangely calm. Where was the passion he'd shown only moments before? "But we'll be victims of it. You know now that when I sold those baskets I didn't think that anything was wrong with them. You know as well that Jasha and I have done what we could to help you find them and the witch who made them."

Q'Daer turned at that. "The other merchant did. I'm not so certain about you."

"I've done everything I could!" Torgan said, his voice rising so that he finally sounded a bit more like himself. "I did my share in S'Vralna! And I've lost everything I had! I've been punished enough!"

Q'Daer regarded him sourly, as if regretting that he'd responded at all. "Like I said, it's not my place to decide your punishment. We'll see what the a'laq has to say."

"By then it will be too late! If I wind up back in your sept, I'm a dead man, regardless of what I deserve. You know I'm right about this!"

Q'Daer looked at Grinsa wearily. "I have no time for this right now. I'm going to check on the other one to see if he's ready." He started to walk in Jasha's direction. "Next time, keep this one away from me."

Grinsa eyed Torgan as the merchant watched Q'Daer walk away. "I could have told you it would go that way," he said. "Q'Daer is devoted to his a'laq. He'd never presume to go against E'Menua's wishes, and that's just what you were asking him to do."

Torgan didn't answer. He didn't even look Grinsa's way. Instead, his eyes wandered the area around him before coming to rest on Q'Daer's mount. "I haven't eaten yet," he said. "Can I get something from his travel sack?" He cast a quick look after the Fal'Borna who was out of earshot by now. "Much of it was my food to begin with," he said. "Mine and Jasha's."

Grinsa felt much as Q'Daer did at this point; he wanted nothing more to do with this man.

"Yes, fine," he said, turning to his own sleeping roll. "Get some food and then get yourself ready." He glanced over at the merchant. "No more delays. You understand?"

"Yes," Torgan said sullenly. "I understand perfectly."

He took several moments to get food from the young Weaver's bag. In fact, he was there fiddling with Q'Daer's belongings for so long that Grinsa finally turned to look to see what he was doing. But by that time Torgan was replacing the sack of food and putting a piece of dried meat in his mouth. Grinsa shook his head and turned his attention back to what he was doing. He did look up again as the merchant walked back to his horse. The man hadn't said anything more to him, or even grunted a thank-you. But he did seem to have accepted that he had no choice but to ride with them back to the sept. And from what Grinsa could see, his hands hung loosely at his side. No more fists. That was something at least.

They rode out a short time later in their usual formation: the Qirsi riding in front, the merchants behind them, and the Mettai bringing up the rear in their cart. Sirj approached Grinsa just as they were leaving to inform him that he and Besh would continue to journey with them.

"We may turn eastward in a few days," the man told him. "But for now we'll remain with you."

Grinsa told him that they'd be happy to have the Mettai with them for as long as they wished to remain, but inwardly he feared they were making a terrible mistake. He also lamented the fact that Sirj and not Besh had come to speak with him. He was afraid that he had offended the older man, and he resolved to make things right as soon as possible.

They crossed the Thraedes a short time after midday, leaving the Horn behind them, and then turned due south, continuing to follow the river.

They pushed their mounts hard and covered a fair amount of ground before stopping for the night. None of them spoke much. Torgan had gone back to brooding in silence, and the Mettai kept to themselves.

They ate a small meal as darkness settled over the plain, and soon were unrolling their sleeping rolls beneath a cloudy sky that glowed faintly with moonlight. Q'Daer said something about remaining awake to speak with E'Menua. Grinsa was exhasted from having been awakened so early in the morning. He lay down and fell asleep quickly, only to wake up some time later to an odd sound. He sat up, rubbing the sleep from his eyes, and peered in the direction from which the sound had come, trying to make out a dark shape a short distance off.

A moment later he realized that he'd been hearing someone retch. He glanced at the young Weaver's sleeping roll, his stomach clenching itself into a hard ball. Q'Daer wasn't there.

"Q'Daer?" he called softly.

"Stay away from me!" came the reply. His voice sounded weak, strained. A moment later Grinsa heard him get sick yet again.

Grinsa stood and started toward the man.

"I told you to keep away, Forelander!" the man said, making him stop.

He could see Q'Daer clearly now. He was on his hands and knees, his head hanging low, his breathing labored.

"I've got it," the Weaver said a moment later, all the anger gone from his voice. "I've got the plague."

Grinsa shivered in the darkness. "How is that possible? It's been days since we left S'Vralna. You can't have it. You're just sick."

Q'Daer shook his head. "No. I've been sick before, but I've never felt like this. I can feel the fever in me. I feel myself getting weak." He looked back at Grinsa. "The Mettai did this to me. That's why they wanted to stay with us."

This time it was Grinsa's turn to shake his head. "They wouldn't do anything of the sort."

"Then how did this happen? You said it yourself: We left S'Vralna days ago. This plague strikes in just hours."

Grinsa started to say again that he doubted it was the plague. But then it came to him. Torgan.

"I'll be back," he said, turning on his heel.

As he passed the fire circle he rekindled the flames with a thought, not even slowing his gait. He walked to where the merchants were sleeping and prodded them both with his foot.

"Get up, both of you."

Jasha grunted, turned over, his eyes barely even opening. Torgan, on the other hand, propped himself up on one arm immediately. Grinsa was certain that he hadn't even been sleeping.

"What's the matter?" the one-eyed merchant asked.

"Wake up, Jasha," Grinsa said, ignoring Torgan for the moment.

The younger man took a long shuddering breath. Then he rubbed at his eyes. "Forelander?" he said groggily.

"Yes. I want both of you to come with me."

"Why?" Torgan asked. "What's going on?"

Grinsa was certain that there was a way to do this, something he could say to put the man off for a few more moments so that he might find a way to prove that Torgan had done something to make Q'Daer ill. But he was too enraged and frightened to play games, and too addled with sleep to think clearly enough.

He said simply, "Q'Daer's sick."

"Damn!" Jasha said, instantly sounding awake. "Is it . . . has he got . . . ?"

"Lici's plague?" Grinsa said for him. He started to say that he thought it was, but then reconsidered, his gaze sliding toward Torgan again. "I don't know. We'll just have to wait and see. On second thought, Torgan will come with me. Jasha, I want you to wake Besh and Sirj and bring them to our fire."

The young merchant scrambled to his feet. "Of course," he said, heading off toward Besh and Sirj's cart.

"Get up, Torgan," Grinsa said for a third time.

The merchant stood slowly. "What is it you want with us?"

Grinsa gave a small shrug. "I told you: Q'Daer's sick. I need help caring for him."

Torgan actually took a step back away from him. "How can we help you with that?"

"There's only the six of us," Grinsa said. He sensed the kernel of an idea forming and he followed his instincts. "We'll need everyone's help."

"Well, the Mettai—"

"Besh, Sirj, and I will have to start working on a cure. It's probably not the plague, but just in case it is . . ." He shrugged again.

"What about Jasha and me?"

"I'm going to send Jasha for help. You'll stay with Q'Daer. He'll need water, a compress on his head to keep his fever down. And you'll need to keep the fire burning."

"Jasha can do that! I can get help just as easily . . ." He trailed off seeing that Grinsa was shaking his head.

"You're determined to escape, Torgan. You've made that clear. I can't send you off anywhere." He started walking back to the fire and Q'Daer, leaving Torgan with little choice but to follow. "No, you have to be the one to care for him."

"But I can't be!" Torgan said. "The plague . . . his power will be out of control! You saw what happened in S'Vralna! I'll be killed!"

"We don't know that it's the plague, Torgan."

The merchant opened his mouth, but quickly clamped it shut again.

Grinsa halted and grabbed the man's arm. "Or do we?"

Torgan wrenched his arm out of Grinsa's grasp. "What's that supposed to mean?" he demanded, his voice quavering.

"What did you do to him, Torgan?"

"I didn't do anything!"

Grinsa summoned a bright flame to the palm of his hand and held it just in front of the merchant's face. Torgan flinched, but before he could step back Grinsa took hold of the front of his shirt, wrapping his fist in the cloth.

"You're lying!" he said. "You did it this past morning, when my back was turned and you were rooting around in Q'Daer's things. Now tell me what you did!"

"Nothing! It must have been the Mettai! They're the ones with magic! It was their curse to begin with!"

Grinsa moved the flame closer to his face, so that it singed some of the man's hair. Torgan closed his eyes and turned his face away, wincing at anticipated pain.

After a moment Grinsa let the fire die out and took hold of Torgan's arm again. "Come on," he said, dragging the merchant to where he'd left the young Weaver. This time Torgan didn't fight him.

Besh, Sirj, and Jasha were already standing beside the fire, all of them looking down at the Fal'Borna who had made his way to his sleeping roll. Q'Daer lay on his side, huddled in his blanket, his legs drawn up so that he looked more like a child than a warrior. His face was bathed in sweat and he appeared to be trembling. He had his eyes open and he merely stared at the flames dancing before him.

When Grinsa and Torgan stepped into the firelight, the three who were standing looked up at them. Jasha frowned at the way Grinsa was holding on to the merchant.

"What's going on?" he asked Grinsa. "What's he done now?"

Grinsa indicated the Fal'Borna with a small nod. "I think he's responsible for what's happened to Q'Daer."

"I'm not!" Torgan said. He pointed at the Mettai. "It's them! They created this plague! They're the ones—"

Grinsa slapped his face, silencing him, and leaving a livid imprint of his hand on the merchant's cheek. "Say that again, and you'll get worse."

"You should back away, Forelander," Besh said. "If this is the plague, you can't be anywhere near the Fal'Borna."

"It is the plague," Q'Daer said, his voice even weaker than it had been before. "What else can it be?"

"Please, Grinsa," Besh said.

Grinsa stared down at Q'Daer for several moments. Finally he nodded, releasing Torgan and shoving him toward the Mettai. "Watch him," he said. "He did this. I'm sure of it." He backed away from the fire, but he didn't go far. "Jasha, I want you to search Q'Daer's carry sack."

"For what?" the young merchant asked.

Grinsa shook his head. "I don't know. Anything that might explain this."

Jasha nodded and walked over to where the young Weaver's belongings were piled. But Grinsa watched Torgan, who just stared at the fire, not looking particularly concerned.

Whatever it was wouldn't be in the carry sack. And since Grinsa and Q'Daer had eaten from the sack of food, it wouldn't be in there, either. Which left . . .

"Damn," Grinsa muttered. "Stop looking, Jasha. It's not in there. It's wrapped up in Q'Daer's sleeping roll or his blanket."

Torgan's eyes snapped up to Grinsa's face. He looked away a moment later, but that one instant was enough to tell Grinsa that he was right.

Q'Daer twisted his head to look up at Grinsa, this simple action seeming to take a great effort. "You're sure he did this?" he asked hoarsely. "It could have been the Mettai."

"You see?" Torgan said. "He knows!"

"It wasn't the Mettai," Grinsa said, sensing that Besh and Sirj had both bristled. "Torgan was in your things this morning. He said he wanted food and I let him get something from your bag. At least that's what I thought I was letting him do. I'm sorry. This is my fault."

"Here it is."

They all turned toward Jasha, who was holding up what appeared to be a small scrap of basket. It was burned at the edges—blackened, like that shadow Grinsa had seen on Torgan's hand—and it was small enough to be hidden in the merchant's fist.

"Where did you get that?" Grinsa demanded glaring at Torgan once more.

"I told you, I didn't—"

"Don't say it, Torgan!" Grinsa leveled a rigid finger at the man. "I swear I'll snap your neck if you do! Besh and Sirj wouldn't do something like this. But if they had, they'd have used magic. They'd have no need to use a piece of one of those baskets. Now, where'd you get it?"

Torgan said nothing.

"It's from that village we found," Jasha said, examining the scrap in the firelight. "I remember seeing this one."

"Is that true?" Grinsa asked.

Torgan had the look of a cornered animal. His eyes flicked back and forth between Jasha and Grinsa, and his mouth opened and closed repeatedly, as if he wanted to speak but feared what would happen if he did.

"I can compel you to answer," Grinsa said. "I have magic—mind-bending it's called—it will make you tell the truth."

"Don't do it that way," Q'Daer said, closing his eyes. "Use shaping. Break his fingers one at a time. Break his ribs."

Grinsa nodded. "All right."

"No!" Torgan said. He licked his lips. "It's true. That's where it came from. That village. I knew you were going to kill me eventually. This was the only chance I had."

"You bloody idiot," Jasha said, shaking his head, a look of disgust on his face. "You're a dead man for sure. And good riddance to you."

"We can punish him later," Besh said, turning to Grinsa. "And whatever you decide in that regard will be fine with us. But what are we going to do to save your friend?"

Grinsa gazed at the Fal'Borna. He seemed to be fading by the moment. And Grinsa knew that it was only a matter of time before he lost control of his magic. Once that began to happen, they'd have little hope of keeping the man alive.

"You and Sirj need to find some way to combat this curse of Lici's. No one here blames you for any of this, but the magic that created it was Mettai, and so the answer is going to lie in your powers, not mine."

Besh nodded. "Very well. You'll stay away from him?"

Grinsa nodded. He didn't feel at all sick. He'd been fortunate beyond measure; he had no intention of endangering himself by getting too close to Q'Daer. "Yes, I'll stay as far away as I am now. But even from this distance, I can use my healing magic on him. It may be that I can cure him, or at least keep him from getting worse."

Chapter 24

✦✝✦

Besh had always considered himself an accomplished conjurer. Whenever he needed to use magic, he found the correct spell to achieve what he set out to do. He couldn't recall the last time he had tried a spell that failed. Even when he was fighting Lici, having to meet her assaults with his defenses, he had managed to ward himself and, ultimately, to defeat her.

Unlike some Mettai he knew, however, he had never considered himself a student of blood magic. Some Mettai spent goodly amounts of both time and blood experimenting with spells, teaching themselves new conjurings, perfecting the magic they already knew. Besh had never done any of that; to his knowledge, neither had Sirj.

Now, suddenly, they not only needed to create a new spell that would combat Lici's plague, but they needed to do so quickly, before the young Fal'Borna succumbed to the disease. Besh wasn't even sure he knew where to begin, though he did have an idea.

Once more Grinsa entrusted the two Mettai with keeping watch on Torgan, and for good measure the Forelander instructed Jasha to go with them as well.

"I'll join you soon," Grinsa told Besh. "I still believe our best hope for finding a magical cure lies in combining our powers. But I need to try this first," he went on, nodding toward Q'Daer. "I may be able to give us a bit more time."

Besh frowned. With all that he had seen in S'Vralna, he couldn't help thinking that Grinsa should remain as far from the Fal'Borna as possible. "Are you sure this is a good idea?" he asked.

"I told you, I won't go near him. But my healing magic can work at a distance. I can help him without endangering myself."

The man sounded very sure of himself, and Besh knew almost nothing about Qirsi magic. But still, something about this troubled him. He remembered hearing . . . *something*. He couldn't recall the words, though he could almost make out the voice.

"Besh?" Grinsa said.

"I wish you wouldn't do this," the old man said, cursing his faulty memory.

"I wish I didn't have to. But I do."

Besh shook his head slowly, trying to remember. But at last he gave up. "All right then," he agreed. "We'll do what we can to undo Lici's curse."

He beckoned to Sirj, intending to go back to their cart and the small fire they had built beside it. Torgan followed reluctantly, and Jasha turned to leave the Qirsi's fire. But as he did he appeared to lift his hand, as if to toss something into the flames.

"No, don't!" Besh called to him, realizing just in time what it was the man was holding.

Jasha hesitated, looking first at the Mettai and then at the scrap of basket he still held. "Shouldn't I destroy it?"

"It might help us to have it," Besh said. "It's the only piece of Lici's spell that remains."

The young merchant turned to Grinsa. "What do you think?"

"I'd like to see it destroyed," the Forelander said, "but Besh is right. If he thinks it can help, we should keep it."

Jasha stared down at the thing he held and after a moment closed his fist around it. When he walked over to where Besh and the others were waiting, he kept a good distance between himself and Grinsa.

"We have a chance now to get away," Torgan said quietly as they walked. "The Forelander will be busy with Q'Daer. Neither of them will be watching us."

Besh opened his mouth, intending to tell the man to be silent, but to his surprise, Sirj beat him to it.

"One more word out of you, Torgan," Sirj said, sounding more menacing than Besh had ever heard him, "and I swear I'll cut your throat."

"I wouldn't expect you to understand," the merchant said. "Somehow the white-hairs trust you both, despite the fact that this is a Mettai curse that's killing their kind. Magic may be the only thing that matters to any of you, but Jasha and I—"

The blow came so swiftly that at first Besh didn't even understand what had happened. One moment Torgan was walking beside them, and the next he was on his back, his hands raised to his face, blood running over his fingers. Sirj stood over him, both of his fists clenched.

"Say something else," the young Mettai said. "Give me another reason to hit you."

Torgan made no move to get up. Instead he pulled his hands away from his face and stared at the blood covering them. "Look what you did to me!" he said, his voice sounding so thick that Besh wondered if Sirj had broken his nose. "You Mettai bastard!"

Sirj pulled his knife from his belt.

"Sirj, no!" Besh said.

"After all he's done, he deserves to die!"

Besh nodded. "Yes, he probably does. But that's for the Qirsi to decide. If you kill him, you'll have to live with that for the rest of your life."

"I could live with killing this man."

Besh had no doubt that he meant it. But after a moment Sirj resheathed his blade. Then he leaned over and hauled the merchant to his feet.

"Next time I will kill you," he said looking Torgan in his good eye. "Even Besh won't be able to stop me."

"Next time I won't try to stop him," Besh said.

Torgan glared at him. Sirj grinned darkly.

They started walking again, but had only taken a few steps when they heard someone cry out behind them.

Besh and Sirj shared a look.

"Was that the Forelander?" Sirj asked.

Before Besh could answer he heard someone coughing. No. Retching.

Besh closed his eyes, the memory coming to him at a last. It was the n'qlae. That's whose voice he had been hearing in his mind, the words unclear, the warning wasted.

My husband believed that the disease struck at our magic.

Of course. That was how the plague had spread. That was why the children had been spared. That was Lici's genius.

"Yes," Besh said, turning and breaking into a run. "That was Grinsa."

ħe'd been prepared for Q'Daer to fight him. They had been rivals since the day they met, and though at times it seemed that they had reached some sort of understanding, their interactions remained difficult, to say the least. Healing a fever required that he enter the man's mind, and that demanded a level of trust that he and Q'Daer had never reached. He'd also thought it possible that the illness might rob the young Weaver of his senses, so that even had he wanted to be healed he would be unable to recognize Grinsa's touch or understand that the gleaner was trying to help him. He'd even prepared himself for the possibility that it was already too late, that even if Q'Daer allowed him into his thoughts, the disease had already progressed too far to be defeated.

But it never occurred to Grinsa that this would happen. It should have, of course. He knew that the plague attacked Qirsi magic; one needed only see the wreckage that once had been S'Vralna to understand that much. Who would have imagined, though, that Lici's curse could be so insidious?

He had called out to Q'Daer before beginning.

"I'm going to try to heal you," he said, sitting on the ground several fourspans from the Fal'Borna and the fire that burned beside him. "I'm going to try to cool your fever. Perhaps I can even stop the illness from getting any worse."

The young Weaver hadn't responded.

"Q'Daer? Can you hear me?"

Nothing.

He knew the Fal'Borna couldn't be dead. Not yet. Not until his magic poured from his body, and with it his life. There seemed nothing left for him to do but make the attempt.

Closing his eyes, Grinsa reached forth with his healing magic and touched Q'Daer's mind.

He knew instantly that he had made a terrible mistake. Entering the young Weaver's mind was like stepping into fire. Abruptly it seemed that his flesh was burning. Grinsa opened his mouth to scream and he felt his lungs being seared by the flames. Q'Daer stood before him amid the blaze, his skin red and shining with sweat, but not blackened as it should have been, as Grinsa felt certain his own must be.

"You shouldn't be here," the Fal'Borna said.

"I was trying to heal you."

"I can't be healed. And now you've killed yourself."

"Not yet I haven't. We can heal each other. We can pit our magic against the curse."

But Q'Daer shook his head, looking like a ghoul standing amid Bian's fires. "Don't you think I've tried," he said. "I'm a Weaver, too, remember? Our magic does nothing against this plague."

Grinsa refused to give in. He turned his healing magic onto himself, trying to grapple with the fever that already gripped his mind. He had healed others who were ill, fevered, near death. He knew how to quell the flames that might ravage a febrile mind.

But nothing he tried worked against this pestilence. It wasn't that Lici's magic was stronger than his own. It didn't resist him, it didn't overpower him. It simply eluded him. Every time he reached out with his power to take hold of the illness, it seemed to slither from his grasp, like some demon serpent from the Underrealm. He tried to pour healing magic over his entire mind, his entire body, as if dousing a fire with a torrent of water. But the serpent wrapped itself around him, withstanding the deluge. When he had exhausted himself, the beast was still there. The flames still raged around him.

"You see?" Q'Daer said. "We're helpless against this plague. The Mettai witch knew what she was doing. She did what all the Eandi armies of the last thousand years couldn't do. She defeated the Fal'Borna. And now more of her kind march with a new dark-eye force. Our people are doomed."

"Not yet," Grinsa said again. But despair lay heavy on his heart. He thought of Cresenne and Bryntelle and felt that he might weep. How could he have failed them this way? He couldn't even reach for his beloved to apologize, to say good-bye, for surely that touch of his magic upon her mind would sicken her, too.

"There's nothing more you can do here, Forelander," Q'Daer said. "Leave me. Let me die in peace."

He wanted to refuse, but he hadn't the will. Not anymore. He merely nodded.

"Die well, Grinsa. We'll see each other in the Deceiver's realm. May he be kind to both of us."

Grinsa briefly met the man's gaze. He said nothing, feeling that to wish Q'Daer a noble death was to surrender, which he still refused to do. He withdrew from the man's mind.

As soon as he was free of the Fal'Borna's thoughts, Grinsa felt his stomach heave. He opened his eyes, twisted himself onto his hands and knees, and emptied the contents of his stomach onto the grass. By the time he had finished being sick, he could hear Besh calling his name. He looked up and saw the two Mettai running toward him.

"You've got it, too," Besh said, stopping in front of him, looking stricken.

Grinsa nodded, not yet trusting himself to speak. An instant later his body was racked by another spasm of illness.

Besh hung his head for a moment and spat a curse. "I'm sorry," he said. "I should have realized. It's the magic. That's how it spreads."

Grinsa shook his head, clamping his mouth shut against another wave of nausea. "I have no power to fight this illness," he said, when he could talk again. His voice sounded raw, and his throat ached. "I don't understand your magic. I can't touch it. Neither can Q'Daer."

"I'm not certain that anyone can," Besh said. "I've told you before: Lici said that her spell couldn't be undone. I hoped she was lying to me, or that she was simply wrong. But . . . but I haven't much hope."

"You have to try," Grinsa told him, closing his eyes again. He felt so weary suddenly. All he wanted was to sleep.

"I intend to. I'll bleed myself weak if I have to. I'll do everything in my power to defeat this plague."

Sirj nodded once. "So will I."

Grinsa smiled weakly. "Thank you both."

"We'd like to stay with you if we may, Grinsa," Besh said. "We may need to try different cures on you until we find one that works."

"Yes, all right."

Besh turned to Sirj. "We'll need that piece of basket, too."

Grinsa looked at him. "Don't you have it?"

"No. Jasha still has it. We heard you getting sick before I could take it from him."

Grinsa was still on his hands and knees, but now he straightened and looked around, though the effort made his head spin. "Where is Jasha? For that matter where's Torgan?"

Besh and Sirj glanced at one another. "When we heard you we came running," the old man said. "I assumed that they'd follow."

"Damn," Grinsa muttered. He wanted to lie down, but instead he tried to stand, fully intending to search for the merchants.

"Stay there," Sirj told him. "Rest. I'll get them."

"Be careful of Torgan," Grinsa said, forcing himself to his feet and staggering toward the fire.

"He'd best be careful of me," Sirj answered, and walked away.

Torgan watched the two Mettai run off in Grinsa's direction, dabbing gingerly at his nose. It was tender and it still bled.

"I think that bastard broke my nose," he said.

Jasha was staring after the Mettai, looking scared and very young. "We should go over there. They'll need our help."

He started to walk toward the others.

"Wait a moment, Jasha."

The young merchant turned, eyeing him with manifest distrust. "Why?"

"Look, I have a pretty good idea of what you think of me right now. I'll even admit that I feel bad for what I've done to the white-hairs."

Jasha smirked. "Sure you do, Torgan."

"I don't care if you believe me. It's the truth. But it's also true that I begged them again and again to let us go. I told them that we'd be killed if they didn't, and they wouldn't listen. They left me with no choice."

"If you say so." Jasha started away again.

"My point is," Torgan said, striding after the younger man, "nothing's changed."

Jasha stopped again. "What do you mean?"

"They're still going to kill us."

"Yes, well you saw to that, didn't you?"

"They were still going to kill us anyway, you fool! Haven't you been paying attention? There's a war coming! We're Eandi; they're white-hairs! If we stay with them we're dead men!" He glanced in the direction the Mettai had gone. "But this is our chance. The two Qirsi are sick; the Mettai are so concerned with saving them that they've left us alone. We can get away right now."

"We're not going anywhere, Torgan. This is your doing, and we're going to help them in any way we can. And if Grinsa and Q'Daer die, you'll be judged for their murders."

Torgan shook his head. "No. You can do what you like, but I'm leaving. I won't die for a white-hair, or for a Mettai, and I certainly won't die for you." He started to walk away, looking up at the sky briefly to gauge how much longer the moons would light the plain. "Good-bye, Jasha. I hope your death is painless."

He heard the young merchant coming after him, but he didn't slow down, at least not until Jasha took hold of his arm. He halted then, looking the young man in the eye.

"Let go of me, Jasha. I don't want to hurt you."

"I'm not letting you go. Not after what you've done."

Torgan laughed, and then punched him in the face. Jasha staggered back but righted himself quickly. He lunged at Torgan again. The older merchant swung at him a second time, but this time Jasha ducked under the blow, wrapping his arms around Torgan's middle and knocking him to the ground.

They wrestled for several moments, breathing hard, grunting with the effort. Jasha was stronger than Torgan had expected, and he was lithe and quick. But Torgan was bigger and more powerful. In short order he had managed to get the younger man in a choke hold.

"That's enough, lad," he said, as Jasha continued to struggle. "Give up now. I'm leaving and there's nothing you can do to stop me."

Jasha flailed at him with his fists.

"Stop it!" Torgan said. He adjusted his grip on the man so that he held him more firmly, his forearm locked around Jasha's throat, his other hand wrapped in the younger man's hair.

"Let me go, Torgan!"

"I won't until you stop fighting me!"

"Never! You've as good as killed those men! You have to pay for that!"

He had no time for this. Any moment now, the Mettai would realize that he and Jasha weren't there, and then they'd come looking for them. If he had chance of getting away, this was it, and he wasn't going to waste it on Jasha.

"I'm gonna let you go," he said. "No more fighting, you hear me? No tricks either."

He began to relax his grip on the lad, and immediately Jasha went into a frenzy, punching blindly with his hands, kicking his feet, trying to twist his body out of Torgan's grasp.

The one-eyed merchant tightened his hold again. "Damn you!"

It wasn't something he would have done a turn or two before. He wasn't certain that he would have done it yesterday. But circumstances had changed. He had changed. War was coming, and he refused to die here on this blasted plain.

"Forgive me, lad," he whispered.

It took little effort really—it amazed him how fragile the human body could be. A sharp tug with the arm at Jasha's throat; a similar motion but in the other direction with the hand that gripped the young man's head. He heard the snap as clear as a bell and abruptly the man's body went limp in his arms. Torgan released him, and watched the young merchant's form roll onto the grass, where it lay still.

One of the lad's hands fell open, revealing something dark against his skin. Torgan knew immediately what it was.

He started to reach for it, but before he could he heard a voice calling out, "Jasha? Torgan?"

The merchant looked up. Sirj was walking in their direction, though Torgan could tell that the man hadn't seen him yet. He would have liked to kill this one, too; a measure of revenge for the broken nose. But he had no answer for the Mettai's magic, and he sensed that this young, dark-haired man would be a more dangerous opponent than Jasha had been.

Instead, he reached down for that dark scrap of cursed basket, tucked it into his pocket, and crept off into the darkness as quietly as possible, edging toward his mount. He'd be away before they could find him. Given a choice between pursuing him and trying to save the Qirsi, the Mettai would choose the latter. It was their curse; they'd do all they could to keep it from taking any more victims.

That curse was also his greatest weapon. And that piece of Mettai basket would get him back to Stelpana alive.

Besh sat cross-legged on the grass, his knife in his hand, but his hands resting in his lap. He didn't know how to begin. He hoped that that small scrap of basket might help him. There was an old spell, one he'd learned as a young man, that would allow him actually to see Lici's magic as light. Perhaps it would also allow him to measure any effect his own spells were having on her curse. It wasn't much, but it was all he had just now.

"Are you awake, Forelander?" he asked, looking at the man. Even in the firelight, the Qirsi's face looked ashen. His hair clung to his forehead, damp with sweat, and his mouth was open, slack. "I want to try some spells on you and I want you to tell me whether they're having any effect. Can you do that?"

After a moment, the Forelander nodded almost imperceptibly. "Yes. I'm awake. I can help you. How's Q'Daer?"

Besh looked across the fire at the Fal'Borna. He looked much as Grinsa did, though there was little doubt but that he had lost consciousness some time ago. The old man didn't know for certain, but he guessed it wouldn't be long before the magic began to flow from his body.

"He's just as he was before," Besh said.

Grinsa responded with another weak nod. "Where's Sirj?"

"He's gone to get the merchants." He hesitated. Then, "Can you tell me what it feels like, Grinsa?"

"It feels like I'm on fire," the man whispered. "Everything's burning, but I haven't the strength to put out the flames. I can't do anything."

Besh nodded and lifted his blade to the back of his hand. He cut himself, caught the welling blood on the flat of the blade, and picked up a handful of dirt. Mixing the blood and the earth, he began to speak a spell.

"Blood to earth, life to power, power to thought, balm to fire."

As he said this last, he made a motion with his hand and opened his fist, as if spreading seed. The mud in his hand became a fine mist that settled over the Forelander's chest and face and then appeared to vanish into him.

Besh waited a moment or two and then asked, "Did you feel that?"

"I felt something cool touch my face," Grinsa answered. Besh had to lean closer to the man just to hear him, so weak was his voice.

"Did it soothe your fever?"

"No. It just touched my face. That's all."

Besh sat back and nodded. He hadn't really expected it to be that easy. He peered into the darkness toward where he had left Jasha and Torgan. Where was Sirj?

He took a breath, then cut himself again, mixed the blood with more earth, and started a second spell. If he couldn't cool Grinsa's fever, perhaps he could purge his magic of the curse.

"Blood to earth, life to power, power to thought, healing to magic."

Again he threw the mud; again it became a silvery mist. It touched the Forelander and was absorbed into his skin.

"Anything?" he asked.

"Nothing more than last time. Was that the same spell?"

"No, though it might as well have been."

Besh heard footsteps behind him and turned. Sirj was walking back in his direction, his blade drawn. He was alone.

"What happened?" Besh asked. "Where are Jasha and Torgan?"

"Jasha's dead," the younger man told him in a low voice. "I don't know where Torgan's gone. I thought I heard a horse at one point, but I didn't know if you wanted me to follow him, or come back here."

"Blood and bone." He shook his head slowly, staring off into the night. Meeting Sirj's gaze again he said, "You did the right thing coming back. We have to heal these two. That's the most important thing. Did you bring that piece of Lici's basket?"

"I couldn't find it," Sirj said. "It's too dark to look for it in the grass. Maybe when the sun comes up."

"Torgan took it."

They both looked at Grinsa, whose eyes were open and shining with firelight.

Besh knew he was right. Torgan wanted only to get away from the Fal'Borna, to make his way back to Eandi land without being killed as an enemy of the white-hairs. He'd think nothing of using Lici's plague to that end.

"I know a spell," he told Grinsa. "One that reveals magic, lets me see it. I was going to use it on that scrap. Obviously I can't do that now, but I can put the spell on you, that is, if you'll let me."

"Is there any danger?"

"I don't think so. But I wanted to ask you first."

Grinsa nodded, closing his eyes again. "Of course, go ahead."

For a third time, Besh cut himself. "Blood to earth, life to power, power to thought, magic revealed." This time he spread the mist over all of Grinsa's body. As soon as it touched the man it flared brilliantly. Besh and Sirj shielded their eyes.

Upon looking at him again, Besh inhaled sharply and then exhaled through his teeth. He'd known it would look bad, but he hadn't been prepared for this. Grinsa was enveloped in a baleful green light, the color of disease and rot, that flickered softly and seemed to lick at his skin like flame.

"May the gods save us all," Sirj whispered.

"Did it work?" Grinsa asked.

"Yes."

The Forelander opened his eyes again and lifted his hands so that he could look at them. "I don't see anything. What does it look like?"

Besh faltered, but only for a moment. "Like you're on fire, just as you said."

Before any of them could say more, they heard a low groan come from the far side of the blaze. Q'Daer stirred, groaned again, shook his head. And then fire burst from both of his hands, streaking into the night sky, and seeming to burn through the clouds overhead.

"It's starting," Grinsa said. "It's not safe for the two of you to be here."

Besh shrugged. "We have no choice. This is where you are."

"That was just fire magic," the Forelander told him, his voice rising. "And it could have been much worse. He also has shaping magic. Even healing can kill if used the wrong way. There's no telling the damage he could do. You could both be killed before you have a chance to help either of us."

"I'll control it," Q'Daer said in a strained voice.

All of them looked his way.

"Can you?" Grinsa asked.

"I think so. Language of beasts, fire, a wind. I'll keep it from touching my shaping or healing power. And I'll direct the fire into the sky."

Even as he spoke, flames flew from his hands again, bright and angry.

"You haven't much time," Grinsa said, dropping his voice. "He may be a Weaver, but his power won't hold out forever."

Besh nodded. He cut himself yet again, gathered the blood on his blade, and mixed it with the dark fertile earth of the plain.

"Blood to earth, life to power, power to thought . . ." He faltered, unsure of what to try next.

"Damn," Q'Daer said, the word seemingly ripped from his chest.

A wind rose, building from a mere breeze to a keening gale in just moments. The fire sputtered, and even sitting, Besh had to brace himself with a hand to keep from being blown over.

Q'Daer began to shout, a terrible, inarticulate sound that mingled with the cry of the wind. He thrust a hand into the air and for a third time fire streamed from his fingers.

"Try anything," Sirj said, his voice barely carrying over the wind and Q'Daer's roar.

Besh nodded. "Plague to health," he said, throwing the bloody mixture again. It transformed itself into a glittering cloud of dust and settled over the Forelander. The green flame surrounding the man wavered for just an instant, as when a sudden gust disturbs a candle flame. But nothing more happened. The magic around him looked just as it had. His face remained ashen.

"Anything?" Besh asked, knowing already that he'd failed again.

Grinsa simply shook his head.

Besh rubbed a hand over his face and shook his head. Sirj stared at the ground, saying nothing. After some time, the wind began to die away and the Fal'Borna fell silent.

"Q'Daer?" Grinsa called to him, sounding alarmed.

"I'm all right," the man said, his voice little more than a breath.

Besh cast a despairing look at Sirj. "If you have ideas I'm open to them. I'm at a loss."

"There may be nothing you can do," Q'Daer whispered. "I know you're trying, Mettai. But this isn't a battle you can win. The witch who did this was too clever."

"There must be a way," Sirj said. "No spell can be perfect; I refuse to believe that Lici was that powerful."

Besh stared at the fire. "She thought she was. She told me I'd never defeat her spell. She even threatened to make a second spell that would do the same to the Mettai."

"You never told me that," Sirj said.

At the same time, Grinsa raised his head. "Say that again."

Besh looked at him. "What?"

"What you just said; say it again."

"She threatened me with a second spell that would sicken the Mettai."

"And what was the other thing she said?" Grinsa asked. "Her exact words."

Besh closed his eyes, trying to recall just what Lici had said. "She told me that her spell couldn't be undone. And then she said that there was no spell I could make that would defeat it."

"That's it!" Grinsa said. "Don't you see?"

Besh shook his head, wondering if the fever had robbed the Forelander of his senses.

"How would that—?"

"Think for a moment, Besh," the man said. "You can't defeat her spell. You can't undo it. But maybe you can create a second spell that has the opposite effect. It doesn't have to destroy hers. It might just be enough to . . . I don't know, to guard us from her spell. To cover hers, as it were."

Besh considered this for several moments, his brow furrowed.

"Could that work?" Sirj asked.

"I don't know. It would take more than a simple conjuring—eight parts rather than four, I would think. But it might work."

Q'Daer shouted out again. Besh heard the horses whinny and stomp. A moment later he began to hear the howling of wolves and the cries of a wildcat. Owls called to one another. It seemed all the darkness had come alive.

"Language of beasts," Grinsa said. "You have to try it, Besh. Q'Daer will be dead before long. And then it'll be my turn."

Besh nodded. He looked down at the back of his hand, which was scored with fresh, raw scars. Usually the cuts a Mettai made for conjurings didn't hurt, but his hand had begun to throb. What choice did he have, though, but to cut himself yet again? He reached for another handful of dirt.

"Blood to earth," he said. "Life to power, power to thought, earth to mist, mist to magic, magic to plague, plague to shield, shield to Qirsi!" With this last he flung the mud from his hand, watching as it changed to that familiar mist and fell over Grinsa. Once more, the green flame around the Forelander flickered, but that was all. It didn't go out or even dim. From what Besh could see, it didn't change at all.

"Damn!" he said. "Damn! Damn! Damn!"

He had allowed himself to hope that this might work, that perhaps the Forelander had hit upon the one approach that would defeat Lici's evil spell. He should have known better. He looked away, staring off into the darkness. The owls still called to one another; the wolves continued to howl.

What had become of his people? This Mettai curse that couldn't be defeated was sweeping across the land, killing indiscriminately. Mettai soldiers were marching to war with the Eandi, bringing a new Blood War to the Southlands. Everywhere, it seemed, people were in peril, all because of blood magic. Throughout his life, Besh had known how the Eandi and the Qirsi thought of his people. But he had lived his life—a good life, filled with love, marked by loss, to be sure, but happy nevertheless. He had never allowed the prejudice of others to touch him. He had never been ashamed to be Mettai. Until now.

Lici had done all of this. One old woman, bent on vengeance, had brought war and suffering to all the land. She might have intended her curse for the Y'Qatt, but the damage she had done to her own people was far greater than any injury she had dealt the white-hairs. The Mettai had been feared, even hated, but mostly they had been shunned. Now they might very well be destroyed, all because Lici had been so terribly clever with her magic; all because her curse killed every Qirsi it touched, just as it would soon kill these two good men lying here on the plain.

Enraged, aggrieved, frustrated beyond words, his hand aching, his energy spent, Besh felt a tear slide down his cheek.

"I feel something."

He looked at Grinsa again. The Forelander's eyes were open and he was staring up into the night sky.

"What did you say?"

"I feel . . . I think it might be working."

Besh leaned closer to him, eager now, daring to hope. "What do you feel?" he whispered

"I don't know. Something. It's . . . it's changing."

"Besh, look!" Sirj said.

He saw it, too. That sheath of light surrounding the Forelander had indeed started to change color. It was subtle still, a slight lightening of the hue at its base, but there could be no mistaking it. Lici's malevolent green was giving way to a soft, pale yellow, something akin to the color of Grinsa's eyes.

"The fever is lessening," Grinsa said. He actually smiled and turned to look at Besh. "I can feel it leaving my body."

Besh turned to Sirj. "You listened? You heard the spell?"

Sirj nodded. "I think so. Earth, mist, magic, plague, shield, Qirsi."

Besh repeated the words to himself. "Yes! That's it!" He nodded toward the Fal'Borna. "Go! Heal him!"

Sirj grinned and then practically leaped across the fire to Q'Daer's side. Besh turned his attention back to Grinsa. The flame around him was now more yellow than green.

"How are you feeling?"

"Weary still, but better. Much better." The Forelander sat up, though clearly it took a great effort. "You did it, Besh. Thank you."

Besh nodded, his relief so great that he wasn't certain whether to laugh or weep. For so long he'd regretted ever coming on this journey and had despaired of doing anything to undo all that Lici had wrought. Yes, he'd killed the woman, exacting a measure of vengeance for those who had perished by her plague, and keeping her from loosing another curse upon the land. But he had feared that her death would be his only success, a dark victory that would have counted for little had Grinsa and Q'Daer died. Now, though . . .

"Actually," he said, "if it really is working, I've done more than you know."

Grinsa frowned slightly. "What do you mean?"

Besh said nothing; he glanced down at his hand and licked away the blood. Then, facing the Forelander again, he smiled.

Chapter 25

Cresenne knew as soon as the dream began that it was Grinsa, stepping into her dreams as only a Weaver could. She found herself standing on the familiar moorland where she had dreamed of him so many times before, and she turned a quick circle, searching for him.

Seeing nothing, she felt fear grip her heart.

"Grinsa?" she called, taking hold of her magic to ward herself in case some other Weaver had come, intending to do her harm.

But an instant later she heard her beloved's voice.

"It's me," he said. "It's all right."

She spotted him then, sitting on the grassy plain. He looked terrible, worse than she had ever seen him. His face looked haggard and deathly pale.

Cresenne ran to him and dropped to her knees. "What's happened?" she asked, panic rising within her like a storm tide. "Are you all right?"

He smiled and nodded, looking so terribly weak. "Yes. I'm fine now. I was sick."

"Sick? What kind . . . ?" Her eyes widened. "You mean the plague, don't you?"

"Yes."

"But how—?"

The smile returned. "Besh healed me. He and Sirj healed both of us, actually. Q'Daer had it, too. But Besh created a spell that defeated Lici's curse."

"Gods be praised." She put her arms around him and kissed his forehead. "It's still spreading though, isn't it?"

"In a way, yes." He told her about Torgan and the scrap of basket the merchant had used against Q'Daer.

"After all you've risked for him," she said, shaking her head. "Forgive me for saying this, Grinsa, but a man like that—he doesn't deserve to live."

"I'm inclined to agree with you. Q'Daer would like nothing more than to kill him with his bare hands."

"He should."

"He can't," Grinsa said. "Torgan's gone. He killed Jasha, and he left. He still has that scrap of basket."

"Demons and fire. So it's still out there. Even if the plague has run its course, he's still got a way of spreading it."

Grinsa nodded. But then he smiled. "You're safe, though."

"None of us is safe, Grinsa."

"Actually," he said, brushing a strand of hair from her brow, "you are now. Besh was very clever with his spell. He made it contagious, just like Lici did. By touching your magic with mine, I've made you immune. You can do the same for Bryntelle. Touch her with your healing magic. That should do it. Q'Daer is speaking with E'Menua right now. Soon everyone in the sept will be safe."

She smiled, then let out a small laugh. "That's amazing. I hope I get a chance to meet these Mettai you're traveling with. I think I'd like them."

"I'm sure you would."

They sat in silence for several moments.

"You've heard there's war coming," she said at last.

Grinsa nodded. "We heard yesterday. I think that's why Torgan did what he did. He'd been carrying that piece of basket for a long time."

"So you're coming back?"

He smiled. "Yes. We're still half a turn away, maybe more. But we've already started heading south."

Suddenly there were tears in her eyes. "I've missed you so much."

He wiped a tear from her cheek, concern etched in his face. "Are you all right?"

"Yes, we're fine. I'll just be glad to have you back."

"That makes two of us."

"Three, really," she said smiling, despite her tears. "Bryntelle misses you, too."

He grinned, then kissed her.

"I should sleep," he said. "We'll ride later today, but we've had a long night."

"Of course. I love you."

"And I love you."

She felt that he was about to leave her dream, and she said his name, stopping him, though she wasn't certain what she wanted to say.

He gazed back at her, a question in his eyes. After a moment, though, he seemed to understand. He leaned forward and kissed her lightly on the lips.

"We'll be careful," he said.

The next moment she was awake, blinking in the pale grey light of early morning. She stretched, looked over at Bryntelle, who was still asleep on her small pallet.

Cresenne sat up and watched the child sleep for several moments. Then she took hold of her power and touched the child with healing magic. Bryntelle stirred, her eyes fluttering open briefly. Then, with a soft sigh, she settled back into her slumber.

"There you go, love," Cresenne whispered. "That's a gift from your father."

Characters

+‡+

Qalsyn (an Eandi city in Stelpana)

JENOE ONJAEF, a marshal in the lord governor's army

ZIRA ONJAEF, Jenoe's wife

TIRNYA ONJAEF, Jenoe and Zira's daughter, a captain in the lord governor's army

MAISAAK TOLM, lord governor of Qalsyn

RIYETTE TOLM, Maisaak's wife

ENLY TOLM, Maisaak and Riyette's son, lord heir of Qalsyn and a captain in the lord governor's army

STRI BALKETT, a captain in the lord governor's army

OLIBAN HERT, a lead rider in Tirnya's company

QAGAN FAWLER, a lead rider in Tirnya's company

DYN GRATHIDAR, a lead rider in Tirnya's company

CROW, a lead rider in Tirnya's company

From Kirayde (a Mettai village in the northern reaches of Stelpana)

BESH, an old Mettai man, a member of the village's Council of Elders

LICALDI, also Lici, an old Mettai woman

EMA, Besh's wife, now deceased

ELICA, his daughter

SIRJ, Elica's husband

MIHAS, Sirj and Elica's elder son

ANNZE, Sirj and Elica's daughter

CAM, Sirj and Elica's younger son

PYAV, a blacksmith, head of the Council of Elders, addressed as "Eldest"

SYLPA, Lici's foster mother, now deceased

On the Plain of the Fal'Borna

GRINSA JAL ARRIET, a Weaver from the Forelands

CRESENNE JA TERBA, Grinsa's wife

BRYNTELLE JA GRINSA, Grinsa and Cresenne's daughter

E'MENUA, a'laq of a Fal'Borna sept in the Central Plain

D'PERA, n'qlae of E'Menua's sept and E'Menua's wife

U'VARA, E'Menua and D'Pera's eldest daughter

Q'DAER, a Weaver in E'Menua's sept

L'NORR, a Weaver in E'Menua's sept

T'LISHA, a girl in E'Menua's sept, L'Norr's concubine

F'SOLYA, a Fal'Borna woman

I'JOLED, F'Solya's husband

F'GHARA, a'laq of a small Fal'Borna sept in the Central Plain

S'PLAED, a'laq of a Fal'Borna sept in the northern plain, now deceased

S'Vralna (a Qirsi city in the Horn on the Central Plain)

P'CRATH, a'laq of S'Vralna

Z'FENI, n'qlae of S'Vralna, P'Crath's wife

B'ASYA, daughter of Z'Feni and P'Crath

The Merchants

TORGAN PLYE, an Eandi merchant from Tordjanne

JASHA ZIFFEL, an Eandi merchant

BRINT HEDFARREN, an Eandi merchant from Tordjanne, also known as Young Red

LARIQENNE GLYSE, an Eandi merchant from Stelpana, also known as Lark

TEGG LONSHER, an Eandi merchant

ANTAL KROST, an Eandi merchant

R'SHEV, a Qirsi merchant on the plains of Stelpana

Other Mettai Villages

KENITHA, a Mettai woman, eldest of Shaldir

FAYONNE, a Mettai woman, eldest of Lifarsa

Lowna (a Fal'Borna village on the Companion Lakes)

S'DORYN, a Qirsi man

N'TEVVA, S'Doryn's wife

T'NOTH, a Qirsi man, friend of S'Doryn and N'Tevva

T'KAAR, a Qirsi man, brother of T'Noth

A'VINYA, T'Kaar's wife

U'SELLE, a'laq (leader) of the village

JYNNA, an Y'Qatt girl

VETTALA, a young Y'Qatt girl

ETAN, a young Y'Qatt boy

About the Author

David B. Coe is the author of ten epic fantasy novels, including The LonTobyn Chronicle, a trilogy that won the Crawford Fantasy Award for best work by a new author, and the Winds of the Forelands quintet. *The Horsemen's Gambit* is the second volume of Blood of the Southlands, a trilogy that began with *The Sorcerers' Plague*. He lives with his wife and their two daughters on the Cumberland Plateau in Tennessee, where he is currently working on the third and final volume of Blood of the Southlands.